# A WARRIOR'S BURDEN

## SAGA OF THE KNOWN LANDS

### BOOK ONE

*By*

## JACOB PEPPERS

This book is a work of fiction. Names, characters, places and incidents are either the product of the author's imagination or are used fictitiously. Any resemblance to actual persons, living or dead, or to actual events or locales is entirely coincidental.

**A Warrior's Burden: Saga of the Known Lands Book 1**
This book is licensed for your personal enjoyment only. This book may not be re-sold or given away to other people. If you would like to share this book with another person, please purchase an additional copy for each person you share it with. If you're reading this book and did not purchase it, or it was not purchased for your use only, then you should return to the retailer and purchase your own copy. Thank you for respecting the hard work of the author.

**Copyright © 2021 Jacob Nathaniel Peppers**. All rights reserved, including the right to reproduce this book, or portions thereof, in any form. No part of this text may be reproduced, transmitted, downloaded, decompiled, reverse engineered, or stored in or introduced into any information storage and retrieval system, in any form or by any means, whether electronic or mechanical without the express written permission of the author. The scanning, uploading, and distribution of this book via the Internet or via any other means without the permission of the publisher is illegal and punishable by law. Please purchase only authorized electronic editions, and do not participate in or encourage electronic piracy of copyrighted materials.

The publisher does not have any control over and does not assume any responsibility for author or third-party websites or their content.

Visit the author website:
*www.JacobPeppersAuthor.com*

*For my children, Gabriel and Norah
I have been very lucky in my life, very blessed
But out of all the blessings I've received—largely undeserved—
There are none I am more thankful for than the privilege of being
your father.*

Sign up for the author's mailing list and, for a limited time, receive a free copy of *The Silent Blade: A Seven Virtues Novella*.

*Go to JacobPeppersAuthor.com and get your free book now!*

# CHAPTER ONE

*He was a prince, yes, but that was the least of him.*
*More, he was a tradesman.*
*As dedicated to his craft as any smith with hours spent hunched at his labors, his hammer in hand.*
*Yet, his craft was not to create but to destroy, for his tool was his axe.*
*And his trade was death.*
—Exiled Historian to the Crown, Petran Quinn

    The woods were dark and seemed to stretch on forever all around him, the snow a heavy blanket at his feet. The forest was so choked with trees that a man would not have been able to see more than a dozen feet in a straight line, if there had been light. But there was not. None, at least, save for the pale light of the moon overhead, hanging thick and pregnant in the sky. It was full tonight, and that was no good thing.

    A full moon meant danger, meant that those things which lurked in the darkness were stronger, their will pressing close against the world. Or so the man had been taught, long ago, while bouncing on his mother's knee, listening to stories, some of brave warriors meant to engender courage, some of the things they faced, meant to engender caution.

    But he was a child no longer. Those days were long passed, and the man was older now than his mother had ever been, older, too, than his father had been on the night when those stories had stopped being only stories, when he had seen, firsthand, the truth of what the darkness held.

## A Warrior's Burden

He had doubted the stories when he was a child, but the man he had become doubted no longer. The bogeymen of his mother's stories, the demons and devils about which she had warned him did exist. He knew this.

After all, he had seen them. He had watched, helpless, as they had clawed at the foundations of his life, his world, until it had fallen away beneath him, had sent him plummeting into the darkness.

But even had he been ignorant of the truth, even had he not seen it first hand, he would have known that tonight was a night of danger. He could feel the tingle of it in his hands as he worked them against the cold, could taste it in the breath as it went in and out of his lungs. The air was cool, frigid, and full of anticipation, as if the world was waiting. And what it waited for—what it *always* waited for—was blood. It waited, but it did not wonder, for the story had been told countless times in countless places, and the conclusion was always the same. It waited for blood. And it would have it.

There in the woods, with the snow falling, its thick blanket muting all sound, with the shadows of the great trees pressing close around him, it seemed to him that he was the only person in the world. There was nothing else. Nothing—save the man and the corpse at his feet.

And the knife, of course. There was always the knife. The man stood for a moment, not appreciating the stillness of the moment—for the man he had become appreciated nothing, no longer remembered how—but acknowledging it as he had so many times before in so many different places. With so many different corpses.

The frost coating his leggings cracked and shifted as he knelt before the corpse. An elk, a large one. The pride of its herd, with wide, powerful horns, and a thick, muscular chest. He had always thought them majestic, proud beasts, but the arrow had stolen more than just its life, had stolen its grace, its beauty, and now it was just a corpse like so many others. The poets wrote of beauty in death, but the poets were fools. Why else try to put into words those things—love, hate, beauty, death—that must only be felt to be understood?

He drew the knife from the leather sheath at his waist, then stopped, staring up at the moon. He sat that way, unmoving, for several minutes, the knife in his hand a familiar weight. Had anyone been there to see him, kneeling there amid that snow-covered landscape, they might have been forgiven for thinking him some statue, a left-over, forgotten remnant from a time long past., and in so many ways, they would have been right. But there was no one there to see.

He was alone. Alone as he had been for many years. As he had been, it sometimes seemed, for his entire life.

He brought the knife to his throat. He didn't think about doing it, never made the conscious decision, but he did it just the same, and as the weight of the handle was familiar to his fingers, so too was the touch of the blade's flat, cold edge against his skin. He remained that way for the space of several breaths, thinking. It was a game he played with himself sometimes. And now, like always, he did not know how it would go, was unsure until finally his breath plumed out in a great white fog, and the blade drifted away from his throat seemingly of its own accord.

He was not left frightened at how close he had come, and his hands did not shake at that understanding. They had, once, but that had been long ago, and even the memory of that fear was buried under a thousand such days as this. A thousand such games.

He was preparing to bring the blade to the elk's throat, to cut away the membrane there so that he might begin to clean it, when a rustle of movement off to his right somewhere in the trees caught his attention. Any normal beast would have been frightened away by the smell of blood thick in the air, and few from the village would have traveled so far from its borders in the day, even less in the night.

Both of these were true things, but they were not the reason why he spun, the reason why the blade was out of his hand, hurtling through the air before he had even drawn another breath. He knew the knife well, its heft and weight, for he had carried it for years, just as he had long ago memorized every tree of these woods, so long had he stalked beneath them.

Both of these were true things, but they were not the reason why the blade flew so straight, why it found its mark unerringly, as if, from the moment it left his hand, there had been no other possibility. The shadowed figure let out a muffled grunt then collapsed to the ground in a heap. The man, known as Cutter to those of the village, rose from his crouch and stalked toward it.

The man had fallen on his back, and the bow—and the arrow he'd been stringing to it—lay in the snow beside him. The man writhed for a moment, but he did not do so for long, for the knife's path had been true, and in seconds, the corpse stared up at him with vacant, but somehow accusing eyes.

Dead then, and that was no wonder, for the truth—the one he had spent the last fifteen years of his life trying to forget—was that the man the villagers knew as Cutter was good at killing. It was the only thing he was good at.

He knelt down before the corpse and retrieved his knife, cleaning it on the dead man's jerkin with several practiced strokes before returning it to its sheath. He leaned forward, meaning to examine the man's clothes—knowing all too well what he would find—but caught a glimpse of an orange speck of light down in the valley beneath the hill on which he crouched. There for only an instant, then gone.

He told himself it had been no more than a figment of his imagination, for if ever there was a place made for such imaginings, it was the cold, dark, lonesome hilltop. He told himself that. But he did not believe it. He told himself that perhaps that orange flash had been no more than a firefly going past, flickering in the shadows. But that, too, he did not believe.

He rose to his feet once more, turning to stare down into the wooded valley from his vantage point on the hill. At first, there was nothing, only the dark and the stillness. Nothing but the cold and the softly falling snow and the white-coated trees, their shadowed limbs thrust out as if they would claw and rend any who drew too close. There was nothing else, nothing at all.

Until there was.

Another orange flicker, then another. Far away, the sight of it nearly occluded by the shape of the great wooden sentinels in the valley beneath him, but there just the same, and no denying it. He knew what it was, realized that he had known it from the first, no matter how much he may have wished otherwise. Fire. And what's more—torches.

There were all manner of beasts in the world, each with their own dangers—so his mother had taught him on her knee, many years ago, and his life had taught him no different. But out of all those beasts, none, save one, carried torches, and that one was, perhaps, the most dangerous of all. Men. Men walking in the dead of night, and though they were too far to even guess at numbers, their forms, if forms he saw, no more than shadows among the trees, the light of the torches—several now—were not comforting. Lights that grew in number with each moment that he watched, blooming in the darkness as if by magic. But if magic it was, it was a dark kind.

He felt a familiar stirring at the sight of them, those phantom lights seeming to float through the darkness on their own. A stirring he had not felt in a long time. One he had hoped to never feel again. No merchants, these, for none would be foolish enough to travel this snow-blasted wilderness underneath the gaze of a full moon. No desperate traveler who'd lost his way either, not with so many. That left only one real option—soldiers. And there was only one reason so many soldiers would leave civilization behind to come to this place.

They had finally come. He had known this day would arrive, sooner or later, had known that truth just as he knew the feel of the knife in his hands, the touch of its blade against his throat. He had known that a man could never truly leave his past behind, that it stalked him always, a beast with claws readied, teeth bared. He had known. And yet, he had hoped. But then, the darkness was not a place for hope.

He spared one more glance for those approaching figures, still too distant to make out, then started down the opposite side of the hill. He paused only long enough to retrieve his own bow and quiver from where he'd left them propped against a tree, then set off at a jog, back toward the village of Brighton, toward the place that, for the last fifteen years, had served as his home.

He left the corpse of the elk to lie where it was. It felt wrong to do it, went against his father's teachings from long ago, for the animal had given its life to provide food that might sustain him and, as such, should have been treated with respect. Dignity. That, instead of being left to rot on a hilltop, any evidence that it had ever existed at all soon to be covered by the thickly-falling snow.

Still, he told himself that the gods—if they were even still alive, and the experiences of his life had engendered within him some doubt of that—would understand. After all, if he was right—and he knew he was—the dead beast would have company soon enough.

## CHAPTER TWO

*Do not ask me what type of man he is,
For I am not sure if he is a man at all.
Certainly, he is more than a man.
Certainly, he is less than one.*
—Maeve "The Marvelous" in interview with Exiled Historian to the Crown, Petran Quinn

The common house of the village was filled with the smell of smoke, old and new, and a great, gray cloud parted around him as he stepped inside. An inconvenience, the smoke, one that made his eyes begin to itch and tear up almost immediately, but like so many of life's inconveniences, it was also necessary. This far north, on the very edge of the Known Lands, there were no seasons, not truly. There was only cold and colder, and even the warmest of days was far below freezing, cold enough that the unprepared could succumb to exposure within an hour of stepping outside.

Not that such a thing happened often. Those hundred or so people who lived in the village of Brighton had long since learned to be prepared, had buried enough dead to know the importance of it. Freezing temperatures, blizzards, Fey raiding parties from the Black Wood, the villagers had weathered them all, survived them all to come out the other side. A little more battered each time, a little more scarred, and with losses to grieve, but alive. Their lives were, mostly, lives of preparation. Preparing for the inevitable winter storms, preparing for Fey raids or the sickness—chills and fevers—that the cold sometimes brought. They were prepared for nearly everything.

And yet, they were not prepared for what was coming.

He closed the door behind him, forcing it shut against the freezing wind that seemed to cut through a man as quick as a blade. By the time the thing was accomplished, there was a pile of snow within the common room, blown in during those few seconds it had taken him.

He turned and walked to stand in front of the thick, oak table at the center of the room, one hewn from two large trees. No more than two, for such a thing was not done, caused jealousy between the spirits of the trees and put a curse on those who used the product of it. Or so the old ways taught. And here, in this forgotten village, in this frozen wilderness, men and women still listened to the old ways.

"Cutter."

He looked away from his boots, sodden with snow and specked with the dead man's blood, bringing his gaze up to the six people seated behind the long table. All old—or, at least, as old as such a place as Brighton saw—and all of them watching him. Three men and three women, as was custom. Five had been the village elders since he had first come to Brighton what felt like a lifetime ago...or no, that wasn't right. He shared little in common with that man who had traveled to this wilderness so long ago, the only thing, perhaps, the desire they both held, a wish to be left alone. And the loneliness, of course, that came to men with such wishes.

The sixth elder was younger than the rest, his mostly-gray hair still peppered here and there with bits of black. He studied Cutter with a sneer he did not try to hide. Cutter rarely saw the elders—or anyone—as he had built his house some distance from the rest of the village, but this one seemed to always be sneering or scowling. "You summoned me," he said, staring at the woman who had spoken, the eldest—and therefore the leader—of the six who served as the village council.

"It is customary," said the sneering man, "to kneel when you approach the Elders."

He shifted his gaze to the elder who'd spoken. "I do not kneel."

The man looked back to the eldest as if for support, but she stared at him impassively before turning back. "Our scouts have just returned. You were right—there's a significant force coming to Brighton."

She waited, as if she expected him to say something. When he did not speak, she went on. "They will be here in half a day, no more."

He glanced up at the hole in the roof, made to allow the smoke of the fires out—a job at which it only partially succeeded—and saw the morning sky. "They will come at night," he said.

"Is that so?" the sneering man said. "And just what do you know of it?"

Cutter glanced at him, saying nothing, letting the silence speak for him, for while he had his talents, words had never been one of them. After a time, he turned back to the eldest. "Their job will be easier at night. When everyone's tired."

The woman nodded slowly. "Perhaps, they don't mean to hurt us," she said, and although she controlled her features carefully, he heard the hope in her voice. "Perhaps they only come to ask questions."

"Such men as this do not ask questions."

She winced. "Then to recruit some of our young men, perhaps. After all, they have come before."

He didn't answer, didn't bother telling her that they would not send so many, if they intended only to recruit. He did not tell her that those times of recruitment had been during the Fey War, a war which was—at least on the surface—now over. He did not tell her because she—like those others in the common house, with their pale faces and restless, fidgeting hands—knew the truth already.

Finally, she sighed. It was a weak, weary gesture, a world of meaning hidden within it. "Listen, Cutter..." She hesitated, as if unsure. Then, "We in Brighton are many things. We are resourceful, brave, and, I think, able to scrape out a living where few others would—or *could*. But we are not warriors. We are not soldiers."

"No."

She rubbed at her temples with a liver-spotted hand as if she felt a headache coming on. And, the man thought that was a damned shame. After all, a headache wasn't the only—or anywhere near the worst—thing coming.

"What I mean..." she tried again, shaking her head as if annoyed at herself. "Look, I'll be straight with you, Cutter. I don't know your real name, and I've never asked. Since the day you showed up, I figured you wanted your privacy, and I did everything I could to make sure you had it. So when you killed that boar that attacked one of the younglings, and folks started callin' you Cutter, I figured that'd do fine for me. Shit, it still does. But only...what I mean is that it's clear you know somethin' of fightin'. More'n the rest of us anyway. Stones and starlight, a body only has to look at those damned arms and shoulders of yours to know as much. So, I thought I'd ask if—"

"I'm not that man anymore."

The woman opened her mouth as if to speak, as if to argue, but finally closed it again and gave a single nod.

*"Not that man,"* the sneering elder hissed from the other side of the table. "I doubt you ever were. Folks walkin' around actin' like you're some demon on account of you got a lucky swing in with an axe and split a pig in two. Well, you might have them fooled, but some of us ain't as easy as others. You ask me, they ought to call you coward."

There had been a time when the man he'd been would never have stood to be called such things, where he would have settled the matter in blood. But that had been a long time ago, and he was that man no longer, so he only gave a slight shrug of his fur-covered shoulders.

*"Cutter, indeed,"* the man hissed.

"That's enough, Telster," one of the other elders, a stick-thin man with long, stringy gray hair and a quaver in his voice said. "There's no call—"

"You ask me there's more than enough call," Telster spat. "We been plenty good to this *coward* here," he went on, throwing the word at him again as if the second might wound where the first had not, "gave him a place to stay, ain't asked nothin' of him, and now—"

*"Enough."* This from the eldest, and Telster scowled but relented, scrunching his shoulders and glaring at the man called Cutter with eyes that said he wished for nothing more but to see him dead. The problem, though, that Cutter could have told him had he asked, was that wishing accomplished nothing. He knew that better than most.

"Everyone out," the eldest said.

All the elders turned to look at her with surprise, each beginning to protest, each cutting off when she raised one of her frail, liver-spotted hands. "Out," she said again. "I need a moment alone with Cutter."

They filed out, Telster sneering as if he'd like to see him killed, the rest hopeful as if they thought he might save them. They would all be disappointed. Many had tried to kill him in his life—human and Fey and worse—and none had succeeded so far, no matter how much he might have wished they had. And as for helping…well, he was not that man, had never been, and even if he had it would have made no difference. What was coming was far too much for any one man to stand against.

Eventually, they were all gone, the last closing the door behind them, and he was left alone with the leader of Brighton. She still sat at the center of the table, watching him. Finally, she spoke. "You are sure that there's no way to get the villagers to safety?"

He shook his head. "They'd catch you. Once you've seen them, it's too late."

"Yet you will run anyway."

"Yes."

"Will you take the boy with you?"

He felt his eyebrow twitch at that, his mouth opening a fraction.

Not much, but then the man known as Cutter was not known for showing emotion, and what might have been insignificant on another was like a scream coming from his throat.

"Oh, please, Cutter," she said, rolling her eyes. "I'm no fool, no matter what the folks in town think, and if I'm old and addled, then I'm still not blind. Not yet. We don't get many visitors out here in Brighton as you well know. A couple who've never been able to have a child suddenly appear in town with a baby that was five, six months old unless I miss my guess, then you arrive barely a week later? Doesn't take a scholar to sort that puzzle out, does it?"

"I guess not."

"So. Will you take him?"

"Yes. If I can."

She snorted. "You can. The boy practically worships you, you know that."

"He shouldn't."

She shrugged. "The young are young for a reason—they're the best at it and the only ones likely to survive the terrible choices they make. Anyway, should or shouldn't makes no difference. We were all that young once, after all."

"Not that young."

"You'll have to forgive Telster. He's been around a time. Why, I've known him for years, even since before the Fall. We were on the same escape boat together, if you can believe that." She paused, a tear winding its way down one craggy cheek. "We stood side by side, watched the capital be overrun by the Skaalden. By those...those *things.*" She paused again and for a moment, he thought that she would not go on. Then she cleared her throat, giving her head a shake as if to banish her memories, and Cutter wished it were only so easy. "Over thirty years ago, but I can still hear the screams," she went on finally. "What I mean is, Telster, he changed that day."

"We all did."

"Yes," she nodded. "Yes, we did. But some men, when tragedy comes upon them, grow from it, bloom like a flower in shit. And others...well, it's like that tragedy tears at 'em, hollows 'em out 'til there's nothing left but bitterness and the memory of what was taken. You understand?"

He nodded. "I won't give it a second thought."

She studied him then, the corner of her mouth upturned in a humorless smile. "No, no, I don't think you will, will you?"

He understood that she was not asking him just about the man, Telster, not now, but he had no answer he could give, none that might offer her any comfort, and so he said nothing.

After a moment, she gave a heavy, weary sigh. "I'm old, Cutter. Older than I'd expected I'd ever be. Older than my mother was when she died during the Fall. My father too. Fire and Salt, there's only a handful in this village that are older'n me, if you take any two and add them together." She paused, but he didn't speak. "What I'm saying is, well, I don't have any illusions about what's comin' my way. It's been comin' for near on eighty years now. In your twenties, shit, maybe even in your thirties, you're able to fool yourself into thinkin' death, growin' old, those are things happen to other folks, not you. They say you get older, you get more wisdom. I can't say as I rightly agree, except that you get a better understandin' of how fragile life is, yours as much as everyone else's. Maybe that's all wisdom really is, in the end."

"Maybe."

She smiled. "Listen to me, goin' on harpin' as if it'll make any difference. Closin' the barn door once the chickens are out, my pa woulda said. Still, I appreciate you humorin' me. Do you think you can make it? You and the boy, I mean?"

"For a while." He shrugged. "As you say, no one makes it forever."

She nodded at that, her expression growing sad. "You don't mind, I think I'll tell myself you made it all the way. After all, I think it'll make it easier, knowin' someone made it out."

She needed something from him, he thought, some sort of reassurance. But he was no priest—just about as far from it as a man could be—and he had no reassurances to give, so he only stood in silence regarding her. She sighed. "The damndest thing. Seems for the last few years, 'bout all I do is bitch and moan about this new ache or that one. More and more often, find myself thinkin' that it'll be a blessin' to close my eyes and not open 'em again, to be buried out at the edge of the Black Wood, next to my father and mother and brother, Jim, whose been dead goin' on forty years now. But now, now that it's upon me, I'm afraid." She gave a laugh with no humor. "S'pose you must think me a coward."

Cutter shook his head. "No, not a coward. You're afraid, and you're right to be. I've seen it before."

She watched him with a strange look in her eyes. "I believe you. I surely do. Tell me, Cutter. I get the feeling you're somebody, maybe somebody important. Or that you were. Once. Will you tell me? You don't have to, if you don't want, but I promise your secret's safe with me." She gave him a small, wistful smile, one that he could tell cost her something. "Always been shit at keepin' 'em—I like to talk too much—but even I can manage a few hours, I think. After that...well, the dead tell only the one story, and it's long since not been a secret."

He winced. He didn't want to do it, didn't want to see the look in her eyes, the same look he'd seen in so many others for so many years. Hate and awe, fear and disgust all wrapped up together, knit so tightly you couldn't tell one from the other. He wasn't sure why he did it, why he stepped forward and whispered that name—a name that was used as a curse in many places and as a blessing in others—into her ear. The name he had tried to leave behind him for fifteen years. But a man can't outrun his past, his name, any more than he can outrun himself. After all, no matter how fast you go, no matter where you turn up, well, there you are.

She gave a sharp intake of breath and jerked away, studying him. Looking to see if he was lying, maybe. Not joking, for there were some names a man wouldn't say, even in jest. He only watched her, expressionless, leaning back himself and letting her take her time. She rubbed a hand across her mouth, and her skin was pale, ashen. "I...thank you. For tellin' me."

But she didn't, not really. He could see the truth of that in her eyes as he had seen it in others long ago. She wished she didn't know, and he understood. He wished he didn't, too.

He turned to go then, opening the door, the frigid wind striking him almost like a physical blow. It might have been the roar of that wind which made her voice sound so small, so afraid, but he didn't think so. "Cutter?"

He glanced back at her. She had risen from the table. It should have made her look bigger, but it did not. She looked smaller. Afraid. "Good luck."

He thought that some might have known the words to say then, words to set her at ease about what was coming, about what would happen, to lend her some strength she might use in the following hours. But if such words existed, he did not know them. He never had. For his had never been a way of peace but of war, and the only strength he knew was in the swinging of the axe, the only ease he'd ever felt that of victory, when his enemies lay low beneath him. He didn't wish her luck. Luck didn't factor into it, not anymore. They were coming, that was all, and with no doubt of what they would do once they arrived. Nothing to say then, so he said nothing at all, walking out into the heavy snow and shutting the door behind him. She did not follow.

# CHAPTER THREE

*I've heard the stories, the ones painting my brother as some...some psychopath.*
*Some mindless killer who bathes in the blood of his victims.*
*Lies, one and all. My brother is a warrior. A soldier.*
*And he does what he does not because he enjoys it.*
*He does it because he must.*
*—Prince Feledias in interview with Exiled Historian to the Crown, Petran Quinn*

The village was busier, more *alive* than he'd ever seen it. He had seen similar from soldiers who, fearing their deaths in a battle, drank and laughed and lived as hard as they could for as long as they could. There was always an undercurrent to that laughter, one that made it seem as if it might turn into a scream at any moment, and there was always a desperation to the way they drank, the way they lived, as if life were a wash cloth that might be squeezed dry before its time.

But here, at least, there was no laughter, desperate or otherwise. Men and women rushed to and fro, all in a hurry—but some, it seemed to Cutter, having no idea what, exactly, they were in a hurry to *do*. Thinking only that they should be doing something, *anything*. He could have told them that it did not matter, that whatever they did, they would all be dead before the coming night gave way once more to the sun, but he did not. When death was certain, when one had nothing to look forward to but pain and loss, even vain hope was better than no hope at all.

Mothers and fathers fought each other to load their children onto the few carts the town had, hitching them up to the healthiest of horses. Which, Brighton being a snow village on the edges of civilization, weren't particularly healthy. Life in the frozen wastes was hard for anyone, man or beast. Each year in the village stripped a little more of them away. At first, the stripping took only the dross—fat from the body, fat from the mind. All of it extra weight a man or woman dragged behind them through life, often not even aware of it. What was left, then, after a time, was no more than survival, muscle and sinew and bone. That was all.

But the stripping was never truly done. The world was not so kind that it ever stopped taking just because there was so little left to take. Like a greedy miser, it continued to rip and pull and tear, never satisfied with what it had taken, forgetting it, in truth, thinking only of what was left, of what else it might catch in its grip.

The horses, like the people around them, were products of such a stripping. Thin, poor things, as meager as the meals which sustained them. Beasts who may have journeyed to the freezing north fine and full of life, but ones that, over time, became pack animals and, when even such menial labor was beyond them, they were rewarded by being slaughtered and used for food, for in such a place as Brighton, when any wasting might lead to death, there was little room for sentiment.

Still, Cutter told himself that, perhaps, the children might make it away. A false hope, maybe, a vain one, but sometimes that was the only kind a man had. Besides, even those who came, cold and heartless as they were, were not animals. Or so he told himself.

A few of the villagers waved at him as he passed on his way back to his home, but not many. Fifteen years he had lived in this place—if living was the word, existing felt closer to the truth—and while he knew all their names, he did not know *them*. It was strange how a man could live among so many people, and yet remain so alone. He had not gotten to know them, not in fifteen years, and now he never would. Death was never far in a settlement so near the Black Wood, but he was not just near, not now. Now, he walked among them, reaching out his hands to pull them all into his dark embrace, an embrace that no one could deny.

Cutter trudged through the snow, toward his house on the outskirts of the village. Some of the doors of the houses he passed had been latched tight, as if to keep what was coming out. Others had been thrown wide, as if by inviting him in, Death might be swayed to let them pass. But there was no lock strong enough to keep death out, and he was never swayed. That much, Cutter knew. That much, he had learned long ago.

At the base of many of the houses, offerings had been lain Fruits and vegetables—poor, wretched looking things compared to their counterparts in the warmer climates of the south. Food that, the day before, the people of the village would have desperately needed, but tomorrow their thoughts would not be on food or the lack, for the dead had no thoughts or, if they did, they were dark ones. Still, he understood.

Each dealt with his coming death in his own way, the only way he knew how. One was not any better than the other, was only a way of making it to the end. True, the Fey had responded to such offerings once—the sprites and pixies mostly, but sometimes their greater kin. Yet, that had been a long ago, before the war. And even before that, the creatures had always been fickle things, as liable to be offended as grateful, and in either case largely irrelevant. Not that it mattered. The Fey would not show up to accept such offerings, even if they'd had a mind.

They had been driven back, back to the heart of their territory, the Black Wood, and even this close, even on this snow-swept wilderness of a village, they would not risk showing themselves. They had once, had come to greet Cutter and his people with open hands, open talons, and they had not been welcomed kindly. Cutter knew that better than most, for he had been one of those in charge of that welcome, one of blood and steel and death. And betrayal.

Finally, he reached his house. Here, there were no desperate shouts of men and women making what preparations they could, preparations that would, in the end, be pointless. No horses neighed, no children cried for reasons they did not know, only because their parents were afraid. It was only him, and his house, far enough away from the village, far enough away from *life* that he never had to live it.

It was cold inside. He had not bothered to set a fire when he returned, knowing that he would not be staying. Fifteen years he had lived here, yet now, looking around the small room with the simple, coarse mattress, and a table at which sat a single chair, the chest in the corner, it looked like a stranger's home. It could have belonged to anyone or no one, a place that might have been abandoned years ago, the only proof of life a tin bowl sitting on the table where he'd yet to clean it. It would go uncleaned, that bowl, and he thought that was a shame. A small shame, really, in a day of great ones, but a shame nonetheless.

He realized, gazing at that emptiness, that he was not even sure why he had come back. There was nothing here for him, not in this house and not in this village. There never had been. Nothing in life, either, as far as that went. Just emptiness and more of the same. But he could escape that emptiness easily enough. He could walk to the chair, could sit, perhaps clean the bowl. He could not fix the things he had done in his past, but the bowl he could fix. It was tempting, that thought, to sit and be at ease, to wait for the fate which had stalked him for fifteen years, the fate which he had earned many times over, to find him.

Tempting, yes, but it, like the knife, was no more than a game. For as much as he might like the idea of having it all over, of letting it end, he knew he would not. There was still one reason to carry on, to fight. The boy. The same reason which had kept the knife's edge at bay for the last fifteen years. Cutter let out a heavy sigh and moved toward the chest, kneeling before it. He reached for the latch then hesitated.

He had reached for the latch many times over the years, had hesitated many times. But each time, he had taken his hand away, deciding that what secrets the chest held were best left locked away, hoping that by remaining so, they would also keep, hidden in the confines of the chest, the past from which they came. They hadn't, though. Some pasts, some scars, never healed, not truly. But if he did not open it this time, there would be no other. For whatever happened, he knew that he would never see Brighton again. If, that was, it existed at all after the night's work was done, and he doubted that very much.

With a slowness borne not out of reverence but of nervousness, he removed the key he kept on a leather thong around his neck, fitting it into the lock. As he did, he entertained a brief hope that, after so many years, it would not fit, that the key or the lock or both would have degraded, rendering them unusable. But they had not, and the key fit as smoothly as it had when he'd purchased it and the chest so many years before. The key seemed to turn of its own accord, and soon—too soon, for he could feel his heart hammering in his chest now—the clasp fell away, and the lock tumbled onto the ground, the echo of its falling seeming to thunder through the small house.

Cutter was not a man known for being afraid. Any who had known him long ago would have said he feared nothing. That wasn't true, though. He wasn't afraid of dying as some men were, wasn't afraid of pain, of swords or the Fey. What the man was afraid of wasn't, had never been death—it was life.

The top of the chest was heavier than it should have been, heavier than it *could* have been, and it seemed to take all of his prodigious—once legendary—strength to lift it. A small creak of a dirty hinge. That was the only sound to announce his past as it came rushing back at him, rushing and rushing, him running from it, knowing that he could not outrun it, that it would catch him in the end, for there was nowhere to run to. Then, when it caught him, realizing that it had had him all along, and the freedom he might have imagined he felt no more than the feel of the wind whistling in a mouse's ear as the cat tosses it in the air before inevitably closing its jaws around its prize.

Letters lay piled in the box. Dozens, hundreds of letters. A few—those crumpled and stained, the text faded from so much handling—written by others. A man, mostly, one who no longer existed. A man who, in his darker moments, Cutter thought might never have existed at all, had been no more real than a mask one might don one moment only to remove the next. The others, those freshly rolled, untouched, were written in his own hand. A hand that had sought to come to grips with the truth, to try to explain the unexplainable, one which had possessed the courage his own voice lacked, to write his answer to the many questions of his past, an answer he could not speak. In the end though, his hand, like his voice—like he himself—had failed.

He reached a tentative hand toward the letters, hesitating in this where, in the rest of his life and often to his great shame, he had never hesitated before. "*No.*" The words grated out of him, not consciously, but pulled out from a place he had tried to bury deep long ago. A place of blood and pain and memory. He jerked his hand away from the chest and its contents as if they were poison—and they were, of course. The problem was that the poison was already in him, had come even before the letters, and they were not the cause of that poisoning, merely a symptom of it. Sometimes—most times, in truth—he thought it had been with him upon his birth. Eating at him, not making him worse, really, but making him what he was, what he always had been.

He rose, turning away from the letters and moving toward where his thick fur cloak hung on the wall, one he had made himself. It, like everything else in his life, his past the greatest, he had gained from killing, had made from the deaths of others. He reached into one of the pockets lining the inside, pockets he himself had sewn, and withdrew the flint he found there. Then, before he could think better of it, before he could question his course, he strode back to the chest and knelt, striking the flint. In seconds, the contents of the chest were burning, the letters, the truths of his past, raging in their burning, filling the room with smoke.

*If only a man's past could be dealt with so easily. But a man does not burn his past—it burns him.* Of all the truths the man knew, of all those his life had taught him, that was the greatest. He moved back to the fur cloak, pulled it on, and then turned away from the chest, from his home, stepping out into the heaving snow. He did not look back, for there was nothing to look back *for*. He carried it with him. Always.

***

He'd barely been walking for five minutes—could still see his house on the hill behind him, the great billowing plume of smoke rising from it—when he caught sight of the boy on the path. Thin and gangly, the way many young boys are when on the cusp of becoming men, but tall, nearly as tall as Cutter himself, and still with plenty of growing left in him.

"*Cutter!*" the boy yelled, his voice high with an excitement that told the flush in his cheeks was from more than just the biting cold.

Cutter came to a slow stop as the boy ran up to him. "Hey, did you hea—" The boy cut off, looking past him, frowning at the smoke. "Cutter, your house," he said, stunned. "It's on fire."

"Sure," Cutter agreed. All the houses of the village would be before long and what the difference?

"But..." the boy said, confused, but obviously trying for a calm to match Cutter's own, a boy nearly a man but not quite, only playing at being one. "Well, what happened?"

Cutter met his eyes. "I set my house on fire."

The boy nodded slowly, his expression serious, fighting to hold back his emotions but finally failing as all men must, a wide grin spreading on his face. "Did you hear? About the troops?"

"I heard."

The boy was nodding again, excited. "I talked to a few of the other men—Bardic, Felmer, and Ned. We're going to join up."

*Men.* The word said with such ease, such pride, but the village of Brighton was small, and Cutter knew the names of all those who lived there, knew the three to be no more than children themselves, no older than the boy. "Join what?"

"Why, the army, of course," the boy said, nearly panting with his eagerness like a dog going for a bone, too caught up in the moment to realize what it took for a treat was actually a pale snake bathing in the sun, ready to bring the poison within it out into the world.

Cutter realized he should have seen this coming. The boy had been talking about being a soldier since he was old enough to swing a stick and yell "En guarde!" Not that anybody in battle ever yelled "En guarde." It had been stupid then and it was stupid now. Cutter had learned long ago that sometimes children could get away with stupidity, but men rarely could. "Those soldiers aren't coming to recruit, boy. They're coming to kill and that only."

The boy was shaking his head before he was finished. "You're wrong, Cutter. Felmer's dad used to serve in the military during the Fey Wars, and he says that back before we won, there were times the king got desperate, sent troops as far out as Brighton to recruit."

"Felmer's dad is a damned fool that couldn't swing a sword if his life depended on it. The closest he ever came to a battlefield is the lies soldiers tell when they're in their cups. Use your *head*, boy.

Even if the king *was* recruiting—which he ain't—what in the fuck would he worry about Brighton for? He'd make the trip for what, four boys too stupid to know they're stupid, is that it?"

The boy winced, clearly hurt by his words, but that was alright. Cutter had seen his fair share of wounds, had taken far *more* than his share. They always hurt, sure, and sometimes they killed but then, sometimes, they saved.

"But Felmer's dad said that we're going to go to battle with the Fey again, that since we won the last war, they've been trying to—"

"*Won?*" Cutter said. "Look around yourself, boy, used your damned *eyes.*" He gestured widely with a gloved hand at the village of Brighton in the distance. Even the word "village" seemed too fine a thing for such a place. A few thrown-together houses, covered in snow, the inhabitants milling about on the outside looking one bad day away from starving. "Does this look like *winning* to you?"

But the boy wasn't ready to give it up. Like so many of the young—like Cutter had once been himself—he believed he knew more about the world than anyone else, never mind that the only bit of it he'd ever seen, at least to remember, was this snowy, wasted landscape. "But we pushed them back, to the Black Wood, I mean. They say the Fey are too scared to come out now, and even you have to admit we haven't seen any in years."

Cutter shook his head slowly, remembering something a friend of his had told him once, long ago. *Sometimes,* she'd said, *walls built of ignorance prove the strongest. Until they don't.* Of course, he hadn't listened then, and the boy didn't seem ready to listen now. How could you explain to a child, only a year removed from chasing his friends around the village and throwing snow balls at each other, that the Fey didn't feel fear, not the way men did? They didn't *think* like men at all, and Cutter had seen more than a few men die for making the mistake of believing they did. "Listen, lad," he said slowly, "do you trust me?"

The boy hesitated then nodded. "Of course, Cutter, but—"

"Then listen to what I'm tellin' you and listen closely, 'cause neither of us has the time for me to say it twice. Those men who are comin', they aren't comin' to recruit anybody. They're coming to burn, that's all. To burn and to kill."

"But...why?" the boy said, his voice quiet now, losing some of his sureness, and that was good. Confidence could serve a man well, could be a shield against the world, but more often than not, it could also get him killed. "Why would they want to hurt us? We haven't ever done anything to anybody."

His past threatened to rise up in his mind then, but Cutter pushed it back down. He'd had a lot of practice at it, after all. It never went down completely, not all the way, but it was enough. "Doesn't matter why, only that they're coming, and they'll kill anyone they find here. Now, come on. We've got to go."

"Go?" the boy said, as if Cutter had just told him they needed to sprout wings and fly in the air like a bird. "Go where?"

"West."

"You mean...toward the Black Wood? But...they say the Fey kill anyone that comes close."

That was true enough, but Cutter didn't feel the need to say so. "You'll die if you stay, boy," he said simply. "We both will."

He could see the thoughts running through the boy's mind, could see him thinking it over. Scared, yes, but excited too, the poor fool, excited by the prospect of venturing past the bounds of the village, of seeing the Black Wood and living to tell the tale. Of course, that last was almost always the problem, particularly when dealing with the Fey. "Okay," the boy said finally, breathless. "Okay. But I've got to go get Momma, she—"

"There's no time," Cutter said. "Besides, boy, you and I both know your mother wasn't gonna make it the year whether these men came or not—it's time to go. Now."

The boy looked at him shocked, as if seeing him for the first time, then he shook his head. "No, I won't leave her. Look, we'll...we'll catch up to you, alright?"

He turned to go, putting his back to Cutter, and that made it easy enough to withdraw the pan from his traveling sack—a heavy, dented thing, scarred with use, much like Cutter himself—and hit the boy in the head with it. Cutter might have spent nearly the last twenty years of his life living in the village, but the body remembers what it will, and it was a clean strike. The boy collapsed soundlessly on the snow.

Cutter replaced the pan. He glanced once more at the direction the men would be coming from and imagined he could make out the faintest flicker of torches in the distance. Then he knelt and picked the boy up, throwing him over one shoulder and starting west, away from the village. He did not look back. After all, there was nothing to look back for, nothing behind him except pain, except blood and death, and he'd had his fill long ago.

## CHAPTER FOUR

*What do I remember most about him?*
*Hmm...maybe his strong jaw-line?*
*Fine, fine, you're serious but fire and salt what a question.*
*Very well, what do I remember most?*
*I remember that he did not stop. Not ever.*
*Not for fear or mercy, not for pleas or pleasure.*
*He never stopped.*
*—Challadius "The Charmer" regarding Prince Bernard, commonly known as "The Crimson Prince" in interview with Exiled Historian to the Crown, Petran Quinn*

He walked for several hours, his unconscious burden held over one shoulder, watching the sun slowly lower over the horizon, watching the night approaching with all its dark promise. Then, he stopped, deciding that it would be good to get some rest. After all, they had a long way to go yet, the road stretched out before them, its twists and turns beyond sight, yet its destination in plain view as it was for all men who lived and breathed and one day would not.

He set the boy down, then knelt in the blanket of snow and removed his pack from where it hung on his shoulder. He withdrew his bedroll and laid it on the snow that crunched beneath his feet. Then he put the boy on it, covering him as much as he could against the falling snow. He wanted to make a fire, but though they were hours from Brighton now, such a thing would have been foolish. And, more than that, it would have been impossible. There were no trees, not here, the miles between the

## A Warrior's Burden

village and the Black Wood nothing but a snow-blasted, featureless landscape stretching on as far as the eye could see.

Instead, he withdrew the blankets from his pack and laid them across the boy's unconscious form, save one which he laid out for himself. Then he sat, waiting, the snow falling around him in a soft curtain, no sound except that of his and the boy's breaths pluming in the frigid air. And there was the wind, of course. The wind which swept drifts of snow across him, across the boy, like some mischievous child who finds enjoyment in cruelty, in adding despair to despair, stacking it on top of what was already there the same way the snow stacked itself around them, until there was nothing but the snow. Nothing but the despair.

The boy roused himself after another hour, coming fully awake. It was a slow thing, the gentle stirring beneath the blankets, a soft, breathless yawn. Cutter watched him, that gentle moment of content confusion that so often follows a long, much needed sleep, watched the contentment leave his face a moment later as his eyes opened and his memory returned.

The boy jerked up, staring around at the featureless landscape. "W-where are we? Where's Brighton?"

"Gone, boy," he said, and the tears which gathered in the youth's eyes showed that he understood the full meaning of that all too well.

"B-but, my mother," the boy said, "I have to go save her—"

He started up, and Cutter rose, catching his arm in a grip that could crush a man's throat. A grip that had. "If you go back, you will die."

The boy's eyes were filling with tears, and his face twisted with rage. "Let me go! I have to protect my mother, have to—"

"She isn't your mother." The words were not said in anger, were not shouted in cruelty as they might have been, but they seemed to strike the boy hard for all that, and he stumbled, his eyes going wide.

"What? What are you talking about, of course she's my mo—"

"Did you never wonder," Cutter said, keeping his voice low and soft, the way a man might when dealing with a scared beast, "why her hair is dark and yours fair? Why she is short of stature and you tall?"

"My father—" the boy began, but Cutter interrupted.

"Was dark-haired too, and as short as your mother, if not more than. No, the woman who raised you is not your mother; she never was."

"You're lying," the boy said, but Cutter could hear the uncertainty in his voice. It wasn't that the truth was often hard to know, when a man saw it—it was simply that more often than not, he didn't want to. Still, whatever he was, the boy was no fool, at least no more than others his age, and as he sat there, frowning, thinking, Cutter saw the realization suddenly come to him. But when the youth looked at him once more, there was an angry expression on his face. "W-what do you know of it, anyway?"

Cutter shrugged, shifting his massive shoulders. "Some. I was the one who gave you to her."

The boy swallowed hard at that. "*Gave* me," he repeated, the tears rolling their way down his cheeks now. "Like I'm a dog."

"Yes," Cutter said. "And I paid her to take you in, to raise you."

The boy recoiled at that, wounded and hurt. Cutter did not like telling it, especially since that last part was a lie, but if he was to have any hope of saving the boy they had to get moving soon, and he couldn't afford to knock him out or chase him down every time he took it in mind to play at being a hero. A lie, yes, but it would make the boy hate the woman who'd served as his mother, the woman who'd taken him in gladly, her husband too, not to be paid but out of kindness. A hate that was unfair, perhaps, but one that would make it easier to leave her and Brighton behind, to accept that they were already dead. Sometimes, Cutter had found, hate was the only way a man got on. Hate for others, sure, but more often, hate for himself.

He could see both in the boy's eyes then. "But...who am I?"

Cutter shrugged again. "I don't know, only a baby found in the road, abandoned." Another lie, but one that was as close to the truth as he would come, as close to it as he *dared* come.

"You mean...even my parents didn't want me."

Cutter had never been good with compassion, with sympathy. There were those, Maeve among them, who had told him often that a boulder was softer, warmer than him, and he had never argued it, but there was no denying the hurt and pain in the boy's eyes, the need to believe he had not been wantonly cast aside.

"Perhaps they were set upon by bandits," Cutter offered, hoping to give the youth a little peace, "or the Fey. There is no knowing."

"And you...took me," the boy said. "Why?"

Cutter did not answer that, only stared at the boy, watched the tears roll down his face, watched some part of him die as he began to accept the fact that the woman he'd known as his mother had not wanted him, that perhaps no one had. "They're all dead, aren't they?" the boy asked. "The folks in Brighton, I mean."

Cutter saw no point in lying. Sometimes, the truth was dark—most times, in fact—but it never did a man any good to ignore it. "Yes."

The lad's mouth worked at that, twisting, and for a time Cutter thought he might burst into more tears. Instead, he nodded, his eyes growing cold, hard. "I wish I was. You should have left me."

"No," Cutter said, and for the first time there was some emotion in his voice as the boy's words cut at old wounds, old scars that had never healed, that *could* never heal. "Death is never something to be courted, boy. Do you understand? It comes for us all in the end—there is no reason to invite it in."

The boy had known him for years and stood in muted shock at the emotion in his words, an emotion he had never seen before in the normally stoic man he had come to admire. Finally, he cleared his throat, wiping an arm across his face furiously, ashamed of his tears, his grief, as only the young could be. The old, Cutter found, knew far too much of grief to be ashamed.

"What...will they come after us?" the boy asked.

"Yes. No doubt they are coming already. The blizzard should cover most of our tracks, but they will find them just the same, sooner or later."

"But *why?*" the boy demanded. "Why did they want to hurt the people of Brighton? Why hurt us?"

"It is what they do," Cutter said simply. There was more to it, of course, far more, but the truth of it sat behind a wall he had erected in his mind, one that had been long years in the making and that, despite his efforts, was threatening to crumble, laying bare the past and the pains it brought.

"I hate them," the lad said. "All of them."

"That's alright, then," Cutter said. "Sometimes, boy, hate is the only way a man gets on."

"So what do we do?"

Saying nothing more about his mother or about the dead, the only people he had known his entire life, but that was not so unusual. It was the shock, that was all, a symptom common enough among those who had suffered a great tragedy, a great loss. Cutter knew that too, knew it better than most, for he had often been the cause of that loss, the reaper of that tragedy. "We continue west."

The boy's eyes went wide at that, and he turned gazing off in the direction. The Black Woods were some distance now, blocked by a horizon filled with snow and that only, but he continued to stare as if he could see them—and perhaps, in his mind, he could. "You mean..."

"Yes," Cutter said. "We cannot outrun them, not for long. If we try, they will catch us."

"And if they catch us..." The lad didn't finish, and Cutter said nothing, letting him come to the conclusion himself, for no truth was as powerful, no lesson as well-learned, as the one a man found on his own. "But the Black Woods..." the boy said finally, "it's...it's where the Fey live."

"Yes."

The boy swallowed hard, no doubt recounting a lifetime of stories about the cruelty of the Fey, the evilness of them, some true, many not. "But if these men, if they want us so badly, won't they just...follow us?"

The boy was clever, always had been. That, Cutter knew, he got from his mother, the real one. "They will not go so far as that," he said with more conviction than he felt. In truth, there was no way of knowing, yet the Woods were their only chances of survival, so he didn't bother telling the boy as it would have served no purpose, only fill him with fear when what was needed was cold, hard strength.

"It will be dangerous, won't it? Going into the Black Wood, I mean."

"Living is always dangerous," Cutter said. "But it is the only chance. There is no other. Now come. It is past time we left."

They walked for hours, the snow falling around them in a muted blanket of white, the only sound that of their footsteps crunching beneath them and the boy's rasping, tired breaths.

In time, night fell heavy and as silent as the thickening snow around them, and the boy could walk no farther. He collapsed to the ground. Cutter stepped toward him, meaning to bring him to his feet, to tell him that they must go on, but as he had feared it might, the shock chose that moment to wear off, and the boy's face twisted with grief. He did not give words to that grief, did not name it, but then he did not need to, for Cutter had seen it before, a hundred, thousand times, and he knew it as another man might know his best friend—or his worst enemy.

A moment later, the boy buried his face in his hands and wept, shaking his head silently as if to deny the night's events. But the truth could never completely be denied, no matter how much a man might wish it. So the boy continued to weep, looking for solace where there was none, and Cutter turned and stared back at the path they had taken, back toward the direction in which the village of Brighton had once stood—but, he did not doubt, stood no longer.

The heavy snow had done much to obscure their footsteps, destroying any evidence that they had ever trod upon the surface of this white-blasted world, that they had ever existed at all. That's all men were, he thought, in a rare moment of introspection, all men left behind them. Footprints, indentations which might be covered in a moment. It was a dark thought, but that did not change the fact that it was also a true one.

Yet for all the snow's efforts at hiding their passage, he knew that those men who had come upon the village of Brighton would find them, sooner or later. They would not rest until they had. After all, it was for Cutter that they had come. A man could never really outrun his past, not forever, for the past did not rest, did not sleep or drink or eat or laugh. It only trailed after, waiting to catch a man up when he was unaware.

He had set a grueling pace for himself and the boy, as much as he had thought the lad capable of handling and then a little more, but he knew that despite his efforts, they could not hope to outrun those who came after them. Besides, the boy was done in—anyone with eyes to see could tell that much. Exhausted from the march, true, and from his own loss. "Rest." Cutter told him, unslinging a bedroll from the pack at his back and tossing it to him. "Sleep and time are the best medicines."

"D-do they work?" the boy asked through his sobs.

*No.* Cutter only stared at him though, saw the boy's fragile eyes asking him for some words of comfort, of hope. But Cutter had never been good at lying.

"But...but they'll catch us. Won't they?"

"Sleep," he said again. The boy, perhaps because of his shock or his loss, perhaps because he courted death whether he knew it or not, made no further argument. Instead, he took the bedroll and laid it out on the blanket of snow, climbing, shivering, inside.

Cutter watched him, watched him close his eyes and turn his back toward him, toward the village of Brighton where his mother now lay dead, as if such a gesture might banish them from his life, from his thoughts. And, perhaps, it would. For a time. But the past, like a mongrel dog once fed, always returned, sooner or later.

"Sleep," Cutter said for the third time, and moments later, the boy did.

# CHAPTER FIVE

*Blood in the snow.*
*Is there anything more terrible?*
*Is there anything more beautiful?*
    *—Unknown Poet*

It did not take him long to find them. They had made good time, as he'd known they would, and he caught sight of them less than two hours away from where the boy lay sleeping. Six in all, a forward scouting party which would be followed, he knew, by a much larger force. These six were meant to root out their quarry, to keep sight of them until the greater force arrived. It was the way it was done—that, he knew better than most, for it had been he who had decided it was so.

He stood waiting for them in the snow, weaponless. The old him, the man he had once been, would have been offended that they had only sent six. That man would have been furious at the insult, would have been keen to display his rage on the bodies of those he felt had wronged him, would have rushed toward them to do just that.

But Cutter was that man no longer, no longer the berserker warrior with a belly full of fire. He was not angry or furious, not eager at the bloodshed to come...he was only tired. That and nothing more. Not too tired to run, if he'd had a mind to, but he did not—was still, in that way, the same as the man he had once been. So he stood in the heavy-falling snow, watching the vague shapes of their forms approach. And he waited.

Another several minutes passed, and they were about a hundred yards away before they became aware of him, a fact made apparent by the way they began to spread out, meaning to encircle him, to surround him and offer no means of escape. Not that he would try. The old him would have gripped his axe in anticipation as he watched, fanning the flames of his love of violence as he did, but Cutter had no axe, not any longer, had no love for violence any longer either, so he only stood and watched. And waited.

They continued to spread out as they drew closer until they formed a circle, a circle of snow-covered specters. He could not see their faces, not yet, but he did not mind. Perhaps if he had, he might have recognized them, might have known them as men he had once shared a drink with, perhaps ones he had saved on one battlefield or another. But he did not see their faces, and he did not care.

He would see them later, he knew, when he slept and the dreams came as they always did. Dreams in which a procession of the dead marched before him in endless number, all saying nothing, at least not with their mouths, but all watching him with dead, sightless eyes which nevertheless made their thoughts clear. *It should have been you,* those eyes said, *you should have died, and the world would be better for it.* And then, like now, he would only stand, saying nothing in return, for there was nothing he could say, no argument he could make—not when he believed them to be right.

They drew their blades, those specters, and started toward him, the sound of their approach masked by the thick snow, so that everything was silent save for his own breath which plumed in front of him in the cold. He shifted, rolling his shoulders to loosen them and the frost which had gathered on the fur covering him cracked as he did. He flexed the fingers of his gloved hands, working what warmth he could into his numb body. He did not fear—that, then, was another thing he shared with the man he had once been. Perhaps he would die and perhaps he would not. If he prevailed, he would continue on with the boy into an uncertain future, and if he did not...well, perhaps that would be better, for the dead have no regrets, and they alone reside in a place where the past cannot follow.

They approached in unison, warily, their blades held in front of them. Professionals, then, disciplined men who had done this before and who would likely do it again. Only, they would not. For while the men were soldiers, probably some of the best—after all, only the best would be tasked with such an errand as they now followed—he was not. He was a killer. Marching and holding lines, standing in a shield wall and following commands, these were the things at which soldiers excelled. Killers, though, had only the one talent.

He remained still as they drew closer until they were only a few dozen feet away, spread out around him like the end-spokes of some great wheel, one which had turned since before his birth and would continue to turn long after he had faded to dust. They all hesitated, as if surprised to find him unmoving, then one of them motioned with his hand, a gesture just barely visible in the driving snow, and they started forward once more. Six men with six swords. But he did not fear. They, after all, were only men. He had faced far worse.

He stood watching as the men crept closer, slowly, ever so slowly, for they would have been told who their target was, would know the lethality of the beast they'd been set to hunt. He remained still, watching them, watching until twenty feet turned to fifteen, until fifteen turned to ten.

Then he moved.

Poets and bards the world over often likened a warrior's movements to wind or rain, smooth and graceful, and perhaps they were even right to do so. But Cutter was no warrior. He was a killer and a killer only, so he charged toward the nearest man who waved his sword in a defensive pattern. Truly a professional, one meaning to stall until his fellows arrived. But Cutter's father had told him and his brother, long ago, before they had become the men they were, that when faced with a job to do, a man had best get it done. And so he did. Instead of allowing himself to be slowed by the man's attacks, he charged directly into them, batting the sweeping blade away with a forearm covered in thick fur, fur which did much to keep the keen edge of the blade from his flesh. Much, but not all.

He felt the kiss of steel along his forearm, but paid it no attention as he dove forward into the man, lifting him up with both hands by the front of his tunic and jerking him toward him even as his head lunged forward, crashing into the man's face in a crimson shower of blood and teeth. He dropped the man—unconscious or dead—and lifted his sword in time for two more to be on him. The sword was not his weapon of choice, a weapon made for finesse and skill, and he wielded it with both hands, swinging it in vicious, deadly arcs that would have looked more at home on a lumberjack at his trade.

The men were well-trained, and parried the way they should have, but no matter what stories they had heard of him, they were not ready for his strength, a strength which knocked the first soldier's blade out of his hands and then powered his own sword as it cleaved deeply into the man's face and forehead.

The soldier screamed, but abruptly grew silent as Cutter ripped the blade free and, with a horizontal slash, lopped his head free of his shoulders. He let the hilt of his sword loose with one hand as he did, grabbing the headless corpse and spinning, interposing it between him and his other attacker just in time for the blade which had been darting at his back to stick into the corpse instead. Then he flung the impaled corpse into this new attacker, and both man and dead man were sent tumbling over.

It would have been sporting, then, to let the man rise, to let him clamber his way free of his dead companion, but Cutter had never been a sporting man, just as he had never been a soldier, and he brought the blade down in a two handed stab that pierced corpse and man alike before driving into the snow-laden ground and sticking deep into the earth. He left the man there, screaming, writhing, and turned to face the remaining three, weaponless once more.

They hesitated, spread out in front of him, shocked, perhaps, by the violence which had occurred or maybe thinking of the best way to get at him. He didn't give them time, for hesitation, he knew, got more men killed than anything else. He drove at the one on his left in a loping run. He could see the shock, the fright in the man's eyes as the soldier raised his sword in front of him, not to attack, really, but only in an attempt to fend off the wild beast he had cornered.

Cutter ducked under the attack, but not enough to avoid the steel kissing his back in a shallow cut. He ignored this wound as he had the first, bowling into the man with enough force to knock the air out of his opponent's lungs, then lifted him up in the air before slamming him down on the ground. The snow was soft, but the man struck hard, and he was still stunned, trying to recover, when Cutter brought his boot down on his face. Once, twice, something crunching beneath it each time. On the third, the man stopped moving, his features all but unrecognizable.

Footsteps behind him, and he spun in time to catch the wrist of this latest attacker before his sword could cleave into his collarbone where it had been aimed. With a growl and a savage twist, the man's wrist snapped, and he screamed, dropping his sword. Cutter scooped it from the ground and brought it around in a two-handed arc that struck the man in the back of his knee then passed through it, severing his leg in half. The man's screams turned to tortured wails as he fell to the ground, blood fountaining from the stump of his leg and staining the snow a crimson that was almost black in the moonlight.

He turned to see that the final one had sprinted away, back in the direction of his forces, no doubt intending to get help, to tell them of this demon he and his companions had found in the driving snow. But demons were not so easily escaped, that Cutter knew, for he had more than his share. He knelt calmly beside the legless man, his screams now a low, pleading moan, and withdrew a hatchet from where it was sheathed at the man's belt. Then he turned, watching the back of the fleeing man.

The driving snow and poor light did much to obscure his form, making of him a vague outline that could have been anyone, anyone at all. Cutter pivoted, bringing the hatchet back over his head and with a grunt, spun, letting it go. It struck the running man in the center of his back, the blade digging in, and the figure in the distance screamed as his back arced in pain, before collapsing.

The old him might have been pleased at this victory, but Cutter felt no pleasure, had not felt any in years. He felt only a need, the need which had driven him to Brighton in the first place, the need—ill-defined even to himself—which had made him always refuse the temptation to take his own life. He looked at the sword he still held, coated in blood, then he sighed and started after the final man.

The man was moving slowly, hobbling a few steps only to stumble and fall, shooting glances back each time which showed his terror even in the poor visibility. In a few minutes, Cutter was on him, staring down. He didn't know what he felt, in that moment, knew only that it was not victorious. The man couldn't find the strength to rise now and was busy scraping at the snow, dragging himself forward, fighting the inevitable as sure as every man did when his time came around. And that time, Cutter knew, *always* came around.

"Let it go," Cutter said. "It's done with now."

The man didn't listen, though, only continuing to drag himself forward, crying and whimpering, his words unintelligible, coated as they were in his own agony.

"You will die before you reach them," Cutter said, trying again, "even if you were allowed to make the attempt. It is over. You can rest now."

"P-please," the man said turning awkwardly on his side to stare at Cutter with eyes as wide as the moon overhead. "Please. Y-you can save me."

"No. I know nothing of saving. Only killing."

"Oh gods. Gods help me."

"Yes," Cutter said, raising the sword overhead. "Gods help us both."

# CHAPTER SIX

*Guilt always tastes better on a full stomach.*
*—Common saying of the Known Lands*

Matt, or Matty as his mother called him, woke to the smell of meat cooking. It was a good, pleasant smell, familiar, too, and for a time he forgot the past day's events, thought he was at his mother's house once more, and the smell was that of her cooking. She had always loved to cook, his mother, before the sickness took her and robbed her of her strength. She had been great at it, too, and plenty of days had seen the villagers of Brighton making some excuse to come by around meal time. His mother had never turned them out, had only welcomed them before turning to him, offering him the smile she had always reserved for him and him alone. "Matty, look, it seems we'll be having company for supper, how's that?" she'd say.

He could hear her voice, even then, and he felt himself smiling in response. But then he opened his eyes—a job made more difficult than normal for all the frost accumulated on his face—and saw that the previous day's events had not been some terrible dream after all. He lay in a bed roll, all of him covered in thick blankets save his face. Snow was falling all around him, and he turned to see that the smell he'd detected wasn't his mother's cooking after all but Cutter. The man's massive back was to him as he tended the fire. Not his mother, then, and he was Matty no longer. He had always hated it when she'd called him that, always thought it had sounded like a kid's name. Now, though, he thought he would do anything to hear her say it one more time. But she never would, would never say anything again, and there would be no more visitors from Brighton, for the village was as dead as his mother. Or at least, the woman who had pretended to be his mother, only, according to Cutter, because she'd been paid for the trouble.

The anger washed away the last vestiges of sleep. Had she only ever pretended to love him? Had he only ever imagined that smile, the one that he had thought meant she loved him? And what of his father? He had spent years crying for him after he died—how long had he spent counting the coins he'd been paid to take Matt in?

"Ah. You're awake then. Eat."

Matt was pulled from his thoughts to see that Cutter had turned from the fire and was offering him a bowl of stew. It smelled delicious, and he was all too aware that the sun was beginning to rise on the horizon, meaning it had been nearly twenty-four hours since he'd last eaten, a breakfast he'd prepared himself and whatever talents his mother had when it came to cooking, he had, unfortunately, not inherited them. *But of course I wouldn't have, since she's not my real mother.*

As hungry as he was, he wasn't yet ready to let his anger go, and he crossed his arms, turning away sullenly. For while his mother and father had been guilty of taking him on for money, it had been Cutter who had paid them to do it, dumping Matt off as if he were no more than some lost mongrel found in the street. "I'm not hungry."

"Eat anyway," the man said, reaching it out farther. "It could be the last meal you'll have in a while. Animals won't stray close to the Black Woods. Not normal ones anyway. Fact is, we're lucky to have this squirrel."

Matt studied the man's eyes carefully. Cutter had always been kind to him, in his way, but the man always seemed to him to be on the edge of violence. Once, his friend Beldin's father had bought a dog from a traveling merchant. The dog had seemed kind enough, gentle, even, lazing about mostly, and all of the village kids had loved it—in the outskirts of the world like Brighton, pets were a luxury few could afford. They had loved that dog, doted on it, right up until it had bitten Beldin one day. Matt had been there. Beldin had done nothing to deserve it, had only been walking by the dog, but it had been vicious, exploding at him like a beast, chewing and digging at Beldin's leg. It had taken over a minute for Beldin's father to rip the dog free, and Beldin had walked with a limp ever since.

Of course, Beldin would walk with a limp no longer, for he, like the rest of Brighton, was dead. Still, in many ways, Cutter reminded Matt of that dog. He could be kind, could be gentle, but there seemed to be a violence within him, one only waiting to erupt to the surface. His anger, he thought, was like a caged beast, calm and docile on the outside, but on the inside, waiting for its moment, the moment when some careless onlooker might draw too close, the moment when he would lash out. Beldin's father had put the dog down, but, somehow, Matt did not think he would have found it so easy to do the same with Cutter.

He took the offered bowl.

Cutter studied him for a moment with those cold eyes, eyes that could have hid anything—or nothing. For a moment, Matt thought he might have somehow read his thoughts, thought that the beast might have worked its way free of its cage. The man, though, only grunted and rose, turning to stare back into the falling snow, back toward Brighton.

Matt released a breath he hadn't realized he was holding, thankful that the big man's attention was no longer on him, like a weight crushing him. Then, belatedly, he realized what he had failed to notice in his surprise. "You're...you're hurt."

Cutter turned to regard him and, sure enough, he saw the cut on the man's left arm, the bandage which had been wrapped around it stained lightly with blood. Not a deep cut, then, but a recent one. Cutter grunted again. "It's nothing."

"But...what happened?"

The man seemed to consider that, then. "I fell."

It was a lie, that much was obvious, but it was just as obvious that the man wasn't going to say anything more. Yet another lie, then, to add to the lies which had made up Matt's entire life. "You're not going to eat?"

"I already did."

Matt frowned at that, glancing around the fire, but if there was a second bowl, he didn't see it, and the small pot Cutter had used didn't appear to be much bigger than Matt's bowl. Had the man only eaten before him, or had he given it all to Matt? After all, one squirrel wasn't much split between two people—wasn't much for one, really, as Matt found that he was still hungry—but he thought there had been a surprising amount of meat in the stew, enough to account for a single squirrel, surely.

And there it was again—that kindness. The kindness he had seen from the man before, a sort of off-handed kindness which he never acknowledged, which he would have likely preferred no one acknowledge. Which was real, then? The anger or the kindness? Both?

"Do you think they'll catch us?" Matt asked, following the man's gaze. He could see nothing but snow, everything else more than a few feet ahead obscured from view by the heavy curtain of white, so that the men could have been less than a hundred paces away, and he would have never known it.

"Not before we reach the Black Wood," he said.

Matt frowned. Yesterday, the man had been sure that they would be caught, but now he seemed confident that they would make it to the woods first. What had changed? Whatever it was, he had a feeling it had something to do with the cut on the man's arm. Had he gone out in the darkness to hide their trail or lay a false one? Matt knew little of such things, but he thought that it would have been a pointless effort as any false trail he might have made would have likely been covered in snow less than an hour later. So what then?

He wondered at it, but not for long. Mostly, he thought of the Black Wood, of what awaited them there. He'd heard the stories, of course. Everyone had. His own mother—and father, before he'd passed—had refused to tell him any, claiming the stories painted the Fey as evil, like demons, when in truth they were just creatures acting according to their nature as all creatures must. Felmer's dad, though, had enjoyed telling them, and more often than not, Matt had spent those nights when he'd stayed over at his friend's house lying awake, terrified, sure that the Fey would appear at any moment and eat his insides or chop off his face and wear it like a mask, the way Felmer's dad said they had during the war.

A war which, Felmer's dad told him, wasn't over, for while a treaty had been signed between the mortals and the Fey following the Fey king's death, it was said to be an uneasy peace, one in which each side nursed the anger its losses had kindled. There were a thousand creatures which had, barely a lifetime ago, lived in the entire country and which now were said to all lurk inside the Black Woods, plotting their revenge for being driven from their lands. Boughdins and Berdocks, Walers and Wuvias, and a thousand others. All manner of creatures of all shapes and all sizes, yet all of them, according to Felmer's dad, sharing one very particular, very nasty characteristic—the consuming of human flesh.

Matt felt a chill run up his spine at that, one he could not wholly blame on the cold no matter how much he might want to. He glanced up at Cutter who was now packing everything away for the journey. If the man felt any fear at the prospect of entering the Wood, he did a good job of hiding it.

"Finished?" Cutter asked, glancing at him and holding his hand out for the bowl.

In truth, Matt could have eaten another two bowls just like the first, but considering that there was nothing left and that he was more than a little sure that the man had foregone his own meal so that he might eat, he tried a smile. "Yes, thank you. It was good."

Cutter grunted—it seemed the man had a policy not to waste any words when a grunt would do—then took the bowl, stowing it in the pack.

Matt moved to help him, but Cutter waved him away. "Get your fur coat—the one in your pack. There's a freeze coming." He paused, sniffing the air, once again putting Matt in mind of some predator, perhaps one questing for prey. "Won't be long now."

"Okay," Matt said. He walked over to his pack and withdrew the fur coat he'd placed inside the night before when he'd lain down to sleep. Then he paused, looking at it, a stab of sadness, sharp as a razor, cutting through him. His mother had made him the coat years ago, from a bear Cutter had killed. It was a fine one, finer than any of the fur coats any of the other villagers had, for his mother had been as skilled with a needle and thread as she had been a cooking pot and spices. Tears were running down his cheeks before he realized it, and he wasn't sure how long he stood there, only that, after at time, he felt the big man's hand on his shoulder.

Gentle, but he could feel the strength in it, strength that he thought could have crushed his shoulder if the man had taken it in mind to give it a good squeeze. "Come on, lad," he said. "We've got to go. We'll need to be in the forest before the snow comes. Might be we can find some shelter."

"Does it ever stop?" Matt asked, still staring at the coat he held. "The guilt, I mean?"

"Guilt?"

"The villagers," Matt said, turning on him. "Brighton. My m— the woman who raised me. We let them all die."

"You have nothin' to be guilty of, boy. I made you come, remember? Besides, even if you had stayed, you could have done nothing but die with them. That's the same for both of us."

Matt nodded slowly. "But does it ever stop?"

Cutter watched him for a moment, those eyes, so pale blue as to be almost white, studying him. "No. But sometimes, you forget it. At least for a while."

"Only to remember it again?"

"Yes."

# CHAPTER SEVEN

*Some men think the Fey evil and therefore believe that their home, the Black Wood, must be evil also.*
*They are wrong on both counts. The Fey are not evil, not anymore than a winter storm or a summer hurricane is evil.*
*Not anymore than men might be said to be evil.*
*Not evil, then. But are they deadly?*
*Oh yes. In all the worlds, there are few things deadlier than the Fey.*
*—Exiled Historian to the Crown Petran Quinn excerpt from "Coming to the Known Lands"*

It felt as if they walked forever, as if they trudged through some gods-forsaken land of the damned in which there was no rest or comfort. And no warmth, that most of all. Matt had lived his entire life—at least as much of it as he could remember—in Brighton. Had believed, at least until yesterday, that he had been born there and that he would likely die there. And, for the most part, that had been okay, that belief.

But now things were different, everything was different. There was no Brighton, his mother was not his mother, and though he'd spent his entire life in the cold climes of the edges of human civilization and had thought himself largely inured to the miseries such a climate provided, he was realizing that he was wrong. And he was cold. Cold inside and cold outside. It was as if he had forgotten what heat was, as if the world itself had forgotten. There was nothing but the white emptiness, white but somehow dark, too. A white that did not sparkle beautifully but that drained the world of color, of life, and though the land spread out before them in a vast emptiness that a man could get lost in, it was also suffocating, oppressive in a way that was hard to define. Matt had never felt like that before about the snow, but he felt it now. Perhaps the emptiness had always been there, but he only recognized it now because of the emptiness inside him, one that matched it.

It did not help that Cutter had said nothing for the last several hours as they trudged through the ever-thickening blanket of snow which lay across the world, the only sound the crunching of the forest beneath their feet and their ragged breaths. It didn't make sense to Matt that a man could be cold and hot at the same time, could not feel his nose and face for numbness but could be sweating inside the fur coat his mother—or the woman who had raised him—had made for him. But then, nothing since he'd woken up the day before had made sense, and he was beginning to think—to know—that nothing ever would again.

"How much farther?" he asked, more for something to say than because he expected any answer.

He wasn't to be disappointed then as Cutter only glanced back at him, his face a mask which gave away no clue as to his thoughts. "Farther," he said.

And that was about the best conversation they had for the first half of the day.

There was nothing for him, then, nothing but the snow and his harsh breaths and a companion who said nothing, who didn't even seem human, but like some automaton taking step after step not because it hopes to reach a destination or because it even wishes to leave another but simply because it knows nothing else. Nothing, then, to distract him from the thoughts which plagued his mind—a confusing jumble of hatred and anger and self-pity mixed with more than his share of guilt and shame. He wanted to scream, wanted to shout that it wasn't fair and that the gods were devils, really, and that Cutter was the biggest devil of them all. What kept him from it, what silenced the scream before it ever reached his throat was that he was afraid the man would agree with him, and what could you say to such a thing as that? What could anyone say?

Nothing. He had nothing, was part of nothing, belonged to nothing, and when all those things were true what was there to say? Nothing. So he walked, an automaton in his own right, a puppet pulled along by motivations he understood no better than the marionette its strings.

Finally, his breath rasping in his lungs, his fingers and face too cold to *be* cold anymore, feeling as if they belonged to someone else, he stopped. "P-please," he stammered. "Please, we have to stop."

Cutter turned, and if the man was weary at all from their hike, he did not show it. Nor did he scorn or taunt Matt which might almost have been better, at least it would have been *something*, something other than the silence. Instead, the man said nothing, only nodded and crouched on the ground, his thick, fur-clad forearms draped over his knees as the snow fell around them and Matt panted, trying to catch his breath.

It was not comfortable, that rest, for he could feel the man waiting on him, and though he did not look at Matt, but behind them, as he always did when they stopped, he could feel the man's gaze on him anyway, judging him, thinking him weak. And the worst was that Matt *felt* weak, weak and afraid and no more than a child. Hard to believe that only yesterday he and Felmer and his friends had been talking about joining the soldiers. Children pretending to be adults and doing a terrible job, fooling themselves and no one else, all of them wanting to show the other, to show *themselves* how tough they were, how brave.

But if the last day and a half had taught Matt anything, it was that he was not tough, he was not brave. Cutter was tough, brave, too, but Matt was not like him, could never *be* like him. The man seemed scared of nothing, moved by nothing, and Matt was scared of everything. He had nothing in common with such a man, no matter how much he wanted to. "You can fight," Matt said, suddenly overcome with an idea.

Cutter glanced up from where he'd been studying his hands as if trying to divine some secret there. He said nothing, only watched Matt, watched him with something that might have been dread hidden in his pale, icy gaze. Or, just as likely, it was nothing.

"I mean, you know how," Matt said, suddenly uncomfortable under that stare.

"Everything that breathes knows how. Men more than most."

Matt winced. "That's not…what I mean is you've been trained."

Again, the man said nothing, only watching him, waiting for what he would say, and Matt shifted, uncomfortable under that scrutiny. "I mean...you could train me. To fight."

"No."

A single word, but spoken roughly, nearly in a growl, and Matt found himself offended by the man's quick refusal. "No?"

Cutter said nothing, and dangerous man or not, Matt was angry. "Damn you then," he hissed. "Damn you for everything. I hate you."

The man did not snap back, as Matt almost wished he would, did not retort or argue or even threaten. He only stood, watching Matt and weathering his words and his anger the same way he had weathered the travails of the last day and a half—in expressionless silence.

"Damnit *say* something!" Matt yelled, hating the way his voice cracked.

"What would you have me say?" Cutter asked quietly, in a voice that was far more terrifying than it would have been if he'd raised it in anger. "You're not a fighter, boy, that's all. Sure, I could teach you enough that you probably wouldn't stab yourself, but even if I wanted to—and I don't—we don't have the time. You're not a killer, that's all. There's nothing to be ashamed about—most people aren't."

"You don't know what I am or where I come from!" Matt shouted. "No one does. Not even—"

Suddenly, Cutter spun to look into the distance from where they'd come.

"What? What i—"

"Quiet," the man growled, holding up his hand for silence.

"Don't tell me to be silent," Matt said, not ready to let it go, "not after—"

"Shut your fucking mouth, boy," the big man growled, and Matt did, his jaw snapping shut. "Shut up and listen."

Matt did, but he could hear nothing. "What is it? I don't—"

But Matt forgot what he'd been about to say as suddenly the blinding snow that had continued since they'd set off that morning stopped as if it had never been. Matt had lived his entire life in the frigid temperatures in and around Brighton, and he had never before seen a snowstorm stop so abruptly and so completely. One moment, the air was covered in thick flakes, so many that you could barely see in front of your face. The next, the snow was gone, and there was no noise at all, only a deathly silence that, for reasons he could not explain, made the hairs on the back of his next stand up.

"We're here."

Suddenly Cutter turned and started off in the direction they'd been traveling. Matt followed his gaze then froze, his breath catching in his throat. He had been able to see nothing during the blizzard, nothing at all except the falling snow. Only moments ago, he had despaired that he would ever see anything else, had wished to finally reach the Black Woods as they, however bad they were, could never approach the terribleness of the featureless white landscape. But gods, how he had been wrong.

The woods lay in front of them, no more than thirty feet away, and even with the snow that had been falling, Matt could not imagine how they'd gotten so close without him seeing any sign of them, would have bet any amount of coin that the woods were still a great distance away, out of sight. But there they were, close, and he felt as if someone—or something—had been creeping up on him, felt that same feeling that sometimes overcame a man, that he was being watched, even though he knew there was no one else in the room with him.

Somehow, though he knew he stared at the woods, he found it difficult, despite the closeness, to make out individual trees. Instead, what he saw was a terrible black *smear* across the landscape, as if an artist, having completed his work and found himself displeased, dipped his thumb into the black paint and dragged it angrily across the canvas.

"Fire and salt," he breathed, "it's...it's terrible."

Cutter followed his gaze, staring at the woods the way a man might gaze upon a familiar—and unliked—visitor suddenly arriving on his doorstep. "Yes. The Woods have always been an important place to the Fey, a sacred place. They are the heart of their power. It is the only reason, many believe, why they signed the treaty in the first place, sacrificing so much of their lands to at least preserve the Black Woods. Though, of course, they do not call it that. That is a name we chose for it."

"You sound as if you think they're the good guys," Matt said, frowning. "But I've heard the stories, the things the Fey do. They're evil."

Cutter shrugged. "Perhaps. But then all things act according to their nature, even men. The Fey would not think of themselves as evil just as men do not—they are simply different than we are. As different from us as we are from the trees or the rocks. And know this—it was not the Fey who destroyed Brighton. It was men."

Matt snarled. He was angry, angry at his fake mother and fake father, at this man who had sold him as if he were just some commodity to be gotten rid of at a good price. "If you love them so much, why don't you go and live with them?"

Cutter spun on him quickly, a hard, cold look in his gaze, and Matt thought that he had gone too far after all, that the man would soon wrap those massive hands around his throat and choke the life out of him. Instead, he slowly turned back to stare at the Black Woods, at that dark smear across the landscape, and shook his head in what might have almost been sadness. "I would not be welcome."

"Why?" Matt said, his curiosity getting the better of his anger, at least for the moment. "What did you do?"

The man was silent for a time and Matt was just beginning to think he wasn't going to answer when he finally spoke. "What all beasts do," he said in a voice barely loud enough to hear. "I acted according to my nature. Now, let's go—there is another storm coming. A bad one."

Matt frowned up at the sky. He had lived in Brighton all his life and knew well the signs of a storm, had been taught from an early age, for more than one person—child and adult—had been lost to the storms over his lifetime, their bodies often found only a short distance away from the village, yet in the blinding snow they had been unable to make their way back to safety. None of those signs were present now. "I don't see any sign. How do you know a storm's coming?"

Cutter grunted, settling the pack on his shoulder as he rose from where he'd knelt. "I always know."

# CHAPTER EIGHT

*Revenge is a sour drink and no surprise considering its ingredients. Hate and rage, pain and loss...how can it be anything else? Yet, as sour as it is, as bitter, there is one more truth to know— Men will never stop seeking it.*
—Rodarian Dalumis, Poet, excerpt taken from "The Ramblings of Life from a Rambling Life"

He sat atop his horse, a massive beast with flanks rippling with muscle, and which stood a foot taller than any of the other mounts standing nearby. The beast had been a gift, long ago, from the Fey king, a king who was now dead and gone, a beast born in a kingdom that hardly still existed and that, in large part, thanks to him.

But it was not the magnificent beast beneath him of which he thought, not then. Now, as always, he thought of one thing and one thing only. Vengeance. He studied the scattered, broken bodies silently, his gauntleted hand flexing as if he might crush the object of his hatred in his grasp. He was not aware of this just as he was not aware—and would not have cared even if he had been—of the troubled looks his men shot him from a short distance away.

"Sire."

Feledias Paterna, known as "Stormborn" to his men—thanks in part to the jagged birthmark, resembling a lightning bolt, which ran down one side of his face and, more recently, in part, to his temperament—turned to regard the scout. The man was covered in sweat, his dark pony-tailed hair lank with it despite the frigid temperatures this far north. He fidgeted anxiously in his saddle as Feledias watched him. "What?"

"T-they're gone, sir. These here, it seems, were *his* work."

No need to say who "he" was, for they all knew, no need for any of it, really, for any fool could see the man was gone just as any who had known him would have recognized the corpses and the attendant savagery as his work as clearly as any signature. And Feledias Paterna knew the man better than anyone else could have. After all, he was his brother. Or had been. Once.

He was tempted, then, to draw his sword from its sheath at his side and make his displeasure and annoyance clear by lopping off the scout's head, but he resisted the urge. Barely.

After all, there were more important things to think about than some fool scout. He was close now, close to the vengeance he had sought for over fifteen years. The closest he had ever been.

"It seems he flees to the Black Woods," the scout finished, licking his lips anxiously, though whether that anxiety came from fear of his prince's famous wrath or from the woods themselves was unclear.

"Then we will follow him."

There was an uncomfortable rustling from the men at that. "Sir," his second-in-command, Commander Malex, said, easing his horse forward and away from the two dozen others, "perhaps it's unwise to...that is, he knows the forest. He has been there before. And according to the terms of the concord, we are not to set foot inside the Black Woods. Perhaps we could set pickets, wait him out, or—"

"A coward's course," Feledias said, meeting his commander's eyes. "If the beastmen and goblins do not like it, then their blood will be added to that of their kin which feeds the ground. But tell me, Malex, do you seek to deny your prince out of a child's fear of bogeymen, or do you mean to deter me for another purpose? Do you work with him, Malex? Are you yet another traitor?"

The commander was, if nothing else, a brave man, a man who had ridden with Feledias and his brother on many campaigns, but brave or not, he blanched at that, his face going pale around his steel-gray beard and moustache. "No, Your Highness. I am now, as always, your loyal servant. Surely you know as much, for I have ridden with you for many years and—"

"You rode with *him* as well," Feledias said, his eyes narrowing. Then, after a moment, his frown split into a wide smile, and he clapped the other man on one of his broad shoulders, a big man, Malex, with a back nearly twice as wide as Feledias's own leaner frame. "Relax, Malex," he said. "I only jest. I know well your loyalty, know and remember. Just as I know that your caution is only done out of love for me and not fear for yourself, nor loyalty to my brother. Isn't that so?"

The man looked genuinely hurt at that, his broad features scrunching up. "Of course, sire."

"Very well," Feledias said, laughing. "And it is a love, a loyalty for which I am grateful. But now is not the time for caution, old friend. Now is the time for action. The time, as my brother was so fond of saying, for *blood*. Now come, ride with me, all of you. My brother's execution has been a long time in coming—it is past time the sentence was carried out."

And with that, he rode toward the Black Woods, the hooves of his massive charger kicking up great tufts of snow behind him. Those others—near fifty in all—who rode atop their own horses were his honor guard, his most trusted and skilled warriors, men—and two women—who had sworn their lives to him. Yet they glanced at each other, their expressions troubled, before finally turning to their commander who gave a single, gruff nod.

"You heard the prince—we go."

And so they did, fifty horses, fifty men, charging behind their ruler, seeking the blood of the man who had driven him to madness, all of them entertaining the thought—the hope—that perhaps, when the object of their ruler's hatred was vanquished, perhaps their prince would be the man he once had been.

# CHAPTER NINE

*I had the misfortune on campaign to walk beneath those great trees
Their branches dark, even in the light of day, seeming to reach for us
I remember well the suffocating feeling of that place, the oppressive hatefulness that seemed to radiate from it
I remember that just as I remember the sounds of the screams of those who wandered too far away
For when a man—or men—enters the Black Woods, there is always a price
A price those men paid that day.
A price, the gods help me, that I pay still.
—Balus Camin, veteran of the Fey Wars in interview with Exiled Historian to the Crown Petran Quinn*

Mortals had named the Black Woods, given it a title which brought so many negative connotations, but while it was perhaps unkind, it was also accurate. By the time they reached the nearest trees on the outskirts of the forest, the snow had begun to fall again, thicker and heavier than ever, and it was all Cutter could do to see the ground at his feet with each step he took.

The temperature had dropped at least ten degrees in the last hour, and he felt the frost gathering on his eyelashes when he blinked, felt, too, his muscles beginning to grow cold and stiff despite their fast pace. He hesitated at the border, gazing about at the trees. This close, the air of menace they possessed had not vanished but instead had grown stronger, yet it was not the feeling in the present, not the present at all, in fact, which caused him to hesitate.

Instead, it was the past, a past full of memories which he felt looming close, whispering in his ear. He remembered coming here the last time, a very different man than he was now, remembered laughing at the fear on the faces of his comrades just as he remembered, when he'd left, promising himself that he would never return. And not *just* himself, but many others. But if life had taught him anything it was that the world loved nothing more than to mock a man's promises, particularly those promises he makes to himself.

He stepped into the Black Woods.

It was an easy thing, so very easy. But then, so was sticking your foot into a bear trap. It was always the getting out that presented a problem.

After a time, he did not hear the boy's footsteps behind him, nor his flagging breath, and he turned to see that he had stopped just inside the boundary of the forest and was now staring back at the snowy plain behind them. Already, the thickly-falling snow had obscured their footsteps completely, so that they might have never come at all.

He knew well the feeling men had when entering the Black Woods, the abstract fear, as if they had just traveled down the gullet of some great beast, for he had seen that fear etched into the faces of his companions so many years ago. Had seen it, but had not felt it for himself, for the man he had been knew no fear, only hunger, no worry, only bloodlust. He walked back to where the lad stood.

Here, beneath the boughs of the thick trees with their limbs which seemed to twist as they reached in all directions, as if meaning to swallow the entire world, the curtain of falling snow had vanished, caught up above in the forest's mantle. So then, he could see clearly the emotions twisting the boy's features, a mixture of fear and grief and anger and finally, resignation.

He said nothing as they stood there, for there was nothing he could say. He had never been good with words, had been good at very few things, in fact. Only the one. Finally, the boy turned to him. No tears in his eyes, as Cutter had expected, and he couldn't decide if that were a good thing or not. He was growing, then, had grown much in the last two days and, unfortunately, the world had a way of shaping a man that was akin to a blacksmith shaping metal. Turning him into a weapon or into a useless scrap to be discarded as if of no use.

The boy met his eyes then turned once more to stare at the frozen wilderness beyond the forest's borders. Was it sadness in his eyes? Sadness for what he left behind? Or was it something else?

"It...seems so far away," the boy said.

"Yes."

"It's as if...as if it's a world away."

In many ways, Cutter thought it was. After all, he had been here before, knew that the magic of the Fey was thickest here, in their sacred place, a place seemingly made to ensnare any who dared enter without invitation. A place where danger lurked around every corner and where a man could not trust the things he saw or heard, could not even trust that, should he turn to look behind him, the path on which he had trod would remain. When last Cutter had come, he had come with fifty other men, all brave, skilled warriors.

In the end, though, it had only been him, his brother, Commander Malex, and less than half a dozen others who had stumbled out once more. The Black Woods took their price—that much of the stories, at least, he knew to be true. Still, telling the boy as much would do no good, would only frighten him more, so he grunted. "Come—the storm is growing worse. We must find shelter and soon, or we will die."

The boy turned back to him and hesitated, perhaps deciding if dying was the better course. Certainly, it was the easier, for to live, Cutter knew, was to feel pain. In the end, though, the boy only nodded, saying nothing.

Cutter understood that too. After all, the world being what it was, what could a man say? What answer could he give? He could do nothing but walk the path before him. "Come," he said, "this way."

The air felt thick around them, oppressive, and each step Cutter took felt as if it was in the face of a high wind, one that pressed against him, trying to eject this trespasser from a place in which he did not belong. The forest around them was silent, too, far more silent than any wood he'd ever been in before, but he knew that that silence—like so much else in the Black Woods and having to do with the Fey at all, in fact—was no more than an illusion, just as the feeling that they were alone was an illusion. He did not doubt that even now, their progress was being marked, that it had been marked since they'd first set foot in the wood.

But like a dream, knowing a thing was an illusion did not mean that a man could peer behind the curtain, that he could see exactly what—and who—it hid. So, he did the only thing he could do: he walked on, checking behind him from time to time to see the boy with his shoulders hunched, his head tucked down against the frigid wind that whistled through the trees. He knew they could not go much farther. The temperature had grown colder still, seemed to drop a degree for each step they took into the forest, and the boy would not survive much longer. Neither would he, for that matter, but he had long since come to grips with his own impending death, and it was not for himself that he still lingered.

The boy, though, had barely lived and was too young to face death. That was not the only reason why he wished him to live, but it *was* the only reason he was prepared to be honest with himself about. The other brought back too many memories, and memories brought back too much pain. It was enough that he would keep the boy alive, if he could. He knew what he was, knew that he was not the man to save children from monsters lurking under their beds or in their closets. Knew, in fact, that he was the monster. But while all monsters had their fangs, their claws, there was nothing that said they could not use those on other monsters.

He knew what he was—had known for over fifteen years, was haunted by the memory of that knowledge, the memory of his greatest crime. Better for everyone, perhaps, if he was dead, but he would not die yet, not until the boy was safe, though what that meant, the world being what it was, he had no idea.

He heard a shuffling sound behind him, a breathless gasp, and turned to see that the boy had fallen. "I-I can't," the youth gasped, his breath pluming in great clouds as he sat on his hands and knees, his head hanging low. "I can't."

Cutter could have lifted him—he'd lifted heavier, that was sure, and scraping out an existence in the wilderness, even in a town like Brighton, didn't leave a man, or a boy, a lot of fat on him—but he knew that doing so would not be a favor. Instead, he stopped, frowning. "What do you intend to do, then?"

The boy raised his head, panting. "What?"

"You said you can't go on. So I'm asking you—what do you intend to do? Will you lie there and die? Will you weep and moan like some whipped mongrel?"

The boy's face twisted with grief, and for a moment, it looked as if he might cry, then his eyes flashed with anger, and it was a battle between the two to see which would win out. Cutter watched, curious, his blank stare doing nothing to reveal just how invested he was in the outcome. In the end, the boy chose anger as he had hoped he would. "Burn you," he hissed. "You're a bastard."

"Yes. I'm a bastard, the air is cold, and you're lying there whining about it."

The boy let out a growl then rose to his feet with a strength he hadn't looked to possess a moment before, drawing a small knife, the kind used for gutting small game, from his belt as he did. He tensed, as if he would come at Cutter, as if he meant to kill him, and Cutter waited, wondering whether or not he'd let him. In the end, though, the boy only slid the knife back into its sheath and stared at him, his face red with fury. "I hate you."

"You're not the first. You're angry now, and that's good—I can handle anger. The world bein' what it is, I don't understand a man who isn't. Better that, better you hate me, than I have to listen to you whine and mope anymore. Now, are you finished? The storm's going to get a lot worse before it gets better, and if we spend much more time out here, we won't come out the other end of it."

The boy's mouth worked, thinking over some biting remarks to say, maybe, but in the end, he only nodded. "I'm ready."

"Good. Now, come on."

***

As they walked, Cutter glanced around them, surveying the trees, their trunks far thicker around than any normal tree. Oddly, while there was snow covering the ground here as it had on the plain, none of it stuck to the trees, as if even the precipitation itself sensed the wrongness that seemed to emanate from them.

And emanate it did. Cutter was not a man known for his feelings or his sensitivity, but even he could feel the wrongness here, could feel it like pinpricks on his skin, taste it like ash in his mouth and smoke in his throat. It had been the same the last time, that feeling, of being watched, yes, but of being hated, too. Hated by the very trees which loomed overhead, by their roots, deep and old which snaked through the ground beneath their feet, like great veins pumping the blood in the heart of some malevolent beast.

"How about...there?"

The boy's voice cut through the stillness, seeming somehow profane or perverse, but Cutter turned, following his pointing finger to a ledge of ground underneath which was a very large hole, as if one of the massive trees surrounding them had been uprooted long ago. Cutter scorned himself for not having noticed it, for allowing himself to be so distracted by his own thoughts, by his surroundings, to even notice. It was important, he knew, for a man to keep his wits about him in the Black Woods. He had seen several companions who had not, who had allowed themselves to become distracted just as he had and who had paid for it with their lives.

"That will do nicely," he said. "Good eye, boy."

He saw the boy smile as if pleased at the compliment, but he chose to ignore it, walking toward the cut out. They made it there a few minutes later, and upon closer inspection it turned out to be much smaller than it had first appeared. The boy hesitated, glancing at him, obviously wanting to take the spot first but not wanting to be impolite. Cutter wanted to tell him that there were far worse things than being impolite, freezing to death for one, but there were more important things that had to be done before they slept, so he only nodded his head. "Take it, boy."

"But...but what about you?"

"What about me?" Cutter growled. "You gotta learn, boy, to look after yourself and no one else. The world doesn't give a shit about you or anyone. The best you can hope to do is survive."

The boy clearly wanted the spot, but still he hesitated. "My mother said that an act of kindness comes back to a man as ten down the road."

"And if he's dead down the road, by the time the kindness makes its way back? Just take the spot, boy. You're shakin' like a leaf already. That's bad, but when the shakin' stops, that'll be a whole lot worse."

"B-but I can help you to build a fire."

"A fire? Here, in the heart of Fey power? No, boy. It wouldn't catch, believe me, and if by some unlucky miracle it did, we wouldn't get to enjoy it long. There are powers in this wood, lad, many kinds, some very old and some not easily stirred. But lighting a fire here, in this place, would stir them sure enough. Now, here. Lay out your bedroll and get some sleep. We won't be goin' anywhere until the storm passes."

"But what about the men?"

"If they come for us now, in this, they'll die the same as us if we try to go on any farther. Relax. You're safe."

"Safe," the boy said as if it was a word he had not heard before, one to which he did not know the meaning, then he blinked groggily and began laying out his bedroll. He started to lie down, but Cutter caught his arm.

"Not yet. There's a few things we need to talk about first."

"Like what?" the boy asked, his voice sounding slurred.

"There are things here, in these woods," Cutter said. "Probably you can feel that, have felt it since we came here. True?"

The boy nodded. "Yes. It...my skin itches. And there's...I feel something, like someone's looking at me or watching me or..."

"That's because they are," Cutter said. "Make no mistake, boy. You might not see them, but they're there, and they know that we're here."

"But...what can we do? What do we do if they come?"

*Die probably.* But that wasn't the sort of medicine the boy needed now, so he lied. "They won't come. You're safe, boy. Lie down and get your rest while you can. Once the storm passes, we'll have to head out. We won't go too deep into the forest; the deeper in you go the more dangerous it gets, the oldest, greatest dangers lying at its center, but we have to go deep enough to lose the men that will be coming. Anyway, what I need you to understand is that you might hear things, during the night. Might see things. Ignore them. Whatever else you do, ignore them. Do you understand?"

"They're not real, you mean? Just...magic?"

"No, boy," Cutter said. "They're real, alright. The Fey may love their illusions and their tricks, but *they* are real, and if you let them, they'll show you just *how* real. Do you understand me?"

The boy nodded, his eyes drowsing as he moved toward his bedroll, but Cutter caught his arm again. "Tell me you understand. If you hear anything, if you see anything, tell me you'll ignore it."

"I understand," the boy said angrily, pulling his arm away. Cutter let him and watched as he lay down to close his eyes.

He had told him. Just as him and his companions had once been told and like those companions, like himself, the boy said he understood. The problem, though, was that some of those men who had said they understood vanished during that first night in the Woods, vanished and never came back again. At least, not all of them. Sometimes, during the days that followed, he or one of the others would stumble on little pieces of them, left like grisly trophies or prizes in their path. A finger, a toe, a tongue, an eye. The Fey were creative bastards, if nothing else.

Those were old memories, ones associated with others which he had spent years trying to forget and, recalling them as he now did, he decided that he would have to stay awake, no matter that he had gotten little sleep over the last three days, and that he was exhausted. He would stay awake as best he could to look out for the boy, to make sure that nothing happened to him. He sat with his back against a nearby tree, determined to stay awake, for it was the only way to make sure that the boy was alright.

He was asleep in less than five minutes.

# CHAPTER TEN

*What are the Fey, you ask?*
*That is not a question easily answered, for you see, they are many things.*
*They are beautiful and ugly, they are kind and cruel, they are clever and foolish.*
*They are like men, then, and, like men, one thing, above all else, might be said of them—*
*Whatever else they are, they are deadly.*
*—Exiled Historian to the Crown Petran Quinn*

Matt dreamed of fire. Fire and blood and smoke rising in great, dark churning pillars all around him. He dreamed of the sound of metal striking flesh. And the screams, of course. At first, he had no idea where he was, some hellish inferno where the attackers screeched like demons, swooping in on the villagers who ran and cried and begged. But no matter what they did, the men came for them, the sword came for them, and the answer to their pleas, to their cries of "Why? Why?" was always the same—blood.

All of it taking place around him but none of it touching him, so that he felt like a man who had bought a ticket to some demented show. And looking around, he began to see things he recognized. There, on the wall of a half-burned home, was a deep groove in the stone where he remembered himself and some friends trying to carve their initials but giving it up after seeing how long it would take. On his left, he could see the village's single well, one his father, before he'd died, had helped repair and maintain. Countless other small, trivial things, enough to let him know where exactly he was, and that knowledge immediately brought regret.

Better to not know, better to think he had been cast headlong into some violent, terrible city of the damned and that those poor souls who suffered and died were strangers than to know them by name, to know the village—or what was left of it—by name. Better to be dead, he thought, than to witness Brighton burn.

He ran then, with no idea where he was going, only meaning to go away, to *get* away as quickly as possible, but his feet refused this simple command and, in time, he was standing twenty feet away from his own home, the home he had lived in his entire life. Standing there, looking at it—or, at least, what was left of it—fear gripped his heart in an icy fist. The door had been stoved in, but, perhaps kindly, the inside of the house was obscured by thick, roiling clouds of smoke and shattered debris. Was his mother in there somewhere? Was she lying in bed, weak and feeble as she had for the last year? If he walked inside, would she smile at him, the smile that lately seemed to cost so much? Or was she dead already? If he walked inside, would he find her body lying there, mutilated as the villagers' had been? Broken and cast aside, the best thing in his world—perhaps the only really *good* thing—destroyed by the village's attackers with no more thought than a man might give to swatting a mosquito?

He thought that maybe he would, was terrified that he would, and he decided he did not want to go into that house, *dared* not go. But again, his feet betrayed him, acting of their own accord, and the next thing he knew he found himself slowly walking toward the broken, burned shell that had once been his home but was that no longer. Walking and moaning at the same time, "*No, no, please gods no,*" over and over in a litany that offered no comfort, in a plea that went unanswered.

He thought that things could get no worse, was sinking into a pit of despair, one from which he thought he would never emerge, one from which he thought he would never *want* to.

Then he heard the voice.

A child's voice, a girl's by the sound, screaming for help. Not so uncommon, not in that hellish place, for there were many screams, many pleas, but somehow this one was clearer than the rest, cutting through the din the way the brutal winter winds sometimes whistled through the village, sounding almost alive. Or at least *had* whistled, for they would whistle through Brighton no more, and anyone happening by a week from now would find no more than the broken remnants of a place where people had once been born and lived their lives. Any such traveler, a year hence, might wonder what had happened to this place, might wonder at its name, but that name, along with the lives of those who had once lived there, would be lost to time, covered in it the way shrubs and stones might lie covered deep beneath a winter snowfall.

"*Please, help me,*" the voice called again, and finally Matt seemed to regain some semblance of control over his own body. He turned in the direction from which the voice had come, grateful for any reason, any means of avoiding what lay in his home, of what he might find there. He feared for a moment that his feet would turn back to the house again, but they did not, and soon he was walking, rushing past villager and attacker alike, all of whom ignored him, as he made his way toward that voice.

He climbed out of the cutout from where the great tree had fallen. Cutter, sat with his back propped against the trunk of a great tree, his eyes on the cutout and on Matt. Or, at least, they would have been had the man not been sleeping, his head sunk low on his chest. Even asleep, Matt was surprised by how intimidating the man seemed. That menace was not lessened by the fact that he was covered in snow and frost, frost which clung to his dark beard, his eyebrows and eyelashes, but was somehow instead enhanced by it. He was like some ancient warrior frozen in time but waiting for a moment when he would be woken once more to reap a bloody harvest.

The chill that went through Matt's spine at that thought wasn't just from the cold. He had once thought this man his friend, the quiet man who lived up the hill, rarely speaking but, when he did, always seeming to say something of value. Gruff, sure, blunt and little concerned with politeness, but possessed of a deep, abiding kindness beneath all that, beneath that cold, blue stare so pale as to be almost gray. Now, having seen him in the last few days, how he moved through the snow relentlessly, as if a blizzard was just a challenge, one which he would inevitably overcome, after having seen how easily he had left those people in Brighton to fend for themselves against their attackers, now Matt was not so sure.

After all, whatever the man had told him, he believed that he could have helped. He didn't know what exactly Cutter was, had no idea who he had been before he'd come to Brighton, apparently carrying with him Matt, a baby then, but he knew that the man was not a normal man, at least not in the way that his father—or the man who had claimed to be his father—had been a normal man. He could not imagine Cutter bouncing him on his back and playing "horsey" as his father had, could not picture him sitting at dinner with his family, laughing and telling jokes.

He pictured him, instead, for reasons he did not know, standing on a slight rise in the middle of a great field, a field in which lay thousands of countless dead. And he, Cutter, the only one standing. He pictured him holding some great, massive weapon, a sword, perhaps, or a club. No, that wasn't it. He pictured him with an axe, a great, double-bladed axe with a haft so thick and a blade so heavy most men wouldn't have been able to lift it. A black-handled axe with a black blade. He pictured him lifting the axe above his head easily in one hand, tilting his head back and roaring in mad glee as the blade dripped crimson drops onto the ground.

That image was so powerful, so all-encompassing and altogether terrifying that, for a moment, Matt forgot what impulse had dragged him from his bed. Worse than that, he thought he could almost hear the man's wild, roaring laughter, the laughter of some demented god bent on destruction. Then the voice came again.

"*Please, help me,*" it pleaded. Not it, though—her. The worst of the storm had passed, the snow had stopped falling and in the stillness, in the quiet that often followed such storms, Matt could hear her clearly. A girl, alright, and a young one by the sound of it. He wondered for a moment, how such a one had managed to find herself here, in the Black Woods, wondered what possible reason she would have had to come, what terrible tragedy might have driven her here. But then, it had been tragedy that had driven him here too, hadn't it?

He considered waking Cutter, but in the end decided against it. The man's presence—while frightening in its own respect—might have went some way toward calming his nerves, toward banishing the strange, otherworldly feeling of dread pulling at Matt's heart, but he dared not wake him. Cutter, he'd discovered, was a man of a single mind, a single purpose, and it was likely that, should he wake him, the man would refuse to go help the girl and would keep Matt from doing so as well.

Then she would be left alone, much as he was alone, for while Cutter was many things—many things, Matt thought, that he even now did not guess at—the man was not much for companionship. Not a friend. A person would have a better chance of befriending a bear and, Matt thought, would probably have less chance of getting mauled.

"Please."

The voice was closer now or seemed to be. "I'm coming!" Matt yelled. Cutter might have been a cold-blooded bastard, but he was not, and he'd be damned if he was leaving anyone else to be alone, especially a little girl. Matt glanced around him at the great, black trunks of the trees, seeming to almost throb perversely in the moonlight, then started in the direction from which the voice had come. He would show Cutter—show himself, too—he could be brave. He was no child, not anymore, even if he had been a few days ago. He was nearly a man grown, and no man save perhaps Cutter would leave a child in the wilderness alone.

Luckily, there was a path through the trees that seemed to run in the exact direction from which the voice had come. That was a good thing—it meant that the girl was clever enough to stay on the path, knowing that was her best chance of being found. How she had survived the night he couldn't imagine, but Matt knew she couldn't be doing well, a thought reinforced by the weak, thready quality of her voice.

He walked for a few minutes then stopped, frowning. It was ridiculous, of course, but by some trick of the darkness and the pale moonlight, the trees seemed to have slowly crept closer, seemed to be crowding in around him.

He felt a twinge of panic but fought it down. "Say something!" he shouted, doing his best to remain calm, in control. They were only trees, after all, nothing to be frightened of.

"Here! Help, please!"

Matt's frown deepened. That was strange. The voice seemed to have come from somewhere close behind him—which was impossible. After all, he'd only walked for a few minutes, and the voice had seemed much farther away than that. He couldn't imagine how he could have walked past her, but he must have done so without realizing it, no doubt due to the darkness. He turned to start back down the path only to have the breath catch in his throat as he realized that the path which he had walked only moments before was no longer there. In its place, thick undergrowth choked the forest floor, seeming to glow in a pale, sickly translucence in the moonlight.

"No, that's ridiculous," he muttered. Of course the path was there—it had to be. He'd just *walked* down it, after all. "Damn this darkness," he cursed. Darkness that made it near impossible to see his hand in front of his face. He hesitated, studying the undergrowth crowding in all around him, thinking. He had gotten turned around, that was it, that *had* to be it. After all, in the darkness, such a thing was easy to do and his mother and father had often warned him of just such an occurrence when venturing outside of the relative safety the village of Brighton provided to go hunting or gathering berries as they sometimes had.

The night played tricks on even the most perceptive, and even expert trackers had gotten lost in such darkness, never to be seen or heard from again. In the darkness, things looked different, that was all. That was a truth even children—perhaps *especially* children—knew. After all, it was children for whom, in the night, coat racks became bogeymen lurking in the corner of their rooms and empty shoes peeking out of their closets became the great furred feet of some monster. Children's thoughts, children's fears, yet they sent a superstitious shiver of fear through him, and Matt hissed, giving his head a shake. "Relax," he whispered, rubbing his hands in front of his face in a vain effort to bring some warmth back to them. "You're not a child to be scared of make-believe monsters."

He took a deep breath then began pushing his way through the undergrowth in the direction of the voice. The bushes stubbornly stood in his path, seeming to cling and pull at him as he forced his way through, but he continued to make steady—if slow—progress. After he'd been shoving his way through the undergrowth for around five minutes he stopped again. It was weird. The girl's voice had sounded close, and even with the time he'd lost forcing his way past the bushes, he would have thought he'd come upon her by now.

The bushes seemed to be crowding closer, pushing toward him as if intent on suffocating him and despite the fact that he knew the thought was a childish one, Matt held his hands out, slowly spinning in a circle for some superstitious fear that the bushes *were* moving, only doing it when he wasn't looking. "Hello!" he shouted, unable to deny the crack in his voice now, thinking less of saving than of being saved. "Where are you?"

"I'm here."

Matt jumped, spinning. The voice had seemed to come from right behind him, and there had been something strange about it, hadn't there? It had been the same voice, that much he knew, but it had sounded different, somehow...older. No, that was silly. It was just the night, that was all, just the night and his own fear working at him, making his mind play tricks. "Where?" he asked breathlessly. "I can't see you."

"This way," the voice said, and it was strange that the more panicked he felt the less panicked the voice seemed to sound. "Just a little farther."

Suddenly, the choking pressure of the bushes—imagined pressure, no doubt—eased, and, turning to the sound of the words, Matt saw that he wasn't surrounded after all, but that there was a path, one small enough he must have overlooked it in the near-darkness, leading in the voice's direction. "I'm coming," he said, "just...just don't move anymore, alright?" *Please. Please don't move.*

"I won't," the voice assured him. "I'll wait for you. Just come...a little...closer."

But despite the voice's assurances, it seemed to be growing farther away with each word, and Matt found himself rushing down the path, eager to find the girl. To save her, yes, but also to no longer be alone in the darkness with the trees looming all around him and the bushes seeming to creep in the moment he turned his back. He hurried forward, shoving errant limbs out of his way and then suddenly the ground vanished from beneath his feet, and he let out a cry as he stumbled and fell and began to roll.

Pain shook his arm and legs as he tucked his head in, rolling down a hill in a bumping, painful fall. He finally came to a panting, groaning rest on his back, blinking up at the night sky, a sky which seemed devoid of any stars at all. There was only the moon, a moon which seemed huge in his sight, so big and close that he was overcome with the certainty that, should he reach out, he would be able to touch it.

After the worst of the pain and his own shock had subsided, he became aware of a sound. It was the gentle, gurgling sound of water. Frowning and swallowing hard, he sat up and turned to the source of the noise to see, to his astonishment, that what he'd heard was the sound of a small stream less than a dozen feet away. A gentle, burbling stream that seemed to sparkle in the moonlight as if millions of diamonds lay just beneath the water's surface. And on the bank of the stream, sitting with her back to him, was a little girl.

She wore a bright white dress that would have looked far more at home on some noble child having dinner in her father's manor than in the middle of a forest in the dead of night. And, perhaps stranger still, there wasn't so much as a speck of dirt on the dress which seemed to almost glow. Matt thought that was odd considering she'd been lost in the woods for the gods alone knew how long, but he brushed the thought aside. Now that he had found the girl, Matt could admit to himself that he was just glad to not be alone any longer, to have a companion, in this place, even if it were only a small girl that no doubt still hid under her blanket when she felt scared.

"Hi," he said, slightly breathless.

The girl turned and in the darkness, her face was largely covered in shadows that seemed to shift and writhe. "Hello, child," she said in a surprisingly forceful, surprisingly older voice.

Matt frowned, hesitating from where he'd been walking toward her. "I'm sorry, what?"

"I'm just a child," she said, "and I'm frightened. Please, will you help me?"

That sounded normal—at least, the voice sounded as it should, and Matt gave a soft laugh. "Gods, but it's dark out here, isn't it? And cold too. You must be freezing." And that was true. In fact, the temperature seemed to have dropped since he'd stepped outside of the undergrowth and came to stand beside the stream. Even now, his breath plumed in front of him in great white clouds.

"It's always cold here," the girl said, her voice quiet and with a sort of sing-song quality to it. "*I'm* always cold."

"Always?" Matt asked. "How long have you been here?"

There was a sort of shifting, a blur it seemed as if too much to follow, and the next thing Matt knew, the girl was standing, facing him, her hands clasped in front of her in a gesture that might have seemed sweet in other circumstances but somehow, in that moment, didn't seem sweet at all, seemed menacing in a way he couldn't define. "Me?" she asked. "I've always been here. Will you help me?"

The girl was acting strangely, that much was certain, talking strangely, too, but that was no great surprise. He'd heard of people caught in the elements acting strangely before, shock it was called, and was that any real surprise? The girl had been wandering in the Black Woods for the gods alone knew how long, in the cold, alone. Was it any wonder, then, that she was a little off? Matt had been wandering around for only a few minutes...he paused, glancing at the moon with a frown, a moon which seemed to have moved far in the sky, indicating that he'd spent far more time searching for the girl than he'd thought. An impossible amount of time. Anyway, he'd been out here for only a short while, however long, and he was already beginning to feel a little crazy. "Of course I'll help you," he said.

"You'll take me?" she said, studying him with eyes that seemed almost too large for her face and in which, with the darkness, he could discern no pupils. "Out of the wood, I mean?"

"Soon," Matt promised. "Only, I have a friend with me, and I'll have to talk to him, to see—"

"The *other* you mean," she said in what sounded almost like a hiss.

"Another," he said, assuming he must have heard her incorrectly, "that's right. We came here for a reason, but I know we won't be staying long. We can meet up with him and—"

"Leave him."

"I'm sorry—what?"

She gave him a small smile. "Leave him," she repeated. "It would be better, if you did. Easier. Easier for everyone."

Matt gave a soft laugh. "I can't leave him he's my..." Well, "friend" actually didn't sound quite right, but he shrugged.

"Anyway, look. I know you're scared, okay?" he said, kneeling down in front of her and grabbing her thin shoulders, shoulders which, despite their small appearance, felt somehow strange beneath his touch. "But this man, he won't hurt you or me…" *Probably.* "Besides, he can help me. Help us, that is. He's been here before."

"*Yes,*" she said, and for a moment he caught only a brief flash of her teeth, teeth that almost seemed sharpened, as if they had been filed down to points.

"Yes," he repeated. "So you'll come? To see my friend?"

"I will come," she said, smiling, and this time, her teeth appeared normal. His mind, then, playing tricks. Perhaps he was not so far from that frightened child as he had thought.

"Will you hold my hand?" she asked. "I do not want to lose you."

"Uh…sure, of course," Matt said. He took her small hand in his own and instantly felt repelled, for it was clammy with sweat and cool to the touch with a strange, greasy quality to it. Still, touching a clammy hand was by far the least of his problems, so he did so, offering her a smile he did not feel. "Ready?"

"Ready," she said, smiling again.

It was only then that Matt realized, looking down at her, that the girl wasn't wearing any shoes. She must have lost them somewhere along the way, before or after she herself had gotten lost. That brought some semblance of thought back to him, and he shook his head. "I'm an idiot, sorry. Tell me, who were you here with?"

"I'm here with no one," she said. "It is only me and you." She finished the last in a voice that he would have almost thought sounded coy had it come from someone older.

"Right," he said slowly, "that is, what I mean is who were you with before you got lost?"

Some expression—anger or annoyance perhaps—flashed across the little girl's face but was gone in another instant, so quickly that he was left wondering whether or not he had imagined it. What replaced it was a look of confused terror, and her lip began to tremble. "I…I don't remember."

*Fool,* he inwardly scorned himself. *Why not just remind her of her situation?* "It's okay," he assured her. "I've got you. We'll get you safe and warm, then we'll find whoever you were with, how'd that be?"

"I don't know," the girl said seriously, the tears which had threatened nowhere in evidence. "I've never been warm before."

Something about that sent an uncomfortable shiver down him, and Matt decided he'd had enough talking for now. Besides, if they didn't make it back to Cutter by the time the man woke, there was no telling what he might do. Likely, he'd abandon Matt, leaving him alone with the girl. That, for reasons he couldn't quite put his finger on, was a very frightening prospect, one perhaps even worse than the idea of being left alone in the woods in general, and suddenly he felt a very powerful urge to break into a run, to leave the girl and her perfect, somehow stainless dress with her bare feet with not a speck of dirt on them, to go and find Cutter as quickly as possible.

But no. That was something a child would do, something the frightened boy he had been a few days ago would have done, and he had promised himself that he would be that boy no longer. So instead, he kept the girl's hand in his, took a slow, deep breath, and started back the way he had come. The undergrowth was as thick as he remembered—an oddly reassuring thing, considering how unusual the night had been—and his task was made more difficult by the fact that he could only use one hand, his other held in a tight grip by the girl. He tried to pull it away once so that he could heave a dead tree branch out of the way, but she refused to let it go, and he was forced to climb over the obstacle instead, helping her along a moment later.

As he worked his way through, the girl behind him, a silent presence, he began to think that he had taken a wrong turn somewhere, began to feel the first ticklings of panic as he imagined what it would be like to be lost in this undergrowth forever, stuck in the darkness with this silent girl and her cold, clammy hands. He paused, his breath rasping, and allowed himself a moment to rest. As he did, he caught a whiff of something foul.

Growing up in the wilderness, in a village like Brighton, a boy was, at an early age, disabused of certain sensitivities and notions that a city child was able to maintain. One of those sensitivities came in the form of butchering livestock. Often, Matt had helped do exactly that as someone in the village needed help with it, and therefore he was no stranger to the smell of dead flesh. There was a hint of that, in the smell, but there was something else, too. This was not just dead flesh, not just some beast that had recently died. No, this smell was different, worse. It was the smell of meat that had been butchered and left to bake in the hot sun until it was rancid and foul.

He glanced back to the girl who looked up at him from beneath her long dark hair with those big, wide eyes. "Do you smell something?"

She said nothing, only studied him, and so Matt grunted, turning back. It was a dead animal, that was all. That was not so odd an occurrence, surely, certainly not in the woods where some animals were predators and others prey. Likely a wolf or coyote had only been disturbed in his meal by some thing or another and had left the remnants of the unfortunate animal somewhere nearby. He told himself it did not matter, that it was no cause for concern. And, partly, he even believed it, enough, at least, to gather his will and continue on, pushing his way through the bushes crowding around them.

By the time they finally emerged from the dense thicket, his clothes, his arms and face were pocked and scratched by the many thorns and twigs he'd had to force his way through, and he paused, giving himself a chance to get his ragged breathing under control. "I just...need a minute," he said, kneeling down and wincing at the cold rasp in his throat. He was surprisingly exhausted, likely not just from the exertion but also from the stress of being out here in the darkness, stress at the way it seemed to press in all around him, like some beast meaning to swallow him up.

Still, the girl would not let go of his hand, but he was too tired to care about that, was too focused on catching his breath. The only consolation he could find was that, soon, he would reach Cutter. Whatever else the man might be, he would be a great comfort now, and he was looking forward to hearing the man's growling, gravelly voice, which normally sounded so menacing, but now would be a pleasure, even if it was used to scold him for his foolishness. A man like Cutter was not scared of the dark or of trees, that much was certain. A man like Cutter wasn't scared of anything.

Matt found himself really looking forward to that, even to the man's disapproving growl when he saw that Matt had gone off into the darkness and had come back with a young child. But when he finally got his breath back enough to glance at his surroundings, he realized that he—*they*—were not where he had thought they would be. "There's...it can't be," he said softly in a breathless voice. He blinked, gave his head a good shake, but nothing changed.

The bank, where he had first found the girl, was only feet away, the stream gurgling past below it. The same stream which he was sure should be at their backs. But as much as he knew it was impossible, the stream did not move, only continued to be right in front of him, exactly where it should not be. "We must have gotten...gotten turned around or...or something."

"Or something."

He glanced back at the little girl who was standing there, smiling at him, not looking frightened in the slightest, not now. Maybe her calm, her smile should have reassured him, but it did not. There was something about that expression he didn't like, something sly, knowing, as if she possessed some great secret that he did not. "Come on," he said, starting toward the underbrush once more. He thought that perhaps the girl would let go of his hand—almost hoped for it—but she did not, only held on and allowed herself to be pulled toward the bushes once more.

At least, for a little while. Then suddenly, her grip tightened on his hand with a strength he wouldn't have credited her with, and he winced in pain, turning. "Look, there's no time, okay? We have to go." He started forward again, but the girl's grip had gotten even stronger, incredibly strong, in fact, so that Matt cried out, feeling as if the bones in his hand were going to snap.

"We have come far enough," a voice said from behind him, one that sounded nothing like a little girl's voice at all. It was far too guttural, that voice, too deep, with a hissing quality to it he did not like, not at all. He heard something strange behind him, squishing sounds mixed with loud, cracking ones. He'd heard such a sound once before. He'd only been a child at the time and one of the older boys in the village had fallen from a tree, fallen in such a way that his leg had broken. It was like the sound of a tree limb snapping in the frost but far louder, far worse, and despite the fact that he'd only been a kid, Matt remembered it clearly.

He heard that sound now, over and over again, just as he heard the mewling hisses from behind him, hisses that seemed like sounds of pleasure and pain all at once. Matt wanted to turn, knew he *should* turn, but he was suddenly frozen with fear, terror which made it impossible for him to move, nearly impossible for him to think at all, and he understood in that moment why elk sometimes froze at the sight of their hunters and the bows they carried. He'd always wondered why they did that, from time to time, why they did not run and try to save themselves. Now, though, he understood.

The grip of the hand holding his tightened still further, seeming not just to tighten but to grow so that it engulfed his entire hand up to the wrist, wrapped around it in some slithering, sickening way, and he screamed as pain lanced through the bones of his hand and up his arm. Then, he heard a shockingly loud sound from behind him, branches snapping as someone—or something—crashed through the undergrowth. There was a terrible, keening wail from behind him, the sound of something striking flesh, and in another moment the pressure on his hand vanished as if it had never been.

Matt finally coaxed up the courage to turn and froze again, staring in horrified silence at the scene before him.

Cutter stood only feet away, his great chest heaving in breaths, blood inexplicably splashed across his face and arms. In one hand he held a torch which blazed bright in the darkness, dazzling Matt's eyes. In the other, he held a tree limb, one so thick that Matt would never have been able to hold it in one hand even if he could have somehow lifted its weight, which he doubted. The end of the limb was shattered, broken off, and the blood coating it was as odd and confusing to Matt as the blood on the big man's arms and face. At least, that was, until he followed Cutter's gaze to his feet.

Some *thing* lay there in a bloody mass just where the young girl had been moments before. But it was not the young girl nor anything that resembled her. Instead, it was a creature unlike anything Matt had ever seen, a monster or demon out of nightmare. The creature's skin was pale but that didn't cover it— in fact, it was translucent, so that Matt could see veins running through it, thought he could actually *see* the blood pumping. It had very short, incredibly thin arms, like a child's, but attached to those arms were thin but very long fingers with claws like daggers on the end of them. Even that, though, wasn't the worst of it. It had legs, too, of a sort, long, spindly legs which were completely disproportionate to the rest of its body. But what caught Matt's attention—what he could not look away from, even though he wanted to—was its mouth. The creature's mouth was ten times as large as a human's and was opened in pain to reveal several rows of teeth which were nearly as long as its claws, all of which came to a sharp point.

"W-what is it?" Matt gasped.

"Your death, if I hadn't come along," Cutter growled, staring down at the monster which mewled in obvious pain as its blood continued to pump out onto the snow-laden bank. "But if you're asking for a name—their own kind call them Gretchlings, though you might have heard them called Doppels."

Matt's eyes went wide at that, and for a moment it seemed as if he couldn't catch his breath. "I...I didn't think they were real. I didn't think—"

"No," the man growled, looking at him and standing there, covered in blood, making an even more terrifying visage than normal. "You didn't think. I *told* you, boy, to stay in the cutout, to listen to nothing. Do you remember?"

"But...but I thought she needed help. I thought...I mean..."

"That *you* could offer that help?" Cutter challenged, then made a growling sound that might have been considered a laugh, assuming bears could laugh. "Look at you, boy. We're on the run from men seeking to kill us—to kill *you*—and you thought, what, you would go and play the hero? Gods, you're a fool."

Matt cowered, he couldn't help himself. He wanted to be outraged, to shout back, but the problem was that he did not feel outraged. What he felt was scared. He had never seen this side of Cutter before, this anger. He had thought it was there, of course, had seen hints of it the way a person might catch hints of their reflection in a rushing river. He had suspected it existed, but he had never actually *seen* it and in none of his suspicions had he ever thought the anger would be directed at him. He was scared, yes, but he was also hurt, surprised by how much the man calling him a fool pained him. He had not realized, until that moment, how much he had always craved the big man's approval. Ever since he'd been a child, a wink or a rare, small smile from Cutter had been the greatest of treats to him and now he felt ashamed. "Yes," he managed.

Cutter's chest heaved as he took in a great breath and the anger, the fire of his wrath, suddenly left his gaze, and he studied Matt with his cold, gray eyes. "You have a picture of yourself, boy, of who you want to be. It's a picture you carry around, lookin' at from time to time, so that whenever you find yourself in a situation where you're unsure of what to do, you ask yourself what that man in the picture might do, what he might say. Most people have a picture like that. They carry it around and study it and try to be the person they see there. To say what they would say. To do what they would do. And most of the time, no one's the worse off for it. But you forgot something today—something important. You're *not* the man you see in the portrait. Do you understand? You're not him, and you never will be. You're not a hero—no one is. If such men ever existed, they're long gone now. It's time you put the picture away. Do you understand?"

"I understand," Matt said softly. "Cutter...I'm sorr—" He cut off at a whimper louder than the others from the creature, and he turned to it, his shame forgotten for the moment as he stared at the mass of blood and broken limbs, at the shattered pieces of the tree limb where Cutter had beaten the thing. "Is it...I mean...will it die?"

"If left alone?" Cutter asked. "No. It would heal—the Fey are survivors if nothing else. It would survive to eat the next fool stupid enough to be lured in by its tricks."

"So...what do we do then?"

"The Fey are difficult to kill, but they *can* be killed. And the best way? Well. The best way is fire."

"*No, no please,*" the thing gurgled, its broken, bloody body writhing on the ground. It's voice was muffled, sounding mushy and unclear, but Matt could still recognize the voice of the small girl it had pretended to be as it spoke, could hear, clearly, its terror. "*P-please, anything but that,*" the creature begged.

Matt could not bring himself to look at it. Even though he knew, now, that the creature had intended to eat him, he could not stand that voice, that pitiful, pleading voice of a child, and he found himself feeling bad for it no matter what it had meant to do. After all, according to Cutter, the creature , like all Fey, like all *men,* for that matter, had only acted according to its nature, searching for food the same way a lion or a bear might. And now, it was lying broken and battered, clearly dying, yet begging for a small kindness, the way a man might. "Maybe we should—" Matt began, but it was too late.

Cutter, apparently, either saw none of the resemblances to a human the creature showed or chose to ignore them, for he did not hesitate, bringing the flaming torch down to the creature's flesh. The creature let out a terrible, shrieking wail and began to writhe and twist, its body shifting and changing, its pale flesh morphing from one thing to the next, as the smell of burning meat filled the air. Suddenly, the face of the young girl appeared in that mound of bloody, burning flesh. *"Please,"* the girl begged in a hoarse voice, full of unimaginable agony, *"please, don't—"*

But Cutter was deaf to its pleas, digging the torch in further even as the creature wailed and screamed in pain. The flames ate at it hungrily and soon its whole body had caught fire. Matt stumbled away, unable to look any longer, but the sound of it dying, the *smell* of it was bad enough. He collapsed to his knees and began to retch, heaving up what little contents his near-empty stomach had in a steaming pile onto the fresh snow.

Eventually, it was over, the screams vanishing, though Matt thought he could still hear the echoes of the agony of the creature's last moments in the air. Then he felt more than saw Cutter move to stand beside him. "Come on," the man said, his voice as cold and as harsh as a blizzard. "Others will have heard. They will come to investigate."

"Y-you," Matt began, his voice a choked whisper, "you killed it. You...murdered it."

"Yes."

And without another word, the big man turned and started away. Matt ran an arm across his mouth, looking after the big man's back, willing to look anywhere so long as it wasn't at the steaming remains of the Doppel. A thousand thoughts flashed through his mind then, a thousand ideas of what he might do, where he might go, all of which revolved around leaving Cutter, of striking out on his own. But then, he had tried that, hadn't he? And it had taken him all of five minutes before a creature out of nightmare had decided to have him for lunch, *would* have if not for Cutter.

In the end, he rose and followed the big man into the darkness.

# CHAPTER ELEVEN

*They called him the Charmer, and I can think of no better title.*
*Except maybe "bastard." That'd suit him fine.*
*And you want to know what I think that bastard's best magic trick is?*
*The fact that he's still walking around breathing and no one's stuck a knife in his back.*
*Someone will, though. Mark my words—it's just a matter of time.*
*—Feller Chall, farmer and father to three adult daughters in interview with Exiled Historian to the Crown Petran Quinn.*

Challadius, or simply the Charmer as he had once been called, woke to a hand on his shoulder shaking him roughly. He blinked, bleary-eyed, and yawned, wincing at the taste of stale ale in his mouth.

"Alright," a voice said, "time to go."

Challadius—or Chall, as his friends called him, which, to be fair, were few and far between these days—blinked up at the woman standing over him. At first, he had no idea where he was or how he'd come to be there, but a quick survey of his surroundings showed that he was in a tavern—or at least what passed for one in the poorest quarter of Laydia—specifically, that he had passed out at one of its tables. He seemed to vaguely remember a crowd, but now the tables around him were empty, the entire common room was empty, in fact, save for himself and the innkeeper. "Uh...hi."

"Save your 'hi,'" the woman said, planting her hands on her rail-thin hips, her hard face scowling and making her sharp, unfeminine features even less appealing. "It's time for you to go.

# A Warrior's Burden

Past time. Now, are you goin' to leave, or am I gonna have to wake one of my lads, get them to see you out?"

Chall winced, working his tongue around in a mouth which felt incredibly dry. "How about one drink? For the road?"

"How about you hit the road before you get hit?" the woman asked. Gods, but she was an unattractive specimen of the mortal species, that much was certain. It was enough to make a man swear off the fairer sex forever. Or at least until he got a few ales in him. Ale was good. It helped a man forget his past—at least for a time—and helped the present look far more appealing, softening the worst of its hard edges.

"Oh come on..." He hesitated, groping for the name, a task made more difficult by a stuffy cloudiness that the ale had left in his mind. "*Shelly,*" he said finally, trying his best smile which, it had to be said given his headache, wasn't as good as it might have been.

The woman scowled. "It's Palla. And you have something in your teeth."

"Of *course* it's Palla," he said, pausing to dig at his teeth with a finger. "I was just...well, I was testing you, wasn't I? A test which I am pleased to say you passed admirably."

"You were testing me," she said flatly. "As if I could forget my own name."

He finished picking at his teeth and tried another smile. This one, he thought, certainly better than the first. "You'd be surprised—why, I guess it has been at least a dozen blessed times when I've forgotten my own."

"Blessed indeed," she said. "Now, there's no drink for you here—get out."

"Oh come now, Falla—"

"*Palla,*" she growled.

"Right, that's what I said. Anyway, this is an *inn,* isn't it? Why should I leave when I can rent a room, save myself a trip and you can make some coin in the process, how'd that be?"

"What coin?" she said, scowling.

He coughed, clearing his throat. "Well, admittedly, I'm a bit short up right now, but if you'll take my stay on credit, I'm sure that soon something will turn—"

"No."

"No?" he asked, blinking.

"You heard me. I've extended you as much credit as I've a mind to, far more than I normally do. Now, if you've got coin—real honest coin, for I find that spends far better than promises or excuses—then we can talk. Otherwise, it's time for you to leave."

Chall didn't like the idea of walking out of the inn just then, of trying to see past the fog of his drink-addled thoughts to find the back alley he called home. In fact, given how numb and uncertain his legs felt even sitting as he now was, he wasn't sure if he was capable of it. So, figuring that the third time's a charm, he gave her one more winning smile and leaned forward. "Palla, have I ever told you that I'm a bit of a magician?"

She sighed. "I've heard this tale, more than once. And you're right—I'm pretty well convinced you've got some magic. Otherwise, I figure you would have been knifed in some back alley by now and the world better for it."

He clapped a hand to his heart—or meant to, but due to lack of coordination from the drink, it instead landed on his, it had to be said, ample stomach—and sat back. "Oh, but you wound me, Palla. Truly."

"Not as much as Herb will, I have to wake him," she said, then raised an eyebrow. "So tell me, *magician,* do I have to wake him?"

"Herb..." he said, trying to remember. "Ah, right. Big fella, scowls a lot? Got a chin like a battle axe?"

She flashed him a smile without humor. "That's the one."

"Ah," he said, clearing his throat again. "Well, I'm sure that's not necessary. A big man like that, I have to assume he needs his sleep. Still," he went on, glancing around and leaning in confidentially as if preparing to tell her some great secret. "I wasn't lying before. About being a magician."

She rolled her eyes. "I'm losing my patience. That line stopped being cute months ago, right about the time your tab started getting outrageous. Now, if you're finished—"

"*Watch,*" he interrupted, holding his hands up and to the sides in a grand gesture of presentation like some performer in a traveling troupe. Which, of course, he was. Or, at least, had been, many years ago before the world had gone to shit and he right along with it. He focused, turning his mind inward to that space in him from which the magic had always come, reached for it mentally, like a hand questing out. He smiled in satisfaction as he felt it beneath his grip then frowned as it seemed to pour out of his grasp like water from a sieve. "*Damn ale,*" he muttered. "Just a minute more," he said, giving her a shaky laugh, "I'll get it, just…well, just a bit out of practice is all."

"No doubt not out of practice in getting black eyes, though," she said, smiling. "I reckon we're about to find out." She turned to look at the stairs. "*Herb—*" she began.

But just then, Chall managed to catch hold of the magic, gripping it tight as it thrashed around like an oily eel in his grasp. He focused his attention on it and then the magic was there, forming in his mind as clearly as it ever had, creating that which he had meant to create. At least, mostly. What he had meant to do was to create a dozen roses—always a sure fire way to a woman's heart, at least, that was, when coin wasn't an option. Instead, he was left holding a single, rather wilted lily.

She turned from the stairs, scowling at him and then at the lily then back at him for good measure. "And what? I'm supposed to be impressed that you carry a wilted flower around with you, that it?"

"What?" he said, frowning. Fire and salt, but roses would have been better. "No, that is—look, I just made this, you see?"

She opened her mouth again, likely to yell for Herb, so with a quick, practiced flourish, he made the flower disappear. Only, the flourish wasn't quite so much a flourish as a panicked gesture—Herbert really was a big man—and it had the side effect of also making a half-empty ale cup vanish to shatter on the floor a moment later. He winced, expecting the black eye she'd promised from her if not from the hired help, but the innkeeper was left blinking at him, apparently unaware or uncaring about the glass he'd broken. "How'd you do that?"

"I told you," he said, smiling triumphantly past his increasingly bad headache, one which a bit of prestidigitation always made worse. "Magic."

She frowned doubtfully but, at least, refrained from shouting for her bouncer, so that was something. "Do something else."

He grunted. "Want a free show, is that it? Well, I can't say that I'm inclined to—"

"It's good enough, maybe I'll let you stay the night. If it ain't, you can take your ass outside and sleep in the street for all I care."

Chall considered that. He hadn't performed much magic in the last few years, having largely found his "gift" to be more of a curse than anything. Besides which, he knew that doing so would make his headache worse than it already was. Still, he'd tried sleeping in the street plenty and didn't particularly care for it, so he nodded. "Of course. Tell me, Palla," he said, smiling his best flirtatious smile, "is there a man in your life? Or, better yet, one you *wished* would be in your life? Or, at least, your bed?"

She scowled. "My personal life's my own business, charlatan, just as my lovers are. Now—"

Chall thought she was being far too optimistic if she thought he—or anyone sober enough to still be conscious—would believe that she had not only one lover but *multiple.* But he didn't think that was the most politic thing to say, so he held up his hands to show he meant no harm. "You don't need to tell me anything about him—or her, who am I to judge? All I ask is for you to picture this man—or woman—in your mind, alright? Just an image."

She frowned. "And then what?"

He smiled. "Then, prepare to be amazed."

She studied him for several seconds then finally sighed. "This had better be good." Then, she closed her eyes.

Chall studied her for a moment. She really was unattractive. Rail thin with hands calloused from work, her hair a dull, lank brown. A man would have to be a far more powerful magician than he—or anyone, come to that—to see her womanly charms. Certainly, she had no curves to speak of, no softness neither in her body, nor in her manner. A damned miserable excuse for a—

"Well?" she demanded.

*Oh, right.* He took a slow breath, calling on his magic again. This time, it answered more quickly, if still somewhat reluctantly, and he winced as he performed his working and a fresh spike of pain lanced through his temple. "Okay, open them."

When she did she let out a satisfying gasp. "*Faerie dust*, but you were telling the truth."

Chall grunted. Of all the curses his people used, that was probably his least favorite. He'd had some run-ins with the Fey—far more than he'd ever wanted, in fact—and knew there was no such thing. Unless, of course, people referred to dust actually *made* from faeries after they'd been set ablaze, and somehow he doubted it. Still, the last thing he needed was to get on her bad side, so he sketched a bow—the best of which he was capable still seated at the table with his gut pressed against its wooden edge—more of a nod, really. "I said as much."

She smiled, and there was some slight warmth to it. She stared at him then, and he was about to ask her what was wrong, if maybe he had a booger or had messed up the nose—the damned nose was always the trickiest part—but then he realized that nothing was wrong. At least, not with him. She was trying—and failing miserably, it had to be said—to give him a seductive look. But doing so as if she had only read about it in some book or maybe not even that. All in all, a thoroughly shitty job. "So," she said in a seductive voice which was at least as bad as the look, "you were saying you wanted a room, that it?"

Chall considered that, considered whether the price of said room would be worth it or if he'd prefer the street after all. It took over a minute, and he would have kept considering it if a frown hadn't slowly begun to spread on her features. "Well?"

"Oh, right," he said, giving a sickly smile, "of course."

"Well," she said, offering him her hand, calloused and all, as if offering him some great treat. "Come on then."

Chall allowed himself to be pulled to his feet—well, he was a big man now, too many ales, so he had to do quite a bit of helping and there was grunting involved all around—but he paused as she tried to lead him up the stairs. "One thing, though," he said, unable to help himself now, as always, in feeling that he was a charlatan just as she had claimed. For now, as always, he felt that he had messed up the illusion, somehow, felt that there was some terrible flaw in it.

His friends—or, maybe better to call them coworkers—had always given him a hard time about that, about how he always thought there was something wrong with the products of his magic, but they could never understand. A painter might, or a poet, any artist that knew exactly those heights to which their work reached just as they knew that they were inevitably doomed to fail. True, a layman, looking upon their art, might see only what had been done right, but they, like Chall, would know that something was always wrong with it, that it had fallen short somehow, even if he could not pinpoint where the flaw lay. "Do I look like him? Your would-be lover, I mean?"

She grunted. "Don't look like yourself anyway, and that's a plus. Now, come on—let's see about that room."

***

*Two men stalked through the darkness. Great trees loomed up around them, radiating malice, their shadowed limbs seeming to reach for these trespassers in their home, meaning to scoop them up and devour them. One of the men, young, little more than a boy, really, took note of this and was afraid. He walked behind the other, casting furtive glances around him, thinking that he was in danger. He was right to be afraid, for the place where they trod was an old place, one of old jealousies and old scores. It was a place of death, and it did not take kindly to the living.*

*The man who walked in the front was a big man with wide shoulders, with arms and hands that looked as if they could crush boulders. There was a grim expression on his face, not because of their circumstances, but simply because it was the only expression he seemed to know. This man carried no weapon, yet he exuded a primal energy, a ferocity which only the world's greatest warriors did, and any who saw him would know that he needed no weapon, for he was one. This one did not seem to take note of the danger they were in or, more likely, simply did not care, for his life had always been one of danger and murder and death, and he had thrived, going on when so many others had fallen.*

*The men walked. And the forest watched.*

*Then, the vision shifted, changed, and the men walked through the wood no longer but stood at its very edge, gazing out onto fields covered in pale yellow and brown grass, signs of winter's coming. Others crouched amongst that waist-high grass, but the boy was still too busy gazing back at the forest anxiously to take note of them. The other man, too, did not notice them, for his gaze was distant, and it seemed that he gazed back at some far different and—by the expression on his face—far worse, time.*

*And so the two set off into the field, the grass rasping and crunching beneath their feet, and the others—at least fifty all told—waited, positioned so that the two would walk into the midst of them, would be caught unawares and surrounded, cut down by the blades the waiters held ready.*

*One of those who crouched in the grass was familiar to Chall, and he recognized him immediately. He had been a good man, once—perhaps even a great one—that man, but he, like all things, had changed, and he was that man no longer. He was, instead, something altogether...different.*

*The big man with the thick rippling muscles and the grim expression was also one he knew, one he had counted a friend, long ago, at least as much as anyone might have counted such a man a friend. He, too, had changed, his dark hair now with specks of gray, but his eyes were the same, eyes so pale blue as to be almost gray. Eyes that showed no compassion and no mercy. Killer's eyes, Chall had always thought, and looking at them now only reaffirmed that belief. Killer's eyes, yes, but eyes which did not see the trap into which he and the boy walked, a trap which was only moments away from—*

Chall woke with a gasp and a snort. He jumped up in bed, or at least intended to, but there was something—or someone—lying on his ample stomach, and his movement did no more than serve to send that something—or someone, definitely a someone, given the shout of surprise—flying off the bed and onto the floor to land with a clatter and a curse.

"The fuck is wrong with you?" a woman's voice demanded.

"Not me," he said, finding it difficult to breathe. "Not me."

"What?"

"*Them!*" he shouted, his voice hoarse and afraid. "Don't you get it? They're waiting for them, they've set a trap and they're going to walk right into it!"

"*Who?*" the woman demanded. As she climbed back to her feet, the swirling fog of panic which had clouded his thoughts faded, and Chall remembered that the woman he had so unceremoniously—perhaps even *rudely*—dumped onto the floor was the owner of the bed and the whole inn in which he found himself. The same woman who, just then, was staring at him like he was a particularly ugly bug she'd particularly enjoy squashing.

"It...never mind," he said, "i-it doesn't matter." But of course it did. It mattered a lot. He had thought that a lot of his feelings, what he now considered his misplaced loyalty, had faded over the years.

The big man with the rock-crushing hands was his problem no longer. Let him be someone else's problem, let the blood he spilled stain someone else's clothes for a change. Chall wanted nothing to do with it. He hadn't wanted anything to do with it then and he certainly didn't now. And yet...

"No," he told himself. "Not this time." There were a thousand reasons not to get involved and not a single good one to do so. *Not. A Single. One.* And yet..."Shit," he muttered. "You damned bastard."

"What did you call me?" Palla demanded.

"Wait, what?" Chall asked, realizing he'd forgotten the woman was there at all, thinking maybe it was time he gave up drinking. "No, not—forget it."

She snorted. "That shouldn't be too hard," she said, shooting a pointed look at his stomach and down past it where the covers had been draped over his waist, covering his member—not that hard a task, he had to admit. A doily would have served well enough. Still, the blankets didn't cover his ample gut or spindly legs, and even he had to admit that the parts which did show weren't all that impressive. Maybe even grotesque.

"Look, there's no cause for that, alright? I mean..." He paused, giving his own meaningful glance—never let it be said that Chall couldn't give as good as he could get. "It's not as if anyone's coming by to pin a ribbon on you anytime, unless there's a livestock competition in town that I haven't heard about."

"You son of a bitch," she growled, then turned toward the door. "*Herb!*" she screamed. "Get up here! We've got some trash needs takin' out!"

"I'll tell you what's trash, your lovemaki—" Chall froze in his insult—not his best, maybe, but certainly not his worst—as the woman grabbed a candleholder off the nightstand and stared toward him. He leapt off the bed—or would have done, if his leaping days weren't far behind him. What he did, instead, was a panicked roll which sent him spilling onto the other side of the bed from the enraged innkeeper. The next few minutes were spent in a mad, painful scramble as he tried to put on his clothes and fend off the mad woman and her candlestick at the same time.

By the time he was out of the room and into the hall, one trouser leg on and his shirt hanging from about his neck, aching in several spots where he was quite sure there would be some livid

## A Warrior's Burden

bruises later, he had to count it a failure on both counts. "Crazy bitch," he muttered, walking toward the stairs with what dignity he could muster while several other of the inn's guests—no doubt woken by the woman's screams and threats, how could they not be the way she was carrying on?—looked on.

"Everything okay?" an older man asked. "Thought I heard someone cry out."

"Everything's fine," Chall assured him as he moved past, "just an upset woman, is all."

"Sounded like a man."

Chall turned to scowl at the man. "Crazy bitch," he muttered again, then he started toward the stairs.

"What's that, you son of a bitch?" the woman screamed, and then she was in the hall, and Chall was forced to abandon what dignity he'd managed to gather—along with his trousers—as his stately walk turned into a mad dash for the stairs, stairs which he took two at a time—very nearly all at a time as his foot caught on one and he only just managed to save himself from falling.

He made it down them though and reached the door, turning and meaning to shout some rejoinder, some answer to his current state, at the woman. He had even begun, getting so far as "You filthy ha—" when something which looked and felt suspiciously like a bronze candlestick struck him in the head, and he abruptly forgot what he'd been about to say. Hag, maybe? Or had it been harlot? He wasn't sure as the first blow drove the thought from his head, and the second drove him out of the door, rolling down the inn steps to plop very unceremoniously—and with no signs of dignity anywhere in sight—in the dirt of the village road. Or, at least, it would have been dirt had the gods not seen fit to send what had apparently had been a real bitch of a storm the night before.

Lying there, staring up at the pale morning sky, Chall consoled himself with the fact that mud was far softer than dirt and that he had never really liked those trousers anyway. They were only his second favorite pair. Of course, he only *had* the two pairs...one now. "Shit," he muttered.

"What's that?"

He turned his aching head to glance dumbly over at the woman standing in the doorway, some poor bastard's blood on the candlestick she held. She was still naked, and the early morning light didn't do her in favors, that much was certain. He considered saying that, then remembered the way the candlestick had felt and decided against it. Instead, he picked himself up—with a bit of groaning and more than a bit of cursing, and stared at her—and the dozen or so onlookers that had gathered behind her in the doorway—raising his nose with as much dignity as he could. "My lady, I have found your establishment...inadequate and your hospitality, such as it is, appalling. I, then, will remove myself from the premises at once and take my business else—"

"What *business?*" she snorted. "And say one more word," she went on, stepping out of the doorway to reveal a man that, while not as big as the man from his dream, certainly seemed plenty big enough to make sure a man's day went to shit and fast, "and I'll get Herb to show you exactly how I feel about you and your *business.*"

Chall opened his mouth to do just that, to launch into some scathing remark involving wrinkles or fence posts but in the end—and as was so rarely the case—greater minds prevailed. He told himself that his lack of speech had absolutely nothing to do with the big man with his arms folded across a chest so big he could have made barrels jealous, and everything to do with taking the high road. Then he turned and walked down the street, leaving the inn—and his trousers—behind him.

The dream, though, could not be left so easily, and despite the people staring at him as he walked—including a guardsman who frowned suspiciously at his lack of trousers—Chall found himself remembering it, found the vision replaying over and over in his mind. Dead men stepping into dead fields—couldn't be much more of an obvious omen than that. The other men crouching in the tall dry grass, waiting for them, their blades ready.

He had seen the big man overcome incredible odds—impossible odds—but taking on fifty men, all of whom were armed and had the advantage of surprise? Even calling such odds impossible would have been far too optimistic. He told himself that it didn't matter. The man's problems were his own, had ceased to be Chall's many years ago, and it would be the height of stupidity to make them his again. After all, what was the point of a man faking his own death and creating a new life for himself if he was wound up making the same mistakes he had the first time around?

Better to make all new mistakes, better for the worst danger he faced to be an innkeeper's hired tough instead of soldiers and Fey creatures with murder on their minds.

Besides, it wasn't exactly as if it were a surprise that the man had people looking to kill him. It seemed he always did, certainly, he had in the past. Live a life like *he* had, and the only people you knew ended up being ghosts and those who wanted to make you one. Only made sense that, sooner or later—sooner, if the urgency the vision had made him feel were any clue—he'd be joining them. A city of the dead, one which he had populated himself with each swipe of his axe.

No, Chall told himself that the man's fate was his own, that he didn't care, just as he told himself that who the boy was and why he traveled with him made no difference. The problem, though, was that while Chall had always been good at lying, he—like a chef who despises his own cooking—had never been able to swallow his own lies. He had tried, of course, had tried for years and years so that, until the dream, he had been able to entertain the fantasy that he had even succeeded. But like the light shining on the innkeeper's flesh—and his own, for that matter—there was one truth that could not be denied. Close scrutiny often reveals ugly truths.

"Shit," he said for the third time since waking. Then he saw the guards—four of them now—approaching, and he sighed, holding up hands which had moments before been busy trying to wrangle and conceal his dangling bits. "Hi there," Chall said as they walked up. "I'm looking for a place to rest. Tell me, do you know if the dungeons have any spare rooms?"

# CHAPTER TWELVE

*The guests were eating and drinking, celebrating the treaty with the Fey.*
*That was when the Crimson Prince walked into the dining hall.*
*But it was not he—not even his blood-spattered clothes—which drew the gaze of everyone present.*
*Instead, it was the macabre bundle he carried before him.*
*A bloody, severed head. But not just any head. No, this was the head of the Fey king, Yeladrian.*
*The same Fey king which had granted us a place to stay here, in the Known Lands.*
*The same Yeladrian with whom Princes Bernard and Feledias had so recently signed a treaty.*
*That was how the Fey Wars began. With a bloody head in a dining hall.*
*—Exiled Historian to the Crown Petran Quinn*

His hand ached. It was a strange feeling, that ache. Perhaps he had felt it before, surely he must have, but he didn't remember it. And as he walked, the boy trudging along silently—though not so silently as to make his misery and disapproval unclear—Cutter realized that the ache wasn't just in his hand but all the way up his arm. An uncomfortable ache. And there was something else, too, something that wasn't just physical, something that the old him would have mocked. It was a stirring in his chest that he hadn't been able to define at first and that, after some consideration, he thought must be guilt. Guilt and maybe shame at what he had done to the Fey creature.

He had thought he had left the man he had once been—the man whose rage had sought blood unending—behind him. He had thought himself scoured of any such feelings as anger or hate, joy or love, but then he had seen the creature changing behind the boy, showing its true self. He had known what it had intended, what it had meant to do, and the rage had come rushing back as if it had never left. And now he realized that perhaps it had not, had only been sleeping the way a bear might in the winter, waiting for when it would be roused to wakefulness once more.

He told himself that he had saved the boy's life—which was true—told himself, also, that he had not enjoyed doing it, had done what he'd done only out of necessity, not for any sort of perverse pleasure. On that second part, though, he was uncertain, and it was that uncertainty which plagued his footsteps as he walked, which made him feel the boy's sullen stare on him as an uncomfortable pressure when the him from the past would have laughed such a thing away as if of no consequence.

Foolish, he knew, to start caring about what people thought of him now. He was what he was. Perhaps he had been born to it or perhaps he had molded himself into the shape he now was over the years the way a sculptor molded his clay until he got the exact shape he wanted. In the end, it didn't matter. What did was that he was a killer, that and nothing else. A monster, in truth, and no amount of regret or shame would change that.

He told himself that it didn't matter. The boy was alive—*that* was all that mattered. Alive and breathing, though considering the odds they faced, there was no way of knowing how long that would remain the case.

"Where are we going?"

This from the boy, each word colored in disapproval. "Farther," Cutter said, not bothering to turn.

"*Farther,*" the boy repeated. "How *much* farther?"

Cutter gave him no answer, for he had none to give. He knew that each step they took into Fey lands increased their peril, knew that, by now, the creatures of the Black Woods would have found their companion dead and would be stirring to action. He did not doubt that some of them watched him and the boy already, marking their progress, scheming schemes and plotting plots. But they could not turn around, not yet, for he knew also that the men—his brother no doubt among them—were following, just as he knew that his brother's hatred would not allow him to balk at entering the Black Woods, that he would not so easily watch his prey escape. No, he would come, he and his men, and should Cutter and the boy stop, should they turn around now, it was only a matter of time before they would be found.

So, then, he made one bad choice to avoid making another. Sometimes, it seemed to him that that was all his life had ever been, choosing one evil over another. Or, perhaps, it was that evil men who lived evil lives only found themselves confronted with evil choices. The how of it didn't really matter, though. What did was putting as much distance as he could between the men pursuing him and the boy, of keeping the boy safe for as long as he could. It would not be forever, he knew, perhaps would not be more than a day, but he would do it for as long as he could. There was nothing else.

He would do it because *she* had asked him to.

*Come no further, Destroyer. Kingslayer. You are not welcome here.*

The words were not spoken, as such, but floated to him as if carried on the breeze, formed in the soft sway of tree branches overhead and the rustle of their leaves. It did not sound like a man but seemed as if the Woods themselves had been given a voice. The boy heard it too, evidence of which could be seen in the surprised sound he made. "Cutter?" he asked, his voice sounding soft and frightened and far younger than his years. "What was that?"

Cutter heard the rustling of undergrowth as the unseen speaker moved toward them, but even had he not, he would have felt its presence as it drew closer, so he only waited, saying nothing. The boy would have his answer soon enough and, if Cutter was any judge, he doubted it would be one he liked. Most, ignorant of the Fey and their ways, would have called what appeared out of the trees, less than a dozen feet away from where Cutter and the boy stood, a demon. They would have been wrong, of course, but he could not have blamed them for thinking so just as he could not blame the boy for his panicked gasp.

The creature was ten feet tall at the least, dwarfing Cutter the way he normally dwarfed other men and women. Its body was a deep, vertiginous green, its face an ebony darker than night itself and its eyes—which were three or four times larger than a man's—were of a deep, vibrant green which made Cutter think of great massive forests with trees which had existed since the beginning of time. A forest in which ancient things moved and roamed. An incredible creature, terrible and beautiful at the same time, and a creature who Cutter recognized.

"Shadelaresh," he said.

The creature shifted, its green eyes flashing a deep dark green so dark it was almost black. Its great mouth opened wide displaying teeth which looked as if they were made of bark. It yawned open, that portal, and the creature tilted its head back. A voice began to emerge, though without any movements of the creature's mouth. And not a single voice but what sounded like dozens, all whispering together, slightly out of sync so that it made a fading sort of echo.

*No one has called me that name in fifteen of your years, mortal. None since your great betrayal.*

"Cutter," the boy said, stepping up beside him, "we should go. There's only the one and—"

Cutter put a hand on the youth's arm. "It's too late, lad. They're all around us now. Only look in the trees."

The boy did, but Cutter did not bother. He knew well what he would see there, figures shifting and moving at the trunks of the trees, figures which might have been thought to be just trees themselves, if not for the intent in their green gazes. They were creatures similar to the one before him, though much smaller, much younger than this being who had lived for countless centuries and which was now regarding him with unmistakable hatred despite its alien appearance.

"What does he want?" Matt whispered.

"Not a 'he,' lad."

"It's...a woman then?"

"No, not as such. The Fey often do not have genders, not at least as we think of them." The boy opened his mouth, clearly preparing to ask another question, dozens of them, likely, but Cutter held up a hand, silencing him, as he looked back to the creature. "What would you have me call you, then?"

The creature studied him with those deep green eyes for what might have been over a minute then it tilted its head backward and its mouth yawned open once again. *I want nothing from you Kingslayer, Enemy of the Fey. Nothing except your death.*

The creature started forward then in a stride several times longer than a mortal's, and as it did the wind began to pick up. Cutter, had he been alone, might have stood and let the creature have its way, would have allowed it to do with him what he would, perhaps even thanked it, before the end. He was not alone, though. The boy was with him, the boy who was ignorant and innocent of the past and who would, if the creature was allowed to work its will, suffer for crimes he did not commit. Crimes which could be laid solely at Cutter's feet.

"Shadelaresh, I hereby claim my boon," Cutter said quickly. "I call on the faithfulness of the Fey."

The creature froze, its hands working at its sides, its green eyes flashing as if some great storm raged behind them. *You dare.*

The words came hissing on the wind, and Cutter stood as snow drifts rushed around him, carried on the heavy gust. *You who have so wronged the Fey dare demand a boon, dare question our own faithfulness. No, Destroyer. Your boon will be an end, an end in which your bones are crushed, and the great sentinels shall look on, their branches swaying with their laughter. And my promise, out of my faithfulness, is that it will be a long time coming, that eons will be dedicated to your suffering, that mortal and Fey alike will blanch when they hear of it, will whisper cautionary tales to their little ones until parent and child alike lie frightened in their beds at the very thought of such an end.*

Words to inspire fear in the bravest of men, yes, but Cutter had long since stopped thinking of himself as a man. He was far less than that. A monster and that only, and monsters had little to fear. "Huh," he grunted. "I had not thought so little of Fey promises as that. Certainly, your king, Yeladrian, when granting me the boon from saving his life, spoke in great length about the faithfulness of the Fey. I must admit I am sad to see that this is no more true than so many of the other stories of your people."

The wind grew even more powerful then, and the boy stumbled, would have fallen, had Cutter not reached out and steadied him. Clouds began to gather in the previously clear sky, impossibly fast, great dark shapes full of menace and power. Cutter said nothing, only waited, watching the creature as the impossible storm grew worse and worse by the moment. Then, as abruptly as it had come, the storm vanished, and as the snow—kicked up by the gusts—slowly settled to the ground once more, he was left staring at the creature, feeling its hatred, its fury, radiate from it in waves.

*What do you want? Have you come for your weapon? Have you come seeking the Breaker of Pacts?*

"No." The word was out of his mouth before he realized it, growled in a harsh hiss.

The creature cocked its head the slightest amount, and he could feel those great green eyes studying him. What did they see, he wondered? And how much? He did not doubt that they saw far more of him than most who looked upon him, saw more of him, he suspected, than he knew himself. Finally, the creature tilted its head back again, and another gust of wind kicked up, though this one was far different than the ones before. This one sounded as if it carried laughter on it, the laughter of thousands.

*I see,* the creature said.

"What?" Cutter asked, unable to help himself despite the fact that he was afraid of how it might answer. "What do you see?"

*Much, Kingslayer,* it said. *I see much. You, Destroyer, seek to be something else, someone else. You search for it, this new self, here in these woods, as you have searched for it in that backwater village among the scattered outliers of your kind. But you did not find it there, Destroyer, and you will not find it here. For wherever you go, no matter how far you journey, you bring yourself with you. You will never be anything more than what you are—a killer. That and that only. You are the Destroyer and you will always be thus. You are who you are. You are Kingslayer. You who has made the world bleed, the sound of whose arrival is announced by the wailing of babes. You whose people called you "hero" until even they discovered the truth of what you are and exiled you.*

And then, although there was no obvious change in the creature's posture or regard, it was obvious that its attention had turned to the boy. *Tell me, boy, do you know with whom you travel? Do you know the truth of who he is? Of what he is?*

"I..." the boy began in a terrified voice, "I don't..."

"Leave him out of this," Cutter growled. "He is under my protection and is no concern of yours."

Another great rush of wind, another chorus of whistling laughter. *Protection. What protection can be found, Destroyer, in the bear's jaw or the lion's teeth? What safety is there in the storm? No, Destroyer, you know naught of protection. It is not how you were made. You are the Destroyer. You will not be—can never be—anything else.*

"And yet he is under my protection just the same."

*And these others who have followed you into the demesne of my people? These who seek your head? Tell me, Kingslayer, is it these from whom you would protect this youth?*

"It is."

*And who, I wonder, will protect him from you?*

Cutter said nothing to that, for there was nothing he could say. Instead, he only waited.

The creature regarded him for some time and several minutes passed in silence. Then, finally, its great mouth yawned open once more. *When first I heard of your coming, Destroyer, I meant to crush you, to rip your heart from your chest, to grind your bones to ash and feast on your flesh. Now, though, I see that you are all but dead already, that there is little life left in you and what life there is knows only pain. You have called on the Boon of the Fey to grant you safe passage through this sacred place, a boon given by the very greatest of our kind, he that you slew in traitorous combat. Very well, then. Let it never be said that the Fey are not faithful. You shall have your boon, Destroyer. But you shall have more besides.*

The bushes on Cutter's left, less than a foot away, shifted and moved, parting like a curtain to reveal a familiar sight lying in the snow-laden grass. A familiar, terrible sight, and Cutter found himself taking an involuntary step back. "No," he whispered.

*Oh yes,* the creature answered, turning to regard the black-hafted axe, the black blade which seemed darker than night. *Take it, Destroyer, your weapon, the same weapon with which you slew so many of my kind, carving out a place for the invasion of your people here, in our homeland. The same weapon with which you slew MY KING.*

The last words came out in a great thunder that seemed to shake the very ground beneath his feet, but it was not the creature's voice which gripped Cutter's heart with fear. Instead, it was what lay on the ground, so close that he could kneel down and pick it up. He remembered well the feel of the axe in his hands, hands which knew the weight of it down to the ounce. "Please..." he began, trailing off, unsure of how he would finish.

*Oh, you will take it, Kingslayer,* the creature answered. *Else, you will be rejecting the boon granted you and if you reject it in this, then you reject all of it. Were you to do that, your life and the life of the boy who travels with you would be forfeit. And I promise you that his death will be a long time coming, I vow that you will wake each day to view his suffering as my people carve piece after piece from his flesh. Take it, Destroyer, for without it you are like a bear without its teeth, a lion without its claws. Take it for it is a part of you—it always has been, and it always will be.*

Cutter saw no choice, yet still he hesitated. He did not doubt the creature's word, for while the Fey often made use of illusions to disarm their prey and, more than that, simply because it was in their nature and they could no more stop doing so than a tree could stop its roots growing, he knew that, in their way, they were far more honest than any mortal ever thought to be. If he did not take the axe, the boy would die. And not just die—suffer.

And he, Cutter, would be forced to watch, to endure that suffering. But the greatest of his pains would come not just from that but from the breaking of a promise he had made long ago. He had made other promises before, of course, had broken most if not all of them. And yet...

It lay there in the snow, a double-bladed head, forged of a black metal which was unfamiliar and unworkable for any human smith. It had been a gift from the Fey king, Yeladrian, before the war began. A gift of great power, a weapon, the king had told him, beyond equal. And on that, at least, Cutter had to agree, for he had wielded it in many battles, far too many to count, just as he could not count the number of souls it had reaped. *The Breaker of Pacts,* Shadelaresh had called it, and on that, too, Cutter had to agree. Its sharp edge—keener than any other blade and one which never needed to be sharpened—had severed many pacts, had many times broken the vows Cutter had made to himself.

And how many promises, how many such vows would he break now, should he take it in his hands once more? Would he, as if by some magic—for it was a blade forged by the Fey and the Fey were known for their magic more than anything else—become the man he had once been? The man who had thirsted for blood above all else, who'd had such a thirst that it might never be sated? But then, he thought of the Doppel at the stream, the one he had killed so brutally, and he wondered if maybe he always had been that man, that the change he thought had occurred in him had been no more than a fantasy, a dream which must be abandoned upon waking.

Shadelaresh had laughed when he had called himself the boy's protector, and he had been right to. His were not hands meant to hold, to protect, but to destroy. Perhaps the gods had fashioned him thus; perhaps he had fashioned himself. In the end, it made little difference. It only mattered that he was what he was, an edge as sharp now as he had been fifteen years ago, a weapon that, like the Breaker of Pacts, would never lose its keenness. Still, he did not want to take the weapon, and he looked at it lying there like some great serpent, one which meant to swallow him whole.

If he left it, he could go on pretending that he was that man no longer, at least for a time, could continue dreaming. Perhaps, if he were lucky, the dream would last until his death. But if he did that, if he refused, the boy would suffer, would die for it.

He took the axe. It felt right in his hands, natural, as if some missing part of him had been restored. And that felt very wrong.

*Ah, there, Destroyer,* Shadelaresh said. *Now, you are complete once more. The serpent has his fangs returned to him. Go, then, and know that the Boon promised you by our king has been fulfilled. Should you set foot in the Black Wood again, your death, like your life, will be a thing of nightmare. Do you understand?*

"I understand," he grated, his eyes still on the axe blade, on the blackness of it that seemed to shift and roil like shadows. He took a slow, deep breath, then turned to Matt. "Come, boy. It's time to go."

He started away, the boy slowly following, casting his gaze between Cutter and Shadelaresh as if there were a thousand questions he might ask, but ones that he could not seem to put into words.

*Tell me, Destroyer,* the creature said from behind him, *now the serpent has its fangs returned, who, do you think, will feel their bite first? Not the serpent itself, no—I can hear your thoughts, but that will not happen. You cannot just as the serpent cannot. But someone will feel the bite, for the serpent* must *bite, Kingslayer. It is all it knows how to do. Will it be one of those men who hunts you even now, who trespasses into our wood, so great their need to see you dead? Or...will it be the boy?*

Cutter ignored him, walking on, his shoulders hunched, feeling as if he carried some great weight. But that weight was not the axe. Now, as ever, the weapon felt as light as a feather in his hands, and he felt the weight of it no more than a man might feel the weight of a part of himself. No, it was not the axe. And yet...it was.

He didn't think it was evil. That would have been ridiculous. A weapon could no more be evil than a horseshoe or a hammer could. But then horseshoes had not tasted the blood the axe had, and hammers were used to create while the axe was made to destroy. And destroy it had. Did its edge remember the taste of the blood it had spilled, Fey and mortal alike? Had it enjoyed it, that taste? Cutter knew it was ridiculous and yet he thought that maybe it had, thought, also, that it wanted to taste more.

"What did he mean?"

Cutter grunted in surprise, for he had been so distracted by his own thoughts that he had nearly forgotten the boy was there. "What?"

"The...the demon thing, back there. He called you Kingslayer and Destroyer...he said that your people called you a hero. What did he mean?"

Cutter met the youth's eyes, saw the question in them, the desperate, hungry need to know. But he shook his head. He had never been much of a liar, preferred to cut to the truth as quickly as he could. Some truths, though, did not need to be spoken of, for speaking of them would do nothing to change them, only force him to relive them and that he was not ready to do. He shook his head. "It was just talk, lad. That's all. The Fey are very strange creatures, and often their meanings are impossible to decipher."

The boy frowned at him. "His meaning seemed clear enough. He didn't like you, not one bit. He said you betrayed them."

"Yes."

"But you're not going to tell me, are you? What he meant?"

"No. Now, come. We need to travel as much distance as we can today. We have to get out of the forest soon and my broth—that is, those men will be searching for us. If we don't make it far enough, they'll find us, and I promise you, boy, you do not want that." *None of us do.* It wasn't because he was afraid, at least not of dying. All men died, sooner or later. He had seen enough death—*caused* enough of it to know that it was a journey no man could avoid no matter how much training or luck he had. No, what he was afraid of, more than anything, was seeing his brother again. Fifteen years it had been, and yet it felt as if it had been no time at all.

For Shadelaresh had been right about another thing too—he was a traitor. Yet for all its ability to see to the heart of things, to know the truths men left unspoken, Cutter doubted even the Fey knew just how right he had been.

# CHAPTER THIRTEEN

*They were an odd bunch, the Crimson Prince's inner circle.
Odd but powerful, some of the most dangerous people I have ever met, save only the prince himself.
But their talents at their own respective crafts were not what amazed me about them.
Instead, it was their loyalty to him, a loyalty that survived test after test.
I do not know where that loyalty came from.
In truth, I doubt they knew themselves.
—Exiled Historian to the Crown Petran Quinn*

"Ah, there it is," Chall said, smiling from where he lay as the woman above him went about her trade with an energy that could only be described as...energetic. Well, he wasn't the poet of their team, he'd known that then and he knew it now. *Their team.* He didn't know where that thought had come from, but he wished it would pack its shit and go back there, wherever there was.

*Their team.*

What a thing to think about, and now of all times. They had never been a team, not really. Any fool with eyes to see would have known that much. What they had been were fools, puppies following after a master that was destined to turn around and kick them sooner or later. Only, the master hadn't been satisfied to just kick them, had he? No, instead he'd decided to go sticking his wick where it most certainly *did not* belong and getting a price on their heads high enough to give some mountains self-confidence issues.

Chall gave his head a shake, trying to focus on the woman above him, to let himself forget, for a time, about the dream he'd had, about the two men and the field and their dooms come upon them. It didn't work, of course, it never did. What it *did* do, however, was snap him out of the first pleasant dream he'd had in some time, and he opened his eyes to discover that the form on top of him—the one which had so pleasantly been rocking back and forth moments ago—was not a beautiful prostitute with a perfect body and the face of an angel. Instead, it was a pig, a very big, very fat pig with a very big, very fat body and with the face of...well, a pig. And the pleasant, wet, tingling sensation Chall felt on his cheek turned out not to be from the woman's fervent kisses. Instead, it was from the pig, its rough tongue wet and slimy along his face.

Abruptly, Chall's moans of contentment suddenly changed to sputters of disgust as he struggled out from beneath the hulking beast, desperately pawing at his tongue—the pig hadn't been the only one doing the licking—and kicking his way backward until he fetched up against something hard. That something, as it turned out, was the side of a wagon bed and, just like that—as if by magic, a particularly assholey, bitchy kind of magic—he remembered where he was and how he'd come to be there.

As for the where, he was in a wagon currently traveling toward the village of Celdar and as for the how, well, that had been a rather unpleasant night spent fleeing half-naked down the street from guards, a few minutes spent stealing a pair of trousers which were, unfortunately purple and were also, at it happened, far too tight for him, then a morning sneaking his way out of the city. He had seen city guardsmen ignore some terrible atrocities in his time—robbery, certainly, muggings absolutely, even a few kidnappings. But apparently, they drew the line at a trouserless fat man running down the street as if such a man would possibly have wound up there on *purpose.*

"Ah, you're awake."

"Unfortunately," Chall muttered, turning to look at the man riding in the front of the wagon, the skin of his face so tanned and leathery that it looked like some animal's hide—though not a damned pig, that much was sure.

The man frowned, adjusting the piece of grass in his mouth. "What's that s'pose to mean?"

"Nothing," Chall said. "Never mind. Anyway, are we there yet?"

The man studied him for another few seconds with narrowed eyes, then hocked and spat, somehow managing to keep the green stem of grass in his mouth as he did. "Nearly. Celdar's right over that hill, yonder," he said, cocking a thumb ahead of them to indicate an incline in the road ahead. "With the gods' graces, we ought to be there in half an hour."

"You ask me, the gods stopped handing out grace a long time ago," Chall said, working his tongue around on his teeth to try to get the last remnants of pig hair off. "Who knows, maybe they ran out. Or took a holiday."

The farmer frowned again. "Don't much care for that kind of talk, mister. You aim to blaspheme, you can do it on someone else's wagon, understand? Or finish the trip with a walk, if you've a mind. Though"—he paused, flashing a look of disgust at the purple trousers Chall wore—"who's to say whether or not you'd be able to walk in those things."

It was Chall's turn to frown. Sure, maybe the trousers weren't exactly the best fit—fact was, he would have laid even odds that he would have burst out of them by now—but they were certainly better than him walking around with his fruits dangling for everybody to see. "I can walk just fine, thank you. And—" He cut off, slapping at a pig's snout as the thing sniffed at him. "Get off me, you damned beast."

"Alright," the man said, "that's it." He clucked at the donkey, giving a tug on the reins, and the beast came to a stop, casting a look over its shoulder as if to see what all the fuss was about. "Go on then," the man said. "Off with you."

"Fine," Chall snapped, doing his best to maintain his dignity and—more importantly—avoid several fresh piles of pig leavings as he climbed out of the back of the wagon. "Tell your wife I said hi—or nevermind." He cast a look at the half a dozen pigs milling about the wagon. "Just tell me which one she is—I'll say it myself."

The next thing he knew, he was sitting on his ass in the road, the purple trousers riding up into some unwanted places so aggressively Chall had a thought to call the guard. Not that there was likely to *be* any guard in a shitty little town like Celdar. There was the farmer, though, the man standing over him even now, his fisted hands on his hips as he stared down at Chall. "Don't much appreciate folks talkin' about my wife. Now, you best learn you some manners, fella, before somebody learns 'em to you."

"What does that even—you know what?" Chall sighed. "Never mind. I'm sorry, alright? About the thing I said about your wife. That wasn't kind." And then, because fools will be fools and he'd never claimed any different, he turned back to the pigs. "Sorry, ma'am."

It took him a bit longer to lower himself to a sitting position the second time. The farmer was still there, watching him. He didn't look angry, as he had before. Or, at least, not only that. He was staring at Chall in a manner usually reserved for insane people. Which, considering that Chall had not ignored the dream but had chosen instead to go find Maeve, probably was just about what he deserved. "What's your deal, fella? You got a death wish?"

Chall considered the dream he'd had, considered, too, the time he'd spent with his team, Maeve and all the rest, and he started laughing. The man hadn't meant it as a joke, of course, but in his experience, the best jokes were the ones men didn't mean to tell. He laughed loudly, falling back onto the dirt road and letting the tears of mirth stream down his face. It wasn't that funny of a joke, maybe, but then the jokes the world told to a man were often not funny unless, that was, the man had a particularly dark—and suicidal—sense of humor.

The farmer shook his head, frowning. "Well. I ain't got time to be sittin' around here watchin' you lose your mind. There's things need doin'. Now, I'll take my payment now." He held out a hand and Chall slowly sobered, blinking at it.

"Payment?"

"That's right, like we agreed. Three sovereigns for the trip."

Chall grunted. "And how much for the punches? Or are those extra?"

The farmer raised an eyebrow. "Oh, they're extra. Matter of fact, I got another one lyin' around here somewhere, if you want it. And you keep flappin' your gums like you are, I'm gonna assume you want it."

"No, no," Chall said, holding up his hands and deciding that he really needed to work on his interpersonal relationships, read a book on it, maybe. "That won't be necessary."

## A Warrior's Burden

The farmer snorted, satisfied. "Didn't figure it would be. Now. My coin?"

Chall grunted, licking his lips. He wanted to tell the man he was an idiot. After all, what fool, if he had money, would pay for the privilege of riding in the back of a pig—and pig-shit—infested wagon? But since his nose already felt a bit loose, and he still hadn't recovered from the candle-stick beating he'd taken at the hands of the ugly innkeeper, he decided to let it go.

Instead, he reached into his pocket, fingering the small pebbles there, pebbles he generally always kept in his pockets—at least those times in which he *had* pockets—for situations just like this. He closed his eyes for a moment, concentrating, calling on the magic.

"Well?" the farmer demanded. "Now, look here, if you lied and you ain't got no money, you'll get a ride from me alright, right to the constable in Celdar, see what he has to say about folks as don't pay their debts."

"No...lie," Chall said, focusing then, a moment later, producing several pebbles from his pocket. Pebbles which, just then, looked like coins. Except for the flaw, of course. He stared at them, looking for it, not seeing it but knowing it was there, then decided to let it go. Not perfect, certainly, but close enough for the farmer to believe that he was holding several coins. The magic would dissipate in time—half a day, no more than that—but until then, the farmer would think he'd gotten a steal. "Here," Chall said sweetly, "take an extra. For your trouble."

"Kind of you," the man said, snatching the coins away so quickly that a person might have been forgiven for thinking he was a magician in his own right. He looked at them then paused, frowning. "What are you playing at?"

"Hmm?" Chall said, just now picking himself to his feet. "What do you mean?"

"You tryin' to cheat me with fake coin, that it?"

Chall held a hand to his chest. "You can't be serious. Me? I'm as honest as they come. Now, what would even make you say such a thing?"

"This," the farmer said, turning the coin to face him, and Chall did his best to hide his surprise. "Now, I ain't gonna claim to be the richest bastard in the world, but I've seen a few sovereigns in my time. You tell me—this look anythin' like old King Reinhart to you?"

The nose. It was always the damned nose. The man was right, though. The nose on the king's golden face looked like a huge, bulbous mass, as if he had some terrible infection. "That's strange..." Chall said, doing his best to hide his nervousness. "Can I see the coin?"

The man frowned deeper then handed it back. Chall took it, staring at the face, focusing on it, then closed his eyes. When he opened them again, the nose was as it should be, a large, prominent nose that was common among the aristocracy. "There you are," he said, offering the farmer his best smile as he handed the coin back. "Must have been a smudge of dirt."

The man frowned. "A smudge."

"That's right," Chall agreed, glancing at the pigs. "One can't imagine where it might have come from." The man scowled, but he took the coin, snatching it away.

"Well. I guess that's alright then." And with that, the pig farmer swung himself back into the front of the wagon and Chall was left staring after him, waving a hand in front of his face in an effort to bat away the dust the wheels kicked up behind the wagon.

"Bastard," he said at normal volume when he'd judged the wagon was far enough away that the man had no way of hearing him. Then, he glanced down the road, in the direction the wagon was traveling, and asked himself, once again, what he was doing here. And once again, himself had no answer—at least none that didn't involve him being a complete fool.

He could have just turned around then, probably should have. He could have gone back to the city, found a good tavern and a good ale or, failing that, any tavern where he didn't have an extended line of credit already—surely there had to be one out there, it was a big city after all—and if good ale wasn't on offer, he'd be satisfied with any with alcohol in it. Why should he let a little thing like a vision of impending doom falling on an old comrade—if anyone could be said to be comrades with such a man—make him uproot his life, such as it was, and travel to see a woman who had always hated him anyway? He shouldn't, that's what, just as he shouldn't allow a little thing like being banned from said city keep him from relaxing and having a nice pint. Or two.

The problem, though, was that the city was over two days' travel behind him now. A long way to go just to have the guards throw you into irons as soon as they saw you. A long way to go even if there was a warm bed and a cold ale waiting on you, and unless dungeons had changed considerably in the last month or so since he'd last visited one, neither would be on offer.

The village of Celdar, though, was only an hour's walk away, give or take, for he could see it in the distance, the smoke rising from the chimneys. Well. Maybe a few hours considering the trousers. Either way, far closer. They would probably have ale, maybe even beds, though in a backwater village like that he thought it just as likely they all slept in the dirt and drank their own piss.

Still, Maeve was there. Maeve who he had not seen in fifteen years. Maeve who, if memory served, had threatened to kill him if she ever saw him again. Though, to be fair, he'd had many people—women in particular—say similar things to him over the years and some of those he had seen again and, while it had to be admitted that though he might not be flourishing, he was, at least, still alive. Probably the woman had only meant the death threat as a jest. Not that he could ever remember Maeve going in for many jokes.

Either way, there was no choice, not if he wanted to save the doomed man and the doomed boy—something he still wasn't sure about. He might know what was coming to them, but he had no idea what he should do to help them—committing suicide by charging at fifty armed men didn't seem like a particularly tempting option. The sad fact was that he'd never been much of a planner. Or a doer either, come to it. He had always considered himself more of a dreamer. Not the type of man who *did* incredible things, true, but the type of man who saw them, maybe, or heard about them over a nice pint and appropriated the best bits for his own.

Maeve, though, she would know what to do. She always had, in the past. The woman might have been a bit of a bitch—the gods could attest to that, surely—but she was also clever. Cleverer than she had a right to be. He'd seen that cleverness in dozens of her schemes over their years campaigning, even if their leader—the man currently walking toward his doom, though he knew it not—had nearly always overruled them and chosen instead the path of blood, as was his way.

He would go to her, then, and tell her of what he had seen in his vision. She would no doubt come up with some plan—assuming she didn't kill him, of course, or neuter him as she'd joked on more than one occasion, doing a bang up job of keeping a straight face and not breaking a laugh or smile. A plan that would, no doubt, somehow enable them to save the boy and the man against all odds. As for Chall, well, that would be the end of his involvement. Once he had told her, once she had been warned, he could wash his hands of the whole affair and get back to...well, get back to getting kicked out of taverns and womens' beds, that was what, his biggest worries bouncers and candlesticks, not swords and pissed off princes. Although, there was no denying that the bed part was becoming less and less frequent of late having, he suspected, some inverse relationship with his growing gut.

Then, resolved—or, at least, as resolved as he ever really got—Chall started down the dirt road toward the village of Celdar, pausing from time to time to defend himself against his recently-acquired trousers.

# CHAPTER FOURTEEN

*You ask me why I chose this path?*
*Very well, I'll tell you.*
*My father was a farmer. My mother too. Their lives spent digging in the dirt, their backs hunched at labor and for what? For more than one night when we were forced to go to bed hungry.*
*No, I will never be a farmer. Better to do anything than that.*
*Better to die.*
—Maeve the Marvelous following the Battle of the Barrier Mountains

Maeve knelt in the dirt of her garden, digging her hands through the fertile soil to create a small pocket, a pocket in which she laid a seed. Then she gently pushed the dirt over, covering it. It was nothing now, nothing but a small seed that might be easily lost or forgotten. But in time, it would grow into a tomato plant, a plant which would produce food that could be eaten. A small thing, perhaps, but then small things, she told herself often, could make all the difference.

That was true, but it wasn't the real reason why she spent so much time in her garden. She knew enough of herself to know that much. No, her reasons were much simpler than that. She liked the feel of the soil in her hands, liked the texture of it, liked, too, the knowledge that hands which had once spent so much time destroying could also create, could help make and sustain life, not just take it away.

It brought a certain peace that had been so rare in her life, one that she had desperately needed. And dirt, it had to be said, washed off far more easily than blood. So, she went about her task, smiling, even whistling a song, one she could not remember the name of.

*Chall would know it.*

She frowned, pausing at that thought, the tune she'd been whistling faltering. Strange, that she would think of the mage now, of all times. For fifteen years, she hadn't given him or any of the others from her past a thought. Or, at least, she'd tried not to and, most of the time, she had even succeeded in that. Lately, though, he had been on her mind a lot. And not just him. Sometimes, the past could trick a person into thinking it was well and truly in the past, that it had forgotten about them and, therefore, they might be allowed to forget about it.

But then, on other nights, the past would snuggle close as she lay in bed, unable to sleep, so close that she could feel its breath on her neck. And she would see them again, all of them as they had been fifteen years ago. She would see the blood, too, would smell it. And of course, there were the screams. Screams the echoes of which she thought she could almost hear even now.

She gave her head a shake and pushed her hands into the soil once more and with a bit more force than was technically necessary. That was when she heard the voice.

"Hi, Maeve."

She knew it at once, that voice, had heard it often enough that it would have been hard not to, and never mind that fifteen years had passed since last she'd heard it. Still, she told herself that it couldn't be, that it was impossible. Yet, when she looked up, there he was. Chall the Charmer, as he'd once been called. A man whose handsome looks had only been eclipsed by his honeyed tongue. But there was little left of the charmer to him now. The years, she saw, had not been kind. *But then, are they ever?*

He stood in tight, purple trousers that looked as if they were prepared to burst, and his shirt was stained with what she would have guessed was spilled ale. Different in so many ways from the man he had been, but the smile he gave her, one that at once seemed flirtatious and mocking, was one she remembered well, one that had often made her want to kiss him and kill him at turns. "Chall," she said, sitting back and letting her arms rest on her folded knees. "You've gotten fat."

He smiled ruefully. "Same old sweet Maeve. Sure, I might have put on a few pounds—"

"Fifty at least."

He sighed, rolling his eyes. "Anyway, it isn't just me that's changed, is it? I never would have thought to see Maeve the *Marvelous* wrist deep in dirt. And on her knees, too, though perhaps that last bit isn't so unusual."

She frowned. "I always hated that name."

"I know."

It was her turn to sigh. "So. What are you doing here—" She was interrupted by the sound of a heavy trod behind her.

"Loretta?" a voice asked in a low growl, like a bear warning someone away from its territory. "Who's your friend?"

She turned back to see her husband scowling, his big arms folded across his thick barrel chest. "Ah, Hank," she said, "I thought you'd gone out drinking with your friends."

"The *boys,* Lorrie," he corrected. "I told you, they're not *friends.* They're the boys."

"Of course," she said. "My mistake."

He gave a snort, glancing at Chall. "Women. If it weren't for what was between their legs, we'd have gotten rid of 'em ages ago, ain't that right?"

Chall grew pale, glancing at her as if he expected her to draw a dagger—admittedly, she used to keep several secreted on her person—and cut the apology out of Hank's flesh. "I uh..." He hesitated. "That is, I've always found myself appreciative of what's between their ears." Hank only stared at him, blinking, and Chall chose to clarify. "You know, their minds."

Hank stared at the fat magician as if he were some alien species, then noted the pants with a grin. "Well, wearin' trousers like that, can't say as I'm surprised. What was her name?"

"I'm sorry," Chall said, "whose name?"

"Well, the woman you stole those trousers from, of course," Hank said, barking a laugh at his own joke.

Chall gave what might have been a laugh, if one ignored the sarcasm and disgust in it. "Oh, it's hard to say. Women, you know? I don't usually bother keeping up with their names. What's the point, right?"

Hank frowned at that, as if trying to decide whether or not he was being mocked which, knowing Chall, he most certainly was. Then he turned back to her. "Who is this fucker, Lorrie?"

She scrambled for an excuse. She had never told her husband about her past, had never told anyone, in fact, having no desire to unearth memories she'd been trying to bury for years—or, for that matter, to risk someone taking it in their mind to get the not insubstantial reward that was offered for her head or the heads of those she'd once traveled with. "Tax collector," she said finally, wincing inwardly as she did.

"Tax collector?" Hank said, frowning suspiciously at Chall. "We've already paid our taxes."

"Right," Chall said, as quick as he always was—thankfully, being grossly overweight didn't interfere with the speed of a man's thoughts, "well, this isn't for taxes, see, more to assess the profit potential in earnings for some of the outlying farms."

"The fuck are you talking about?" Hank demanded. "Do we owe any money or not?"

Chall glanced at her in disbelief then back to Hank, giving him a sickly smile. "You…do not."

Hank grunted. "Well, why not just say that then? Anyway, all tax collectors dress like you?"

"Oh yes," Chall said, nodding, a sober expression on his face, "it's the new uniform."

Hank shook his head. "Damn this world we live in. Folks getting weirder and weirder every day."

"And dumber too," Chall offered, nodding.

Hank scowled again, still trying to decide if he were being mocked. Then he made a point of eyeing Chall up and down. "Well. Maybe I ought to get into the tax collectin' business. You ain't starvin' that's for damn sure. Anyway, I thought you folk usually came around in twos, with a partner."

"Oh, that. Well, I'm afraid I got hungry," Chall said dryly. "I had to eat him."

Hank stared at him for several seconds, and Maeve was left wondering how she would intervene if he decided to give Chall a black eye. Wondering, too, if she would intervene at all. "Anyway," her husband said finally, turning to her, "I had to come back to get some more money—it's my night to buy the rounds."

"Getting an early start are you?" Chall asked, glancing up at the early afternoon sun.

Hank let out a growl—one Maeve had heard before—and started toward the magician, but Maeve stopped him with a hand on his arm. "Please, Hank, no trouble. Did you find the money you needed?"

Hank continued to scowl at Chall for several seconds before turning back to her. "I did, never mind that you tried to hide it under the bed. Honestly, Lorrie, sometimes I think you ain't got any sense except what I beat into you."

She gave him a smile. "Sorry, Hank. I wasn't trying to make you angry. Only, we'll need to buy groceries soon, and I was trying to keep—"

"Never mind what you were tryin' to keep," he snapped. Then he glanced back at Chall. "You're still here."

"Um...yes," the magician said, fidgeting. "Yes, I am."

"Right," Hank said. "Well. Best not be. Off with you, fat man."

Chall turned to her, incredulous, but she gave a slight shake of her head. "Best leave, Cha—sir. Everything is in order here. We pay our taxes every yea—"

"I had a vision, Maeve," he interrupted. "Of *him*. He's in trouble."

Maeve felt as if she'd been struck by lightning, and she stared at the mage in shock. Chall always enjoyed joking—was notorious for it, in fact—and she'd long since lost track of the men and women who'd wanted to kill him thanks to his "jokes." But the mage was not laughing or smiling now, and if it was a joke, it wasn't a very funny one, even for him. Instead, he only stared at her, the import of his words obvious in his steady gaze.

A vision. Chall was many things—a philanderer, a fraud, and a liar chief among them—but he also happened to be a powerful illusionist, perhaps the best who had ever lived, and that wasn't all. He was also blessed—or cursed, to hear him tell it—with the ability to sometimes see into the future, to catch glimpses of it. Often these glimpses were unclear were, according to what he'd told her years ago, like catching sight of a fish's ass before it swims away. But this vision, whatever its contents, had obviously been clear enough to drag him out of whatever brothel or farmer's daughter's bed he'd been sleeping in and bring him all the way here, purple trousers and all. That worried her. She had told herself she was done with her past, done, too, with all those people who had been a part of it. But then, she had always been good at lying to herself.

"Go on and drink with your friends, Hank," she said, so worried by Chall's tone, by the worry in his gaze, too, that she didn't take care to honey her words as she often did with her husband.

He noticed. In another moment, Hank was jerking her up by her shirt sleeve. "Who you think you're talkin' to that way, Lorrie?" he demanded. Then he shook his head. "Damn me, but I thought that the last lesson I taught you would *be* the last. Seems like you're just too stupid to learn."

She brushed his hand free with a practiced flick of her arm. "Not now, Hank," she said. "We'll talk. Later, alright? But not now, now I—" She cut off as he slapped her a ringing blow across the face, and she stumbled, nearly falling.

"Hey—" Chall began, stepping forward, but she held up a hand, stopping him. The magician was many things, but a warrior was not one of them. She tasted blood in her mouth—Hank was a big man, strong, and, as everyone in the village knew, prone to use his fists instead of his words.

"I'm sorry," she said, "look, Hank, I didn't mean anything, alright? I'll just finish talking to Cha...to the tax collector here and then get back to work. Please, go have a fun time with your friends, okay?"

"No," he growled, his fisted hands on his hips like some obstinate child. "No, I don't think I will. You've got a lesson comin', Lorrie. Had one comin' for a while, it seems, and high past time you learnt it."

He reached out to slap her again, but this time, Maeve did not let him. Sometimes, the body remembers what the mind forgets, and she ducked underneath the telegraphed blow with ease, then rose, bringing the ridge of her hand to his throat, pulling the blow at the last moment to keep it from being lethal. Hank grunted, stumbling away as a hand went to his throat, but instead of stopping, he let out a roar like some angry bear and charged her.

Maeve was impatient to hear about what news Chall brought and so she decided she didn't have time to waste humoring her fool of a husband, not today. He grabbed for her, but she pivoted, slapping his arms away contemptuously before grabbing a handful of his fruits and giving them a squeeze. *That* stopped him quickly enough, as it did all men, and he gasped in a sharp intake of breath.

"Enough," she growled at her husband who was watching her with wide, terrified eyes, looking at her as if seeing her for the first time. "Now, I am going to have a conversation with my friend here, Hank—that's right, my friend, or at least, not a tax collector. And *you* are going to go and drink with *your* friends. Isn't that right?"

"Y-yes," he stammered through the pain. "L-Lorrie, I'm sorry. I didn't mean—"

"Never mind that," she said, releasing him with a shove that made him cry out. "Just go on—away with you."

He stood there trying to scowl at her—an effort made more difficult by the fact that one hand was cupping his fruits tenderly, the other rubbing at his throat. "We're goin' to have a talk about this later, Lorrie," he growled. "A long talk."

She sighed. "I don't doubt it. Now go."

He scowled at her, then at Chall as if he had murder on his mind, but thankfully he turned and started away. Maeve watched him go then gave a shake of her head. "That'll be trouble later."

"Seems to me that's trouble all the time," Chall said. "Gods, Maeve, what happened to you?"

She looked at him, feeling a bit defensive. "What happens to all of us, Chall—time. That's all."

"Still," he said, "I wouldn't have ever thought to see you let yourself be bullied by some...some *ape* that looks too stupid to know how good he's got it. Or even read for that matter."

She gave him a smile at that. Chall could be sweet sometimes, too—though always, without fail, only when he didn't mean to be. "No," she said, "maybe not. But it's better than a public torture and an even more public execution."

"If you say so," Chall said dubiously, staring off in the direction her husband had gone.

She waved a hand dismissively. "Forget Hank. He's a fool, but fools are easy enough to control. Now, why don't you tell me why you've come."

He gave her a wink. "Missed me, did you?"

She stared at him. "I refused your proposal and married an ape. What does that tell you?"

Chall winced at that. "Right, on to business then. Though," he went on, getting that shifty look he sometimes—nearly always—got, "it's a bit of a tale, and I've had quite a walk, and I'm a bit thirsty. I wonder if it wouldn't be possible, that is, if maybe you had something…"

She sighed. "Hank had *the boys* over a week ago. I'm pretty sure they left something or another."

He smiled. "It's good to see you, Maeve."

She stared at him, fat and in purple trousers, his shirt and pants covered in dust from the road, and found, to her surprise, that despite everything, despite all the times she had considered strangling him, it *was* good to see him. She shook her head. "Come on, you bastard."

***

A short time later they were sitting at the small table in Maeve's home, using the only two chairs which had survived Hank's regular drunken rages. She held a cup of hot tea in her hand while Chall took a large, unceremonious gulp from the half-drunk bottle her husband and his friends had left. He opened his mouth as if he would speak then paused, beginning to brush dust off his shirt and pants, straightening his droopy, stained collar, making a big production of it. One of the things she most definitely *hadn't* missed about the magician was his need to primp and be the center of attention, even if that attention led to black eyes and headaches—black eyes for him and headaches for anyone who happened to be unfortunate enough to listen to his ramblings.

She took a sip of her tea then frowned, putting it down. Never had liked the stuff. She'd tried it often enough, but like so many aspects of her life, she could never seem to do the thing that she knew was best for her. Proof of that much, at least, sat directly in front of her, purple trousers and all. "You figure you'll get around to the story anytime soon, or should I take a quick nap?"

Chall paused from where he was running a finger across his teeth and winced. Then, finally, he proceeded to tell her about the vision, having to be prodded, from time to time, to get back on track and stop cursing some random innkeeper who he had apparently—and to no one's surprise but his own—managed to piss off enough to take a candlestick to him. As Maeve listened to him take forever dancing around the point as if it were a game he was playing, she found herself envious of the woman as she wouldn't have minded taking a few swings at him herself.

But once he'd finished, she was no longer envious. Instead, she was worried. Worried and mad—furious, really, though at who or at what she wasn't sure—and more than a little confused. It was difficult, in fact, for her to know what exactly she was feeling, so twisted up were her emotions. On the one hand, she had told herself that she was done with all of that, with all those people. From that side, she thought it was only right that someone was trying to kill her ex-commander, thought that it was a wonder there wasn't already a career path for that exact thing, that folks couldn't take classes on it. On the other, though, she found herself worried, worried for him, mostly, and that, she believed, was what made her angry. He was a murderer. A cruel murderer, an adulterer, and worse, a man who had gloried in his own sins. She should not care what happened to him at the least or even should have wished to help those seeking his life.

But she did care. Partly this was because the same men which sought his life sought hers as well. Mostly, though, it was because she cared for him. For reasons she could not explain even to herself, she cared for him, and the thought of something happening to him did not sit well with her, not at all. And that wasn't even to mention the boy, whatever poor youth had found himself sucked up in the man's wake, much the same way that she and Chall and the rest had. It wasn't that they had *chosen* to follow him exactly. Certainly she did not remember ever making a conscious decision to do so. Instead, it was as if the man were some great whirlwind or cyclone driving its way across the land and she and those others who they had traveled with—some alive, most not—had simply been pulled along by the force of him, had been swept up by his drive and his personality which, while it could have never been said to be kind, was certainly powerful.

Chall watched her silently, a question in his eyes, one which he voiced a moment later. "What do we do, Maeve?" He paused, smiling mischievously. "Or should I call you Lorrie? It's what the ogre called you, isn't it? Lorrie?"

She frowned. "Do you really think this is the most pressing thing right now, Chall?"

He shrugged. "Just never thought of you as a 'Lorrie' that's all. Though I also never would have thought to have found you on your knees in the dirt, picking weeds either. And I don't even want to get started on the way that big bastard talked to you. The Maeve I knew—"

"The Maeve *you* knew," she interrupted, "has a price on her head that could beggar some of the realm's wealthiest noblemen, thanks in no small part to you and your constant inability to keep your mouth shut when you should. After all, not all of us are illusionists who can fake our deaths. I wonder, did you go to your own funeral? It seems like the sort of thing you would do."

He winced. "I'm afraid I missed the whole affair. I was, as I recall, a bit drunk at the time."

"Surprising," she said dryly. "Anyway, I wouldn't worry about it—I was there, and it seems to me that just about everyone missed it."

"Fine, fine, so maybe I'm not exactly overburdened with friends. Still, to see you like this—"

"No, Chall," she growled. "No. I won't talk about my husband or about anything else with you. That's my business and mine alone. We've all dealt with our past in our own ways, found paths to move forward in our own ways. Yours, it seems"—she paused, glancing at his protruding gut—"mostly in the form of ale and food."

"And prostitutes," he offered without a hint of shame—it seemed the bastard still didn't have any—"let's not forget that."

She sighed. "Have I told you just how pleased I am to see you?"

"Believe me, I didn't want to come here..." He trailed off as she frowned. "I mean, I wanted to see you—of course, who wouldn't, you're such a pleasant person. But...what I mean..."

"I know what you mean," she said. And that was true. She knew exactly how the vision's contents made him feel, for she thought it likely that she was feeling much the same herself.

They trailed into silence then, both of them thinking their own thoughts, and just for something to do, Maeve took a sip of her tea. Terrible stuff, normally, but she could taste none of it now.

"What are we going to do, Mae?" Chall asked quietly.

No one had called her that in a very long time, no one had *ever* called her that, in fact, except for Chall. She'd always hated it, that name, and had long since lost track of the arguments they'd had over it—more than a few of which had ended when she'd finally had enough and reached for one of the knives she'd always kept. Now, though, she found that after fifteen years, she'd missed it. She had not, however, missed the way he was staring at her now, the same way that a child might stare at a parent when they'd had a bad dream. The child confident that the parent would know what to do, that the parent could make the monsters go away.

*What are we going to do, Mae?* A single sentence, uttered in a moment, but one that threatened to turn her life, the one she had spent the last fifteen years building, on its head. "What life?" she muttered.

"I'm sorry?"

She shook her head. "Nothing." And that was an answer not just to his question, she realized, but to her own as well. What life? Nothing. No life at all, that was the truth. She realized, then, that she had been so focused on staying hidden, so focused on keeping her life that she had traded it one piece at a time in the name of safety, a particularly large part on her wedding day to Hank. For years, she had tolerated the man's drunken pawings and drunken rages, pretending to be a meek, frightened wife because she thought that, in this way, she would keep herself safe, so that she might live. After all, as Chall had pointed out, no one could have ever expected to find Maeve the Marvelous in a shithole of a village, meekly accepting the constant rebukes of her overbearing husband. She had sought to keep her life and, in seeking it, had lost it.

She realized another truth then, a particularly unwelcome one. In the last fifteen years, she had done very few things of which she was proud, very few things which she could look back on with anything but shame. Over fifteen years, she had transformed herself, had metamorphosed the way a caterpillar might turn into a butterfly. Only she had not turned from an ugly insect into a beautiful butterfly. Instead, she had turned herself from a confident, brave woman, one after whom men lusted even while they were terrified of her, into a mewling, scraping wife, one who was, in fact, little better than a servant.

Chall had asked her how the Maeve he had known could marry Hank, could put up with the things she did, and the fact was that such a woman could not. So she had allowed herself to become something else, something worse. Years ago, before her head had such a price on it, and she had exiled herself from civilized society, Maeve had done many things. She had been known throughout the land—Maeve the Marvelous, they had called her, and though she had always hated that name, it had stood for something. *She* had stood for something, something more than pulled weeds and being a punching bag for her husband when he had it in mind to vent his anger and she was closest at hand.

True, she had done some terrible things back then, but she had done some fine ones too, ones which her position and her power—not to mention her reputation—had allowed her to do. For the last fifteen years, she had hardly done anything at all, just watched her life slip by as if it were someone else's, watched it like it was sand in an hourglass. "What are we going to do?" she asked, the decision already made, feeling better, more *herself* than she had in a very long time. "I'll tell you what we're going to do, Chall. We're going to help them."

He gave her a small smile that looked more like a wince, as if he had known what she was going to say long before she said it. And, likely, he had. Chall was many things, but a fool was not among them. "How?"

No arguing, no telling her that he would have nothing to do with it and that it was on her, only the simple question. She loved him, in that moment, for perhaps she had turned herself into a caterpillar but now, she would turn herself into a butterfly once more, if she could. And *if* she managed it, she would have Chall to thank, for he, and his coming, was her cocoon. She brushed the disgusting cup of tea off the table, oblivious to the sound of the small cup cracking as it struck the wooden floor, then she leaned forward, eyeing him. "I'll tell you how."

# CHAPTER FIFTEEN

*People tip-toed around him, scared to talk, that they might say the wrong thing, scared to remain silent, that he might take offense. But they did not know him, none of them, at least not as I did.*
*For as terrifying as his anger was, it was not the worst of him.*
*No, he was not at his most dangerous when he was angry.*
*For when he held the Fey king's head before him at feast, gobbets of blood dripping from it onto the table, he was not growling or cursing, not shouting or threatening.*
*No. He was laughing.*
—Excerpt from journal of Maeve the Marvelous regarding Prince Bernard, known as "The Crimson Prince"

Matt followed the big man's back as they trudged through the snow-laden ground of the Black Woods. They had traveled so for over a day, heading south. He knew that much only because his father—or the man who had claimed to be his father—had taught him to read the stars long ago, in case he ever got lost. He did not know *why* they headed south just as he did not know the answer to the thousands of other questions pressing on his mind. He had tried to ask Cutter, at first, about what the green demon had said, what it had meant when it called him Kingslayer and Destroyer and Hero, but Cutter had avoided the question. Since then, he had not bothered even doing that, choosing instead not to answer Matt at all.

And so, they walked in silence, as they had for the last day and a half, the big man saying nothing except for the night before when it had been time for them to break camp and then only, "We'll stop here." That and nothing else.

Being here, in this place, in the cold that seemed to penetrate him all the way into his bones no matter how many clothes he wore or how much he bundled up at night, with only his silent, brooding companion for company, Matt missed his family, his loneliness a terrible ache in his chest. He was not angry, not any longer. He was only sad. Perhaps they had not been his *real* family. Perhaps they had even taken money to watch over him as Cutter claimed, but what did that matter? They *had* watched over him, after all, had treated him as family, had loved him—or at least pretended to—as much as, perhaps even more, than any of the other parents of the village had loved their own children.

He missed his mother's smile, the one he had always thought of as just for him, missed her asking him what he wanted to eat for breakfast. He missed his friends, too, missed carefree days spent fishing in the summer thaw, laughing and telling jokes and lying about which village girl they'd kissed with no bigger worries than that someone would call them on it. He had always hated his life, envied those other boys whose mothers and fathers had decided that life in the remote village of Brighton was not to their taste and who had chosen to take their chances among civilization. He had watched those families leave angrily, angry mostly at his mother who had refused, who had told him that their place, *his* place, was in Brighton.

He had always asked her why, why they must stay in such a gods-forsaken village with snow and nothing else, and she had always refused to answer. Except, that was, for one time when she had grown cross at his insistent, petulant demands, and had finally told him that they stayed because of a promise. She had clearly not meant to say it—that much had been obvious in her expression—but no matter how much he had pestered, she had said no more than that. And now, he would never know.

He wasn't aware he was crying until the wind struck his face, and he felt the cold dampness on his cheeks. He glanced up at Cutter, terrified that the man would notice, as for reasons he could not explain, even to himself, the man's regard mattered more to him than he cared admit. He needn't have worried, though. Cutter only trudged forward, the axe slung across his back in a sling he had fashioned the night before when Matt had lain down to sleep. He marched forward as if there was nothing else in the world, as if he had no hopes or dreams, no regrets or any feeling at all except for some unknown impetus which drove him onward.

Matt had had a family once, and truly his or not, it had been a family. He'd had parents that loved him, a mother that sang him lullabies when he'd had a bad dream, and a father who'd bounced him on his knee and played horsey. Now, he had nothing. Nothing except for the man in front of him who seemed as cold, as unforgiving and unfeeling as the landscape which surrounded them. "I miss them."

The words were out of his mouth before he realized it, and Cutter turned regarding him with a blank expression. He might have been thinking anything. "Yes."

"We should have left," Matt said, finding that now that he'd started, he was unable to keep himself from speaking, if for no other reason than to derive some small comfort from the sound of a human voice in this strange, alien place.

"Left what?"

"The village!" Matt said, shouting the words. "I told her, my mom, a hundred times that we should leave. I wanted to go to the city, to see the world, not spend my life stuck in some backwater village like Brighton, but she refused. She always said we couldn't, said it wasn't safe."

"She was right to say so."

"But what does that *mean?*" Matt demanded. "Sure, it wasn't safe, but we weren't safe in Brighton either, were we?"

He fell to his knees then, overcome with emotion, and the tears rolled freely down his face. He did not bother wiping them away. After all, what was the point? More would come, that much was sure. And so he knelt there, on the cold hard ground, and he cried.

For a time, the big man said nothing, *did* nothing but stood there, regarding him. Matt, however, barely noticed, for his face was buried in his hands, the tears which he had struggled to hold back for the last several days, tears for all that he had lost, all that had been taken from him, coming freely now. Then, suddenly, there was a hand on his shoulder. A rough hand, with callouses he could feel even through his heavy shirt and jacket, and though the touch was gentle he could feel the strength behind it. "Why did she do it?" Matt sobbed. "Why did she stay?"

At first, he didn't think the man would answer, thought that, like the several days previous, he would only let the silence speak for him. When he did finally speak, Cutter's voice was rough and soft, as if it held back some great emotion. "Because I made her promise she would. Her and your father too, before he died."

Matt's sobbing cut off at that, and he raised his head, staring at the big man. "What?"

Cutter turned to fully face him now. "Your mother and father stayed in Brighton because I made them promise to when I gave you to them."

Matt's head was suddenly full of confused, jumbled thoughts. "So what then? You paid them for that too?"

The man's eye twinged, a small, almost imperceptible gesture that might not have even been noticeable on another person but which, on him, stood out as a break in his unfeeling, uncaring façade, a crack in the armor he wore over himself against the world. "I never paid your mother and father."

"But...but you said you paid them to take me in, paid them so that they'd keep me."

The big man's shoulders shifted in what might have been a shrug. "I lied."

Matt had thought himself drained of anger, had thought that all he'd had left in him was sadness and pain and regret. He'd been wrong. "So *what?*" he said, rising to his feet, his fists clenched at his sides. "You let me believe that my mother and father, that they just took me in because you paid them like some trader paid for a service, let me *hate* them?"

"Yes."

"But *why?*" he yelled, not caring, for the moment, that they were in the middle of the Black Woods, not worried in that instant about drawing attention to himself.

"Because I needed you to get up and walk," Cutter said simply. "And you did. Sometimes, boy, hate is the only thing that keeps us moving."

Matt was shaking now, his entire body trembling with rage, and before he knew it, he let out a scream and charged at the man. He'd been in a few fights over the years—mostly with the village boys with whom he would be best friends the next day—and he had always accounted himself well. His mother had told him, during such times when she'd nursed his hurts and scolded him for the use of violence, that it was "in his blood." Had told him, too, that a person could fight what was in their nature, could rise above it. But while fighting might have been in his blood, while *violence* might have been in his blood—whatever that meant—it was in Cutter's entire body, as if he were an avatar of violence and war.

He felt a terrible rush of glee when his first punch struck home in the man's stomach, but it felt like hitting a tree trunk, and Cutter did not so much as move, only let out a soft groan. "That's enough, lad," he said, not sounding hurt in the slightest, only sounding like a man trying to calm down a wild beast.

That made Matt even more angry, and before he knew it, he'd punched the man in the face, a blow that made Cutter's head turn at the impact. "I hate you!" Matt screamed, rearing back for a third blow.

"I said that's—"

But he wasn't listening to the man. He'd listened to him already, and had left his village, his *mother* to burn because of it. No, he was done listening now. He swung again, wanting nothing more in that moment than to feel the man's nose break beneath his fist. But Cutter suddenly moved, and the next thing Matt knew he was hurtling through the air, upside down, to land hard on the snowy ground with such force that the wind was knocked out of him.

He lay there panting, gasping for breath and trying to understand what happened. He was still trying to work it out when Cutter's big form loomed over him, staring down. There was a slight trickle of blood running from his mouth, one which gratified Matt to see, warming him in a way that he had not been warm in days. Perhaps his mother had been right after all; perhaps violence was in his nature, but then she had been wrong to tell him to fight it. For seeing the small trickle of blood, knowing that he had caused this man, this object of his hate, pain, was a good feeling. Maybe even a great one.

"That's enough, lad," Cutter said. He reached out a hand to help Matt to his feet. Matt took it, allowing himself to be hoisted up. Once he was standing, he reared back and punched Cutter in the gut again, but like the first, the blow hurt his hand while seeming to have very little effect on the big man.

Except, that was, that the big man's eyes flashed with anger, and Matt felt a surge of panic before Cutter leaned forward and, almost casually, planted his fist in Matt's stomach.

Pain—terrible, excruciating pain—ripped through Matt, and it felt as if the man had punched a hole right through him. The next thing he knew, he was on his hands and knees, retching the meager contents of his breakfast—another squirrel, one Cutter had managed to find—out onto the cold snow where it steamed in a gross, revolting puddle.

"I said *enough*," Cutter growled, and there was such fury in his voice that Matt cowered away. He glanced up and saw the big man studying him, his cold blue eyes seeming to burn in their sockets with rage. The man said nothing, his thick chest heaving, his fists working at his sides, and though he did not speak, Matt had the feeling—the terrible, helpless feeling—that the man wanted to kill him, that it was all he could do to hold himself back.

Finally, though, the moment passed. Cutter's breathing slowed, and his eyes turned cold once more, like chips of ice in their sockets. "I made your parents promise not to take you out of the village, boy, because it isn't *safe*. Do you understand?"

Matt scooted away on his butt, suddenly frightened to be too close to the big man in case that terrible rage, the rage of which he thought he had only glimpsed a small fraction, like an iceberg's tip seen above the water, might return. "I-it isn't so hard a journey," he rasped. "Troy's father and mother have made it several times, it—"

"It's different for you," the big man interrupted.

"What...what does that mean?" Matt wheezed past his aching stomach. "Why?"

The big man stared at him as if considering something, then he finally gave a dismissive shake of his head. "It doesn't matter. Just know that it is dangerous for you to go out, boy. Dangerous for you in ways it is not dangerous for anyone else. Do you understand?"

"How can I?" Matt demanded, hurt and angry all at once. "You haven't *told* me anything."

"I've told you enough," the big man said. "Now, get up. We need to cover more ground before dark. Shadelaresh has so far kept his people from accosting us, but he will not do so forever. If we linger much longer in the Wood, they will come for us, boon or no boon."

Matt wanted to argue, wanted to scream and tell the man he hated him, that he hoped they did come just so long as he got to watch them kill Cutter first. The problem, though, was that, for one, he feared the man might grow angry again, and he was terrified to see that part of him once more, would have given much to keep from seeing it. But it wasn't just that. It was also the fact that he feared that should he tell Cutter he hated him and that he hoped he died, the man wouldn't care, might even agree with him.

So, instead of saying anything, he only rose. Cutter watched him for a moment, as if waiting to see if there was going to be another outburst. When none came, the big man turned and started away again. And, left with no choice—as always—Matt followed.

## CHAPTER SIXTEEN

*It is said, by the followers of Raveza, Goddess of Temperance, that the road to peace is taken one step at a time. A true saying, or so I believe, but we must remember something. Yes, the road to peace is taken one step at a time.*
*But then, so, too, is the road to damnation.*
*—Ex-priest of Raveza from his prison cell.*

"It appears to be a relatively fresh kill, sire. Perhaps no more than a day or two."

"So it does, Malex," Feledias said, staring down at the Gretchling corpse. He had seen their kind before, during the war, had even seen a few in their natural form—a form they only chose to take, perhaps only *could* take, once they had died. Though, it had to be said, he had never seen one in such terrible shape as this, the creature's body so mutilated as to almost be unrecognizable. "This is *his* work," he said quietly.

Malex, along with the other soldiers, shifted uneasily at that, but Feledias paid them little mind. After all, they had all spent the last day acting uneasy, had done so since they'd first entered the Black Wood, as if afraid, like children, that the monsters would come for them during the night. The Fey would do such things, of course, for he had seen it before, but they had not done so yet, though they could not have missed the passage of him and his men in their lands. To Feledias, that must mean that they approved of his quest for his brother's head and did not wish to hinder him in the carrying out of it which was good for him—a wise choice. For he had been seeking his brother for many years now and would slaughter any who dared become an obstacle in his path. The fulfilling of his vengeance, of the vow he had taken, was close, and he would not allow anyone to hinder him.

"Where did they go?" he asked, turning to Dalen. The grizzled tracker adjusted the furs covering him, clearly uncomfortable with Feledias's attention.

"Not so easy to tell, Highness," he said quietly in a dry, croaking voice that sounded as if he never used it. A fact which Feledias could attest to, for he had ridden with the man often and had rarely heard him speak. "The snow covers most tracks."

Feledias frowned. "What am I paying you for then? Perhaps, it would be better if I chose, Dalen, to forego your services. What do you think of that?"

The man blanched, as well he should, for anyone with the sense the gods had given him knew what Feledias meant by that. He was the prince of the realm and, as such, men were not allowed to leave his service, not voluntarily at least, and he made sure, as a rule, that should he wish for them to leave, they would never work with anyone else again. Or breathe, for that matter.

"Covers *most* tracks, Highness," Dalen said hurriedly, "but not all." He knelt, studying the tracks carefully as if his life depended on it—which it did. Finally, he nodded. "They went this way, Highness," he went on, pointing further into the forest. "Prince Bernard and the…the other."

Feledias let out a growl, reaching out and slapping the man ringingly across the face. Dalen cried out in surprise, falling to the ground and staring up at him with wide eyes. "He is *not* your prince," he growled at the man as he bled from his mouth. "Not any longer. Not since he lay with that adultering whore, not since he *betrayed* me. He is a traitor to the realm, a traitor to *me*. That and nothing more. Do you understand me, Dalen?"

"F-forgive me, sir," he said, "I meant no offense. I-it was a mistake."

Feledias watched him, considering reaching for the blade at his side, the fury and rage which had been his constant companions for fifteen years roiling within him like a storm. "A mistake," he said, his voice a harsh whisper. "Very well, Dalen. I will forgive you, this time. But know that should you ever refer to that—that *traitor* as a prince again, I will not be so kind, and it will be the very last mistake you make. Am I clear?"

"O-of course, sir."

"Very well," he said. "Now, stand up and tell me what you have learned."

The man climbed to his feet, bowing his head. "I apologize again, Highness, I did not mean—"

"Never mind what you meant," Feledias growled. "Speak quickly, Dalen, for I have little patience left."

"Yes, sire. As I was saying, I scouted ahead. The two went that way"—he motioned into the forest—"but then they turned around and are now traveling south."

"South," Feledias said thoughtfully, running a hand across his chin. What would his brother be planning? There had been a time when Feledias would have been able to guess his intentions easily enough, for the man had been little more than a beast, akin to a bull who saw red and so whose only thought was to charge at the nearest enemy and, if one weren't forthcoming, his nearest ally, with bloodletting on his mind.

But it had been fifteen years since he'd last seen the man, more than that, in fact, and had he still been the same person as before, he would have heard of Feledias's hunt for him and come to finish matters the only way a brute such as he had known—violence. The fact that Feledias had not seen or heard anything of him—neither, until recently, had his many agents scattered across the realm—meant that the man had changed. At least enough to fight his baser desires, those which were no doubt even now urging him to fight, to kill. But, somehow, for some reason, he was ignoring those desires, had ignored them for the last fifteen years.

Feledias could only imagine that the man was afraid for his life, and it was this fear which kept him from facing him. Of course, he was right to be afraid, for when Feledias found him—or any of those others who had aided him, whom he had called friend—he would make an example of him, would carve the price of the man's betrayal out of his flesh.

He forced his anger down, forced himself to think. Yes, he would exact his vengeance from the man and his companions, but he had to find him first. He was close now, closer than he had been for the last fifteen years, and he could not afford to let his anger get the better of him. He frowned, looking around them.

His brother wanted to live, cared only for his own safety, that much was obvious. He wanted to live, and he was heading south. Where would he go, though? What refuge might he seek to avoid...Feledias hissed in a breath as the answer became obvious. The Fey would not long suffer the man in their lands. After all, it had been he who had lured their king to parley under a flag of truce only to chop his head from his shoulders with that great axe he carried. He would not turn around and head north, of that much Feledias was confident. After all, there was nothing there for him to head *toward.* Nothing, that was, except the burned-out skeleton of the village that had dared shelter him, the corpses of its inhabitants, traitors to the crown one and all, likely still smoking. And if he tried to go past that, to travel farther north, he would only reach the Barrier Mountains, their very name originating from the fact that they could not be crossed, far too high and too cold for any man to survive the journey.

No, he was going south, that much was certain. And if he did not wish to remain in the Black Wood for long, he would be forced to abandon their relative safety soon. But he would not do so without a plan. No, he would head for the safest place he could. Feledias grinned, turning to Commander Malex. "Get everyone on their horses—we ride for Valaidra."

Commander Malex looked perplexed. "Sire?"

"He will not tarry long in the Wood, Malex. No, my brother is like an animal on the run and seeks only safety. If he cannot disappear into the wilderness—and he cannot—then he will try to hide in plain sight, to be only another face among thousands. And as you well know, Valaidra is the only city of any size near us. We will wait for him outside the Wood and will catch our quarry when he leaves the Fey lands."

The man bowed his head. "As you command, Highness." Then he stepped away, motioning to the troops and growling orders. In moments, the soldiers were preparing their kits, mounting their horses.

"Not you, Dalen," Feledias said, and the tracker turned.

"Sire?"

"You will continue to follow them, discover where they are, exactly—see them with your own *eyes,* do you understand?—then bring news back to me. I believe I know what my brother will do, but I could be wrong, and something as important as this cannot be left to chance, do you understand?"

"Of course, Highness, but there is a risk…should I get too close. Your brother is known for his cleverness, for being difficult to catch, and if he senses—"

"You are worried about what my brother might do to you, is that it, Dalen?" Feledias demanded.

The man paled, but said nothing, made no move to argue with him.

"Oh, but you need not be, Dalen," Feledias said, his voice an angry simmer, "for if you do not do this thing for me, or if you should fail, then whatever fate my brother might have chosen for you will be eclipsed a thousand times by the pain and suffering I visit on not just you but your family. You have a sister living in the capital, do you not? Perhaps I will have my men pay her a visit, to take the measure, you see, of her hospitality."

The man swallowed hard, quivering with fear or rage or both. "I will leave at once, sire."

"I thought you might," Feledias said dryly. "Now go. And leave your horse. The beast will give your position away."

"As you command, Highness," the man said, bowing his head.

Feledias watched him disappear into the wood, then he turned to the rest of his soldiers, all waiting on their mounts. He strode to his own beast and in one smooth motion leapt into the saddle. Then he turned and nodded at Commander Malex. In another moment, they were riding out of the woods, an anticipatory grin on Feledias's face.

## CHAPTER SEVENTEEN

*The Fearsome Five, they were called.*
*The number was not always correct—sometimes there were more, sometimes less, for even the world's greatest heroes might die in battle.*
*And heroes they were. There were others, of course, during the Fey Wars, but none so respected, so feared, as Prince Bernard and his closest companions.*
*And wherever they went, men and women bowed and scraped before them.*
*Heroes, yes, men and women of incredible prowess in battle.*
*But sometimes, even heroes can become villains.*
*—Exiled Historian to the Crown, Petran Quinn*

"Ah, but I've missed the smells of the city," Chall said from beside her, taking in a long, deep breath.

Maeve frowned over at him. She was annoyed. For one, her tailbone hurt, and she was sore in places she didn't remember ever being sore before. She was not accustomed to riding in the back of jouncing wagons, and her body ached from a day and a half of it. She told herself she was going soft, that the last fifteen years had done her no favors, but it wasn't only that. Even back when she had traveled with her companions, during the Fey Wars, she had never been reduced to riding in the back of wagons.

Indeed, no one in their right mind would have ever expected to find Maeve the Marvelous so humbled. No, she had ridden at the front of great companies of troops, only surpassed in her majesty and the love of the crowd by her lord. They had ridden into cities—those they had conquered and those they had saved—to the adulation, sometimes real, often feigned, of its citizens, and flowers of all colors had been thrown at the feet of their mounts. While Maeve regretted many things of her past, and while she was glad to have most of the features of those days long behind her, existing now only in memory, she could have done with some flowers just then, would have even settled for a simple pillow for her aching backside.

And she decided then that it wasn't just her backside that hurt, but her pride, too. She hadn't thought she'd had much of the stuff left, to be honest, had thought she'd left it behind her, if not when she'd fled like a coward in the night when the truth of her lord's betrayal had come to light, then certainly abandoned at the altar when she'd chosen to marry Hank. But as it turned out, her pride, like so many of her sins, had followed her, refusing to give her a moment's rest.

She thought that Chall, given his gross overweightness and the trousers which she did not think she imagined were already beginning to peel away at their tortured seams, must have surely enjoyed the trip even less than she, yet he was not complaining now. Instead, he stood beside her, just inside the city gate, smiling widely at the buildings and those who passed them like a fool, either unaware or uncaring of the laughter his—and no doubt her—appearance elicited. After all, they were both covered in dust and hay from riding in the back of a wagon, and there was a stain on Maeve's skirt which looked—and smelled—suspiciously like animal shit. "Missed the smells, did you?" she snapped. "And what smells are those? Despair and unwashed bodies?"

"And *ale,* dear Maeve," the magician said, still smiling widely, apparently unwilling to be put off so easily. "Pray thee, do not forget the ale. Now," he went on thoughtfully, looking around, "the real question is, which tavern would be the best for—"

"We didn't come here so that you could drink ale and ogle barmaids, Chall," she growled. "You know that." "Oh, come on," he said, his voice whiny, "just a little ogle?" He must have seen some of her disapproval in her stare—hard not to as she was scowling just about as hard as she could—for he heaved a heavy sigh. "Fine, no ogling at all, though it's a shame, if you ask me, to leave such beauty unappreciated."

"No one did ask you."

He shook his head sadly. "No, no I suppose they didn't and that should serve as proof enough that the world is a cruel, ignorant place. Anyway, you shall have your way—we will only make a quick trip into a tavern, just a stop off, an opportunity to catch our breaths, you might say, and...perhaps to slake our thirsts."

"One more word from you about stopping by a tavern," she warned, "and I'll be slaking my thirst for blood, you understand?"

"Oh, come now, Mae," he said, smiling once more. "People change—you are no longer the cold-blooded, assassin-beauty which sent so many fantasizing men to bed in a mixture of fear and admiration. Why, I'm quite certain you do not even have a knife—" He cut off as she produced two knives from inside her dress, not quite as quick as she once might have, perhaps, but pretty quick just the same.

"People don't change that much, Chall," she said.

He moaned. "Very well, Maeve—you make a particularly...sharp point. Why, I certainly would not wish to feel the *edge* of your anger, for it is both sharp and cutting and—"

"One more jibe, Chall," she said, "and I'll show you just how cutting it can be."

He sighed again. "You really do have a way of taking all the fun out of being hunted by the entire realm and throwing ourselves into even greater peril, you know that?"

"The gods weep."

"Well," he said dryly, "if they don't, they most certainly should. Anyway, what's your plan then? I suppose go hunting for our erstwhile companion, perhaps stop by some establishments—I said *establishments,* damn you, not taverns—and introduce ourselves, tell them who we are and who we search for?" He gave a humorless laugh. "Perhaps we could even lay odds on how long it will take someone to call the guard and how long after that it will take before our execution is scheduled. Not long, I'd wager. Not long at all."

"I'm not stupid, Chall," she said.

"Could have fooled—"

"And while my mind isn't the greatest—time, the bastard, has seen to that—I'm still not quite ready to part with it, and the rest of my head, quite yet. Anyway, he shouldn't be so hard to find."

"Oh, don't be silly, Maeve," Chall said. "You've got a wonderful head. At least, parts of it. Why, there's a spot just there, right above your hairline, where it hasn't gone to gray yet and—"

"I *will* stab you, Chall."

"Very well. All I mean is, I'm not entirely certain we should have come here in the first place. Why bother? There's a good chance he isn't even here anyway. What, you said you heard that how long ago? Five years? He could be anywhere. For all we know, they've set up a convent for all the world's pompous assholes in some far away country—the gods can hope *very* far away—and put him at its head. Certainly I can think of no other person more deserving of the honor."

She sighed. "You never did like him. I think probably because he didn't pat you on the back and buy you a beer every time you bragged about your latest conquest, as if bedding farmer's daughters was so remarkable."

"There's an art to it," Chall said defensively. "Anyway, not just 'not every time' but not *any* time. The bastard never did give me my due."

"Listen," she said, glancing around the street at those walking around them before leaning in, "there are more important things at stake here than your wounded pride."

"Yes," he said, "dehydration comes to mind."

"Oh, I wouldn't worry overly much, Chall," she said. "When you die, I don't think it'll be dehydration that causes it. Blood loss, likelier than not. Now come on—if I remember right, there's a church near the center of town, one dedicated to Raveza."

"The Goddess of Temperance," Chall said, rolling his eyes. "Might as well be the Goddess of Unicorns and Assorted Mythical Creatures."

"Not bad," Maeve said, smiling despite herself, "though I'm not sure if it'd fit on the statue plaques."

"And wouldn't that be a terrible shame?"

Maeve stared at him for several seconds. "Are you done?"

Chall frowned. "Yes, Mae. I'm done."

"You're sure?" she asked, raising an eyebrow, "because, who knows, if we hang around talking much longer, we might end up making some of the guards suspicious. Why, we could even be recognized, though given your current...weight—sorry, I meant state, of course—that could be in some doubt. Still..." She shrugged. "It's all the same to me. If you want to hang around, see if anyone calls the guards on us, we can. Then, I expect you'll have some bigger things to bitch about than what appears to be, judging by the state of you, your personal quest to bring down the Goddess of Temperance."

He had a hurt look on his face. "You know, you should really leave the jokes to me—they're not supposed to be cruel. Only funny."

"Oh, Chall," she said, "how can I ever be expected to leave the jokes to you? After all, the world has its own jokes and, if you ask me, they're rarely funny and are always cruel. Now come on, damn you. Let's find him so we can get out of here—so many people looking at us makes my skin crawl."

"You know what makes *my* skin crawl?" he began. "Men—or women, I'm an equal opportunity despiser—who thins they're so damned holy that their shit smells like plum pudding..."

He went on after that, but Maeve wasn't listening. Instead, she turned and started down the street, confident that the magician would follow, confident, too, that he would bitch the entire way. People changed, sure, but in her experience, they didn't change all that much.

# CHAPTER EIGHTEEN

*What to say of Valden Abereth, the man known simply as "Priest?"*
*This historian has rarely met a wiser man, a kinder one.*
*During our travels, we sometimes sat in council, the two of us, and, more often than not, the conversation turned to his goddess, to what a man might expect when moving beyond life's veil.*
*Valden seemed to know much on the subject, particularly about the world beyond this one.*
*But then, I suppose that is no great surprise, for he sent many there himself.*
*For Valden Abereth was a kind man, a wise one.*
*And he was also, as it happened, one of the world's most talented killers.*
*—Exiled Historian to the Crown, Petran Quinn*

The boy stood before him dressed in filthy rags most people wouldn't have allowed their dogs to lie on. Valden bowed his head to him, retrieving a hard piece of bread from the basket beside him and offering it to the youth. "The road to peace," he said.

"Is taken one step at a time," the boy responded instantly. He, like those two dozen or so other street waifs standing in line behind him, knew what was expected of him, for he had said it often enough when Valden or one of his brothers or sisters came to the poor district to hand out food. Likely, the poor souls said it not out of some true belief but out of a simple wish not to anger the man on whose food they had come to rely, but Valden did not mind. Perhaps, in time, they would say the words enough that they might even come to believe them. And if they did not? Well, that was fine as well, for at least they would be fed. He could not give them a place to live, could not give them coin with which to buy the things they needed—for he had no coin himself just as he had no personal possessions as none of those within his order did—but he could at least make sure they ate. Not every day, perhaps, but today.

The boy did not thank him, did not even offer him a smile, only hurried away, clutching his chunk of hard bread against his chest as if it were some great prize he was in fear of losing or—more likely—having taken from him. Cradling it to his chest as if his life depended on it. Which, when one was a starving orphan living on the streets, it did. Valden wanted to help the boy, wanted to take him aside and tell him that Raveza loved him—which was true—and that everything would be okay—which may or may not have been. In the end, of course, he knew that Raveza would take all of those who passed from the tortured veil that was the mortal world into her loving embrace, but among the many promises she had made to mankind, there was not one that they would not suffer or feel pain before their day came.

*The path to peace,* Valden told himself, *is taken one step at a time.* He could not save the boy—he could only do what he could. He took a moment to offer up a silent prayer for the boy then took a slow, deep breath, and turned to the next in line, this one a young girl. *How many times,* he wondered, *can a man's heart break? How many times can he witness the world's suffering and not despair?* But though he did not feel it, he forced a warm smile onto his face, reaching into the basket—the basket which, he could see at a glance, did not contain enough bread for those in line—and handed it over. "The path to peace," he said.

"Is walked a step at a time."

Valden smiled. "Taken, young one."

"Sure," she said, then she snatched the bread and hurried away at a jog.

Valden watched her go, gave a heavy sigh, and reached into the basket for a third time, withdrawing a piece of bread. "The path to peace—"

"Fuck your peace, old man. Give me the food—now."

Valden frowned, looking up. He was surprised to find that, at some point during his distraction, the line of children had vanished, scattering like mice before a flood. In their place stood three men—boys, really, who looked to be in their late teens, perhaps early twenties. Boys, but ones at that most dangerous age, the age where they believed they were men grown. Old enough to think themselves capable of making their own decisions but not old enough to understand that so many of those decisions would inevitably turn out wrong. "I know that you are hungry," Valden said, "but this is not the way, lads. Darkness, heed me, is an abyss, one which a man might easily fall into with but a single misplaced step. And should you fall, it is very hard to—"

"Shut your damned mouth," the second snapped. "Nobody's got time for your lessons, *Priest.* Now, hand over the bread, or—" There was a pause of several seconds as he fumbled at his ratty trousers, finally producing a small, rusted knife of the kind fishermen used to shear their lines, "or I'll cut you."

Valden glanced at the knife then back to the boy. "Of course you may each take a piece of bread and with my blessing. Only, I ask that you leave some for the little ones. It is not so easy for them to find food to eat as strong men like yourselves. Please, out of kindness—"

The third jerked him up by the front of his robe—white once, but now stained with dust and dirt to a washed out brown—"We ain't gonna just take one piece, you old fucker. We're takin' all of it, you hear me? Try to stop us, you'll get hurt."

"Curses are the crutch of a man crippled within his own mind, young one, and violence not a pet to be tamed but a master to any man who seeks to claim it. Do you understa—" He cut off as one of the boy's reached out and slapped him across the face. It was an awkward, ungainly blow, clearly with no training or skill behind it, and Valden ran a hand across his mouth where a trickle of blood was starting down his lip. "There is really no need for this, young men. I will help you any way I can, only leave enough for the children, I beg."

But the youths were not listening. One reached for the basket beside him, snatching it up so quickly that several of the pieces of bread fell out onto the street. A second began scooping them up, cursing his companion as he did, while the third continued to hold his robe, giving him a shake. "Now the money, you old bastard."

"I don't have any coin, young man. We followers of Raveza forego our earthly possessions so that they might not hinder or weigh us down in the quest for peace."

"Save your bullshit for someone else, Priest," the boy growled, pawing at his robe, "tell me where it is, where's the money, or by the gods I'll cut you and see if the shit you're full of comes pourin' out."

Just then, something caught Valden's attention, and he glanced up to see two strangers standing in the street a short distance away, regarding him and the young men. A heavy-set man in purple trousers and a woman with dark hair, some of which had gone to gray. She was older, then, perhaps in her late forties or early fifties, but possessing a majestic beauty that shone past the few wrinkles she had. There was something regal about her bearing, while the heavy-set man's mouth was turned up at one corner into a small, almost imperceptible smile as if he were about to laugh at some joke only he knew. And while his body might have been heavy and awkward, there was a sharp intelligence in his eyes, one shared in the eyes of the woman, and Valden realized that they were not strangers after all.

"Maeve," he said, smiling. "Challadius."

"Priest," the woman said.

"Who the fuck?" one of the boys growled. "Get out of here, old woman, and take your fat man with you before you both end up getting hurt."

"If you would like to wait at the church," Valden offered, "I will finish my business here and meet you both there shortly."

Challadius made a sour face, snorting, and Maeve glanced at him before rolling her eyes and looking back to him. "We just came from there, actually. We asked them where we could find you."

"Very well," Valden said, "then if you will only give me half an hour, no more—"

"It's important, Valden," Maeve interrupted. "We would not be here otherwise. *He's* in trouble."

Valden felt a surge of something go through him, some undefinable emotion. Was it panic, perhaps? Fear? Or something else? "You're sure?"

She grunted. "Chall dreamed it."

He glanced to the big man who still had a sour expression on his face, but he nodded to confirm the truth of it.

"*Enough,*" the youth holding him growled. He turned to his two companions who had finally managed to scoop up the pieces of bread. "Go and get the fat man and the bitch—might be they got some coin on them."

Maeve's eyes went wide at that, and Valden was moving before he realized it, his hand flashing out, the ridge of it catching the young man holding him in the throat. His attacker gasped, letting loose his hold, but Valden did not hesitate, following up with a knee to the man's midsection and then he pivoted, sending two rapid blows into the boy's face. The youth fell like a poleaxed ox, collapsing on the ground.

The sound of his fall alerted his companions, and the two of them turned, their eyes widening as they realized what had happened. Then they cursed and attacked. The first one charged him, swinging an unpracticed punch which was easily avoided. Valden ducked the blow, placing three rapid strikes in the youth's stomach, then spun, his leg sweeping out of his robe and striking the youth in the back of his knees, causing him to collapse in a wheezing heap on the ground. The third growled, reaching for him, but Valden swayed to the side, avoiding his hands and placed two punches in the man's side. His attacker groaned, bending over, his hands going to his floating ribs, and Valden spun, bringing his own fist in a fast uppercut which caught the man under the chin and sent him sprawling.

He took a moment, surveying the three men on the ground, unconscious or close enough as to make no difference. Then, he turned back to Chall and Maeve. "When did this vision occur?"

*\*\*\**

Chall stared at the three unconscious men, blinking. Time had changed them in many ways. He'd grown fat—there, he'd said it. Maeve had grown older—still attractive, and still looking like she'd just as soon take a knife to him as talk to him most times. Even Priest looked older, and the man had already looked damned near ancient when Chall had met him twenty years ago. But whatever else time had robbed them all of—or added to them, in Chall's case—it had clearly stolen none of the man's skill in unarmed combat. A skill which was the main reason why he'd so often held his tongue when the old bastard started lecturing him on morality or simply giving him that disappointed gaze he so often did when Chall had arrived late at a meeting, usually with some farmer's daughter—or farmer's wife, depending on what was on offer—to blame.

"Damn," he said, the word coming out of his mouth without him meaning it to.

And *there* was the disappointed look. "Curses," Priest said, "are the crutch of a m—"

"Man crippled within his own mind," Chall interrupted, rolling his eyes. "Yes, I seem to remember that little nugget of wisdom." Hard not to when he'd spent five years hearing it practically every day, along with a few hundred other empty platitudes that the man wielded arguably with even more skill than he did his fists.

"Ah sarcasm," the older man said, nodding as if he'd expected as much, "ever the shield of the unvirtuous against wisdom."

"Speaking of unvirtuous," Chall said, glancing at Maeve, "now that we've found our conscience, do you think we could stop by a tavern? I've got a mighty thirst."

He expected to get a rise out of the man—at least, *hoped* to, knowing it was childish but hoping it just the same. Instead, the older man only smiled, walking toward him and, in a moment, he was wrapping Chall into a tight hug. "It is good to see you again, Challadius."

Chall hated being preached at, hated being called "Challadius," also, a name far too pompous, too assuming for him. But to his surprise, he found that he did not hate the hug so much found that, in fact, he had missed the man. "It's good to see you too," he mumbled.

Priest let him go, smiling widely, then turned to Maeve, taking her hand and giving it a gentle kiss that was in no way flirtatious or strange but which seemed completely natural even given that he was no nobleman but a priest in a dirty robe, and they stood not in a ballroom but in a back alley currently littered with the unconscious forms of three young men. "Maeve. I see that the years have stolen none of your beauty but have, instead, served only to enhance it."

Chall watched her smile widely and wondered how the old man always seemed able, even now, after so long, to so easily elicit such an expression from the woman who smiled so rarely while he himself generally only managed to get an angry scowl and a curse.

"And I see that you have lost none of your talents," she said, eyeing him then turning her gaze meaningfully to the three unconscious figures.

Priest looked ashamed at that, wincing as he stared at the men. "Would that I had. Violence, after all, is the—"

"Weapon of the unwise?" Chall guessed. "Tool of the asshole?"

Priest smiled humoringly. "Not untrue, perhaps, though not how I would have said it. I would have said instead that violence is the last recourse of men who have failed to find wisdom."

"Damn," Chall said, "so close."

"Still," the old man went on in a musing tone, "the goddess teaches that exercise is good for the heart and the soul, and a wise man will not allow his body, the letter upon which his life is writ, to fall into…" He paused, turning to regard Chall, and Chall didn't think he imagined the way the man's mouth quirked up at one corner in the hint of a smile. "Shall we say, disrepair?"

Chall thought then, as he had so many years ago, that beneath the pompous, arrogant and downright haughty exterior, the priest was also a bit of an asshole. "I like the robe," he said. "What color is that—mud brown?"

Priest grinned, not put off or angry at all, the bastard. "I believe so, though not so extravagant as your trousers, I'm afraid."

Maeve burst out a laugh at that, and Chall frowned. Maybe more than just a bit of an asshole after all.

"Anyway, Valden," the woman said, her voice growing somber, "to answer your question, Chall had the vision less than a week ago and—"

"Wait," Chall said, "Valden?"

They turned to him, Priest with a smile, Maeve a frown. "Do you mean to tell me that after all the time we spent together you don't even know his name?"

"Of course I know his name!" Chall said, feeling a touch defensive. "Why, it's Prie—" He cut off, frowning. "Oh. Right."

"Unbelievable," Maeve said.

Chall felt his face heat. "Look, it's not my fault. I didn't know the man actually *had* a name. For all I know, he gave it up with all the rest to join his cul—I mean church. You know, handed it over along with his dick and his joy—the two, in my experience, being closely linked."

"Chall," she said wearily, "do you really have to be such a pri—"

"Please, Maeve," Priest said, holding up a hand, "there is no need. Yes, Chall, to answer your question I have a name, though it is true that most prefer simply to call me Priest. As for the rest...I respect your opinion, but I am curious—you, I believe, have given up nothing, have joined no 'cult' as I believe you meant to say. Would you say, then, that you are happy?"

"Ask me once I've had a drink—assuming, of course, that this city of yours actually *has* any ale and has anybody to serve it, that is if they aren't busy lecturing each other on how to take a shit virtuously or wipe their asses wisely."

Not his best jest, perhaps, but certainly not his worst. Priest, though, did not grow frustrated or annoyed or angry, only tilted his head back and roared with a hearty, warming laugh like that of a loving grandfather. "Ah, Challadius, but I have missed your wit."

Despite the fact that most of the time he would have enjoyed strangling the man—or at least getting him shit-faced drunk and finding a scribe to record it—Chall found his face flushing with pleasure at that. He turned to Maeve, cocking an eyebrow. "You hear that? He says I have wit."

"Yes, well," Maeve said dryly, "even priests aren't perfect."

That elicited another hearty laugh from the man, but he sobered quickly. "Forgive me, but in my joy at seeing the two of you I find that I have neglected, most grossly, your reason for coming. The vision you spoke of—when will it occur?"

They were both looking at him now, expecting him to have all the answers and wasn't that the most damning thing? All they had to do was glance at him and the purple trousers he was wearing to see that he wasn't a man with any answers at all, just a lot of questions, the answer to most of which, he suspected, was "and he died terribly, terribly alone, and terribly fat."

He sighed. "It's not as if someone just sent me a message with all the details, is it? They didn't bother marking it on a calendar, you know."

"Ah, but someone *did* send you a message, Challadius," Priest disagreed. "I believe, in fact, that we may have had this discussion before. Your gift—your wonderful gift—is quite clearly a blessing from the gods themselves."

"Great, this again," Chall muttered. "Honestly, Priest, if the gods were handing out gifts, do you think I'd be at the top of the list? Or anywhere on the damn thing for that matter? Why, you've said yourself that I'm nothing but a philandering, womanizing wastrel with a heart of coal and ale instead of blood pumping in my veins."

"I...do not recall ever having said that," Priest said slowly.

Chall grunted. "Well. You probably thought it. Anyway, that's not the point! The point is that if the gods *were* handing out powers, they certainly wouldn't be handing them out to me. I mean, *look* at me for gods' sake," he said, spreading his hands. "Do I look like some champion of the gods?"

The Priest hesitated at that, opening his mouth several times only to close it again. Finally, he spoke. "The gods see far more clearly than mortal eyes, Challadius. And with that greater sight, they have seen something within you, something buried deep—"

"*Very* deep," Maeve interrupted in a voice that sounded on the verge of laughter.

"Inside of you," Priest went on, "a goodness, perhaps even a greatness of which even you yourself are not aware."

"Then the gods are fools," Chall said. Something—anger perhaps, or when it was in a priest's gaze was it called something else? Divine retribution, maybe—flashed in the man's eyes then, and Chall thought he had finally found the man's limit and that he would soon be decorating the alley cobbles along with the three would-be criminals who were still snoring away in blessed unconsciousness.

"Enough," Maeve said, drawing both of their attention—including the priest's dangerous stare for which Chall could only be thankful—"we don't have time for this. What Chall is trying—and, as usual, failing miserably—to say is that he does not know the exact time, only that it will be soon."

Priest nodded, rubbing at his chin thoughtfully, and Chall watched, surprised by how anxious he was to hear what the man would say, whether he would agree to come or not. On the one hand, the man was an absolute, pompous busy-body who, if he had his way, would have likely chosen to perch on Chall's shoulder and spend his days remarking on all the many ways in which he failed. On the other, Chall knew that despite a promise he'd made to himself fifteen years ago when he'd left their band—or been forced to leave...fleeing might have been more accurate—a promise to never once again allow himself to be embroiled in conflicts that had nothing to do with him and risk his head over it, it looked as if that was exactly what was happening.

Soon now, likely depressingly soon, he would be putting himself in danger, sticking his neck out for a man who had become famous—or infamous, more like—for chopping heads off. And if that was the case, there was no denying that he would like to have a man like Priest at his side. After all, whatever else the man was, he was a great fighter, a great scout, and perhaps the greatest archer of his generation, if not all generations. Sure, he was a pain in the ass, but he'd also managed to save Chall's on far too many occasions for him to count, so if there was going to be blood—and he was not so optimistic to believe that there was anyway out of this without it—then Chall would want the man at his side.

Priest did not ask any more questions, did not argue that it was not his concern. He only nodded, glancing between them. "When do we leave?"

Chall let out a breath he hadn't realized he'd been holding as a mixture of relief and annoyance rolled through him. He glanced at Maeve who shook her head at him, turning back to the older man. "You're coming?"

"Of course," the man answered as if were obvious that he should risk his life, that they should all risk their lives, for a man they had not seen in fifteen years and could have only loosely called friend. But then, judging by the fact that the three of them were standing there, perhaps it was.

Maeve grunted in clear surprise. "I am glad. Then, I suppose, we will leave just as soon as you gather your things."

Priest nodded thoughtfully, then looked around the street, walking over and bending down to pick up a small, dull copper chain that had apparently been ripped off his neck when the youths had accosted him. He closed his eyes for a moment, as if saying a silent prayer, then gently tucked the chain into his pocket before turning back to them. "I'm ready."

# CHAPTER NINETEEN

*They came in the darkness, the mist rising up around them as if it was theirs to command.*
*We did not know what they were at first, these giant beings who seemed to appear all at once, all over the kingdom.*
*We did not know. But we learned. They were the creatures out of nightmare, creatures told of in our oldest stories.*
*They were the Skaalden. And they were death.*
*—Excerpt found scrawled on the desk of a priest in his chamber before he took his own life.*

Dalen had grown up in the woods, had spent practically his entire life there, back before he and his people—led by their two princes—had been forced to flee before the Skaalden. Creatures out of nightmare who healed from any wound, who did not require drink or sleep and who ate nothing save human flesh.

He and his people had tried to fight, of course, but they had not been prepared, had lived long on the land and grown fat from it, spoiled and weak, and so they had been driven from their homes, across the great ocean to this gods forsaken place dubbed "The Known Lands." Here, they had at first been offered peace by the Fey but then, when the war began, they had been forced to call on the bitter lessons of war, ones taught them at the hands of the unstoppable Skaalden, to defend themselves against the Fey.

It had been over thirty years since they had abandoned their homeland to the Skaalden, over thirty years since Dalen had walked the lands of his father, and his father's father before him, going back to time immemorable. Yet, he thought of those woods often, and it was only in such a place, in the forests that this new land offered, where he could ever find surcease from the nagging guilt and self-loathing which had plagued him since he and the rest of his people had abandoned their land, their *birthright*.

But these woods, this forest, known as the Black Woods, were different. There was no peace to find here unless it was the peace of the dead rotting in their graves, and there was no contemplative silence in which a man might consider the world and his place in it. The silence, instead, was a brooding, living thing, as if some great beast regarded him as he made his way through the forest, following the near-imperceptible signs of the man and the youth's passage. A beast which might, at any moment, rouse itself to action and swallow whole this interloper who dared set foot in its demesne.

There was no love lost between his people and the Fey, that much Dalen knew. When they first arrived, fleeing the Skaalden invasion, the Fey had welcomed them with open arms, had even sympathized with their predicament so much as to offer them lands on which they might live and raise their children. At first, the princes had seemed to accept, and Dalen, along with the rest of his people, had been in a state of terrible relief and wonder. After having their homeland taken from them and seeing so many of their friends and loved ones killed—Dalen's father among them—it had been almost too much to believe that they would now be given a chance to rebuild, to survive.

The princes, though had seen it differently, and no sooner had they organized a parley, a peace talk with the Fey king, than they had betrayed the magical creatures. Accounts varied on what had actually happened during that feast, one meant to celebrate the new friendship and alliance between mortal and Fey, but what could not be argued was that, at its end, the Fey king was dead, his head forcefully separated from his body.

What followed had been years of bloody struggle and, in the end, after heavy losses on both sides, the mortals had carved out a piece of land for themselves in this place, a piece, as it happened, that was smaller than the one they had originally been offered, pushing the Fey back to what came to be known as the Black Woods.

No, there was no love lost between Fey and mortal, not anymore, whatever bond had once been forming between the two peoples shattered irrevocably at that traitorous meeting, and even had he not known the history, even had he not *lived* it, still Dalen would know the hatred of the Fey. For he could feel it emanating from each branch and each leaf, could taste it in the air which was crisp with winter's coming, yet somehow foul and unclean.

And yet, he was here. Here at the behest of his prince, and if that was not terrible enough, then he was forced to confront the fact that he had been sent on the unenviable task of tracking down what was perhaps the world's most accomplished killer. A man that was known for his brutality and viciousness in battle, for his complete lack of mercy or kindness or anything at all but a thirst for blood that could never be slaked.

Once, in better times, his prince would have never sent him on such a mission, for Feledias had been known by all of his people as the exact opposite of his brother. Kind where his brother was cruel, merciful and warm where his brother was cold as winter's coming. Wise and compassionate, and Dalen, along with all the rest of his people, had hated only that the man had been the younger of the two and therefore not the brother who would be granted power once their father, the king—who had been aged and sick with the fever that would eventually kill him—passed beyond the veil.

Then, it had happened. In the span of a day or a week—certainly, it had seemed no more than the time it took to draw a breath—something had changed. What that something was Dalen, like the rest of his people, did not know. All he knew for sure was that Prince Bernard vanished, never to be seen again, and Feledias *did* take over rule of his people. Only, the peace and joy they had expected if such a lucky event ever transpired did not come, for the Feledias they had known, the prince they had loved, had changed.

No longer was he the kind, loving prince who always had time for even the lowliest of his people, who spent his idle hours handing out food to the hungry and coin to the poor. Instead, he became a vicious tyrant, worse, perhaps, even than they had feared his brother might be, a tyrant who bent his entire will—and the entire energy of his people—toward finding his vanished brother and those who had been closest to him and making them suffer.

Yet for all of his prince's efforts in the last fifteen years, only one of the men he'd deemed traitor had been found, a youth, really, one of no more than nineteen years, a boy who was said to have served as Prince Bernard's squire, the youth given the unenviable task of cleaning the constant blood which coated it from his lord's axe, of carrying his weapon when it was not in use. On that score, at least, he'd had an easy time of it, for it seemed that the prince had never been far from his weapon. It was, after all, the arbiter of his will, the one and only answer which he gave to any who dared to question him, gave even to those, like the Fey king, who had offered no question at all, only kindness.

Dalen had been there when Prince Feledias, had extracted the price of what he'd deemed his treason from the youth. He had not wanted to be—would have given anything to have been anywhere else for even now, so many years later, the visions and sounds he had witnessed from the young man haunted his dreams—but had been forced to attend, his duty as one of his king's honor guard. The youth had been made to suffer terribly before he had finally found what peace death offered, suffered not under the hand of a skilled torturer but at the hand of his very own prince, a man who the youth had loved deeply and to whom he had been forever loyal. And while it had been terrible, the worst event in a life that Dalen sometimes thought was full only of terrible events, even now he had to admit that whatever training he lacked in the ways of a torturer, Feledias had made up for with cruel vigor and an energy which he brought to bear using the many tools and implements of the torturer's trade until the young man was no longer recognizable.

Only a pile of bloody, mewling flesh that had, finally, been allowed to die. No, Dalen did not want to anger his prince. Whatever possible fate he might face at the hands of his prince's brother—a fate which made his normally sure feet uncertain beneath him—even that paled in comparison to what he knew Feledias was capable of, should he fail him.

So, with the forest looming close around him, and with memories of the boy's screams and pleas and questions of what he had done—all of which went unanswered—echoing in his mind, Dalen stalked through the forest, following the tracks of the man and the youth. There were surprisingly few, and those he did find

Dalen thought must have come from the boy while the big man, despite his size, seemed to move across the land like a ghost, leaving neither hint nor track of his passage.

But whatever skills in woodcraft he possessed, the youth did not share them, and it was only because of this that Dalen was able to track them at all, carrying on the unenviable task set him and tracking down the most notorious warrior in the world.

It was difficult to mark the passage of time here, beneath the boughs of the great trees, and it felt as if the world of men, the world of which Dalen was a part, did not, *could not* exist in this place, as if conceits such as time had no meaning. Yet, he knew that it was late in the evening, perhaps even the early morning hours, and he was surprised to find that his targets had not yet stopped to rest. He had heard the stories, of course, of Feledias's brother—there was not a man or woman living who could claim otherwise—stories which had served sometimes as cautionary tales and other times as horror stories, but he knew, too, that the man, despite the stories, *was* just a man and that like every other man, he would need to stop, to rest, sooner or later. And if not him, then certainly the youth who traveled with him.

Yet as he continued to work his way through the Wood, hurrying to catch them up, to have this part of the task done so that he might leave this blasted forest behind and return to the relative safety of his prince's company, Dalen began to doubt. Did they intend to travel through the night then? Leading him a chase that would last forever, one in which they never stopped, one in which they continued to outdistance him despite the efforts he put in—even foregoing some of his usual caution in favor of speed?

Or—and this was a far worse thought—had he lost their trail, somewhere? Was he now following the meanderings of some animal of the forest or some Fey creature out of nightmare? Would he grow lost in the Wood, tracking someone—or something—which was not even his target? Was he lost already? Dalen was not a man to panic, was known for his courage among his fellow soldiers, for trackers such as he spent much of their time alone, braving the elements and enemy forces without any help from their comrades. But now, he did not feel brave, and while he might not have normally been a man to panic, he felt some panic now, a churning, unsettled feeling in the pit of his stomach.

He moved faster, trying to be as quiet as he could, to move through the forest while disturbing as little as possible, yet accepting those small, inevitable noises he made as sacrifices made in exchange for speed, a speed which he hoped would pay off by him finding his quarry and then being able to put all of his fears and unfounded worries to rest.

And indeed, no more than an hour had passed when he began to feel that his rush through the woods had been worth it. The signs of his quarry's passage began to seem fresher, and he even chanced upon a few footprints left on the ground, footprints that the falling snow had not yet managed to cover. It was then that he cautioned himself to slow down. It was difficult, though, knowing that his quarry was close now, that soon he would be able to accomplish his errand and leave this damned place behind him, hopefully never to return.

Still, his heart racing with a mixture of anxiety and excitement, he crept through the woods and soon came upon a small clearing. It was still dark, only a small amount of moonlight filtering its way through the trees to illuminate the clearing, and he sat and watched, trying to pick out things in the darkness.

He felt a great wash of relief as he saw two bedrolls spread out in the clearing. One, judging by the size of its occupant, belonging to the youth who was turned with his back to him, a back which slowly rose and fell with the breath of sleep. The other was beyond his sight line, lying as it did in a patch of shadow, and so Dalen could not make it out, but that was alright. It was them—that much was certain. The two his master had sent him to find, to track.

Now he could return, could leave his fears and doubts and—

He froze at the sound of what sounded like a twig breaking behind him. Then, slowly, Dalen turned to see a great, hulking figure standing behind him, no more than two feet away. How the man had come upon him without him hearing, he could not imagine, for it was a feat he doubted he could have duplicated despite the fact that he had spent nearly his entire life in the woods.

He wondered for a panicked moment who the figure was, but that curiosity did not last for long, not long at all, for he recognized the man standing before him, looming over him, in truth. And as he stared at the grim, cold expression on the man's face, at the cold, pale blue eyes which studied him and the massive battle axe clutched in one fist, Dalen realized something. He realized that here, this close, no amount of stories did the man justice, and that those stories, as he had thought on occasion, had not been exaggerated after all, but, if anything, fell far short of the truth.

"Hi," the man said in a voice that somehow reminded Dalen of the sound of trees snapping in the frost. Then, there was a sudden movement, a burst of speed from him that Dalen would not have thought possible from a figure so big.

*I should not be here.* It was the last thought that Dalen had before the axe the figure held flashed in the moonlight. It was the last thought, in fact, that he ever had.

***

Matt woke with a gasp, sitting up in his bedroll and throwing it aside. He spun, looking around, but at first saw nothing, heard nothing to account for his sudden wakefulness. But that did not make him feel any better. He did not feel relief, not at all. Instead, he felt alone. A great, terrible loneliness. He looked over to where Cutter had laid his own bedroll, desperate for some sort of companionship in the darkness, even if it was from the man whom he thought he was growing to hate. But the big man's bedroll was empty.

The sound of something rustling behind him made him jump, and he spun to see some monstrous beast appearing out of the woods. Only after a moment, the figure stepped out of the shadows and was not a monster or some strange, alien Fey creature after all. It was Cutter.

The man had a grim expression on his face which was not particularly surprising as it was pretty much the only expression he ever seemed to have. "Cutter," Matt said, still out of breath. "I-is everything okay? I thought I heard something. A scream, maybe."

"Everything's fine, lad," the big man said.

Matt frowned. "Then why do you have your axe?"

Cutter grunted. "Just patrollin', that's all, make sure nothin's creepin' up on us in the dark. The Fey, as I think you've seen, do love their tricks. Anyway, if you're awake, we might as well get movin'."

Matt blinked. "But we only just stopped...didn't we?"

"A few hours gone now," Cutter said. "But we need to make it out of these woods soon. The Fey might have patience—though it's likely even that is stretched thin, just now—but the men chasing us do not. We have squandered too much time already, and if we waste more, they will find us."

"But *why* are they chasing us?" Matt said. "I don't understand it, any of it. What did we ever do to them?"

"Later," Cutter said. "For now, pack your things. We're moving."

"More *secrets*," Matt hissed angrily.

"Yes," Cutter said. "More secrets. Now, come on."

# CHAPTER TWENTY

*Why do I fight?*
*Why does anyone do anything?*
*Fine, if you insist. I don't fight for honor and glory—that much is sure.*
*You can't eat them, honor and glory, you can't drink them.*
*You ask me why I fight? Fine, I'll tell you—*
*Whores aren't free.*
*—Challadius "The Charmer" in interview with Exiled Historian to the Crown Petran Quinn*

The three of them sat atop their horses—at least, Maeve and Priest did, for Chall it was all he could do to keep from falling off the ornery beast—and stared at the Black Woods. He did not want to go into that place of Fey magic. Some believed that magic had originated from the Fey, magic which included his own, and perhaps that was even true, yet he did not care. Certainly, that sense inside him, the sense gifted him by his magic, rebelled at the thought of entering, for the Wood was an ancient place, a place steeped in magic and age, one which bore a hatred for mankind that it was impossible to ignore.

"Maybe we shouldn't," he said, trying to keep the squeak of fear from his voice and not altogether succeeding. "Maybe there's another way. We could send a message to him or..."

Maeve barked a laugh without humor. "A message? And who would carry that message, Chall? You know as well as I do that no messenger would travel into the Black Woods, not for all the gold in the world."

"Which just goes to show that not all men are fools after all," he snapped.

Maeve sighed. "Look, we've come this far. Anyway, it isn't as if we intend to cut down some trees, maybe build a house—"

"Don't even *joke* about such things!" Chall snapped. "Damnit, woman, these are not normal trees, don't you get that? And this is no normal wood. These trees think, and what they think…" He shook his head, heaving a ragged sigh.

"Oh enough bitching," Maeve said. "Anyway, this is where you said he'll be, right? According to your vision, he should be close to the edge—with any luck, we won't have to take but a few steps in until we find them."

"With any luck," Chall muttered, "we wouldn't be here at all."

"Forget it," Maeve said. "Priest and I will go. You just stay here, how's that? Who knows," she went on, grinning evilly, "perhaps Feledias will be along directly. I imagine he'd be pleased to see—what was it he called you again? Oh, that's right, his brother's 'pet magician.' Who knows? Maybe he'll throw a ball for you—or an execution. After all, unless my memory fails me, I seem to recall your name being on the list of those of us he means to kill."

Chall shuddered at that, scowling at the pleased look on the woman's face. "And what of the Fey?" he challenged. "Somehow, I doubt they'll exactly welcome us with open arms—why, I'm certain that if they find us, they'll kill us just as quick as Feledias would and with just as much energy."

Maeve grunted. "Best we not be found then, isn't it? Now, come on. Daylight's burning."

With that, she gave her horse a kick and after shooting him a look of compassion, Priest did the same. Chall watched them for a minute, thinking that, if he somehow survived the next day or so, he was really going to have to make some better, safer friends. Like a pack of wolves. Or a bear, maybe. Then, he gave his horse a soft kick, and the beast snorted in anger, trying—and nearly succeeding—to buck him off before starting toward the forest. A stupid animal, that was sure, but not so stupid that it didn't hesitate, requiring another kick, before it walked into the forest. Which was fine—Chall just wished there was someone there to kick him.

***

They were heading east, now, toward the forest's border. Cutter had led them south for as long as he dared, and he knew that coming out of the wood should put them into the fields outside Valaidra. He should know, after all, for years ago, during the war with the Fey, he had traveled the lands often on one campaign or another, most often at the head of an army.

The boy had said nothing for a while, but then he did not need to, for Cutter could feel his anger, his hate, coming off him in seething waves. He told himself that was fine. Let the lad be angry, if it helped him. What was important was that he lived to *be* angry.

The forest was silent as always, the only sounds that of him and the boy breathing and their footsteps crunching in the snow. They had been traveling east for several hours when another sound intruded on that silence, and he held up a hand, ordering the boy to stop.

"What?" Matt asked. "What is it?"

"*Quiet,*" Cutter hissed. He unlimbered his axe from the sling at his back and turned, glancing back. "Stay here," he mouthed. "Don't make a sound."

And then he was moving. Cutter's father, long ago, had insisted on training his sons in woodcraft the same way in which he had insisted on training them in so many other things, and so his footsteps were nearly silent as he moved through the woods, using the great trunks of the trees as cover as he inched forward.

He walked this way for several minutes, was beginning to think that he had imagined the whole thing, when he heard another noise, what sounded like a muttered curse. He ducked low, turning, and caught a flash of color, what might have been purple, from a short distance ahead. Then it was gone again, covered by the thick trees and undergrowth.

Men, that much was sure. Another, in his position, might have waited, might have let whoever it was go by, but Cutter did not, for he knew that any mortals who dared venture into the Black Woods could only be there for him and the boy. Feledias must have sent another scouting party, that was all. After all, the man had plenty enough resources as well as the motivation to do so.

So instead of waiting, Cutter charged, running on the balls of his feet to make as little noise as possible. The man was guiding a horse. There was another, a woman, walking in front of him, but Cutter paid no attention to her. One at a time—it was the only way to get the thing done. The man let out a squeal as he finally became aware of Cutter's approach and spun—or at least tried to. Cutter grabbed him, bringing the axe blade unerringly to within inches of his throat as he spun him, interposing him between Cutter and the other companions so that his back faced him. "Who are you?" he demanded.

The man froze, letting out a mewling sound of terror. "W-wait, just hold on a minute, alright? I don't know—"

"Wait a minute," Cutter said, grunting with surprise at the voice, for even squeaking as it was, it was one he recognized. "Chall?"

He spun the man around and, sure enough, was shocked to see the magician's pale expression staring back. Fatter than before, older but undeniable for all that.

"H-hi."

"What are you doing here?" Cutter said, letting the axe drop, then he turned to the woman and was unsurprised to find that her face, when she turned to regard him, was one he also recognized. "Maeve?"

"Hello, Prince Bernard," she said calmly. "How have you been?"

Just then, there was an almost imperceptible sound behind him. "Priest," he said, turning to regard the old man who had stepped out from behind the cover of a nearby tree, and was holding a bow that he released the tension on, smoothly sliding the arrow that had been nocked to the string into the quiver at his back.

"My prince," the man said, bowing his head.

"Not prince," Cutter growled, surprised by how angry it made him to be called that, "not anymore."

"Forgive me, my lord," the man said, "but a man can no more change who he is than a leopard might change its spots. You are a prince, exiled or not, that simple fact remains."

Cutter sighed. "What are you all doing here?"

"Me?" Chall asked, swallowing and pulling at his collar. "Well, just now, I'm thinking that I'm going to have to find a new pair of trousers."

Maeve shot the man an annoyed look. "We came here to help you. Feledias is tracking you."

"I know. One of his scouts found us last night."

"Fire and salt then we're too late," Chall groaned. "The man'll report back to Feledias and—"

"No." Cutter interrupted.

The magician shared a meaningful look with Maeve at that, then seemed to blanch. "Ah, well that's...good, of course."

"We came," Maeve said, rolling her eyes, "because Chall had a vision. It's Feledias, Prince—"

"Do not call me that," Cutter growled, "I go by Cutter now."

Maeve grunted in what might have been amusement. "Well. I can't say that it isn't appropriate."

He winced at that and was about to respond when suddenly the underbrush rustled behind him, and the boy came out of it, his eyes widening as he took in the four of them. "I told you to wait," Cutter growled.

"I heard voices," he said, "and a scream. I thought...I thought something was wrong."

"It wasn't a scream," Chall muttered. "More of a...ah, forget it."

"W-who are these people?" the boy asked, his eyes wide, his voice breathy with nerves. "Is it...the men that are chasing us?"

"No, lad," Cutter said. "These people are different they're...friends."

He turned back to see the three of them staring at the boy, their eyes wide. "Is this...him?" Maeve asked in a breathy voice.

"This is Matt," Cutter said abruptly. "A boy from Brighton. His village was attacked."

"Damn my eyes, but it's uncanny," Chall breathed. "He looks just like her, it's as if—"

*"Enough,"* Cutter said.

"Who?" Matt asked. "Who do I look like? I don't understa—"

"Later," Cutter growled. "There's no time. We have to get out of these Woods and fast. Feledias is not far behind and—"

"We know," Chall interrupted, then seemed to quail when Cutter turned his attention on him. "I mean...it's why we're here."

"Fine," Cutter said, "anyway, we need to leave. We'll head for Valaidra. It's the closest city and—"

"I wouldn't do that," Chall interrupted.

"Oh? And why not?"

"Feledias knows you'll go there," Chall said. "In the vision I had, Pri—" He cut off at a warning look from Cutter, then paused, swallowing, before continuing, "What I mean *Cutter,* is that he's waiting with his men. He plans to ambush you once you leave the Black Woods."

Cutter hissed. "Very well. There's another place—a small village by the name of Ferrimore. It's a bit farther south."

"Ferrimore?" Maeve said, frowning. "I've never heard of it."

"Nor would you have," Cutter said. "It isn't on any of the maps—only a few hundred people if that. Still, it will get us out of the Black Woods and give us time to figure out our next move. Now come on—we've wasted enough time already."

***

Maeve watched her prince's back as he led the group of them out of the Black Woods, and she wondered at many things. She wondered at why he had just assumed they would follow his plan without bothering asking their opinions on the matter. Wondered, too, based on how she and the others did exactly that, if he were wrong to do so. Most of all, she wondered if she was a fool. Probably, she was. After all, who else would so easily fall back into the rhythm—a rhythm which had gotten her and the others exiled with a price on their head to beggar kings—of following a man such as he?

She told herself, though, that this time was different. Years ago, she had followed her prince—the man who now styled himself as Cutter—for several reasons. For one, he had been her prince, after all, and to have disobeyed him would have been treason. Another part had been swept up by the force of his personality, but now, walking in the quiet of the Woods, the only sound that of her and her companions' footsteps, she had to admit to herself that there had been another reason, too.

Yes, her prince had been eager for bloodshed, had seemed to wish to drown in it. He had been brutal and cruel and callous, preferring to prove his right through the strength of his arm and the keen edge of his axe. And while she had hated him for that— still did, in fact—she realized that she had not been so very different. After all, no matter how much she might like to look on the past and find herself blameless, she could not help but admit, at least to herself, that she had *enjoyed* the reputation they had carried with them. A reputation which had meant that men and women fell prostrate at their approach, men and women who scrambled to do their bidding and went to great lengths to avoid saying or doing anything that might cause them offense.

In short, they had been like kings and queens traveling the land, not respected, perhaps, but feared, and sometimes it was not so easy to tell the difference between the two. But if that were true, then why did she follow him now? She wanted to believe it was because of the boy, this confused, frightened youth who had no idea what was happening, why he was being hunted, for Cutter had obviously neglected to tell him. Not that such a thing was surprising, for Cutter had always preferred bellowing war cries to having quiet conversation, and even at the best of times it was difficult to get more than a few words out of the big man unless those words were threats or gloating over one corpse or another—there had been many over the years.

She looked at the boy now. He was alive—that much Cutter had managed, but she could say no more than that. He walked with his shoulders slumped, his head down, on his face an expression of quiet panic and, behind that, of some great loss. She did not know the exact details of that loss but knowing Cutter—and his brother Feledias—as well as she did, it did not take much to imagine it.

She slowed her pace until she came to the back of the line where the boy walked. "I'm Maeve," she said, offering her hand.

The boy started, looking up at her and gave her a sickly smile. "I-I'm Matt," he said, taking the offered hand and giving it a weak shake.

She gave him what she hoped was a reassuring smile. "I know."

He frowned. "*How* do you know, though?"

She opened her mouth to answer then glanced up to see that Cutter had turned back and was watching her, his cold blue-gray gaze seeming to see into her thoughts, then he turned and started on again, saying nothing. Maeve turned to the boy, giving her head a shake. "Best if I let him tell you that."

The boy rasped a laugh without humor. "He's not much for telling people things, I think."

She smiled again, this time the expression feeling more natural on her face. "No. No, he is not."

They walked on in silence for a few minutes then, the boy clearly having questions, but she not wanting to press him, to let him ask them in his own time, in his own way. Then, "You knew him, then? A long time ago?"

Maeve considered the question. "I knew him as well as anyone did, I expect," she said finally.

The boy nodded. "What was he like?"

She turned to regard the big man, once the greatest warrior of their people, their prince upon whom all of their hopes had relied until he had become bloodthirsty, a danger greater even than their enemies, and she frowned. "Much the same, I expect," she said slowly. "But...angrier, perhaps."

The boy blinked at that. "Angrier? I don't want to argue, but I have a hard time imagining that. He pretty much always seems angry now. Angry at me, in particular," he finished in a mumble.

*Oh, you poor boy,* Maeve thought. "Yes," she agreed, "but it was a different kind of anger. A different...there was a time, Matt, when Cutter's fury was a terrible sight to behold, when he burned like a great flame, one that threatened to sweep over the entire world."

"Oh," he said softly. "And...now?"

She shook her head slowly. "He is different. Still angry, yes, but it seems a cold anger, one that waits instead of rushing in...and to be honest, I do not know if that is better or not."

The boy was looking at Cutter now, and she saw something in his gaze that worried her. It was not adoration, not exactly, but it was not far from it either. She saw the need in his gaze, a need she understood all too well for she had felt it too, once upon a time. That, too, had been one of the reasons why she had followed the man. And that need, that desire to find his approval for reasons she could not understand, even now, had brought her no end of grief.

She wanted to tell the boy that, to try to reassure him that there were other places out there, better places, better *people* in which he might find that approval, but now was not the time, so she only walked on. Walked. And worried.

# CHAPTER TWENTY-ONE

*The Fey are not people and to think them such would be a great mistake.*
*They are beings from another world, another place.*
*Yet, there are some things that they share with mortals.*
*Joy, for instance. Friendship too.*
*And of course, anger. That, perhaps, most of all.*
*—Excerpt from "The Workings of the Fey" by Scholar Kelden Marrimore*

Eventually, they reached the edge of the Black Wood, and Maeve breathed a heavy sigh of relief to be out from underneath the boughs of those great trees that seemed to mark each step they took, to tally them as transgressions that would one day be paid. It was a short lived relief, however, as she was confronted with the undeniable fact that, once again, she had fallen into the role of following what was perhaps the most dangerous man in the world—to his enemies and, if the past was any indication, his friends as well.

Chall, too, showed obvious signs of relief, grinning widely and staring up at the sky as if he'd thought to never see it again. Even Priest wore a small, contented smile on his face, though the truth was that, in Maeve's experience, the man nearly always did. It was as if he thought the world were some magical place of wonder and joy, when from what she could tell, it was by and large an elaborate torture device created by malicious gods.

The youth, Matt, seemed much as he had before, worried and scared and beaten down, though perhaps with some small spring in his step. The only one who seemed to have taken no notice that they had left the Black Woods behind was Cutter. The big man only continued to trudge down the path with a walk that somehow seemed weary and threatening at the same time, as if he could do with a good nap but was more than willing to shatter any obstacle that had the misfortune to find itself in his path before then.

Maeve thought it was funny how fifteen years could pass and a woman could find herself in almost the exact same circumstances she'd thought far behind her. Or maybe it wasn't funny at all, but one of those cruel cosmic jokes which, if it elicited laughter at all, elicited the kind that sounded so very much like screams.

They'd traveled for less than an hour when the fields of grass began to change to crops, corn and wheat. Maeve recognized them well enough from her time spent working—or, if she was being particularly honest with herself, hiding—in her garden. She expected to see men and women bent at the labor of working the crops, but the fields were empty, devoid of any life, the only sign that people called the village home coming in the sign of pillars of smoke rising in the air ahead of them.

Minutes later, they crested a ridge, and she was able to see what must have been the village of Ferrimore that Cutter had told them about. Or at least what was left of it. As she stared at the distant village, Maeve realized that the columns of smoke she'd seen, ones she'd taken, at the time for evidence of fires lit to fight off the chill of winter's bite, had, in fact, a far grimmer source.

As she and the others stood there gazing at the smoking husks of what once had been homes and shops, she realized why she had seen no men or women working the fields. Those who might have were no doubt far too busy at repairing their homes. If, that was, they were alive at all.

"Fire and Salt," Chall breathed beside her. "What happened here? Is it...is it Feledias? Did he somehow realize we were coming?"

Cutter grunted. "I don't think so."

Maeve frowned, for she had been having much the same thought as the mage. She turned to regard the big man. "If it wasn't Feledias, then who? Who would have done th—"

"Come on," Cutter said grimly, and he started down the path leading toward the village.

"Are you...are we sure that's a good idea?" Chall asked, his unease clear in his tone. "I mean...this place doesn't look like a great one to take shelter in just now. Perhaps there's another—"

"There isn't another place," Cutter said, turning to regard him. "Not for miles. Unless, that is, you want to take your chances with Valaidra."

Chall winced, glancing to Maeve as if for help, but she had no help to give, felt just as confused and unnerved as the mage, and after a moment of silence Cutter nodded. "Let's go," he said, and he started toward the village once more.

Left with no other options, Maeve and the others followed. As they drew closer to the village of Ferrimore, Maeve began to pick out more signs of destruction. Most of the village's buildings had been made from stone and so still remained, though few were those that were not charred and scorched from flames. Their roofs, though, most which would have been made of straw or wood, had not fared nearly so well, most completely gone while a few seemed to have retained some small bit of their materials.

And if the sight of such devastation—though what might have caused it she couldn't imagine, the only one who might have seeming to be Cutter who, as usual, chose to remain silent—wasn't enough, there was the smell which clung to her nostrils. Smoke, yes, but something worse than that, a smell she had not smelled in some time, one she had hoped to never smell again. Blood. A lot of it.

The youth walking beside her paused, glancing into the field beside the path. "Maeve?" he asked. "What...what is that?"

Maeve stopped, following his gaze, and saw a form lying in the field, partially obscured by the grass. Partially, but not completely. A corpse. A woman's judging by the size, though the grass made most of her identity a mystery. Maeve had seen such corpses before, the remains of battles, ones which stood as mute argument against those who managed to be alive following such a battle, which lay in silent accusation of any who might claim the day a victory. A quick glance around showed other such forms in the grass on either side, lumps of fabric that, obscured as they were, might have been taken for no more than clothes—most bloodstained, which had been scattered about. She took the boy's hand. "Best not look at them, lad," she said softly as she led him on down the path after Cutter who, while he could not have failed to notice the devastation and the bodies, did not deem it worth pausing to notice.

The boy hesitated for a moment but then he allowed himself to be led away and, a moment later, was walking past her, lost in his own thoughts. "I don't like this, Mae," a voice said softly from beside her, and she glanced over to see that Chall had walked up. "Not at all. Something's happened here. Something bad."

Maeve glanced sidelong at him. "Oh?" she snapped. "Cast a magic spell to figure that one out, did you?"

Chall recoiled, obviously hurt by the harshness in her voice. "Sorry, Maeve," he said, "I only meant—"

She sighed, waving a hand dismissively. "I'm sorry, Chall. You're right, of course. I don't like it either."

The man nodded but said nothing else, perhaps worried that to do so would be to risk her ire once more, and Maeve watched him drop back to walk with Priest, scolding herself. The man had wanted reassurance, that was all, and instead she had bitten his head off. The problem, of course, was that she had no reassurance to give, for she felt the same worry that had been writ so plainly on the mage's face. And not just worry, either, but guilt. Guilt for how she'd treated the mage, yes, but not just that.

She felt guilt for the village—or what was left of it—before her. Felt that, somehow, she and those with her were responsible for it. She had no proof, could not imagine how that could be the case, but that did not change the way she felt, did nothing to answer the guilt roiling through her, guilt which she could see on the mage's face as well. She'd felt such guilt before, of course, but had thought she'd left that behind her along with her old life. Say what you wanted about being married to an ass of a husband and spending your idle hours knelt in the dirt tending a garden which never seemed to produce well no matter how much you tried. Boring, maybe, but no one's life depended on whether or not her tomatoes grew well.

Worry and guilt, yes, but as she stared at Cutter's back, the man walking on toward the ruins of the village, either not noticing or not caring about those bloody lumps scattered in the fields around them, she found that she felt something else, too—anger.

Before she knew it, she was speeding up her pace until she was walking beside the man who had once been her prince. He turned, glancing at her, his expression unreadable, before turning back to the trail. "You know something," she said, not bothering to try to hide the accusation in her tone.

"A few things," he said. "You'll have to be more specific."

She frowned. "Something about *this*, I mean," she said, waving her hand in a gesture meant to encompass the village and the corpses scattered about it like broken dolls.

"Yes," he answered.

She waited, thinking there would be more, but the man said nothing else, only walking onward.

Maeve felt her anger rising to a boiling point. She glanced back at the others, the youth with his pale face, his lip trembling as if he were on the verge of tears and just managing to hold them back; Chall walking with his shoulders slumped as if he carried the weight of the world on them and looking little better. The man might act as if he cared for nothing but ale and whores, but Maeve knew it to be a lie, one he closely guarded, for the man's problem was not that he did not care but that he cared too much.

Even the normally unflappable Priest looked troubled, his eyes roaming the fields and each corpse as if he meant to commemorate them to memory. All of them, then, affected by the grim scene. All, that was, save for Cutter whose expression betrayed nothing—except perhaps impatience. "*Well?*" she demanded, her anger overriding a caution which would have normally warned her off of talking to the man in such a way, for she had seen how the man dealt—nearly always with a bloody finality—with people who he felt disrespected him.

But while many aspects of the man before her felt infuriatingly the same, it was clear that the years had worked some changes in him, for he only glanced at her, his expression not one of fury but one which was still unreadable. He studied her for a moment, as if thinking, then he seemed to make a decision. "Did you notice the corpses?"

She glanced back, making sure that the others were out of earshot, then leaned close. "Of *course* I noticed them," she hissed. "How could I not? Corpses are a lot of things, but they're generally not subtle."

He gave a single nod, seemingly oblivious to her anger. "And did anything about them strike you as odd?"

"Call me crazy," she said, "but I'm always a bit put off by an entire village being slaughtered."

"Not an entire village," he said.

"*What?*"

He nodded his head in the direction of the village, and she followed his gaze to see figures moving about the smoking ruins in the distance, and she clenched her fists at her sides. "Oh, right. So a few survived. Well, that's okay then. Maybe we should have a celebration, throw a party."

"You're angry with me," he said, with no more feeling in his voice than if he'd been commenting on the weather.

"And here I thought I was hiding it so well," she said. "You know, an entire village—sorry not an *entire* village, but a damned far amount of it from what I can see—has just been slaughtered. It might do you good to show a little bit of damned feeling."

"And would doing so bring the dead back to life?" he asked. "Would it close their wounds and take away their grief?"

"That...well, no."

"Then what good would it do them?"

"You're right," she said, "why bother, you know, being human? Better to be some unfeeling brute who doesn't pay attention to anything at all, is that it?"

"I pay attention, Maeve," he said softly. "Now, the corpses. Have you looked at them? Closely, I mean?"

Maeve wanted to snap at him then, to tell him that, as a general rule, most people, *human* people, avoided looking closely at corpses whenever possible. But she didn't have the energy, felt exhausted, so instead she only sighed, turning to glance around the fields again, searching for one of the unfortunate souls who'd been slaughtered. It didn't take long to find one, this one the body of a man who appeared to have been in his fifties. "Yeah, they're dead," she said. "I don't see what—" But she paused then, her words failing her as realization struck.

Cutter nodded beside her. "You see it now, don't you?" he said. "The claw marks? The insides torn open, some of them missing? You asked me what I knew, Maeve. Now, I'll tell you. Swords don't leave those sorts of marks and soldiers don't kill that way."

Maeve's breath caught in her throat and she stood, stunned, trying to understand. Cutter walked on, but she was barely aware of it. Instead, she stared at those corpses littering the field, seeing them with new eyes, making out, too, their weapons—pitchforks and shovels mostly, and several burned out brands that could only have been torches as well—lying near them. Cutter, damn him, was right. Swords did not make those sorts of wounds and soldiers cared nothing for digging through the entrails of their victims. But the Fey did.

She turned to look at Cutter's wide back as he continued down the path. The Fey had been here, that was the truth he knew. The Fey who had been content to spend the last several years in the Black Woods, had chosen now, of all times, to renew their hostilities with the world of men. A time which had just so happened to coincide with Cutter's entrance into and subsequent departure from the Black Woods. Coincidence? She wanted to believe that it was, but as much as she might wish to, she could not convince herself of that.

After all, it was well known that the Fey held no love for Cutter, the prince who, along with his brother, they had invited into their homes, with whom they had made peace only to have that peace shattered when Cutter had killed their king, tearing his head from his body with that great axe of his. She did not know what had transpired in the Wood with Cutter and the boy, did not know why they had been allowed to pass through the Fey's domain without assault, but she did know, without knowing the how or why of it, that whatever fate Cutter and the boy had avoided at the hands of the Fey had been transferred to Ferrimore and its citizens instead.

She thought that she should feel surprised at this realization, perhaps even shocked. But what she felt, more than anything, was weary. After all, wherever Cutter, wherever her *prince* walked, death followed. It had always been thus, and while many things changed, some, unfortunately, did not.

# CHAPTER TWENTY-TWO

*Revenge is bloody, thirsty work, the results of which no one, including—perhaps especially—he who seeks it, cares to contemplate.*
—*Unknown Poet*

Cutter could feel Maeve's eyes on his back, could feel her disapproval like a weight on his shoulders. He did not doubt that she had come to some conclusions about why the Fey would have attacked Ferrimore and, as clever as he knew her to be, he did not doubt that they were the right ones. Which meant that her disapproval, her anger at him, was also right, and just as he could say nothing to address the boy's sadness or Chall's worry, neither could he say anything that might satisfy her anger. So instead he said nothing at all, only continued forward.

Shadelaresh had granted him his boon as he'd asked, for the Fey—as a general rule and despite the many illusions upon which their kind relied—never broke their oath. He was not even sure if they entirely understood the concept of such a thing, though now, he did not doubt that after their dealings with men, they were beginning to. And so, Shadelaresh, despite his fury at Cutter, fury engendered by the slaying of his king, had kept to the promise of that same king, resisting the no doubt powerful urge to do harm to Cutter and the boy with him.

Ferrimore, though, had been given no such boon to protect them and so it seemed that Shadelaresh had chosen to vent his rage upon the unfortunate villagers, men and women who'd had no part in Cutter's past crimes. And had the Fey spirit somehow known that Cutter's journeying would bring him this way, despite the fact that he himself, at the time of their meeting, had meant to go to Valaidra instead? Cutter thought that probably he had.

He did not know how the Fey had known that he would come here, to this place, for the Fey and their ways were largely inscrutable, but clearly they had, and they had left the shattered remnants of this village to serve as testimony for Cutter's crimes.

*How many?* he thought.

How many had died because of his sins over the years? Far more than had ever been cut down by his axe, that much was sure, and that number was already one which weighed heavily upon him. He felt the urge to despair then, to quit, to toss down his axe and walk into the Black Woods, never looking back, only forward, searching for the death which had searched for him for so long. He thought, too, about the knife sheathed at his waist, about the game he had so often played with himself over the years. It was sharp, that knife, for he always kept it so, and he knew that it would be quick. Sure. The easiest thing in the world. The hardest thing in the world.

Yet he knew that he would not seek his death in the Black Woods just as he would not seek it at the end of his knife. In part this was because he knew that the dead feel no pain, and he deserved to feel far more, deserved to be crushed beneath his own guilt, to be ground beneath it into ash. More than that, though, there was the boy. Chall and Maeve and Valden—the man they had long since taken to calling Priest—would do their best to protect him, of course, should Cutter choose the coward's way out, yet it would likely not be enough. Cutter might not have been good for much. Certainly he was not a shoulder to cry on, and he never knew the right thing to say. Killing, though, was something at which he had always excelled. And if the lad had any hope of being safe, then he thought it likely that there would be more killing that needed doing. Probably a lot more.

No. He would remain, he and his guilt, until the boy was safe. Then and only then would he allow himself to die.

A stone wall ran around the village. A small one, no more than three feet high. A wall not meant for defense but crafted to keep out wild animals, one that would have proved of little use against the forces which had come against the villagers. A quick glance showed that the stones had been toppled in several places, and even as he watched men and women were at work restacking them, carting in more to make the wall higher. Others milled about the buildings, raking through shattered belongings in search of anything salvageable, while still others pushed wooden carts laden with dead toward a great fire which raged somewhere near the village center.

He and the others followed the path to a break in the wall where, judging by the shattered wooden remnants scattered on the ground, a gate had once stood, but stood no longer. Still, there was a man stationed at the gate, his clothes, like those of the rest of the villagers, living and dead alike, were stained with blood and ash. There was a vacant, stunned look in his eyes, one which Cutter had seen often over the years, nearly always following a battle. It was the vacant, confused look of a man who had believed the world to be one thing and had discovered, in one brutal day or hour of bloodshed, as he'd listened to the screams of his friends and family as they died, that it was something very different, something far darker.

The guard was so caught up in his own thoughts, his own dark musings, that he didn't notice Cutter and the others approach until they were within ten feet of him, then he roused himself, brandishing his weapon—not some soldier's blade, this, but a pitchfork, the tines of which were stained with blood—and focusing his unsteady gaze on them with an effort. "The fuck do you want?" he asked in a voice that was meant to be intimidating but was belied by the tremor in his hands as he held his makeshift weapon.

Not a warrior, this, nor a killer, a man who went out searching for blood. No, this was a normal man, a farmer, perhaps, one who cared nothing for wars or battles but who cared only for tending to his crops and protecting his family. One who had not gone out in search of violence and yet, as was so often the case, violence had found him anyway.

Cutter held out his empty hands in what he hoped was a soothing gesture. "We're only travelers, friend, seeking shelter. We mean no harm."

The man let out a laugh that sounded in danger of becoming a scream. "Shelter, that it?" he said in a voice that trembled with grief and mad humor. "Well, you ain't picked the best day to visit

Ferrimore, stranger. You and your group'd be best to turn around and go back where you come from."

Considering that Cutter and the rest had just come from the Black Woods, he might have argued that, but there was no point. He was still thinking of what to say instead when Matt stepped forward.

"What happened here?" the youth asked, glancing at Cutter in challenge before turning back to the man.

"What happened?" the guard asked. "What *happened?* Well, I'll tell you, lad. The Fey came, that's what. The abominations came in the darkness." His eyes glazed over with the pain of the memory. "I've lived here ten years gone, me and my w..." He cut off, letting out a strangled sob before choking it back. "Lived here a long time," he went on, sniffling and running an arm across his nose. "Got some folks here fought in the war. I'd heard the stories, of course. We all had. I thought—*we* thought—we were ready. But...we were wrong. Gods help us, we were wrong."

The man went silent then, his expression twisting with grief as he relived what must have been the terrible events of the night past, and Cutter glanced to the youth. "Satisfied?" he growled.

Matt said nothing, only stepping back to stand with the others. Cutter watched the grieving man, feeling more uncomfortable, more unsure than he had ever felt on the midst of a battle, locked in a struggle where his life hung in the balance of each passing moment. He did not know what that said about him, that he should be far more at ease in the midst of a life or death struggle than faced with a man's naked grief, but likely it was nothing good.

The man continued sobbing, and Cutter continued standing there, unsure of what to do, until Priest stepped forward, putting a gentle hand on the man's shoulder. He whispered some words to the man—too low for Cutter to hear. The guard's sobbing slowly began to quiet, and he looked up at Priest with watery eyes filled not just with grief, not now, but with something like gratitude.

Cutter found himself wondering what the man had said, was suddenly possessed of the feeling—ridiculous, probably, but there none the less—that if he only knew those words, if he only understood them, perhaps he could change, could leave the killer behind and become...something else.

But the guard did not share them. Instead, he only nodded slowly, sniffling, and finally turned back to Cutter. "As I said, Ferrimore ain't as nice now as usual, but if you've really no other place to go, you can go to the inn. Berden, the innkeeper, died in the night, but I think his wife Netty's there now. Might be she could find you a place to stay." He let out another sobbing laugh. "The gods know there's far more beds than there are folks to use 'em now."

Cutter nodded. "Where's the inn?"

"Can't miss it," the guard said, swallowing. "It's the only buildin' still has a roof."

"Thanks." He hesitated for a moment, thinking he should say something, but the words would not come, so he only nodded again. He glanced at the others, saw Maeve studying him in a way he didn't like, then motioned them into the village.

They all started forward save Valden who remained with his hand on the guard's shoulder.

"Priest?" Cutter asked.

Priest met his eyes, gave him a small smile. "I will remain here, for a time. I will catch up with you all soon."

Cutter glanced between the man and the guard who had hung his head and was now sobbing quietly, then he grunted. "Very well," he said, then he turned and led the others deeper into the village.

Cutter and the others walked through the hollowed-out corpse of Ferrimore, past men and women who looked as stunned and lost as the guard at the gate. A great fire burned at the village's center, and even as he passed, men and women pushed wooden carts carrying their dead toward the blaze where others waited to haul one body after the other into the flames while the families and friends of those who had died looked on and wept.

Cutter was not surprised to see such a burial by flame. Others who had not fought the Fey, might have thought it disrespectful, but those who had met the creatures knew that the only things they truly feared were salt and fire. So then, the heaving of the bodies into the flame was a promise, one he had seen made several times throughout the war. A promise that those bodies cast into the blaze would never again be ravaged by the Fey but would remain ever beyond their reach.

He and the others paused for a moment, watching the grisly spectacle, then he grunted. "Come on—we need to find the inn. We all need rest."

"Are you truly so cold?" Maeve demanded.

Cutter met her eyes, then looked over to see the boy and Chall, both watching him, waiting for what he would say. He said nothing though, only turned and started deeper into the village. The guard had been right about this much—it was not a difficult thing to pick out the inn. It was the largest building in the village and the only one with a roof. Wounded lay on the ground outside on sheets splattered with crimson stains, some moaning, others blessedly unconscious, as men and women who looked nearly as bad as their charges tended to them as best as they were able.

Cutter had seen the aftermath of a battle—or, in this case, a slaughter—before, had been on either end of it too many times to count. He had seen, had inflicted and suffered, a variety of wounds, and so he was faced with a cold truth. Out of the six wounded being ministered to on the ground in front of the inn, only one would live for sure, with another having a chance—albeit a small one—to pull through. But he did not bother saying as much to those men and women tending them, men and women who, judging by their quiet looks of panic, would have been more at home tending to their livestock than their fellow villagers.

Six wounded. Not so many considering that several hundred men and women called the small village home. But then, another thing Cutter had learned about the Fey from hard, bitter experience was that the Creatures of the Wood never left many.

Cutter stared at those wounded, those dying men and women, and hesitated, frowning. No matter what Maeve thought of him—thoughts for which he, of all people, could not blame her—he was not immune to the pain and suffering of others, and he wished that he could help, that he could offer some healing or, if not that, than at least some hope, vain or not. The problem, though, was that Cutter knew only how to hurt, to kill, and knew nothing of how to save. As for hope, for most of those lying there now, the only hope was that the world beyond the Veil would be kinder than this one, a hope Cutter felt was destined to be shattered, for he had sent many men and creatures on that journey himself, and none, to his recollection, had smiled as they went.

"We should help them," Chall said softly, and Cutter turned to see the heavy-set mage staring at the wounded and those struggling to at the very least make them comfortable. A tear was gliding its way down his cheek.

"Do you know anything of healing?" Cutter asked him.

The mage winced. "No. No, I don't." He glanced with hope at Maeve, and the woman gave a sad shake of her head.

"Neither do I," Cutter growled, "so stop your fucking crying. That, at least, you can do for them."

The mage recoiled as if he'd been slapped, but he nodded, running an arm across his eyes. Cutter gave him a moment to gather himself, then he gave a nod of his own and led them toward the entrance of the inn.

The healers and the wounded paid them little attention as they made their way past, the latter too busy dying and the former too busy trying desperately—and vainly—to stop the inevitable to notice them. Closer to them, their cries of anguish, their desperate pleas, struck him almost like a physical blow, and the smell of blood and death filled his nostrils. Cutter felt something rouse within him. Fury. Rage. A beast which had slumbered for fifteen years. A fitful, uneasy slumber, but a slumber nonetheless, one which the sight of the ruined village, the ruined bodies, threatened to wake it from. And if it woke, that beast which he had carried around with him since, it seemed, his birth, Cutter knew that it would not easily be put down once more.

He took a slow, deep breath to steady himself, forcing his eyes away from the wounded to those with him. They all wore their misery plain on their face, but he saw more than just that. They were not just sad for those who had suffered—they were exhausted. And none more so than Matt. The boy looked done in, looked little better, in truth, than those poor souls writhing on their bloody sheets, as if he might collapse at any moment. And while Cutter did not like seeing such pain on those strangers, seeing it on the boy wounded him, touched him in a way nothing else could. The lad was exhausted, had little left to give—and Cutter understood, for a trip through the Black Woods, at the best of times, felt as if it stripped away pieces of a man's soul, and their circumstances had been far from the best. The boy needed rest, *real* rest, a quiet place to lay his head without the dark shadows of the Black Wood's trees looming over him, without the specter of his own village's destruction or Ferrimore's slaughter in his mind.

Unfortunately, Cutter could not give him that, no matter how much he might wish to, but he could, at least, make sure the boy had a chance to rest, however fitful that rest might be, however plagued by dreams of blood and death. "Come on," he growled. "Let's go find this innkeeper."

Another angry look from Maeve, and an expression on the boy's face that was a mixture of hurt and anger, but that was alright. Let him be hurt, let him be angry, just let him be alive. Cutter turned and led them into the inn.

The common room of the inn had been turned into a makeshift healer's tent. Tables which, in happier times, would have held the ales of men and women. In such a small village, those who would have normally set at the tables would have all known each other. Perhaps they would have laughed and drank as they told interesting stories and more interesting lies about the week's events. Now, though, no one laughed, and the tables did not hold ales. Cutter was surprised to see that they held more wounded, these also tended to by people who, judging by the quiet desperation on their faces, had no idea what they were doing.

Nearly two dozen wounded at least, most of them badly. The beast within him stirred once more in its fitful slumber, not waking, not yet, but close. Too close. The Fey did not usually leave wounded, for their victims served another, darker purpose than just as corpses to them, and they were not often wasteful. Neither would they ever be stalled in one of their attacks by villagers with pitchforks and shovels and a three-foot wall as their only defense. Which meant that this had been intentional. The ruined village, the wounded suffering and dying, all of it was, for Shadelaresh, a message, one meant for Cutter and him alone, one that was impossible to ignore.

The room was in chaos, with people hurrying this way and that, some carrying water or cloth strips cut into makeshift bandages, some seeming only to hurry for the sake of hurrying, their minds too broken from the night's madness and the day's following spectacle to focus on what they meant to do. Cutter understood that, too, the madness that overtook a person when their world had been turned upside down, and they were faced with not just their own mortality, but the fact that the living were all not just made to suffer death, but often to suffer a terrible, agonizing death.

There were others, though, who did not walk with purpose or without, who only stood, unmoving. They gathered in dazed clumps, not speaking to each other, only standing as if they were puppets whose master had foregone their strings, abandoning them. The only person who seemed to have any real idea of what to do was an old woman with a hunched back and one withered hand who moved about the room, seeming to be everywhere at once, and despite her frail appearance, she carried with her a strength of personality, of *will* that was obvious. Obvious, too, to those at whom she barked orders in a voice that did not waver or quiver with fragility or sadness, but one which was resolute, one which was focused not on the dying but on the living, on doing what needed to be done.

Here, then, was their leader. Even as he watched, the woman paused at the huddled groups of those too stunned to do anything but stand there, saying words too low for Cutter to hear. Some of those in such groups, upon hearing her, seemed to blink as if waking from a dream, then set about doing those things that needed to be done.

Not all of them, but enough to bring some order back to the chaos, an order that was threatened every moment by the despair lying thick like fog in the room. Cutter watched with appreciation as the woman shouted orders, noted the sometimes sullen—and quickly covered—stares of those she directed before they inevitably set about the tasks she'd set them. He wondered if they thought her cold, callous, immune by some lack of humanity to the devastation around her. Probably they did. That was a thing Cutter understood, just as he understood that they were lucky to have her.

He had stood among such devastation countless times in his life, far more than any right-minded man should, and in such times he had discovered that it was often the most unlikely of people, shy clerks and elderly grandmothers, who rose out of the chaos as champions of order. In normal times, such a person as the hunched old woman might have passed her life quietly and unremarked, but war and chaos, while it brought out the worst in some people, it also, in some select few, brought out the best. Cutter knew that, just as he knew that he was not one of those, one of those champions of order. He was and always had been an agent of chaos, perhaps the greatest—or worst—of its agents. Still, knowing that did nothing to lessen his respect for the old woman, and he watched her for another few seconds, admiring her humble greatness while knowing he could never share it.

"Cutter?"

He turned at the sound of the voice to see the others watching him. Chall and the lad with curious expressions on their faces, as if wondering what he was about, and Maeve with a small, humorless smirk, as if she knew all too well. Probably she did. Anyone, seeing their group, the group he had led, in the past, might have thought he'd kept Maeve around for her skills with the knives she'd once carried or her ability to seemingly talk anyone into doing nearly anything, but they would have been wrong. Maeve's greatest asset—one which, likely, even she was unaware of—was her ability to see past the superfluous to the heart of things, the heart of people. It was what made her great, what had, once upon a time, made her terrible as well.

"Are you...okay?" Chall asked, his voice tenuous, uncertain.

Cutter grunted. "I'm fine. Come on."

He led them toward the bar where a few stools—those currently not being used by the "healers" scattered about the room—were left empty. He looked around for whoever was manning the bar but the space behind the counter was empty, the shelves where liquor was no doubt normally kept in clean rows mostly empty save for a few bottles lying on their sides, the rest, he suspected, carried away to be used as makeshift disinfectant.

"Might as well have a seat," he said to the others. "This might be a minute."

Chall didn't hesitate, half-sitting, half-collapsing wearily into one of the stools which creaked threateningly under his not inconsiderable weight. Maeve frowned at the mage as he let out a heavy sigh of relief then she, too, slid quietly into another stool, somehow imbuing the simple gesture with a dignity, as she always seemed to do.

The boy, though, looked at the stool guiltily before glancing back at the wounded and those ministering to them. "Sit, lad," Cutter said. "What can be done for them is being done already."

"But...but they're dying," he said, and Cutter winced at the volume of his tone as some of the would-be healers glanced their direction.

"People die, lad," he said softly. "It's what they're best at."

"We're," Maeve said.

Cutter frowned. "What?"

"It's what we're best at," she answered, meeting his gaze with a challenge in her own.

Cutter grunted. "Right. Anyway, what I mean, lad, is that we all have our own journeys and never mind that they end up in the same place. And the fact that others are suffering does not diminish your own. Now, sit. You have had a long journey—you refusing to rest will do nothing to help those you pity."

The boy opened his mouth as if he might argue but something—his own weariness, most likely—decided him and in another moment he sat. Cutter waited another few minutes, watching the lad seem to sink further and further into the stool, as if he were dissolving before his eyes like a snowman in the heat, then he reached out and clapped one of his hands onto the wooden counter.

A moment later, a figure stepped around the counter, scowling at them and wiping bloody hands on a rag that was little better. Cutter was unsurprised to see that it was the hunched old woman who had been commanding those inside the common room moments before. A general among her army and in her command tent no less. "Ain't got time to be pourin' drinks just now," she said. "In case you all hadn't noticed, we're a bit busy at the moment."

"No drinks," Cutter said. "We only need rooms."

The woman stared at him as if he were insane. "Rooms? Here? What is it, you got a death wish? Like those mad bastards go chasin' after hurricanes and the gods alone know what else?"

"No," Cutter said. "Not that. Though I've heard that lightning can't strike in the same place twice."

The woman grunted, glancing over his shoulder at the wounded. "Maybe it can and maybe it can't, though I don't see as it makes much difference either way. You ask me, once is pretty well enough to get the job done. More than. Anyway," she went on, bringing her attention back to him, "I wouldn't hang around here, if I were you. I'm afraid Ferrimore's hospitality ain't up to what it usually is just now. Better you go to Valaidra. A big city, plenty of rooms there, no doubt."

"We won't make it to Valaidra," he persisted, not bothering to share that even if they did, they had Feledias and the gods alone knew how many others waiting on them. "We've had a long journey. We're weary, and we need rooms."

"A long journey, is it?" the woman asked. "Well, last night I watched my husband get torn apart and eaten—at least parts of him—by creatures most folk think are just bedtime stories for when mommy and daddy want their little 'uns to wake up in the night screamin'. We all got problems. So forgive me if I'm not as sympathetic as I might be when you tell me you're tired, maybe a little foot sore, and lookin' for a room."

She watched him, waiting for what he would say, but Cutter said nothing, only watching her back, and after a moment she glanced over at Matt, the boy barely more than a puddle in the stool now, and some of the hardness left her features. She sighed. "Alright. Might be I can spare a room or two. But if you're expectin' warm soup and a bedtime story, hate to say I'm fresh out."

"The rooms will be fine," Cutter said.

She grunted. "Alright," she said, then she reached under the counter and passed him two keys. He glanced up at her, and she shrugged. "Two's all I can spare. The rest are taken up by folks bleedin' or dyin' or both. If it ain't up to your standards, I 'spose you can go sleep in the fields—plenty of room out there."

"Two's good," Cutter said. "Thanks."

"You go on and get some rest, lad," she said to Matt, who mumbled what might have been assent. "And you, big fella," she said, turning back to Cutter, "you want a piece of friendly advice—I'd get yourself in one of those rooms quickly as possible, don't come out 'til you plan on leavin' Ferrimore behind ya, understand?"

Cutter frowned. "No, I don't—" He cut off as he felt a hand fall on his shoulder. Not much to go on, maybe, but it was enough, and he understood even before the man spoke.

"A big bastard, ain't ya?"

Cutter fought down a sigh, turning in his stool to look at the man standing before him. He had the broad shoulders and thick, calloused fingers of a man who'd spent his life in manual labor, and the protruding gut which said he liked his ale more than was healthy. The two men standing on either side of the first and slightly behind him were also big, though not quite as big as the man himself and which, considering that men, when violence was on their mind, were not so very different than wolves, explained their respective positions easily enough.

"Something I can do for you?" Cutter asked.

The man flashed him a grin without humor, glancing back at his comrades. "Oh, I was thinkin' there might be somethin' we can do for you. Or maybe *to* you'd be more accurate."

Cutter had plenty of problems on his plate, and the last thing he needed was to get in a pissing contest with a man who, following the night's events, had found himself with a lot of anger, a currency that only ever spent one way. Blood. "Look, we aren't looking for any trouble, alright? We've been traveling for a long time and are looking for a room, that's all."

"Weren't lookin' for trouble myself, last night when I laid down with my wife. Didn't stop those *things* from comin' in the night, rippin' her out of bed and givin' her a good chew for I bashed the bastard's skull in. Sometimes, fella, trouble finds you whether you look for it or not."

"Oh, let off, Cend," the old innkeeper said with a weary voice. "These folks don't—"

"No, *you* let off, Netty," the big man said, holding up a warning finger. "You know well as I do who this big fucker is. This bastard is the one responsible for what happened last night."

The woman grunted. "That right? He the one that attacked us, that it? He the one that killed your wife and my husband? Got to be honest, Cend, he don't much look like the thing that took my Berden from me. But if your aim is to pass around blame, well, why don't we blame him for my stiff bones too, how'd that be? Maybe blame him for the bad weather or old Frank's horse goin' lame a year gone."

The man's face twisted with rage, a rage only brought on by suffering some terrible loss. Perhaps in normal times, he was a nice enough man, pleasant. Probably his wife had thought so. But rage makes monsters of all men, and he was fully in its grip now. "You shut your fuckin' mouth, you old hag," he said, thrusting his finger at her like it was a sword. "You heard the same shit I heard from that green demon last night. There's a man comin' he said, one responsible for your fate and the fate of your loved ones. He described 'em, shit, and while I was lyin' there half unconscious, well, I listened, didn't I? Listened so close I'd know that bastard, if he came, know him as well as I know my own brother, as I knew my *wife*," he finished, the last word little more than a bestial growl. "And if that weren't enough, that green demon, he said this man, if he showed up, would be carryin' an axe, an axe, friend," he said, staring at Cutter, "much like the one you're carrying."

"Look," Cutter said, knowing it would be worthless but trying anyway, "I'm sorry for what happened to you and your people. But—"

"Damn your *sorry*," the man hissed, lifting him up by the front of his jerkin with a not inconsiderable strength. "Someone needs to pay, you son of a bitch, understand? Someone needs to *pay*."

With his free hand, he drew a knife, a cruel, wicked looking thing, and he brandished it in front of Cutter's face. "I'm owed, stranger. And I mean to collect what I'm owed. I mean to cut the price out of your flesh bit by bit until I'm satisfied, and—"

"Hold on, Cend," one of his companions said, narrowing his eyes and studying Cutter like he was a mystery in need of solving.

"What?" the big man, Cend, growled. "Look, if you don't have the stomach for it, then turn around and—"

"It ain't that," his friend interrupted. "Only look at him, Cend. *Really* look at 'em. Seems I know that face."

The man, Cend, frowned, studying Cutter carefully. Then, his eyes went wide. "Fire and salt, it's him," he said in a voice that was not full of menace, not at that moment, but shock and disbelief.

"Yes," the other man said, nervousness clear in his voice now. "That's the Crimson Prince. I seen 'em once before on campaign, and by the gods, that's him."

"Prince Bernard himself," Cend said, his tone emotionless in his surprise.

"Prince?" Matt asked, his voice weak with exhaustion but still obviously confused.

The men, though, paid him no attention, and Cutter didn't have a moment to spare to explain it to the youth, not that he would have known what to say even if he had.

"Look, Cend," the third man said, licking his lips, "maybe we ought to just leave off, eh? Might be better for everybody if we just—"

"Fuck that," the big man growled, finally getting over his initial shock. "I'm *owed*, damnit. I don't give a shit if he's one of the gods himself, this fucker is responsible for what happened to Kira, he's responsible for *all* of it."

"Yeah, sure, sure, Cend," the second said, "but it's the *Crimson Prince*. Let's just go, alright? There's Kira's arrangements to make and—"

Cend let out a bestial growl, one that, matched with the fury on his face, made it clear that he was past listening, long past. He lifted the blade over his head, and Cutter waited, trying to decide the best way to take it from him, trying to decide if he wanted to take it at all or let the blade finish its lethal arc.

That was when Matt got off his stool, stepping forward. "Please, just leave him alone. We don't—" His words turned into a shout of surprised pain as the man, Cend, backhanded him with the blade holding the knife, hitting him in the face. The youth's lip busted and blood splattered as he fell back, tumbling over his stool to hit the ground.

Some of that blood, of the *boy's* blood, struck Cutter in the face. They had escaped a doomed village, had made their way through the Black Wood, without any harm—physical, at least—befalling the boy and now, here, this angry farmer had struck him for no reason, no reason at all. Cutter turned and looked at the boy lying there, a hand over his bloody mouth. The beast of his fury did not slowly come awake, not in a way that it might be soothed back down. Instead, it *sprang* awake, its teeth already bared, its claws out, as they always were. The man holding him was saying something, but he might as well have been speaking in a different language, for Cutter could not understand it, and he did not care to. Maeve also said something but her words, too, were drowned out by the storm inside him, the storm which was the beast's growl, and he could not make it out.

And he did not try. The beast sprang forward, and Cutter, as ever, was carried along with it.

## CHAPTER TWENTY-THREE

*Some likened him, in his wrath, to a storm, but he was not a storm. Storms might be weathered, might be sheltered against, and there was no shelter, not from him.*
*Some others said he was like a beast in his rage but this, too, fell short of the mark.*
*Most beasts, after all, kill from necessity. The Crimson Prince, though, killed for no other reason than that he enjoyed it.*
*No, not a storm, then, and not a beast.*
*His wrath, his fury, was far worse than both.*
*—Exiled Historian to the Crown, Petran Quinn*

Maeve saw it happening, that terrible transformation. Or perhaps transformation was not the right word, for it was not as if Cutter *became* something else. Instead, it was as if he were that thing all along, and the normal man, the man who spoke softly when he spoke at all, was only a mask he sometimes wore in the hopes that it might hide who he really was, even from himself.

She had seen it before, that change, that *becoming*, and now, like then, she found herself watching with a dreaded fascination as the man took in the boy lying bloody on the ground, as the dull, emotionlessness left his gaze to be replaced by a rage that seemed to threaten to burst its way free of him. "Cutter," she said, knowing it would do no good but knowing, too, that she had to try. "It's fine, the boy's fine, okay? Just a bloody lip, that's all, folks have suffered a lot worse and—"

But then she was out of time. Cutter let out a growl that sounded like it came from some wild, furious animal, and he moved with the devastating speed she had seen him display on multiple occasions, his hand coming up and striking the man, Cend, in his wrist. While his speed was shocking, his strength now, as it had been fifteen years ago, seemed almost superhuman, and as his hand struck the man's wrist there was a loud, ear-splitting *crack*. The tavern tough screamed as his wrist bent at an unnatural angle, and the knife went hurtling through the air, nearly impaling one of the men and women who had moments before been busy at healing but who had now all turned to watch the proceedings.

When he'd struck the man's wrist, the knife had scored Cutter on his hand, and Maeve saw that it was bleeding freely. Cutter, her prince, did not notice though, paying it no more attention than he did anyone else in the room—including the boy. There were only the three in front of him, the three who had dared to harm the boy, only the objects of his wrath.

The big man's cries of pain suddenly cut off as Cutter lunged forward with his entire body, bringing his forehead into the man's face and making of his nose and mouth a bloody, smashed ruin. The big man fell away, and then one of his companions was reaching into his tunic, likely trying to retrieve a knife or blade with which he might defend himself.

He never got the chance. Cutter was on him in an instant, sinking his bloody fist into the man's stomach. The unfortunate man's air exploded out of him in a *whoosh,* and he doubled over as if he were trying to kiss his shoes. Then Cutter growled and brought his elbow down on the back of the man's head, and he collapsed at his feet in a limp heap. The third man let out a shocked whimper and turned to run but he, like his comrades, was far too slow.

He'd only made it two steps away when Cutter was on him, grabbing a fistful of his hair. The man cried out, trying to break free, both of his hands pawing at Cutter's wrist. It made no difference. Cutter took his time, walking toward the nearest table and dragging his hapless victim behind him. Then he paused, lifting the man up, and the man, seeing what he intended, renewed his struggles, screaming and crying for help.

Maeve wanted to help him. After all, these men were just hurting, that was all. They had suffered greatly in the past night, and in the middle of winter, with so many of their fellow villagers dead and unable to contribute to the community as was so necessary in a small village, they would be hard pressed even to survive the coming days. She did not wish to make their lives any harder, wanted Cutter to stop, to let it go, but she, like the rest of those standing in the common room of the inn, was frozen into shocked silence as she stared at the swift, brutal violence of the fight. But then, it wasn't really a fight, no more than the guillotine fought the man lying beneath it, and in due course things proceeded in the only way they could. The one being executed never won, never could win, and this, then, was like that.

Cutter flexed, his thick, muscled arms suddenly writhing with veins as he raised the man's head up and then pivoted, bringing it down into the table with bone-shattering force. The man's panicked whimpers quickly went silent, and he fell backward, straight as a board, to collapse on the common room floor.

Silence followed then save for Cutter's rasping breaths as everyone watched this man, this *beast* which had been let loose amongst them, which had snuck inside wearing the mask of a man. They were afraid, all of them, afraid that this man, this beast who seemed possessed of so much fury might find that fury undiminished in the wake of what he had perpetrated on his attackers and would seek to vent it elsewhere.

Maeve did not blame them, for they were right to be afraid. She, too, felt the icy tendrils of fear spreading through her just as she had so many years ago, and she knew that more than once the man's anger had done exactly what the people gathered in the common room feared—had driven him on past the original target of his ire.

She stood there, hoping that it would stop, that this would be the end of it, but she saw him studying the men lying on their backs and knew that this time, he did not mean to stop. This time, they would not be so lucky. If he was to be stopped, something or some*one* would have to stop him. She had seen it done a few times before, a few when the unlucky man or woman who had dared interpose themselves between him and the objects of his wrath survived the attempt, but usually the man raged on until his own exhaustion brought him down.

She considered waiting on that, for they had journeyed far, slept little, and that, coupled with the fact that he had just fought three men, ought to mean that he must feeling at least some of the exhaustion that she herself felt. True, the man often struck her not as a man at all but some revenant who traveled through the world, never slowing, caring for nothing, stopping for nothing but only adhering to some unexplainable directive, some grim purpose which would see him traveling onward through the world, leaving a path of blood and the dead behind him long after she and those others he knew were dead and gone.

Still, when he made no move toward the men, she had a brief hope that he might let it go after all, that he might be finished. The three men would wake up—most likely, at least—with terrible headaches and some bruises and pains to remind them of how close they had come to death. Miserable, hurting, but alive. Or so she believed.

That was when he reached for his axe.

*\*\**

His chest heaved not with exertion—or at least not mostly that—but with anger. The man lay beneath him. He did not know his name, and he did not care, knew only that he was his enemy, knew only that the beast was loose, and that it was far from satisfied. He reached for the axe hanging on his back, his hand tightening around the handle, preparing to draw it loose, preparing to end the threat the man represented.

That was when he felt a hand on his wrist, and he spun, thinking that one of the man's companions had risen, meaning to resume the fight. He growled, his free hand knotting into a fist. But it was not one of the men standing before him. It was a woman, one that, even in his anger, he recognized.

"No," she said. "It's enough, Bernard. You've done enough."

That name. He had not heard it in a long time—in years, in fact—and the hearing of it pulled him back to himself. He blinked groggily, feeling as if he were waking from a dream. He glanced around him, saw the terrified faces watching him, all of them cringing away as if he might attack them at any moment. He saw, too, the three men lying on the ground. Unconscious? Dead? He turned back to Maeve who was still studying him, trying to decide, perhaps, if he were done, if the beast had chosen, of its own will, to slip back into its fitful slumber for the time being.

How many times had they stood thus, with her watching him, afraid of him and right to be? Bodies lying around them? Too many times, that was sure. Had he really believed he could change? Had he believed he *had* changed, or had it been only some fancy, some gentle lie he had told himself like a bedtime story, one meant to soothe a child to his rest? "They hurt the lad," he said, surprised by how hoarse his voice sounded.

"He's fine," she said.

He grunted, glancing past her to where the boy still lay where he had fallen, his face pale with fear and shock. Cutter let the axe handle go, flexed his hand where he had gripped it so tightly that it ached, then he started toward the boy. "You alright, lad?"

Matt scooted away from him, his eyes wide, and Cutter frowned. "You're okay, boy. They're not going to hurt—"

"You were going to kill those men," the boy said, his voice thick with emotion and accusation, and Cutter realized it was not the men he feared. It was him.

He froze, making no more move to the boy and finally he nodded. "Yes."

"But...*why?*"

Cutter stood there, wondering how many times he had asked himself that same question, wondering, too, how many times he had come up empty without an answer to give.

In the silence, Maeve walked forward, offering the boy her hand, and he did not shy away, taking it and allowing himself to be pulled to his feet. She glanced at Cutter, a world of meaning in her gaze, then looked back to the boy. "Come on, Matt," she said. "How about you help an old lady to her room, eh? I think we could both use the rest."

The boy seemed stunned as she led him up the stairs, watching Cutter worriedly, as if at any moment he might attack him. Cutter wanted to tell him that he would never do that, that out of the many crimes he had committed, the many atrocities, that was one even he would not do. He wanted to tell the boy he was sorry, to somehow make him understand, but he could not find the words, and in another moment they were disappearing up the stairs, Chall following behind, and Cutter was left standing alone in the common room.

"One night."

He turned to see the innkeeper, Netty, standing beside him. "One night," she repeated. "And then you're gone, do you understand?"

"I understand."

She studied him for several seconds then grunted. "Cend and the others are fools, but normally harmless enough ones. They don't deserve to die."

"No," he said. "No, I don't expect they do."

She nodded. "Alright then," she said, then turned back to those others in the room, those men and women who, minutes ago, had been busy tending to the wounded but who were, as one, watching him. "Well?" she demanded. "Did a miracle happen and all those wounds healed themselves and somehow I missed it?"

That got them back to work, but Cutter couldn't help but notice the sidelong, fearful glances they kept shooting his way. How often had he suffered such looks before? Suffered, yes, but deserved them nonetheless. Suddenly, the air felt thick, claustrophobic, and he turned and walked—fled—out of the inn.

# CHAPTER TWENTY-FOUR

*How can one explain, to those so young, the cruelty of war? How can one prepare them, with their hopeful eyes, their excitement at being soldiers, for the inevitable losses and pain that wait for them?*
*You cannot, that's all, and there is no reason to try.*
*After all, they will learn the truth soon enough.*
—*General Malex regarding new recruits during the Fey Wars*

Maeve unlocked the door, motioning the boy in. He shambled inside and sat on the bed, a dazed expression on his face, one that she understood. She glanced back at the mage standing in the hallway, still wearing the ridiculous purple trousers. She'd thought those trousers were funny when she'd first seen them, but they did not seem so funny now. But then, nothing did. The mage looked anxious, and he fidgeted nervously as if unsure of what he should be doing.

He glanced past her at the boy then met her eyes again. "Should I...I mean..."

Maeve sighed. "Go and get some rest, Chall," she said softly. "I'll talk to him."

He winced, obviously feeling guilty but just as obviously relieved. "Okay...goodnight, Mae."

"Goodnight."

She watched the mage walk down the hall to the other room, where he would find his bed and, if he were lucky, get some rest. It was what she wanted as well, some rest, some sleep, the only thing that might put some distance between herself and their circumstances, which would allow her, at least for a few hours, to dream that she was someone else, anyone else. But there were some, like Cutter, whose seemingly only purpose in life was destruction and others whose job it was to pick up what remained when the destruction was finished, to try to piece something back together from the debris they left in their wake. She had never thought herself a good candidate for such a job, but it was a role she was familiar with nonetheless.

The boy still sat on the bed, his eyes unfocused, as she stepped into the room. He didn't look up until she closed the door behind her, a bit louder than she needed to, truth be told. "How we doing, lad?" she asked, moving to sit beside him, feeling, in that moment, very old and very tired.

"He...he was going to kill them, Maeve." He turned, meeting her eyes, and she could see tears gathering there. "Wasn't he?"

"Yes," she said softly. "He was going to kill them."

"But...*why?*"

Maeve had asked herself that question often following one of her prince's killing sprees and now, like then, she had no answer. She doubted, in truth, if even Cutter knew. Still, the youth was watching her, needing something from her, some answer, some way to understand, so she sighed, thinking. "Prince Ber...that is, Cutter, is not like you and me. He's...well, he's not like anyone, really."

"But you follow him."

"Yes."

"Why?"

Another question without an answer, or at least, if it had one, it was one she herself had not been able to discover in the twenty or so years that she had known the man. She glanced at the boy. "Why do you?"

The boy opened his mouth to answer then hesitated, frowning.

She gave him a small smile. "Yes. Cutter's like that. He's not like a man, really. He's more like...a storm, maybe. A storm that just sort of sweeps you up and carries you along with it. Terrifying, sure, something to be avoided, if you want to live in peace, a storm full of lightning and rage and no knowing, at any time, where it might strike. And yet..."

"You're carried along anyway," he finished.

Whatever else the boy was, he was no fool, that much was certain. "That's right," she said. "Like a leaf in the wind."

The boy nodded, not satisfied probably but likely understanding that it was the best answer he was going to get. "Those men," he said, "they called him Prince Bernard. The Crimson Prince."

"Yes."

"So he is? Our prince, I mean? My father and mother didn't talk much about them, the royals, but some of my friends, their parents told them stories about him. He was…he was a hero, wasn't he?"

"Oh yes," Maeve said. "He was, he *is* a hero. It's because of him—his brother too, understand, but mostly him—that we won the war against the Fey and found a place to stay here." Of course, it was also because of Cutter that they had ever been forced into a war with the strange denizens of this land in the first place, for it had been he and he alone who had broken the peace treaty by slaying the Fey king, but she didn't think now was the time to mention that.

"A hero," the boy said slowly, musing over it. "But scary."

She grunted. There wasn't any arguing that, even if she'd meant to, and she did not. After all, she had traveled with the man for years, was as close to him as anyone could claim to be, but knowing him, traveling with him for years, had done nothing to make him less terrifying to her. For as it turned out, being close to the monster, knowing the exact length and sharpness of its claws, having seen its bite, offered no comfort. "Scary," she nodded. "I'd say that's pretty accurate."

"Still," the boy said, something flashing in his eyes that she thought dangerously close to admiration and out of all the things she'd seen in the last couple of days since Chall had arrived at her home, she thought that the scariest yet. "I've never seen anybody fight like that…I never knew people *could* fight like that."

"Yes," she said grudgingly. "He is a great warrior, it's true. I have seen many warriors in my time and none—not even his brother who is known for his skill with the sword—can compare." A great warrior, yes, perhaps from the outside looking in, but she had never thought of him as such, and she doubted Cutter thought of himself in that way. A great killer, sure, one born to it as much as anyone ever had been, that could not be denied.

"Do you think..." He hesitated, then turned to meet her eyes. "Do you think he would teach me?"

Those words rocked her to her core. She had been expecting them, of course, but she had hoped..."Would you want him to?" she asked. "Would you want to be like him?"

The lad hesitated, thinking it through, and that was something. For a moment, Maeve allowed herself to hope, then he frowned, his face going hard. "Men came to my village. They killed everyone in it, my friends...my mom. If I could fight, maybe I would have been able to stop them. I wish I could have. I wish I could have killed them. All of them."

Maeve watched him, feeling very old, feeling very sad. "Will you take a bit of advice from an old woman, Matt?"

He didn't say yes, but he didn't say no either, so she grunted. "Bloodshed only leads to more bloodshed and killing only leads to more killing. You see, killing, hurting, it's a habit a man or a woman gets into. One that is very, very hard to break."

His expression softened for a moment, and she began to think that maybe he had heard her, then his face hardened again, and he scooted away from her. "What do you know?" he demanded. "You're not the one who ran away while your mother and all your friends were killed. They *killed* them, Maeve."

Maeve frowned. "What do *I* know?" she demanded, feeling some anger of her own, feeling, in that moment, closer to the woman she had once been than she had in many, many years. "Do not talk to me of *loss,* boy," she hissed. "I have lived far longer than you, have lost more than you could imagine. You have lost, boy, but do not think for a second that your losses are greater than those of others. You, after all, weren't alive during the Skaalden invasion. You were not forced to watch your home, your entire *kingdom* destroyed. You lost your mother, your friends? I lost my *husband. My daughter.* My *home.* And you would lecture *me* about loss?"

The boy recoiled, clearly frightened, and Maeve felt a heavy wave of guilt sweep over her as she realized that she had screamed that last. It was true, of course; she had lost, had suffered much. Had lost a man who had meant the world to her, the only love of her life and doubted very much if there'd be another. Had lost her young daughter, a child born out of the love that she, in her youth, and her husband had felt for one another. But that did not give her the right to treat the boy so. He was only frightened, that was all, frightened and wounded from recent loss, and here she was lashing out at him while her own losses had long since scabbed over. Not healed, for such losses never healed in truth, but they were scars she'd at least had years to examine, to come to terms with.

"I'm sorry, lad," she said softly. "I didn't mean..."

"No," Matt said, "no, I'm sorry. I didn't know...about your husband and your daughter...I didn't—"

Maeve waved a hand. "Leave it, lad. I'm sorry for what you've suffered, believe me I am. I only...you see, Matt, I have lived a long time—longer than I ever expected to, in truth. And I have seen people's grief turn them into monsters. I would not see that happen to you, not if I could help it. But I understand, I do, understand the desire to defend yourself. So if you really want him to teach you..."

"I asked him before," Matt said softly, his shoulders slumping. "He said no."

She nodded. "Well. Just think on it, okay, lad? Sleep on it. And if, when you wake in the morning, you still want to learn...I'll talk to him. Okay?"

"Really?" he asked, turning to her, and there was no denying—no matter how much she might have wanted to—the hope in his eyes, in his voice. "You would do that?"

Maeve sighed. "Yes. I would, if you really want me to, I will. But I can't promise you it'll do any good. Cutter makes his own decisions—he always has."

He nodded. "Maybe you're right," he said. "Maybe I shouldn't..." But they were words spoken for her, she saw that from his face, saw that they were just his attempt to soothe things over, words meant as an apology. "But, Maeve...can I ask you something?"

"Yes."

"If Cutter really is a prince...then why...why does he care about me? Why did he take me away from the village? Why was he even *in* the village in the first place?"

She winced. "I don't want to keep you in the dark, Matt, I know how that feels. But if you want Cutter's reasons, you'd best ask him yourself."

Matt sighed. "He won't tell me. He doesn't tell me anything."

Maeve watched the boy, feeling sorry for him. A boy with a history he knew nothing about, a bloody, tragic legacy from which he had come. A legacy which would follow him, one way or the other, for the rest of his life. There were those—many—who would see him killed for that legacy, would execute him for crimes he had not committed and for reasons he did not understand. "I'll talk to him," she said finally. Then she rose.

"You're leaving?" he said, looking up at her. Fifteen or sixteen years old. Not a child, not anymore, but neither was he a man, and like a child, he was watching her, frightened at the thought of being alone, and that she understood. After all, children were scared of monsters in their closets, under their beds, but she knew enough of the world, had lived and struggled and suffered within it long enough to understand, as all adults came to, sooner or later, that the monsters they had imagined in their youths were actually very real. Only, the real monsters did not hide underneath beds or in wardrobes. Instead, they walked among men, hidden in plain sight, often behind smiles and soft words, but monsters just the same. Sometimes, those monsters were people you knew. Sometimes, they were your friends, your family. Sometimes, they were your prince.

"Yes," she said, moving toward the door. "You need your sleep—we all do. If I know Cutter, he'll want an early start in the morning, so you'd best rest while you can."

"Okay," he said in a soft voice. "Sleep well, Maeve."

"And you," she said, giving him a wink before turning and stepping out of the room, closing the door behind her. *Sleep well.* Maeve appreciated the sentiment, truly she did, but she doubted that she would sleep well. Doubted, in fact, that she would sleep at all. More likely, she would spend hours tossing and turning, thinking and worrying, and regretting, that most of all. But even that lay somewhere beyond her, minutes or hours, there was no way to know for sure.

No, she would not shuffle to her room to lay and nestle curled up against her regrets and her fears. At least, not yet.

There was something she had to do first.

\*\*\*

It did not take her long to find him. There were others standing surrounding the great blaze, villagers mourning their dead, sending prayers up into the air to accompany the great pillar of dark smoke drifting into the sky. There were other forms, many, men and women who could have been anyone, their forms vague and indistinct in the darkness, yet it was not difficult to pick him out.

For one, there was the fact that he was far taller and wider at the shoulders than any of those others gathered around the fire, but mostly it was because while those others huddled in groups, those who had lost the most sobbing and wailing while those with them did their best to offer what little comfort they could, he stood alone. A lone figure receiving no comfort and giving none, a figure who stood so still that he might have been a statue placed to appear as if it regarded the flames.

She had known she would find him here, had been able to trace her way to him as easily as if she'd had a map. He doubted that, if he were asked, he could have explained what had brought him here to this great blaze within which the corpses of those villagers who had died burned, but she knew well enough. He had come because he *must* come, the same way that a moth must brave the flames of a torch, attracted to it by some imperative which it could not deny. Only fire waited for the moth in its coming, only the possibility of drifting too close and being burned and it was much the same with him, for there was nothing here, nothing but grief and pain.

But it was not grief, not pain that drew him. Neither was it, like the moth, the flame and the heat it provided. No, he was drawn, now, like always, to this place not from the fire or the grief and certainly not the comfort. He had been drawn to it because it was a place of death and now, as in all times since she had known him, her prince was drawn to death, seemed to gather it about himself like a cloak, like some dreaded creature of the night which survived only by the death of others. In the end, it changed nothing that the creature regretted its existence, its need to make use of such macabre fuel to sustain itself, for the creature, like the moth, could do nothing else.

She wondered as she approached what thoughts ran through his mind as he stood staring at the blaze. Did any? Or did he only stand there, absorbing the death, the grief, the way those others around him absorbed the heat of the great pillar of flame?

His back was to her, and he did not turn at her approach. The sound of her footsteps was covered by the cries of the bereaved and the sparking cinders of the dead as the fire crackled and popped, yet he grunted in recognition. "Maeve."

"Prince."

He did turn then, regarding her with a blank expression. "I've asked you not to call me that—I am a prince no longer."

"'Course not," she said, "and I'm not an old woman whose looks, such as they were, have been replaced with too many aches and pains to name. We are what we are, Prince, and we cannot change it just by the saying so. Priest was right about that much. I'm a woman who was once a celebrated beauty and who now is only old and tired and you..." She trailed off then, suddenly unable to finish.

"And me," he said, as if he knew well enough the words she'd left unspoken. "But some things do change, Maeve. Caterpillars turn into butterflies."

"We are not caterpillars, Prince," she said softly, realizing how his words echoed her own thoughts from days before. "We are people and we do not change so easily as that."

"Perhaps you are right," he said. It was not easy to tell—it never was as far as the prince was concerned—but she thought she detected the slightest bit of regret in his voice. She understood that regret, had seen it, heard it, in him before, and now, like then, she had no comfort to offer, so she only stood silently, turning to gaze at the fire.

"But you are not right in all of it," he said finally.

She turned to glance at him, raising an eyebrow. "Oh?"

He gave her a small smile, one that obviously cost him. "You are still beautiful, Maeve. Now as ever."

Despite everything, she felt her face flush with pleasure at his words. Ridiculous, of course, to feel pleasure in the midst of so much death, so much pain, but then she told herself that it was only the way of the world. Tragedies happened, *death* happened. People lost those they loved—she herself had lost many—and they moved on. After all, what else could they do? But even that was not the most ridiculous part of it, for she knew that she was not for him. She had wanted him, once, she like every other woman in the kingdom, for while Cutter might be a killer, might be terrifying, there was often beauty, attraction in terror. It was why people feared the night—rightly so from what she had seen—yet still spent so many hours gazing into it, why so many bards and artists chose it as the subject of their works. Scary, yes. Unsettling. But beautiful.

Cutter had been much the same fifteen years ago, and even now time had done nothing to detract from his allure. A big man, strong and powerful, and what lines time and pain had left on his once youthful, handsome features had not stolen their beauty but served, instead, to accentuate them. Yes, there had been a time when she had wanted him, and if she were being completely truthful with herself, part of her wanted him still. Wanted him in the same way that a woman might, upon seeing a terrible storm heading in her direction, neglect taking shelter, unable to pull her eyes away from the majesty, the horror of it. Yet as beautiful as she had once been, as famous as that beauty had once been, he had never been hers to have, not then and certainly not now.

After all, a woman might appreciate that storm, a moth might seek the flame, but they could not cuddle up against it, and it would not keep them warm when the world grew cold. No, Cutter was not a man for love, or if he was, it was not for her. There had been one woman, once, one who Maeve believed the big man had loved dearly, at least as much as a man like him was capable of loving anything, but that had been a long time ago and it was that love which had led, in the end, to so much tragedy, to so much death.

She knew that he could not love her, not like *that*, yet she found herself wanting to say something, wanting finally to divulge those feelings which she had held so close for so long, the feelings which she had never dared to share for fear of what he might say, what he might do. The words were on the tip of her tongue, threatening to spill out of her in a terrifying, damning, *relieving* flood—then a scream rose in the darkness, one not borne of fear or pain but of terrible grief, and she swallowed, choking the words back.

Now, standing among such grief, with the ashes of Ferrimore's dead rising in the air, was not the time. Perhaps there never would be one, and perhaps that was even for the best. After all, what good would it do? No good for her, certainly, and no good for him. More than that, it would not be fair, not for either of them, so now, like fifteen years ago, she chose to keep that love close, and lest the urge come upon her again, she decided to change the subject.

"He loves you, you know."

"Who?"

Matt. He loves you."

Cutter turned away from her, clearly uncomfortable, choosing the flame, choosing the dead, over the thought that the boy might love him. Others might have found it funny that a man who was at home on a battlefield with enemies seeking his death and a great axe in his hands and blood—his own and that of his enemies—staining him might be so discomfited by talk of love, but Maeve did not find it funny. Mostly, she found it sad.

When it was clear that Cutter would say nothing, she sighed. "He wants you to train him."

He grunted. "I know."

"And yet...?"

He turned back to her then, and though his face remained expressionless, she could see a storm of emotion in his gaze. "No. I...no."

She grunted. "You're probably right. Being who he is, there'll be no shortage of men and women wanting to see him dead, your brother chief among them. Better if he can do nothing to defend himself, if he's only left at the mercy of men who have none."

He frowned. "I would have thought you'd be glad."

"In a perfect world, perhaps. In a world where villages were not massacred just to make a point to one man, in a world where men and women were not forced to feed the bodies of their loved ones to the fire and watch their ashes drift on the wind. But we do not live in a perfect world, Prince, and it is not a kindness to send the boy out into it without the means to defend himself."

He turned away and several seconds passed, so that she began to think he would not answer. But then, he did. "I wanted to protect him, Maeve. I would not send him out into the world, if I could help it. It is why I took him to Brighton in the first place."

"And yet, the world found him," she said. "Your brother found him."

"I tried, Maeve," he said, turning to her. "I wanted...I wanted to keep him safe."

"I know," she said softly. "But no one is safe in this world, Prince, him least of all."

He met her eyes then, and his features twitched, as if the mask he always wore was threatening to come off. "What do I do, Maeve?"

She grunted, startled by the question. She had known her prince for a long time and had lost count of the scraps they'd been in, had lost track of the number of times they had faced seemingly impossible odds and yet had managed to come out the other side. And in all those years, in all those bloody battles, she had never known him to be uncertain. Even when their situation had seemed dire, their deaths imminent—perhaps, even, *especially* then—he had always seemed to know what to do, had been a creature of certainty, of will, and it had been that will which had carried them through so much when others would have, when others *had* fallen. He had braved assassins, armies of the Fey, creatures out of nightmare, had beaten some of the world's best warriors in single combat, and none of that had ever made so much as a crack in his seemingly insurmountable will. But where the world's greatest warriors and most dire threats had not marred that certainty, a young boy had.

A storm of emotions raged in Maeve then as she stared at his face, the mask of certainty gone for the first time she had ever seen, and chief among those was fear. Fear for what it might mean that the mask was finally slipping, for whatever else the man had been, brutal, often cruel, he had always been certain, and it had been that certainty, more than anything, which seemed to make him more than a man, which made him, instead, a force of nature. One that could never be defeated, could never be killed, one that a person could only hope to avoid or, if avoiding was impossible, hunker down beneath the force of it the way a family might hunker down at the approach of an impending storm.

It rocked her, seeing that mask slip, seeing that beneath it all, beneath the thousands of stories told about him, her prince was just a man after all. Suddenly she felt short of breath. She had not realized until that moment just how much she had come to rely on the man's strength, on his certainty even while she'd thought him less than human because of it. And he *was* less than human, that much she still believed, but he was more too. "You talk to him, Prince," she finally said.

He frowned. "Talk to him? What good will that do?"

"More than you know," she said honestly. "You have kept him alive thus far, a task most would have thought impossible, particularly since your brother has been hunting him since he was born. But it isn't enough only to *live*, Prince. We know that better than anyone...don't we?"

"What will I say?"

Asking her as if she somehow knew, he, the world's most feared man, staring at her with fear in his own eyes, waiting for her answer. And here, at least, she would not disappoint him. "The truth, Prince. He has not had an easy life so far, and I doubt it will get an easier. Tell him the truth."

"You mean...about his past? About...his mother?"

"Yes," she said, "for he deserves to know. But more than that, tell him how you feel." She leaned close. "Tell him about his father."

He recoiled at that as if she'd slapped him, his eyes widening with surprise. "The truth," he said quietly.

"Yes."

He considered that, seemed on the verge of agreeing, perhaps even on the verge of tears, a sight she would have never thought to see, but then his features shifted, and the fear and uncertainty left his face, and he was the man, the force, she had known once more. He regarded her with hard, blue, somehow cold eyes. "I will train the boy," he said finally, his voice dry and without any hint of emotion.

She stared at him for several seconds, trying to decide what she was feeling to see the mask in place once more. Was it regret? Relief? Perhaps it was a mixture of both. She sighed. "I think that will be good."

"But even so, that will not guarantee that he will be safe."

"No," she said. "This world, Prince, is full of much—pain and grief and fear. But guarantees, I'm afraid, are in short supply. As long as he is alive, the boy will have those who seek his death. As long as he is alive, Feledias will not stop until he sees him dead."

"You're saying that I cannot keep him safe."

"I'm saying that no one's safe, Cutter. Still, as for the boy's safety...I've got some ideas about that."

"What are they?"

She winced. "You're not going to like them."

He sighed. "No, no I don't expect I will."

"As long as the boy acts like a fugitive—as long as *you* act like he is—then he'll be treated like one. Feledias and his ilk will never stop hunting him, and the price on his head will only continue to increase."

"So what, then?"

She turned to him, meeting his eyes. "A fugitive can be hunted down, can be accosted everywhere he goes. But a prince—"

"No."

The word was a dry growl. The mask slipping again, but this time giving way not before sadness or fear but anger—and that, at least, was familiar. Maeve knew, logically, that the man would not kill her, that she was his friend or at least as close to one as a person like him was capable of having. The problem, though, was that knowing a thing logically and knowing it *emotionally* were very different. She believed she was the man's friend, but then she had thought of him, so recently, as a force of a nature, like a thunderstorm or a tornado. And only a fool tried to befriend either. Her mouth felt impossibly dry, and she cleared her throat. "What I mean—"

"*No*, Maeve," he rasped, and his great chest was rising and falling with suddenly rapid breaths. "I would not wish that on him, not on anyone. Princes are not known for living peaceful lives—that I know better than anyone."

She considered leaving it then. Perhaps only a fool would try befriending a thunderstorm, but it took a special kind of idiot to step into the maelstrom with a thought to challenging it. She was on the very verge of leaving it, in fact, but then she remembered the boy sitting on the bed, the boy who did not understand why so many wanted him dead, who was looking to her for the help he so desperately needed.

Maybe only a pure idiot would spit into a hurricane. And maybe she was that idiot, after all. "Don't you tell me no, *Cutter*," she snapped. "That boy has a birthright. And whether you want him to have it or not doesn't make any difference—that birthright is his, and it's going to follow him all his life. Better that he knows the truth, *all* of the truth. Besides, a fugitive can be hunted, can be killed, with little fuss, but princes are not so easily cast aside. And if his identity becomes known, your brother will not so easily be able to dispatch him, for the people would not sit idly by while a member of the royal blood was slain out of hand."

He stared at her, clearly surprised by her outburst, and she couldn't blame him—she was surprised herself. She waited tensely, holding her breath, to see if he would decide that he'd had enough of her and would reach for the great axe still strapped to his back. He did not though, and after a time, he grunted. "Even if I wanted to prove that he was a prince, it's useless. Feledias destroyed all the records of his birth—you know that as well as I do. As far as the world knows, Matthias doesn't exist at all, or at least he's just another fugitive from the law with a price on his head."

Maeve met his gaze, clearing her throat. "Not *all* the records."

He frowned, clearly trying to figure out what she meant, but she said nothing, only waited, watching him, letting him come to the realization on his own.

She saw it when it came, saw it in the tightening of his features, the narrowing of his eyes. "No."

"Cutter—Prince—it's the only wa—"

"Maeve, in case you've forgotten, the man has no love for me. Besides, last I heard, Feledias threw him in the dungeon. Likely as not, he's dead already, and even if he isn't, he may as well be, for there's no way we'd ever make it to him."

"You know he's not dead," she said. "The people are willing to put up with a lot from their princes, Cutter"—she paused, meeting his eyes meaningfully—"a *lot,* the gods know they've had to, but the people love Petran, and they would not sit by and watch him be executed. After everything that happened, they are already...disillusioned with the royals. To see their Petran killed...it would cause a revolt."

"Maybe," Cutter agreed, and there was no denying the reluctance in his voice, "but Feledias may not see it that way."

She grunted. "I don't have any love for your brother, Prince, but he is the cleverest man, the cleverest *person*—a far greater compliment as, by and large, men are fools while the gods saw fit to grant all the cleverness to women—I have ever met. If I have thought of it, rest assured that he has as well. No, the historian still lives, of that I am certain."

"Fine, probably you're right. But even if he does, the man isn't exactly loyal to the crown and especially not to me. Why would he help?"

"You're right," she admitted, "Petran is not loyal to the crown, but he *is* loyal to the truth, that above all else. It's the reason why the people love him so. He will share the truth of the prince's existence—of his birthright—not in service to you but simply in service to the truth."

He frowned. "Maybe. It will be dangerous."

She shrugged. "The truth is always dangerous, Prince. After all, it's the reason why Feledias saw fit to throw Petran into the dungeons in the first place just as it's the reason why your brother will never—*can never*—stop until Matt is dead."

She could have given him more reasons, a thousand to show him that her idea—while dangerous—was their only option, but she did not. Instead, she only stood silently, watching him, knowing that the tornado chose its path the way it would and no one—certainly not a foolish old woman with her best years far behind her—could leash it and guide it the way another might guide a dog. Besides, while Feledias was always known for his cleverness, for his ability as a tactician and a troop commander and Cutter, his brother, known only as a killer, Maeve knew the man well enough to know that he was no fool himself, possessed of a cunning many would not have credited him with.

Still, he took his time, considering. Then, finally he grunted. "It will not be easy, sneaking into the capital and into the dungeons to free him."

And that was all. For all his faults—and as far as she was concerned, Maeve thought the man had many—one of those things she had always admired about her prince was that, once a task was before him, no matter how grim, he did not hesitate as most did. Instead, as with so many other things in his life, he charged directly at it as if it were some enemy to be conquered. "No," she said, "it won't be easy. But then…when is it?"

He nodded then let out a heavy breath. "Okay. We'll leave tomorrow."

She put a hand on his shoulder, felt him tense beneath her. "You're doing the right thing."

He grunted, turning back to stare at the flame. "I hope you're right."

She watched him then. Others, not knowing him as well as she did, might not have seen the tenseness in his posture, might not have noticed the worry lines in his eyes, but she did, and she knew that that tenseness, that worry, was not for himself but for the boy. The love, it seemed, that he had felt for the mother had been transferred to her son.

"Will you rest?" she said. "If we are to go to the capital, we have a long journey ahead of us."

"Later," he said, and though it was only the single word, she could hear the dismissal in it. Not a rude one, but one that spoke of deep thoughts, one that spoke of the many fears and worries plaguing him.

"Goodnight, Bernard," she said softly. He did not turn or answer, his gaze, instead, remaining locked on the flames, on the corpses burning somewhere inside of them. Life all around him but now, as was so often the case, his gaze was locked on the dead.

She left him there, with the dead and the fire, left him surrounded by weeping villagers and the darkness. The darkness which hid none of the grief, the pain, which could be heard in the sobbing wails of those the Fey had left behind. The darkness that did not hide her worries, her regrets, and her fear, a fear largely surrounded around the way that, for the first time ever, she had seen her prince's mask—that mask of invincibility, of certainty—slip. Would it slip again, that mask? And would that slip happen when they needed it most? In the end, would she and those with her die not, as she had so long feared, because of the monster her prince could be, but because of the man he was?

No, the darkness did not hide her fear or her regrets. It did, however, hide the form of a figure lurking at the fire's edge, just as it hid the deep, dark bruise on his face, one so very recently acquired. It also hid his expression—a mixture of terror and excitement. It hid, too, the man's gaze, locked unerringly on Cutter's hulking form. The man standing, lurking in the shadows, had lost his wife and more recently still, his pride. Some, in the face of such loss, would have crawled into a corner and closed their eyes, doing their best, in their grief, to forget about the world and hoping, too, that it might forget about them. But this man did not do that. In him, those losses, so recent, so fresh, served, as they sometimes did, like chisels, chipping away at who he was, at the life he had built for himself, and when all else was scoured away, there was nothing left but hate. No hope at all—save, perhaps, the hope of revenge.

The darkness hid the man's features as they twisted in anger, but worst of all, it hid his furtive movements as he turned and disappeared into the shadows, heading for the village's edge, leaving one prince behind in search of another.

# CHAPTER TWENTY-FIVE

*The lion does not thank the man who feeds it, just as it does not wonder at the life of that which it devours.*
*It takes the meat, eats it, just as, if the man is foolish and comes too close, it will take the hand which feeds it.*
*To the beast, after all, meat is meat.*
*And men, the gods help us, are not so very different. Not so very different at all.*
*—Words found in a soldier's journal after battle during the Fey Wars*

They lay in the dew-laden grass, their forms nearly invisible amidst the green blades. They had been lying so for hours now, and Feledias's impatience was growing by the second as his anger, his thirst for revenge gnawed at his insides like some voracious, hungry rodent. A hunger which would never be sated until Bernard, his traitorous brother, was killed, he and all those who had chosen to follow him.

They had lain concealed so for hours, yet no one spoke, no one gave vent to the tired yawns which boredom often produced. Neither did they give voice to groans from aches and pains often occurring when men remained so still for so long. Not a single complaint was uttered, a single moan loosed, for many of those near fifty men with him shared Feledias's hate for his brother, had been wronged by him in some way. As for those who did not share his hate, they, too, remained silent, for they knew well what would happen to them should they jeopardize this opportunity—the best they'd had in years—to finally catch and punish the fugitive prince.

And so they lay still, the minutes ticking by, and with each that passed, Feledias's impatience, his anger, grew, until it was a rodent no longer but some great beast writhing within him, ripping and tearing at him in its anxiousness to get the thing done.

And into this silence, into this tense mood of anticipated murder, a man came. The horse on which he rode was a large beast, one considerably bigger than those coursers which the prince had ordered picketed some distance away so as not to reveal their position. A beast used not for war but for hard labor, and the man on it much the same, not a warrior, Feledias could see at a glance, but a man who, judging by his calloused knuckles and protruding gut, was a laborer, likely a farmer or woodcutter.

Feledias, while angry at the man's intrusion, was grateful, at least, to see that though the newcomer rode within a dozen paces of several of his troops, he did not notice him. He considered letting the man pass, had decided to do exactly that—after all, it would be his brother's luck to be happening out of the Wood only to see several dozen men rise from the tall grass and accost the rider—but then the man spoke.

Or, more accurately, yelled, his gaze turning this way and that. "Prince Feledias?" he shouted.

The soldiers nearest Feledias, including Commander Malex, shifted the slightest amount, glancing at Feledias as the man's shouting continued. Feledias was angry now, for even should they not show themselves, if his brother was close, he could not help but hear the man shouting his name, and even if they did not appear, his brother would likely not be willing to risk it, choosing to either go farther south in the Wood before exiting or, alternatively, to back track.

"Prince Fele—" the man started again, then let out a shout of shock as Feledias rose, followed a moment later by his soldiers, all of them seeming to appear out of the grass like phantoms, blades in hand. The man's mount, sharing its rider's surprise, backed up several paces, the man, in his shock, struggling to gain control of it. Feledias understood the man's discomfiture, one minute thinking himself alone, the next being surrounded by armed men, all ill-tempered from hours spent barely daring to move, to do anything but breathe, hours that might well have just been squandered by this fool with the bruised face.

"P-prince," the man said, his eyes wide, trembling.

"I am High Prince Feledias," he said, smiling without humor as he noted the way the man's eyes tracked to his bared blade and the bared blades of his soldiers around him. "And you are?"

"C-Cend's my name, sir, I mean, Prince...my lord."

Some farmer hick, a man who, in the right, natural course of things, would have never found himself in the presence of a royal *horse* let alone the kingdom's ruler. A reminder, if any was needed, of all that was wrong with the world, all caused by his brother's betrayal. "Cend," Feledias said, allowing some of his anger to creep into his tone. "And what, exactly, has brought you here to disrupt me and my men at our work?"

"W-work, my lord?" the man asked.

Feledias bared his teeth. "Bloody work, farmer. Now, before you become a part of it, tell me why you have come, why you ride a cart horse and shout my name."

"F-forgive me, my lord," he stammered, "I did not mean to...that is..."

He trailed off, and Feledias glanced at his troops, sharing an amused smile before looking back to the man. "Out with it, farmer. We are busy men and have little time for your stupidity."

"O-of course, Prince," the man managed, looking far stupider, in that moment, than the weary mount on which he rode, ludicrous really. The peasant cleared his throat, glancing nervously around. "I-it's your brother, my lord."

The dark humor which Feledias had been feeling vanished in that moment. At least, the humor did. The darkness, as ever since his brother's betrayal, remained. "What of him?" he said, moving forward, and there must have been some hint of his sudden change in mood either in his movements or his voice, for the man's face grew pale.

"I...that is, you're looking for him, aren't you, my lord? Your brother?"

Feledias frowned, his eyes narrowing. "And if I were? Speak quickly, farmer. Have you heard some news of my wayward brother's whereabouts?"

"N-not as such, my lord," the man managed.

Feledias let out a growl and, reading his desires, two of his soldiers surged forward and in another moment the farmer was letting out a squeal similar, no doubt, to one of those barnyard pigs he likely raised as he was ripped off his mount and thrown onto the ground, two bared blades poised at his throat.

"Then *why*," Feledias hissed, "have you come?"

"I-I didn't hear of h-him, my lord," the man stammered, his voice squeaking with his fear, his bruised face writhing with panic, "I-I saw him, I did."

"*Saw* him?"

"Y-yes, my lord," the man said, staring at the blades.

"Do not watch the swords, for your eyes will not stop them from doing their work should I order it," Feledias said. "Only your voice might do that. Now, tell me, where did you see my brother? The Black Woods?"

"T-the Black Woods? F-forgive me, my lord, no. He is in my village. Ferrimore."

Feledias frowned. "Ferrimore." He knew the place, of course, knew every town and city, every shithole in the entire kingdom, for even before his Bernard's betrayal, while his brother had focused on killing—anyone, really, on that point he was never particular—it had been Feledias's job to follow behind him, cleaning up the mess, appeasing terrified, grieving villagers who inevitably suffered when his brother passed through.

"Ferrimore?" Commander Malex asked from behind him, his surprise clear in his tone. "But how? Surely he should have went to Valaidra. Why would he have chosen Ferrimore instead?"

"There is only one reason," Feledias said, his hands clenching into fists at his sides. "He knew we were waiting for him."

The soldiers shared uneasy glances at that. "Forgive me, my prince," the commander said, "but how could he? How could he possibly have known?"

Feledias's frown deepened. "I think I know. It is that pet mage of his—I saw him, before, was present when he had one of his...fits. Visions, he calls them. More than once, those visions saved my brother and his merry little band from disaster."

"You mean the mage, Challadius?" Malex asked, surprised. "But...he died, didn't he? Fifteen years ago?"

Feledias hissed. "An illusion, no doubt. My brother's pet mage has a knack for those, if nothing else."

Malex frowned, perhaps doubting it, but that was fine, just so long as he kept his doubts to himself. Feledias, though, knew it was true, *felt* it, inside himself. The mage was back. A foolish mistake, for he could have went on living in whatever pathetic rathole he'd crawled into and done so for a few more years. Of course, Feledias would have hunted him down eventually, once he'd dealt with his brother, but he promised himself now that he would make the taking of the man's life, the tearing apart of it bit by bit, a priority. But first, there was the farmer to deal with.

He turned back to the man. "How long ago did he pass through Ferrimore?"

"B-beggin' your pardon, my lord," the farmer said, "but he didn't pass through. Him and the others with him, they're still there—they took rooms at the inn not a couple of hours gone."

Feledias felt his breath catch in his throat at that, but something the man said caught his attention, and he forced himself to remain calm, forced himself to resist the urge to sprint to the horses and to go riding off in the direction of Ferrimore as quickly as possible. It was something his brother would have done, in the past, trusting in himself—and more importantly, his axe—to carve his way past whatever problems a decision made in haste might produce. Feledias, though, had always been, by necessity, the thinker of the family, the strategist, and so he resisted the compulsion, kneeling beside the farmer instead. "Others? What others?"

The man's bruised face screwed up in thought, no doubt thought made more difficult by the swords at his throat. "There was a young lad, a boy, really, seemed scared of his own shadow, you ask me. And a fat man in purple trousers, the most ridiculous set I've ever seen. And...and a woman."

Feledias frowned. "Woman?"

"That's right," the man answered, nodding quickly. "A woman."

"Well?" Feledias demanded. "What did she *look* like, fool?"

"A...an older woman, my lord," the man said, "in her forties, perhaps. Pretty though. Handsome."

"Maeve," Malex said from beside him, and Feledias turned, giving the man a small smirk.

"Oh, that's right. You and Marvelous had a bit of a tryst, didn't you?" He watched the man carefully. "I trust, Malex, that you will not allow the past to hamper the carrying out of your duty."

"Of course not, my lord," the man said, "I wouldn't think of it."

Feledias nodded, leaning back. "Of course not." He gave a thoughtful hum. "Maeve the Marvelous, it appears, has returned from her self-imposed exile. It seems my brother is getting the whole band back together."

"But why?" Malex asked, genuine curiosity in his tone. "What does he intend?"

Feledias rose. "The same thing he always intends, no doubt. My brother is many things, Malex, but complicated is not one of them. He intends to fight. So come—let us accommodate him. If we ride hard, we should reach Ferrimore within the hour."

He started away but paused when Malex spoke. "And what about…him, my lord?"

Feledias turned back, frowning at the farmer who he had nearly forgotten about in his urgent need to come to grips with his brother and the other traitors who followed him. "Ah yes, our dear peasant. Tell me, man, what do you think should be done with you?"

The man licked his lips nervously, his gaze traveling between the two soldiers above him. Fear was there, in his gaze, but as Feledias watched, something else arose within it too. Greed. "Might be…" The man hesitated, clearing his throat. "Might be…I could get a reward?"

"A reward," Feledias said, musing over the words, rubbing at his chin in consideration. Then he gave a single nod. "Very well. And a reward you shall have, dear peasant." The man started to smile, but the expression froze on his face as Feledias spoke on. "A traitor's reward. For you see, whatever else he is, my brother is still a prince of the realm, and you the man who, out of greed and anger—for do not think me such a fool that I cannot guess at who has done the work on your face—have chosen to betray him."

He glanced at the two guards standing over the man and gave them a single nod. He turned to start away, pausing again when Malex spoke.

"But, my prince," Malex said, "are you sure? He came to help, after all. Had he not come, we would not have known—"

"I'm sure, Malex," Feledias said. "Ferrimore has chosen to aid my brother, to give him sanctuary, and so they must be punished, *will* be punished. And it would be better, I think, if no witnesses remained to tell of what happened." He met the man's eyes. "Don't you?"

"Sir?" Malex asked, a stricken look on his face. "Y-you mean to destroy the village?"

"Me?" Feledias asked. "Of course not. I am a prince of the realm, Commander Malex. Sworn to protect and serve the citizens of our great kingdom. I would, of course, offer no harm to my citizens. The Fey though...well. It seems that they have attacked the village once. I do not doubt that they might do so again. After all, if the Fey are known for anything, it is for their inexplicability. Now…" He paused, glancing back at the farmer once more, the man staring at him in shock as if he still had yet to fully realize what was going to happen. "Finish it. We leave—now."

Feledias started toward where the horses were picketed, his soldiers, save the two left to deal with the farmer, following. He heard the farmer screaming behind him, begging, but there was the whistle of metal in the air, and then only silence. Feledias moved to his horse.

# CHAPTER TWENTY-SIX

*Death is a fickle thing.*
*Sometimes, it comes with a roar, like the thunder of battle cries as armies meet.*
*Other times, it is subtle, quiet, sneaking up on a man before he is even aware of its coming.*
*The flash of metal in the shadows, the whistle of an arrow high overhead.*
*Sometimes, death comes quietly. Sometimes, it comes loudly.*
*There is no way, then, to know how death might come, when it does.*
*As death is concerned there is only one certainty, one inarguable truth—*
*It comes.*
*—Unknown author*

He lay on his stomach on a hill outside Ferrimore, his bow and quiver placed beside him. The tall grass concealed him from any except the closest of inspections, though it also tickled at his skin where it touched his hands and face. But he ignored the urge to scratch that itch just as he ignored the aches in his back and knees. It might have proven difficult for some, ignoring those sensations, but then few had as much practice at it as Valden had himself. His life, after all, seemed to largely consist of such aches, such tickles of grass, and, of course, such hillsides. And now, like those other times, he told himself that it was nothing, that the ache in his back was nothing. After all, while the goddess promised that the path to peace would be taken one step at a time, she never promised that each of those steps would be pleasant, and a man grew in himself more from his pains than his pleasures anyway.

He told himself that, but with the grief of the guardsman still haunting him despite what meager efforts he'd given to assuage it, Priest was forced to wonder why it often seemed, on the path to peace, that each step was harder than the last. Some might have thought that experience would make such hillsides, such naked grief as he'd seen on the guardsman's face and seen so often before, easier, but they would have been wrong. Instead, it felt as if they grew harder each time, but there was nothing to be done except to move forward, or, in this case, to lie still. And wait.

Likely, his waiting would amount to nothing, but he would wait just the same. Cutter was the warrior, Challadius the mage, Maeve, while she would label herself as an assassin, was often the voice of reason, of pragmatism. As for Priest, he was the scout, the man who watched their backs so that his comrades might worry about what lay ahead. And so he did it now, lying on the hillside and watching the road into Ferrimore lest the Fey or, particularly unlikely, Feledias and his men, found them here.

Yet, he did not begrudge the wait, for he knew that his being here would allow the others to get what troubled sleep they may. Not much of a gift, perhaps, just as his compassion, his attempts at sympathy for the guardsman were not much, but it was the best he could give them, and so he would.

He lay there for several hours until he grew certain that the night would pass in merciful, restful quiet after all. He said a silent prayer to the goddess in thanks and started to rise. That was when he caught sight of figures in the far distance, vague shadows in the moonlight, what some might have taken as no more than shadows or figments of their eyes produced by the distance. Priest, though, had seen such shadows before, countless times, and so he knew they were not shadows, nor figments. Knew instead that they were what they were—soldiers. Soldiers on the move, and judging by the uniformed organization of their movements, they were not the Fey returned to torment Ferrimore once more. No, this was an altogether different and, in its way, worse, torment.

"Goddess guide my path," he whispered. He considered his best course, for the men were mounted and while his own mount was tied at the base of the hill, he could see, even from here, that the approaching soldiers rode war mounts while his own was a draft horse borrowed from the village. He would never be able to outrun them or beat them to the village should they take it in mind to give the beasts they rode their head.

Which meant that they needed to be slowed down somehow. Priest said another prayer, this one not searching for a solution but only for forgiveness. Then he rose, lifted his bow from where it lay beside him and withdrew one arrow from his quiver before slinging it over his back. The figures were far distant, they and their horses little more than blurs. Most would have never attempted such a shot, sure of failure, but then Priest had been on this hillside—or at least a thousand like it—before, had taken such shots before, so he did not hesitate.

He drew the string of his bow back, calculating the range before raising the bow so that the arrow pointed almost straight up. He took a slow breath then breathed it out, releasing the string as he did. The arrow flew high into the air, so high that it seemed to be meant to pierce the moon itself, and at such a height, it seemed it could land anywhere. But of course it could not, for once fired, arrows had only one destination, only one result, and the result of this one was to strike one of the rider's at the front of the column.

Perhaps the man cried out, perhaps not. At this distance, there was no way to tell for sure, but Priest saw movement, a slight shifting of the shadows which he took to be the man falling from his saddle. His skills, then, remained even after fifteen years. He did not know whether to be thankful or sad for that fact. Perhaps both.

Saying another prayer for the fallen man, that he might pass through the veil with as little pain, as little fear, as possible, Priest made his way down the hill to his horse. The beast fidgeted as he secured his bow, as if it could read his troubled mood through his touch. He took a moment to gives its muzzle a rub, offering what comfort he could, taking what comfort he could. "It's okay, boy," he whispered. "It's okay."

The horse tossed its head as if to say that whatever things were, they were far from okay, and with no argument to make, Priest swung into the saddle. "Come," he said, "we must be fast now, for there is little time."

And with that, he turned and rode back to the village at a gallop, pushing the beast beneath him to its limit. The arrow, appearing out of nowhere and striking down one of their number, should slow the troops down, but he knew that, when no others followed, they would resume their pace soon enough. He had bought them some time that was all, and he could only hope that it would be enough.

*** 

He stood as the great blaze died down, as those mourners who had gathered around it began to depart, seeking the shelter and the dubious comfort of homes that would, going forward, be emptier than they had. At least of people. There was the absence, of course, an absence they would feel at their shoulders, in their beds, an absence that loomed and brought with it a very painful, very *loud* silence.

They departed bit by bit, in small, grieving knots, and eventually he was left alone with the dead, to breathe air which felt thick with the grief that had concentrated there minutes ago. It lingered, grief, lingered even after the cause of it was nothing but dust. It was a truth Cutter had known for a long time, one he had been taught and had, in his turn and to his shame, taught to many others.

And into that grief, that silence, a sound intruded, the sound of a galloping horse. He turned in the direction from which it came and, moments later, he saw a horse racing toward him, one upon which Priest rode, the archer's face grim. As he brought the horse to a rearing halt and leapt from his saddle, Cutter did not have to ask the man what was wrong, what the cause of his haste, for there could only be one thing.

"How long?"

The man gave a shake of his head, obviously weary. "Not long. An hour. Maybe less. Your brother and fifty men at least."

Cutter nodded grimly. "Go wake the others."

Priest nodded. "What will you do?"

Cutter glanced in the direction of the village gate, the one they had come through so recently. "If I know my brother, he will send a man ahead, a scout meant to locate us, to keep an eye on us. I will go and meet him. I'll catch up with you at the inn."

The man hesitated, watching him for a moment. "The man who comes. You will kill him?"

Cutter rolled his shoulders to rid them of some of the soreness standing still for so long had caused. "Yes."

The man looked as if he wanted to say something more, but in the end he only nodded. "Good luck, Prince."

With that, he turned and started away at a run, leaving his weary mount. Cutter watched him go. *Good luck,* the man had said, and while Cutter was grateful for the well wishes, he did not think that luck was needed, not for this man, at least. After all, the man needed to be killed, and in that, if in nothing else, there were few better than Cutter.

He turned and started toward the gate.

# CHAPTER TWENTY-SEVEN

*The greatest illusions are the ones we cast on ourselves.*
*Trust me—I should know. Gods help me, I should know.*
            *—Challadius "The Charmer"*

She was beautiful, the woman—and why not? After all, while the illusions he cast in his waking hours were always marred by one flaw or another, one often only he could see, the illusions his dream-mind created were far more thorough and, of course...entertaining.

The woman had a thin, toned waist, shapely thighs, and long hair that hung down into his face as she sat atop him. Beautiful, which was good. Eager, which was also good, but the best of all was that the woman did not scowl at him or make him feel like a fool with a single look, not the way Maeve did.

Beautiful enough, eager enough, that he could almost forget that she was not, strictly speaking, real. Her hands were on his chest which, by a trick of the fact that it was a dream and he its dreamer, was more muscular and less hairy than in real life. Her legs were around his waist which, by some slightly more powerful trick, was thin enough for them to fit around.

And her mouth was busy panting and saying things—all nice. Things about him, about how strong he was, how manly, nothing like those things Maeve would say to him, nothing like those sentences, those words which she'd wield nearly as effectively as the prince would his axe, cutting him down with seemingly little to no effort, likely not even being fully aware, at the time, just how deep her words wounded him.

And he would not tell her, not now, not ever. Those illusions created by Chall's magic, those he wove with his spells like a tailor might weave a dress from idle strands of cloth, did not exist for long. But this illusion, the one regarding Maeve and his feelings for her, he had maintained for over twenty years and would continue to maintain it, not by his magic but by his will, by his fear, a terrible, gnawing fear of what she might say should she find out. Would she mock him? Would she laugh? Chall could handle a lot from a lot of people, had been called every name imaginable and, most of the time, had deserved it, but he could not handle that. It was better to maintain the illusion. Better not to know.

Perhaps that made him a coward, but that was no great surprise. He had known that about himself for a long time now, had made his peace with it. And so, he pushed all those errant thoughts aside, focusing instead on the woman on top of him. She would not mock him, not laugh, or taunt, and what pain she caused would be so intermingled with pleasure that a man could not tell where one ended and the other began. In the face of all of that, the fact that she was not real, was little more than a mild inconvenience. After all, every couple had their problems.

Suddenly one of her hands grabbed him more roughly, and he frowned. "Easy," he said. "Take it easy."

The woman continued to smile, continued to rock and tell him how great of a lover he was, but her grip on his chest tightened, and she gave him a rough shake. "Wake up, Chall," she said.

Strange, for a dream to be asking him to wake up. Stranger still for the woman to speak in the familiar voice of Priest, strange and more than a little uncomfortable. "Wake up. Now."

Then he was blinking his eyes open, and it was not the woman he was staring at anymore but the wizened features of the Priest, a grim expression on his face. Thankfully, the man was not sitting on top of him as the woman had been, but was instead standing beside the bed, looking like bad news waiting to be heard.

Chall didn't want to be that someone, would have gone through quite a bit to avoid it, but he sighed and slid up into the bed so that his back was propped against the wall. "Let me guess," he grunted, rubbing an arm at eyes gummy with sleep, "we're fucked."

The other man frowned at the profanity, but apparently his news was important enough that he didn't dare waste time on yet another lecture. That, of course, was a very bad sign, for the man loved his lectures more than anything, so even before he started to tell Chall just how well and truly doomed they were, he'd already risen and started pulling on his boots.

This, of course, made him notice the purple pants he was wearing—the bright color visible beneath dirt stains—and he had a thought that he really ought to take the time to visit a tailor, buy some trousers which were a touch less ridiculous. After all, he was going to make a damned ugly corpse—sooner rather than later, it seemed—and there wasn't any need to be wearing purple trousers of all things. Chall knew he was ridiculous, odd, had largely embraced that fact...but even he had his limits.

"The others?" he asked when the man had finished an abbreviated version of what was happening, possibly short enough to fit on their tombstones.

"Here."

Chall followed the sound of the voice to the door where Maeve stood, and despite his efforts at his dreaming, she was far more beautiful now, even harried and clearly worried, than the woman of his dreams had been. Older, yes, but not lessened by the years. Instead, she had been magnified by them, and what few wrinkles lined her face did nothing to mar her beauty, served only instead to outline it. Seeing her so recently after the dream, after his thoughts of her, Chall felt his face flush with embarrassment, feeling as if somehow she must know exactly what his thoughts had been, a small smile, what might have been a smirk on her face, that seemed to support that.

"We're in a bit of a hurry," she went on, "you know, impending death and all, but are you sure you don't want to take a moment,"—she paused, staring meaningfully at his pants—"maybe change your trousers?"

Chall didn't have any trousers to change into, would have done so long ago if he had, his travel bag, such as it was, consisting of mostly empty bottles of liquor, and a ratty blanket most homeless people would have thrown out long ago. He could have told her as much but, of course, Chall never told the truth when he could lie instead, particularly to Maeve, so he smiled—difficult considering what Priest had just told him. "Why would I do that while these are perfectly fine?"

She grunted. "Not the word I'd use."

Chall glanced between the two of them. "Cutter?"

"Keeping an eye out," Priest said.

Chall grunted. Which meant likely someone—whoever the first of Feledias's troops was—was getting ready to have a real shit day. "And has anyone woken the lad up yet?"

"I thought maybe you'd like to do that," Priest said.

Chall frowned, glancing at Maeve who only shrugged before looking back at Priest. "Why?"

The man gave him that small, knowing smile, the one that always gave Chall the urge to punch him in the face, an urge he would have long since given into if he wasn't quite so much of a chicken shit. "Why not?" Priest asked.

Well, there wasn't time to sit and argue about it, not unless they meant to race to see who died first, so he grunted. "Whatever." Then he turned and started for the door.

\*\*\*

Maeve watched the mage walk out of the door and head toward Matt's room. He did a good job hiding it, of trying to perpetuate the lie that he was fine—few, after all, had more practice at lying than *that* false bastard—yet she knew him well enough to know he was scared. And why not? He, much like her, had spent the last fifteen years of his life trying to avoid a fate pretty much exactly like this one. Had, in many ways, given up his life to save it, and Maeve knew that feeling well. Knew the feeling of never being able to get a completely restful sleep, for the worry was always there, in the back of your mind, the worry that today would be the day, tonight the night, when the fate she had feared for so many years would finally find her.

All that sacrifice just to stay alive, a sacrifice that she was beginning to think wasn't worth it, for what had it bought her but nights spent waking in cold sweats, days spent looking over her shoulder sure that *this* time, Feledias and his men would be there? Chall had sacrificed just as much to live, and while he loved to pretend at selfishness—likely even believed his own lies in that regard—he had been willing to give all of that up the moment he'd seen that their prince was in trouble. Not a selfish man then and not a coward, no matter what he acted like.

She watched until the man—looking thoroughly uncomfortable—stopped in front of the lad's door.

Maeve decided to leave him to it, turning back to Priest. "Why?" she asked, genuinely curious. "Why send him? Do you think that, what, seeing Chall will make the boy worry less?"

Priest gave her a small smile as he started toward the door. "I didn't do it for him—I did it for Chall. He will be brave, confident, for the boy. He will be it because he has to. Now, we had better go—our prince will be waiting.

With that, he walked past her, pausing only briefly to put a gentle, comforting hand on her shoulder, offering her a nod of his head before continuing on.

\*\*\*

Matt woke with a gasp as water splashed into his face, sputtering in a panicked moment feeling as if he were drowning. Then that moment, that fear, subsided, and he blinked up to see the heavy-set man called Chall standing over him. "Hey," he managed, running an arm across his dripping face, "what did you do that for?"

The man shrugged. "You been walkin' a while, lad. Might be no one else is ready to tell you, but you could do with a bath. We all could. But there's no time for one, not now, probably not for a while, so I'm thinking this is probably as close as you're going to get." He set the now-empty glass down. "Well. Best be getting up and putting your boots on. We're set to leave."

"Leave?" Matt asked, confused and still struggling to shake off the heavy sleep that had come over him the second he'd laid his head down. "But...when?"

The other man raised an eyebrow. "When you get your boots on."

"But...but it's still night," he said, glancing at the window where darkness could be seen outside. "I mean...isn't it?"

"So it is," Chall agreed. "Unfortunately, revenge-mad princes have a tendency of not taking others' feelings into consideration as much as they might."

Matt blinked, still struggling to catch up with what the man was telling him. "Revenge-mad princes?"

"That's right. Princes like the one approaching Ferrimore right now, along with fifty or so of his troops. The same one that, the way it's looking, will be here knocking on the door before you *put your damned boots on.*"

That was enough to get him moving, to wipe the remaining cobwebs of sleep away, and Matt jumped to his feet, finding his boots and tugging them on. "W-what do we do?"

Chall winced. "We go and find Pri—Cutter. He'll know what to do. He always does. Now, come on, lad. We're running out of time."

Matt felt terror gripping him, terror and a sense of hopelessness. He had left his home, had watched from a distance as it and everyone he loved was burned to the ground. He had traveled through the Black Woods, a place he'd heard horror stories of for as long as he could remember and, somehow, had come out the other side alive only to find that their pursuers had found them almost immediately. He was tired, exhausted, and he was scared, so he did the only thing he could do—when the other man hurried out of the room and down toward the common area of the inn, he followed him.

The wounded were still there, still being overseen by the innkeeper who, the night before, had terrified Matt, but who now he paid little mind as he was already about as terrified as he was likely to get. But terrified or not, he could not help but notice that there were far fewer wounded—and caretakers—than there had been. He would like to believe that was because many of those the caretakers had been tending to had gotten well enough to leave on their own. Certainly, the Matt from a week ago would have believed exactly that. But then that Matt had not seen his village burned, his friends and family killed. That Matt had not nearly been devoured by a creature out of nightmare, or hunted for days by men who wanted to kill him for reasons he still did not understand.

He wanted to believe that those wounded had gotten better, but he did not. Instead, he thought it more likely that those poor souls had succumbed to their wounds despite the healers' efforts. A dark thought, perhaps, but one that seemed to be substantiated by the grim expressions on the faces of those remaining caretakers—who looked little better than those they tended—and by the innkeeper herself who moved among them like a troupe manager backstage, always there when she was needed to direct, assist or console the wounded and those who cared for them.

He felt a hand on his shoulder and turned to see Chall staring at him, something like compassion in his face. "Come, lad," he said quietly. "There's nothing we can do for them."

"B-but...you're a mage, aren't you?" Matt asked hopefully. "Can't you...I don't know, cast a spell or something?"

The heavy-set man winced. "My magic, I'm afraid, is not the useful kind. Now, come on. The others are waiting for us."

And indeed, they were, for a quick look showed the man, Priest, they'd called him, and Maeve standing by the door. They both looked tense, ready, but if they felt any of the overwhelming terror that was currently gripping Matt then they hid it well.

The mage started toward them. Matt hesitated, looking back once more at those wounded, wishing he could help them somehow. In the end, though, he moved toward the others who were currently engaged in a hushed conversation.

"—haven't seen him, yet," Maeve said.

"He said he would meet us," Priest replied, "and so he will be here."

Chall grunted. "I don't like this, not at all. Feledias is almost here and—"

Maeve glanced over, seemed to notice Matt for the first time, and made a shushing noise, cutting the mage off. "Did you get some good sleep, Matt?" she asked, obviously making an attempt to force cheer into her voice.

"I-I guess," he said, glancing between them. "If they're almost here, the men hunting me, I mean, then what do we do?"

"First," Chall whispered, glancing behind him, "you speak quieter, boy. There's no need to go making a scene. And after that..."

"We wait," Maeve said. "For Cutter."

No sooner had she finished speaking than the door opened and standing in the dark doorway as if his name had called him, was Cutter, the man Matt had known since he was a child and who he was recently realizing he had not known at all, not really. His hulking form filled the doorway, and he was forced to duck under the lintel as he stepped inside. Cutter noted his companions immediately and moved toward them.

As he approached, Matt couldn't help but notice fresh spatters of blood staining the man's front and his hands, noted, too, that the big man's knuckles were raw and scraped.

"We were wondering when you'd decide to show up," Chall said.

Maeve looked the man up and down. "Trouble?"

Cutter grunted in assent. "Feledias isn't on his way to the village anymore, he—"

"But that's great," Matt interrupted, feeling a heady sense of relief. "If he isn't—"

"No, lad," Chall interrupted, watching Cutter's face, the grim expression on it. "He isn't on his way—he's here alrea—"

The door burst open again, and they all spun to see the guardsman from the gate. The man was panting and coated in sweat, and, Matt was surprised to see, grinning. The innkeeper hurried forward. "What is it, Rolph? What's happened?"

"It's High Prince Feledias, Netty!" the guardsman exclaimed through panting breaths, a wide grin on his face.

"The High Prince?" the woman asked, frowning. "What about him?"

"He's *here,* Netty," the guard said.

"Here?" the woman asked, clearly surprised, and Matt couldn't blame her. After all, he had lived in Brighton, a village about the size of Ferrimore, for his entire life, and they had never once had the prince visit. Except, of course, for when he did come and burned the village to the ground.

"Yes, *here,*" the man said, "in Ferrimore. Or, at least, just outside of it. Guardsman Pender was speaking to them when I left, thought I'd come ahead and give you warning, so you could get the place ready or..." He shrugged, taking a deep breath. "Or whatever."

"But *why?*" Netty asked with a frown, apparently not as ready to celebrate as the guardsman. "Why would he come here?"

"Well, it's obvious, ain't it?" the guardsman asked. "He must have heard of our troubles with the Fey, that's all. Must have heard of it and come to help us. He's come to *help,* Netty!"

There were shouts of excitement from wounded and caretaker alike at that, and the guardsman, grinning, moved off toward them, speaking on as those who could gathered around him.

The innkeeper, though, remained, and when she turned to look at Cutter, she was not smiling. She moved toward them, her frown deepening with each step. "Two princes in as many days," she said, watching Cutter as if searching for something. "Ferrimore's never been so popular."

She watched the big man silently, perhaps waiting for Cutter to respond, but he said nothing, only letting the silence speak for him.

The innkeeper grunted, giving a single nod as if she'd just had some suspicion confirmed. "And you lot, it's not just bad timin', you all leavin' in the middle of the night just as your brother's arrivin' at our gates. Is it?"

"No," Cutter said. "It isn't."

The woman nodded again. "Heard some tale about you two brothers bein' at odds, though can't say I know the specifics, can't say I've ever felt the lack of not knowin' either. We got our own life here in Ferrimore, with plenty enough to worry about on our own without gettin' involved with princes and their squabbles. Or, at least we had our own life." She frowned at him. "Didn't we?"

Again, Cutter said nothing, and the woman sighed. "Your brother, Prince Feledias. He hasn't come to help, has he?"

Cutter shook his head. "No."

"He's come for you."

"Yes."

"And as for us? Us lowly non-royal peasants? What sort of greeting might we expect from this royal brother of yours?"

Instead of answering, Cutter turned to the others, meeting Maeve's eyes in particular. "Best get them moving, Maeve. I'll catch up with you in a moment."

"Sounds great," the woman said dryly. "Only, where exactly might we be moving to?"

"Let's start with 'away.' We'll head west, toward the capital. I'll meet you in just a moment."

"Come on, lad," Maeve said gently, putting a hand on Matt's shoulder, "better be on our way."

Matt hesitated, looking at the innkeeper, the woman watching Cutter with hard eyes. There was something, some terrible knowledge looming in his mind like some great monolithic figure in the mist, indistinct yet threatening and full of some unnatural menace. It was a knowledge, a truth, that he thought he could see in the innkeeper's gaze as well. Yet that knowledge, that truth was too obscured by the fog of his own fear, his own desire to run and get as far away as possible from those hunting him for him to understand it.

Swallowing, he turned and allowed himself to be led out of the inn.

\*\*\*

Cutter watched Maeve and the others leave then turned back to the innkeeper, the woman staring at him with undisguised anger.

"Gettin' the boy to leave. Clever," the woman said dryly. "Don't want any folks hanging around watchin' when you commit murder."

"I have offered none of your people harm."

"Thing is, Prince, that ain't exactly true, is it? Cend would certainly disagree, and I think his bruised face and bruised pride are just about the least of our worries right now, considerin' your brother is knockin' on our door."

There was nothing to be said, no way to make it better, for he knew what would happen now, they both did. What *must* happen. "I'm sorry," he said.

Her face worked for a moment, a flurry of emotions chasing their way across her features. Then, finally, she scowled. "Damn your sorry," she said. "These are good people here. People that don't deserve what they're gettin'."

No one ever did, but Cutter didn't think now was the time to say that, so instead he nodded. "I'm sorry."

"Are you?" she asked, watching him closely. "Are you really? Seems to me you're just as heartless as the stories say. A beast, they call you, and I think they call it right. But what do you think, *Prince?*"

Once more he said nothing, for he did not have the words to make it right, to make it okay, even if such words existed. And even if they did, even if he *did* have them, there was no time to speak them, not now. He turned to go, and she reached out, snatching his arm.

"Don't you walk away from me, you *monster*," she growled, nearly shouting it, and he turned back to see her glaring at him, to see that many of the caretakers seeing to the wounded had paused in their labors and their excited whispering to look over, their good moods clearly giving way to confusion at their de facto leader's anger.

He looked past her, and she snarled, turning and following his gaze. "Everything's alright," she said, forcing a false joviality into her tone, "this big fella here just turned down my proposition for a drink, that's all. Why don't you all mind your business, maybe get ready." She turned back to glance at Cutter as she finished. "Got us a prince visitin'," she said loudly. "Reckon we'll want to look our best."

They all grinned, wounded and caretaker alike, and soon they were ensconced in hurried, whispered conversation again, excited as they had a right to be, about a visit from their royal prince. They had no way of knowing, save some rumors which, while they reached far, might not have reached so far as this out of the way village, that their princes were not worthy of their love or their excitement.

"They love you," Cutter said, wondering how such a thing might feel, to engender anything in those you met besides hate or fear and knowing that he would never know.

"Helps that I don't get them all butchered by a revenge-mad prince," she said.

He wanted to say sorry again, to tell her that he had not intended this, but he had said it already, and his feelings would do nothing to save them from the dark fate visiting their village. So he nodded instead, deciding to leave it there. Not a good place to leave it, perhaps, but then when you had just single-handedly spelled the death of an entire village, there wasn't a good way. Another weight, then, to add to that already accumulated on his back, a weight of regret and shame that he had carried with him for as long as he could remember, dragging it behind him.

He turned, heading toward the door.

"He'll find out, you know," the woman said.

He paused, glancing back at the innkeeper.

"The boy," she said. "He'll find out who you are. *What* you are."

"Yes," he said quietly. "He's finding out already." And with that, he turned and walked into the darkness, leaving his victims—still living, still breathing and walking around, but not for long—behind him.

***

They were waiting for him outside, Maeve and Chall and Priest watching him with the knowledge of what was coming in their eyes. After all, there had been other villages in the past, other massacres, some which they had fled, others which they had perpetrated. They knew this, for they, like he, still bore the scars of those slaughters, carried them as constant, daily reminders of how fragile human life could really be. It was as if everything—society, the idea of civilization and being civilized, every human construct—was made of glass. It was not a matter of if it would shatter, for its shattering was as inevitable as death. And when it did, it would reveal that "civilization" was no more than a fantasy, a thin transparent veil that the beast that was humanity draped across itself, imagining—incorrectly—that it covered its shameful nakedness.

Perhaps even managing to, for a time. But the veil would slip—it always did—and what it hid was ugly and cruel and without virtue.

"It's time to go," Cutter said, starting forward.

The others followed, saying nothing, their expressions etched with agony at the knowledge of the villager's fates. Cutter understood, but he understood, too, that to stay would be to condemn all of them to torture and death. He did not mind that for himself so much, for he knew that he had earned such a fate long ago, had bought and paid for it a thousand times over. But he would not, *could not* let the boy suffer for his sins. And so they would run, leaving a bloody trail of the innocent behind them. It wasn't as if they, as if *he,* had not done it before.

They moved quickly and quietly, Cutter's eyes roaming the corners of the burned-out shells that had once been the homes of the villagers before he had brought their first doom upon them. But there were no soldiers lurking around corners waiting in ambush as he expected, proving that Feledias and his men had not yet surrounded the village.

"What will they do to them, Maeve?" a voice asked, breaking the silence, and Cutter turned back to see Matt staring at the woman. Tears were running down his face, tears which meant that he knew, deep down, the answer to the question he asked. Instead of answering, Maeve only turned to look at Cutter, meeting his gaze.

They were all looking at him, regret and self-loathing clear on their features, one that served to accentuate his own. "Best keep moving," he said, his voice harsh.

And on they walked. The boy did not ask the question again, likely fearing that this time, if he did, he would receive an answer. They were in sight of the village edge when the silence was broken by distant screams. Cutter turned back and saw light bloom in the darkness, the orange, ruddy glow of a flame. Feledias beginning his work then, meaning to finish what the Fey had begun and destroy the village completely.

"Prince," Priest began, his own face twisted with grief as if he felt the pain and fear of the one who had screamed, and even as he spoke more screams echoed in the darkness. Not screams of pain, not yet, but of fear and sudden understanding as those villagers of Ferrimore who remained after the Fey attack began to realize that those men they had supposed to be their saviors would be, instead, their executioners.

Cutter stared back at the older man, shaking his head. "We can't, Priest," he managed through gritted teeth. "You know that. There are too many."

The man glanced at the boy, standing there with tears still streaming down his face, then back at Cutter. "You are wrong, Prince. *You* can't, and I understand your reasons. Truly, I do. But *I* can."

The older man moved to Maeve, pulling her into a tight embrace. "Goodbye, Maeve."

There were tears shimmering in her eyes as well, but she pulled him close. "Are...are you sure?"

"I'm sure," he said, offering her a smile as he stepped back. "Good luck, Maeve. It has been a pleasure knowing you."

The woman opened her mouth as if she would say something, but she seemed unable to find the words, and the man smiled, nodding his head to her before moving to Chall. The heavy-set mage shook his head desperately as the man walked to him. "No," he said, his voice a harsh whisper, "Priest, it isn't...I mean, you can't..."

"It is okay, Challadius," Priest said, pulling him into a tight embrace. The mage hesitated for a moment, then hugged him back. "It's okay. All men have their journey, and they can do naught but travel it as best they may. May the gods be with you."

"Oh gods, Priest," Chall said. "I...I'm sorry. Sorry for all the things I said—"

"There is nothing to forgive," the man said, smiling. "But if there is, then you were forgiven the moment you said them. Live well, Challadius. You are a better man than you know."

"Live well," Chall repeated as if the words were in some other language, some language he did not understand. "How?"

Priest smiled at that but said nothing, stepping away. He glanced at Matt, the boy's face covered in tears. "It was a pleasure meeting you, Matt. I wish only that I could have known you better, but, it seems, it is not the goddess's will."

Matt's mouth worked, as if he were trying to speak, but in the end it seemed the words would not come and a moment later Priest stepped past him, meeting Cutter's gaze.

"You will die," Cutter said.

"Yes," Priest said, smiling once more. "But all men die, Prince. It is what gives our lives worth."

Cutter grunted, nodding. "Good luck, old friend."

The man winked. "And to you."

They watched him start away at a jog then, his bow slung across his back, and Cutter felt some great emotion writhing within him, threatening to be unleashed. But he choked it down, that emotion, that feeling, for he could not afford it, not now. Later, perhaps, he would grieve but not now. There was the boy to think about. There was, there *could be,* nothing else.

He was still watching the man's form vanish into the darkness heading back in the direction they'd come when Maeve stepped up to stand beside him. "How long, Prince?" she asked.

He glanced at her, raising an eyebrow.

"How long," she repeated in a whisper, "before our poor tortured souls are turned black, before they become twisted, pathetic things inside of us?" She glanced at Matt, the boy watching the old scout go, an expression of such wretched agony on his face that Cutter could not look at it for long. "He would forgive you much, I think, but he will not forgive you this. Not ever."

Again, the emotions threatened to well up inside him, and again Cutter forced them down, swallowing them back. "Maybe not," he growled, his voice harsh with emotion. "But he will live. And how long, you ask me, Maeve?" he said. "I do not know, and I do not care. The boy will live. That is all that matters. If I must make my soul black, if I must twist and torture it, if I must give it up entire, I will do so, if it means the boy lives. I will do *anything* to make sure he lives. And if that makes my soul black then so be it."

"I know," she said sadly, a lone tear gliding its way down her face. "I know, Prince, for you do it even now."

He let out an angry growl, turning to the others. "Come on, we—"

He cut off, his eyes going wide, feeling a powerful, sharp stab of fear as he looked at the boy. Matt was not standing and weeping now, or at least, not as he had been. He still stood, and his face was still covered with tears, but now he held something in his hand, a knife, and the blade of it was poised at his own throat.

"What are you doing?" Cutter said, taking a step forward before the boy brought the knife closer, less than an inch away from his neck. Cutter froze.

"I-I won't do this," the boy said. "I-I can't. T-these people....it isn't...it isn't right. They're going to die because of us and I won't..." He was shaking his head desperately, so desperately that Cutter feared the blade would do its work without him meaning it.

"Stop fucking around," he growled. "There's no time for this, boy. They'll be here any minute and—"

"No," the boy said, and Cutter was surprised by the strength in his words. "No. I have followed you, Cutter, have trusted you. I trusted you when you said we had to leave Brighton, trusted you when you said it was the only way. Well, now I need you to trust me. I will go back and help them, and if you try to stop me, I will kill myself. I *swear* to you that I will."

Cutter's hands clenched and unclenched into fists at his sides, and he glanced at Maeve and Chall, both of them looking as shocked as he felt. But was there something else in their gazes, something lurking behind that surprise. Was it relief? Was it joy?"

"Damnit, boy," he said, trying again, "don't be a fool. You don't even know how to fight, for the gods' sake. You'll be butchered and for what? What good will it do?"

"I don't know, and I don't care," he said. "And you're right—I don't know how to fight, but neither do the villagers. They're farmers and workmen not soldiers. And if I die...well, better to be dead than to become...*this*. To become *you*."

That hurt him, hurt him more than he thought anything could, and Cutter found himself recoiling back a step at the youth's words. He looked again to Maeve and Chall, but it was clear that there would be no help from that quarter, for they only watched him with baited breath, waiting for what he would say, what he would do.

He was fast, yes, and he was strong, but he knew that he was not fast enough to cover the intervening feet between him and the boy before he did what he threatened, and his strength would not serve to reknit skin broken by a knife's edge. He hesitated, wanting to call the boy on his bluff. The problem, though, was that he knew he was not bluffing, that he meant every word of it. *Trust me*, the boy had said. And he did.

His chest heaved with anger, but at who, he could not have guessed. At the boy? At the woman and the mage who remained silent? Or, perhaps, at himself. He did not know, and it did not matter. All that mattered was that the boy was in danger, and that, no matter how he might wish not to, he believed him.

Still, he had one last tack to try, one last, desperate effort. "You will die, then, but not alone. You will kill Maeve and Chall as well with your foolishness. You will kill me. Do you hate us all so much, boy, that you would sentence us to death because the world is not the way you wish it was?"

"Yes," the boy said, the tears flowing freely once more. "You're r-right, Cutter. The world isn't how I wish it was, but it'll never change if we ignore it. Someone has to stand up, has to do *something*. It isn't going to fix itself."

"And you think you're that someone?" Cutter demanded. "You who have never wielded a blade in anger, you who, less than three years gone, sat playing with tin soldiers in the dirt with your friends?"

"No," the boy said, his face growing hard, determined. "I don't think I'm that person. Maybe I am just a dumb kid, maybe I am useless. But I'm going to go back, and I'm going to help them. And if I can't," he went on, overriding Cutter as he began to retort, "then I'll die with them. If that's all I can do for them, then that's what I'll do."

"You're a fool then," Cutter barked.

"Maybe," the boy agreed, nodding his head. Then he met his eyes. "Thank you, Cutter. For saving me. I'm leaving now. Don't try to stop me. I still have the knife, and if you do, I swear I'll use it."

And with that, the boy backed away slowly, watching him, as if he thought he might lunge forward at any moment and try to wrest the blade from his hands. Which, of course, he would have, if he'd seen the opportunity to do so.

But such an opportunity did not present itself, and he was forced to watch until the lad put a good distance between them then turned and hurried away.

Cutter had seen many terrible things in his life, had been the *cause* of many terrible things, yet he had never seen anything which rocked him so heavily as watching the boy run back into the town, headed to the certain death that awaited him there.

He was so overcome by that feeling, by the terror he felt, that he did not notice Maeve's approach, did not notice anything, really, except for the boy's departing form. "He's brave," she said softly.

"Yes," he said. "Like his mother."

And remembering her, he was reminded, too, of the promise he'd made. Fifteen years had passed since that promise, but it felt as if it had only been yesterday. He glanced between Maeve and Chall. "I'm going back. Thank you both for your help, now and in the past. But you should run. If my brother finds you here, he will not be kind, and I am tired of people suffering for my sake."

Maeve snorted. "As if we'd just up and leave. Gods, but sometimes I think you're the biggest fool I've ever met."

Cutter briefly considered the course of his life and grunted. "Probably you're right."

"Anyway," she went on, "fool or not, we won't leave you, not like this. Will we, Chall?" She turned to the mage, who frowned.

"Well, there is this whore I've heard of who I'd really like to…" He trailed off at Maeve's frown, sighing. "But why seek pleasure when pain is in such abundance?" he asked. "I'm with you, Prince."

Cutter looked between the two of them, surprised and more than a little touched. He wondered briefly what he had done to deserve such companions, such friends, but he did not wonder long. Nothing, that was the answer, for one thing he'd learned over the years was that men very rarely got what they deserved. Still, he realized then that he loved them, in that moment, realized that he always had.

In the past, that love had been too overshadowed by hate, by anger and arrogance, for him to notice it, to feel it, but he noticed it now, *felt* it now. "You're sure?"

"Oh, let's go already," Chall said. "We stand here talking about it much longer, I'm liable to shit myself, and I'd rather not be buried that way, not if I can help it."

"Plus," Maeve said, smirking, "it'd be a shame to ruin such fine trousers."

The mage glanced down at the purple trousers he still wore, frowning. "Sometimes, Maeve, I think you might be the world's biggest bitch."

She grunted in what might have been amusement. "Seems someone else'll have to take up the mantle soon enough."

Cutter found himself grinning despite himself, and he realized he could not remember the last time he'd smiled. Funny, maybe, that it would be here, before their inevitable deaths, that he found a reason to do so but probably for the best. After all, there wouldn't be any more time for it, that much was certain. "Ready?" he asked.

"Yes," Maeve said.

"No," Chall said.

And then they were running.

# CHAPTER TWENTY-EIGHT

*There are none more confident that they know best than the young.*
*And there are none more wrong.*
—*Common saying in the Known Lands*

It did not take them long to catch up with Matt. The youth spun at their approach, thinking, perhaps, that they were some of Feledias's soldiers. When he saw that it was them instead, he fumbled at the blade now sheathed at his side, bringing it to his throat once more. "I-I t-told you not to follow me, that I would kill myself if you tried to stop me. I meant it."

"I know you did, lad," Cutter said, holding up his hands. "We haven't come to stop you."

"No?" Matt asked, clearly surprised and just as clearly relieved. "Th-then why…"

"We've come to help," Cutter said.

The youth's eyes went wide at that. "Y-you mean it? You've come to help?"

"Sure," Chall said with a shrug. "I mean, who'd pass up an opportunity to get tortured to death?"

"And y-you won't…you promise you won't try to stop me?" Matt asked, staring at Cutter.

Cutter was just about to open his mouth to speak, to tell the boy that he would not try to stop him and that while he had lied to him often in the past, this, at least, was nothing short of the truth. But just then there was a shout from nearby, and he spun to see two of Feledias's soldiers moving out of an alleyway, swords drawn.

No doubt, these, like other pairs, had been sent about the village to round up any townsfolk, to also find Cutter and the rest in case they had attempted to flee—which, of course, they had. But what they did more than anything was prove that there was no reason for him to answer the boy. The time for fleeing, for stopping him, had passed.

There would be no running, not now. Feledias had caught up with him. His *past* had caught up with him, and there was nothing left to do but face it. Cutter stepped in front of Matt, protecting him from those men, from his own past as best as he could. He reached for the axe at his back, but before he could close the distance between him and the soldiers, Priest moved, drawing the bow from his back and stringing an arrow to it in one smooth motion. Before Cutter or the soldiers could react, the missile was whistling across the intervening space, and the next thing Cutter—and the unfortunate soldier—knew, it had buried itself in his throat.

The other soldier watched his comrade fall, his mouth opening as if he would say something, but he never got the chance, for Maeve shifted and suddenly there was a knife in her hand. She pivoted with a grace the years had done nothing to diminish, and then the knife wasn't in her hand any longer but hurling across the distance to plunge into the remaining soldier's chest.

And just like that, it was over.

Cutter blinked at the two corpses. It had been some time since he had seen just how skilled the two of them were, fifteen years in fact, but it seemed that the intervening time had done nothing to dampen their talents. Maeve stepped forward to the guardsman who'd fallen on his face, unceremoniously rolling him over and retrieving her knife. She would feel that death later, of course—assuming there was a later—for Cutter knew she always did, had heard her crying herself to sleep many times over the years. But he knew, also, that she would not allow herself to feel it now, not when there was work to do.

Maeve rose, glancing back at Cutter then at Chall who, by the expression of shock on his face, was just as surprised by the speed of what had just occurred as Cutter was himself. "What?" she asked.

Cutter shared a look with the mage and shrugged. "Nothing."

She rolled her eyes. "You're not the only one knows how to stop a man's heart, Prince. And as for you," she went on, turning to glance at the mage, "you just remember this the next time you want to run your mouth."

Then they were moving again, jogging at a fast clip, for all of them were well aware that if they did not arrive soon there would be no point in arriving at all. Feledias was nothing if not thorough. As they drew closer to the inn they had left less than an hour ago, the screams grew louder, the firelight—not from one house now, or two, but several throughout the village as his brother set about the task of destroying the village—brighter.

They fell back into a familiar routine as they made their way through the streets. Priest moved up ahead of them, scouting, ensuring that their way was clear of anymore surprises. Cutter was next, followed by Chall in the middle with Matt, and Maeve last, the woman keeping an eye on their back lest someone try to surprise them from behind.

Soon, they drew near the inn once more. The screams—and the owners of those screams—were close now, very close, just on the other side of a building. Cutter and the others waited while Priest crept forward, making use of his almost supernatural ability to move in complete silence, but it was not just that, for the moment the man stepped away from them, Cutter seemed to lose sight of him, as if he wrapped the darkness of the night around him like a cloak, concealing himself from view.

Several tense minutes passed then as they waited for the scout to return, waited and listened to the sounds of shouting from nearby. He was just beginning to worry that the man had been caught when, suddenly, Priest appeared out of the night only feet away from Cutter and nearly elicited a shout of surprise that would have given them away. "How's it look?" Cutter asked, but as he peered at the scout, taking in his grim expression, he realized he probably hadn't needed to ask.

"It's bad," the man said, confirming his suspicion. "They're burning the village—what little of it isn't already burned, anyway. They're bringing all the villagers to the inn."

"Gods," Chall muttered.

"What?" Matt asked quietly, glancing between their grim expressions. "I don't understand. Why would he bring the villagers to the inn?"

They all looked at Cutter, leaving it to him, and he sighed. "Makes it easier," he said, meeting the boy's eyes.

Matt frowned. "What? It makes what easier?"

"This way," Cutter went on, "there's only one really important fire. He throws the villagers inside, bars the door, and lets the flames wipe out any trace of what happened here, any possible evidence that might point back to him or his troops."

Matt's eyes went wide at that. "Y-you can't be serious. H-he wouldn't...I mean, a person wouldn't...all those people—"

"He would, lad," Cutter said simply. "It's been done before." He did not bother telling the boy that this was almost certainly what had been done in Brighton, his home.

"W-we have to help them," Matt said, meeting Cutter's eyes. "W-we can't let him...we can't."

Cutter doubted very much there was any help they could offer the citizens of Ferrimore, thought it likely that the only effect such an attempt would have would be them dying along with them, but he knew that the boy had meant what he said, knew that he would use the blade he still carried if Cutter tried to drag him away from here. But even that wasn't the only reason he stayed. He found that, now that he was here, he was glad. True, they were almost certainly about to begin a battle that would lead, inevitably and irrevocably, to their deaths, but it wasn't as if he hadn't been in such a place before.

He had tried to keep the boy safe, tucked away, hidden away, but Maeve was right—no one who was alive was safe, not in this world. And if the boy was to die, if they all were, then Cutter could think of far worse ways than giving their lives to try to keep the villagers from suffering the worst of his brother's rage.

Cutter put his hand on the boy's shoulder. "We won't, lad." He noted the look of gratitude that passed over the boy's face at that, but he turned away, looking to Priest. "Show us."

The scout nodded and soon they were moving again, making slower progress now as they focused on stealth. Cutter felt a tightness across his shoulders as they moved. He had never been one given to sneaking or lurking in the shadows, and he felt a growing respect for Priest and his talents. There was an anxiousness, a tenseness that Cutter never felt in the grip of a battle, when a man had made his decisions already and had no more to make, when there were no more choices to make and the only thing that was left was the blood.

In time, the scout led them to behind the burned-out shell of a house, the stone scorched and stained with soot. He put his back against the corner and peered around then turned back to Cutter, motioning him forward.

Cutter crept forward, glancing around the corner.

The scene was much as Priest had described it. Even as he watched, soldiers dragged kicking and screaming villagers toward the inn entrance, throwing them inside while others stood with swords drawn at the door lest any of those terrified villagers peering out of the entrance attempted to make a run for it.

But while this was a terrible sight, what drew Cutter's eye was, instead, the half a dozen soldiers standing in front of the building in a rough semi-circle and, specifically, the man at their front. Feledias. Cutter had not seen his brother in years, not since their falling out fifteen years ago, a falling out which had been his fault and his alone. His brother had aged in that time, that much could be seen in the gray streaks in his hair and beard, could be seen in the hard lines on his face.

Yet, in his features, Cutter could see the child he had once been, the happy, carefree child who had followed his big brother everywhere, who had thought him a hero. Perhaps Feledias was a monster now, but he had not always been so, and if he *was* a monster, then he was one of Cutter's making.

An old woman knelt in front of his brother, a soldier on either side of her. Her lip was split from a recent cut, and her face was marred by a fresh bruise, but despite this, the orange ruddy glow of the torches several of the soldiers held was enough for Cutter to recognize her as Netty, the innkeeper.

"What...what do we do?" Matt asked in a hushed whisper.

Cutter considered that. They were outnumbered with no chance of fighting their way through the soldiers. If they tried, they would be cut down long before they ever reached the inn and the frightened villagers inside it. He glanced at the others to see if they had any ideas, but they offered nothing, only watched him, waiting for what he would say. He knew that, should he ask it of them, they would not hesitate to charge suicidally into the waiting troops. Well, perhaps Chall would hesitate, but the man would go nonetheless, of that much he was certain. Just as he was certain that, if he did, he would die, he and all the others. They would all die at his brother's hands for a sin of which he alone was guilty. His brother hated him for that sin, with a hate so strong that it had warped him, twisted the once kind, benevolent man into a creature who sought only revenge, and who cared nothing about anyone else, would destroy anything or anyone who got in the way of him achieving his vengeance.

Cutter deserved to die for what he had done—there was no denying that. But his companions, his friends, did not. Suddenly, a thought struck him, and he grunted. "I've got an idea—a way out of this, a way we can save those villagers. But we have to be fast."

Matt was nodding quickly, and he could see hope not just on the boy's face but on those of the others as well. Perhaps they would have been willing to charge suicidally into the soldiers, but no doubt they preferred a less painful, less final alternative.

"There's a back door into the inn," he whispered, knowing they had to be fast. "I saw it earlier. Feledias will have it guarded, but not as heavily as the front. You all go, wait for my signal, then, if there are any soldiers left, take them out and sneak the villagers out the back."

"But...where will you be?" Matt asked.

Cutter was aware of all their eyes on him, aware of Maeve's in particular. She was clever, Maeve, cleverer than him by half and always had been. So, he took his time, choosing his words, his tone carefully. "I'll stay here, create a distraction. When I do, you make your move."

"A distraction," Maeve said, watching him carefully, her eyes seeming to see right through him.

Cutter forced himself to nod confidently. "Yes."

"But, Prince," Chall said, "perhaps it would be better if I stayed. With my magic—"

"No," Cutter interrupted, giving his head a shake. "If things go sideways, they'll need your magic to rescue the villagers and make it out alive."

The mage clearly wanted to argue the point, but he remained silent, glancing at Maeve as if for help. The woman, though, was only watching Cutter with her eyes that seemed to see so much. "And what about you?"

He felt their time, their chances, slipping away, but he forced back his impatience, giving as casual of a shrug as he could. "Lead the villagers to the north side of the village—there's a forest a little over a mile away in that direction. On open ground, their horses will catch you and they'll cut you down, but if you can make it to the trees, it will be harder for Feledias and his men to track you. You'll have a chance."

"But what about you?" Maeve asked again.

Cutter shook his head, unable to completely hide his frustration. "I'll catch up, don't worry about that—I don't mean to die today. Now, hurry—there's no more time."

They nodded, turning to start away but Cutter caught the boy, putting a hand on his shoulder. Matt turned, looking at him with eyes as big as dinner saucers in the moonlight. "Be brave, Matt," Cutter said. "Whatever happens, be brave. Do you understand?"

"Y-yes, sir," the boy said.

Cutter stared at him. There were a thousand things he wanted to say, a thousand truths he wanted to tell, not least of which how he felt for the boy, how he had felt since the first time he'd held him, a squalling babe, so small and so fragile in his arms. But there was no time, so he only grunted. "Go on then," he said, offering him the best smile he could. "I'll see you soon."

"Priest," he said, as the others started working their way toward the next building, meaning to loop around to the inn's back.

The man turned back, raising an eyebrow.

"I'd speak with you, for a moment."

Maeve shot one more suspicious glance at him before she, Chall, and the boy started away. Priest walked up to him. "Yes, Prince?"

Cutter frowned. He had not expected his plan to work, for it to have gone so easily. Now that it had, he was having difficulty saying what he needed to. "Priest," he said quietly, "Valden...do you think..." He paused, clearing his throat. "Do you think that the gods, seeing a man's evil, his sins, might give up on him?"

A Warrior's Burden

The man watched him carefully. Maeve was clever, it was true, but so was Valden. "You do not mean to meet us in the forest."

He could have lied, but he saw no point in it. He had never been good with lies. Had never been much good with the truth either, come to it. Some people wielded words the way others wielded blades. His brother had been one such, long ago, but Cutter had never possessed such a gift. So instead of lying, he shook his head. "No."

"You mean to sacrifice yourself."

It was not really a question but Cutter answered it anyway. "Yes. He will not stop, Valden. Not ever. You know that as well as I do. He will not stop until he has killed me."

"And so you travel to your death so that others might be saved."

Cutter shrugged. "I've been traveling to my death for a long time now, Priest. But please...you won't tell the others?"

The man watched him for several seconds then finally shook his head. "I will not tell them. But they will discover it soon enough when you do not arrive. They will be angry."

"I know. Let them be angry. Just let them live. I have done terrible things, Priest, unimaginable things, and there is no counting the number of those who have suffered for what I have done. I would have it stop. I would end it—here. There is a price for my sins, and it is one I pay gladly. Only...the reason I asked you to stay..." He trailed off, suddenly struggling to finish.

"I will look after the boy," Priest said softly. "As best as I am able."

Cutter let out a heavy, relieved sigh. "Thank you. And please...the others, too. Maeve. Chall...he will not understand."

The man nodded at that, and then there was nothing to be said, no more words needed. There was, now, only the doing. Cutter offered his hand to the man who took it. "It has been a pleasure, Priest."

"The pleasure is mine, Prince Bernard," the man said. And with that, he turned and started away, then pausing to look back at him. "Prince?"

"Yes?"

"The gods never give up on us, not ever. Not, even, when we give up on ourselves. Good luck."

Cutter nodded. "And to you."

Then the man was gone, vanishing into the shadows after the others. Cutter watched him go, a small smile on his face. "Good luck," the man had said, but Cutter did not think he needed it. It didn't take much luck, after all, to die.

He found, now that he was alone, that he did not fear his death. The man, Priest, was always fond of saying that the path to peace was taken one step at a time, and Cutter believed that. He believed, too, that when a man was haunted by his past crimes, his very soul stained with them, that the only path to peace was death—and that path, at least, was a short one.

He rose from where he crouched beside the building, staring back at where his brother barked words at the bruised and battered innkeeper still kneeling on the ground. He had lied to them, Matt and Maeve and the others, but not everything he'd said had been a lie. He would create a distraction, that much was true, and what better distraction for a man whose entire life had been twisted on vengeance than the sudden appearance of the object of his rage?

# CHAPTER TWENTY-NINE

*What to say of Prince Feledias?*
*He was all that his brother was not.*
*He was kind where his brother was cruel, warm where his brother was cold.*
*He was the greatest man I have ever known.*
*But that man, that prince, is dead.*
*And in his place...a monster lurks.*
—Exiled Historian to the Crown Petran Quinn

"Where is he?" Feledias shouted at the old woman kneeling in the dirt.

The woman looked up at him, working her mouth before turning and spitting out a gobbet of blood. "Who's that now?"

"You know who!" he barked. "My brother—Prince Bernard. I know that he came here, that he stayed at your inn." He paused, withdrawing the knife from the sheath at his waist, then knelt before her. "You will tell me where he has gone, old woman. One way or the other."

"I s'pose I'm meant to be impressed by that little sticker?" the old woman asked, eyeing the blade. After a moment, she shrugged. "I've seen bigger." She cackled at that, cackled right up until his fist struck her in the face, and she let out a gasp of pain and surprise, collapsing sideways onto the ground.

Feledias growled as the woman slowly climbed back to her knees. "You will die, peasant. I am sure that you have gathered that much, at least, and so I will not lie to you. One way or the other, you die today. But if you tell me where my brother has gone, I promise to make your death quick, painless. If you instead choose to continue to be a fool and cover for a man who has never cared for anyone or anything in his life except himself, well..." He paused, glancing at the blade in his hand. "You would be surprised just how much pain a person can suffer and still live."

He saw the terrible understanding in her eyes as she glanced at the blade, thought that, perhaps, she would finally tell him what he wanted to know, but when she looked back to him, her gaze hardened. "That's it?" she asked. "That's your big threat? I'm over seventy years old, *Prince*. Fire and salt, I have more pain than you could cause with that little toy of yours every time I take a piss."

Feledias's anger, his impatience to find his brother, demanded that he attack the woman, that he carve his fury into her flesh piece by piece, but he forced himself to remain calm, to take a slow, deep breath. He smiled then. "You are a fool, but a brave one, that much I'll grant you. Still," he said, glancing at the open door of the inn and those villagers gathered inside, more being added all the time as his soldiers scoured the village, "I wonder, are these others quite so brave? Would you be so willing to watch them suffer and die because you chose to remain silent?"

The older woman glanced back at the doorway, and for the first time her expression showed something that it had not yet—fear. Feledias smiled. Every person had his weakness, his pressure point. For most, it was simply themselves, fear that they—that who they were—might be altered, might be changed, and it was enough to plant in them the idea of what life would look like with one less finger, one less hand. Or, how they would feel about not living at all. That worked most of the time, but not always.

There were some people—not many, but some—who needed some other sort of motivation, and this nearly always came in the form of their family, their friends. After all, no man or woman walked the world alone, without connection. The closest, perhaps, was his own wayward brother, Cutter, and even he had his weakness.

Everyone did. And once you found it, getting what you wanted from them, making them little more than your puppet, was no more difficult than lifting the strings and making them dance. He had always known this, even before his brother's betrayal, had looked at these different levers a person might pull to get what he wanted, and they had served him well in various diplomatic negotiations. He had been a puppet master then, too, but one constrained by his own morality and society's conventions. Now, though, he entertained no such constraints. He would have his vengeance, no matter what.

"Ah," he said, smiling at the old woman's troubled expression. "It seems we've found the crack in your armor after all."

"Leave them out of this," she said, "they got nothin' to do with it. They ain't none of your business."

"Well, now, that's where you're wrong, peasant," Feledias said. "You see, I'm High Prince of the realm which means that every single person—noble or commoner, even old innkeepers and backwater hicks—*are* my business."

He glanced back at the door once more, at the villagers huddled, frightened inside the inn. He caught sight of one, a girl in her teens, perhaps early twenties. Pretty, for a peasant. He motioned to one of the soldiers at the door. "Bring me the girl."

The girl in question screamed as they approached, backing away, but the soldier grabbed her, dragging her out of the inn to throw her at Feledias's feet beside the old woman.

"N-Netty?" the girl asked, her brown eyes wide and confused, clearly looking for comfort.

"I-it's okay, Emille," the old woman said. "Everything will be okay."

Feledias's grin widened as he saw the fear in the old woman's face magnified as she stared at the girl. A close friend, perhaps? A stand-in for the daughter she never had? "Everything will be okay?" he said, then gave a sad shake of his head. "Oh, but I'm afraid that's just not true." Feledias paused, meeting the girl's eyes. "In fact, my dear, things are very far from okay. You see, your Netty here will not answer my questions, and so you're going to die. Badly, I'm afraid."

The girl whimpered then, her tanned farmer's skin growing pale as she looked at the woman. "Netty," she said. "I don't—"

"Hush now, child," the old woman said, but she was not looking at the girl, was instead looking at him. "Go on, then," she spat. "Ask your questions."

Feledias said, "That's better, isn't it? Now, we can all get along. So tell me, peasant, how long ago did my brother leave?"

The old woman shrugged. "A day? Day and a half? He traveled—"

She cut off with a gasp as Feledias casually reached over and backhanded the young woman. The woman screamed in shock and pain, falling onto her side in the dirt.

"You're lying," Feledias said calmly. "Tell me, lass," he said, looking at the weeping girl, at the undeniably shapely figure beneath the simple linen dress she wore, "have you ever known the touch of a man?"

"Leave her alone, you bastard," the old woman hissed.

The girl said nothing, only looked at him, trembling. "Well," Feledias said, "you will. If your Netty here tries to lie to me again or does anything other than tell me exactly what I want to know, I'll see to your education myself. And when I'm done with that, I'll give you to my soldiers—they are not so kind as me, I'm afraid, not so...gentle."

"An hour ago," the old woman sneered. "No more than that."

"That's better," he said, offering her a smile. "And tell me, where did they go?"

"And how in the name of the gods would I know that?" she asked. "It isn't as if they asked my opinion on it, is it?"

Feledias watched her for a moment then shrugged. He motioned to one of the soldiers, and the girl gave a panicked cry as the man stepped forward, hefting her to her feet.

"I really don't know, damn you," the old woman said. "They didn't tell me."

"Oh, I believe you," Feledias said, offering her a grin. "It's only that, now that I think on it, a roll with a farm girl might be just the thing. Unless, that is, you decide to be a touch more cooperative."

He turned back to her and saw that she was no longer studying him but instead was looking over his shoulder, something like relief and pleasure in her gaze. "Can't tell you where they were going," the old woman said, "but I think probably I can tell you where they are."

"Oh?" Feledias asked, not liking the sudden confidence in the woman's tone, for he did not understand it, and he never liked things he did not understand. "And where is that?"

The woman smiled. "Behind you."

Feledias grunted. "A pathetic ruse, and one which will serve you no purpose," he said, turning, "for if you do not—"

The words were gone. Torn from him by a shock that thrummed through his entire body as if he'd been struck by lightning, a shock which was greater than any he had ever felt or thought to feel. He had hunted his brother for years, ever since his betrayal, and he had known that he would find him one day, that he would make him suffer. Now it seemed, that day, that moment, had come. But in all his fantasies, in all the dreams he'd had of this moment, his brother had cowered before him, weak and broken and afraid, begging for his life.

But he did not look weak now, nor broken, and he did not beg. He only stood, regarding Feledias over the intervening distance between where he stood beside a house wall. Stood as big and imposing—perhaps even more imposing than he remembered—and seeing him standing there, in the ruddy, flickering torchlight, Feledias felt a shock of surprise and something else. Something very close to fear.

"Hello, brother," the hulking figure said, the words like two great boulders shifting against each other.

Feledias's mouth was suddenly unaccountably dry, and despite the many dreams of this moment he'd had, imaginings in which he had cut his brother down with words before he began the cutting in truth, he found that now that the moment had come, he could remember none of the phrases he'd used, and he was left only to stare at his brother.

"It's been a long time," his brother said. "Now, if you have questions, ask me. Not them," he said, glancing past Feledias at the innkeeper and the girl, both of which he had dismissed in his surprise.

*Questions.* That word struck a chord in him, bringing him out of the stupor of surprise and back to himself. "*Questions,*" he sneered, feeling the shock which had clouded his mind departing, vanishing like mist in the sunlight. "Only one, brother. The same one that I have carried for fifteen years. *Why?*"

His brother's features twisted in something like grief, which Feledias knew could not be right, for his brother, the Crimson Prince felt neither compassion nor grief. "Feledias...I am sorry—"

"*Why?*" Feledias asked again, this time aware that he was screaming but unable to stop himself. "*Why did you take her from me?*"

His brother winced. "I was a fool, Fell," he said softly. "A selfish fool. And…and I loved her."

"*Love,*" Feledias spat. "What does the Crimson Prince know of *love?* You betrayed me, brother. I, who was willing to do anything for you, I who was always pleased to be the lesser prince, to watch you accept all the glory and the praise and the love of the common folk. I wanted nothing, *asked* for nothing, except…" He swallowed hard, his mouth dry. "Except her."

"I know," his brother said, so quietly he almost thought he'd imagined it.

"I loved her," Feledias said. "And she loved me. I would have been okay with you having the world, *brother.* I did not mind that you were the famous one, the one everyone looked up to. I was proud of you. But her…"

"I'm sorry," he said. And what's more, it seemed that he meant it.

That took Feledias back even more than his brother appearing seemingly out of nowhere had. He had known Bernard his entire life, had followed him around like a lost puppy for most of it. He had seen Bernard angry, had seen him curse and yell and scream and spit with rage, had seen every variation of fury on his face. But in all that time, in all the many years in which he had known him, in which he had followed him, he had never known his brother to apologize.

He would have said, if asked, that the man didn't know how and that he had no interest in learning it. Hearing the words come from his mouth was like hearing thunder from clear skies or as if a dog had opened its mouth but, instead of barking, demonstrated that it had learned to speak instead. But as amazing as it was, as shocking as it was, it would not bring her back, would not fix what had been broken. Nothing would. "You're sorry," he said.

"Yes."

Feledias had never expected to hear such a thing from his brother, had always thought of him as someone larger than life, not a person, not really, but some force of nature disguised as one, a devil, likely, one sent to the world with one mission and one mission only—death. But now, looking at him, at the hair on his temples that had begun to go white, at the haggard lines in his face where time had scarred him, he realized something. His brother was not a force of nature, not half-god as he had sometimes suspected. He was not like a plague to be avoided, or a mythical figure to be feared.

He was only a man. He was not invincible. He was just blood and bone like everyone else. Just a man. Feledias felt something stir within him—love, perhaps? Affection for his brother, so long lost to him, for his entire life, it seemed, and only just found?

*No.*

The voice which spoke inside his head was his. And yet it was not. It was the voice which the last fifteen years had formed, which had been born in his hate and his rage at all that he had lost, at a betrayal that was unforgivable. It was a voice that knew nothing of love or affection, that knew hate and that only. A voice that demanded satisfaction, a satisfaction that could only be carved out of the body of the man who had betrayed him.

That voice could not be appeased, knew nothing of redemption, only of loss. "No," he said, and though it was not his voice, not really, it used his voice, ragged with grief and rage. "*Sorry*," he hissed. "Do you think that changes anything?"

"No," his brother said. "But I'm sorry just the same."

How long, he wondered, had he sought such a reaction, such *humanness* from his brother? How long had he sought to have a relationship with him, to be, in reality, what they had always pretended in fantasy, or at least what he had, creating and maintaining the illusion, as he had for so long. There had been a time when he had done so well at feeding that fiction that he had convinced nearly every man and woman in the kingdom of the truth of it, that their princes were the best of friends, loyal to each other—and to their kingdom—above all else.

A pretty lie, one that much easier to tell because they had wanted to hear it. Easier to tell because *he* had wanted to hear it, for now he could admit that he had always craved his brother's affection, his love. And for a time, despite all of the atrocities he committed, despite the fact that the Crimson Prince had never cared for anyone except in as much as they might be a victim through which he might vent his unending rage, the kingdom had believed it.

Even though he had laughed and mocked Feledias for his many attempts at building his brother's reputation, calling him "womanly" and "weak" as he sat around getting drunk and reliving battles with his inner circle—always the most bloodthirsty troops in the army, though never as bloodthirsty as Bernard himself, never that—Feledias had, after telling himself the lie enough, come to believe it.

But the truth, as was so often the case, was far grimmer than the fantasy. The truth was that his brother had not killed to save or to build his kingdom as Feledias had always claimed. Instead, he had killed simply because he had enjoyed it. The truth was that instead of appreciating Feledias's efforts on his behalf, his brother had scorned them, treating him like some pathetic dog following him around, eager for any scraps he might drop him. And the truth was that he had been.

But the biggest truth, the one which could not be ignored, was that his brother had taken everything from him, had taken *her* from him. The truth was that the dog, no matter how pathetic, how bent on its master's approval, would bite if it were kicked enough.

"*Damn your sorry,*" Feledias hissed, his voice choked with emotion. "Perhaps it would have mattered before, before *her*...but it does not matter now. Now there is only one thing that matters."

"I know the thing you mean," his brother answered, his voice sounding full of regret, another thing he had never expected to hear from the man, "and blood, death, they never fix problems, Feledias. I know that better than most. They only cause more. A man cannot create by destroying and killing me will not fill that hole in you. That hole you can only fill yourself."

"And you, *brother?*" Feledias sneered. "Have you filled your own?"

"No. But I'm trying."

Feledias stared at the big man standing there by the edge of the building, a storm of emotions raging inside him. And he thought, in that moment, that perhaps he could forgive him, that perhaps together they could heal, could become whole once more. But he realized something as he stood there. He did not want to be whole, did not want healing. He only wanted revenge. "Perhaps you're right," he said finally. "Perhaps killing you will fix nothing. But then, there's only one way to find out, isn't there?"

He smiled then, withdrawing his two swords, sheathed at either hip.

"I do not want to fight you, Feledias," Cutter said.

"*Want?*" Feledias hissed. "Do not speak to me of want, brother. And do not think me such easy prey. You might have beaten me at every sparring match we ever had, might have taken pleasure in embarrassing me, of making me into a joke, but you will find that I am not the same man I once was, and I have you to thank for that."

"Prince," Commander Malex ventured quietly from beside him, "we outnumber him. If we were all to attack at once—"

"*No,*" Feledias growled. "Not another word, Malex. He's mine." With that, Feledias started forward. And then his brother surprised him yet again, doing something he had never seen him do before, something he had never expected to see him do no matter how much he might have changed.

Bernard, the Crimson Prince, the most feared warrior in the realm, known for his bloodthirsty nature and for never backing down from a fight no matter how uneven the odds, gave one final look at his brother, then turned.

And ran.

# CHAPTER THIRTY

*I asked him, after the battle, why he did not retreat, for while the battle was won, it was won at a great, a terrible cost. I asked the Crimson Prince why he did not flee to fight another day.*
*And do you know what he told me? Nothing.*
*He only laughed.*
*And in that, he told me everything.*
*—Exiled Historian to the Crown Petran Quinn*

Cutter did not want to fight his brother, for what was broken between them had been broken by him and him alone. But that was not the main reason he did not draw the axe at his back, did not rush to meet him as he once would have done without hesitation. No, the biggest reason that he chose to turn and sprint into the darkness instead was Matt, him and the others who were even now creeping behind the inn or perhaps there already. They were counting on him, them and all those villagers of Ferrimore who had not perished in the Fey attack. Cutter had chosen the path of violence, of death often in his life—always, in truth. Now, he chose life.

He chose to run.

He turned and sprinted into the shadows. He did not wonder if Feledias would follow him—he knew he would, for the creature his brother had become, the creature *he* had made him, could do nothing else. He knew this just as he knew that they would catch him. Soon.

As he ran, he could hear Feledias shouting furiously at his soldiers, ordering them to spread out and give chase. With so many men after him, it was not a question of if they would catch him, only how much time it would take them. And, more importantly, how much time he could buy the others before the death which had been stalking his steps all his life finally found him.

\*\*\*

"That son of a bitch," Maeve whispered.

"What?" Matt asked from where he and the others, Chall and Priest, crouched behind the burned-out remnants of a house behind the inn. "Did he abandon us? I knew it! He only cares for himself and—"

"Shut your fucking mouth, boy," Maeve hissed. "What he does now he does not do for himself."

Matt recoiled, obviously hurt. "What...what do you mean?"

"Do you not see, boy?" Chall said sadly, his voice soft. "Our prince sacrifices himself for us." He paused, turning to look at Matt. "For you."

The boy was clearly confused, not understanding. But then, he did. "You mean...he's going to get killed?"

Maeve grunted. "Eventually. Feledias has been hunting his revenge for fifteen years, lad. He will not squander his moment."

"And neither, then, should we," Priest said, and they all turned to him. "Our prince buys us time," he continued, "we must use it."

Maeve blinked. "You can't be serious," she said. "You mean to leave him alone? To *let* him die?"

"He is our prince," Priest said calmly, not reacting to her anger. "I mean to obey."

Maeve stared at the man, hesitating as her emotions raged inside her.

"What do we do, Maeve?"

She turned to look at the mage, watching her, waiting for her to make the decision. Then she cursed. "Priest's right. The villagers need us. Come on."

She nodded to Valden. "Best go see what we're up against."

The man returned the gesture and then grabbed hold of the stone wall of the ruined house. Maeve watched as the man scaled the wall as easily as someone else might have a ladder, climbing to the top where he crouched low, taking advantage of the relative height the building afforded him to get a better view.

A moment later, he climbed back down. "There are ten guards at the back, fifteen stationed at the front. And Maeve?" he went on, his expression grim as he met her eyes. "They're stacking wood around the inn."

"Wood?" Matt asked. "Why would they—" He cut off, his eyes going wide in the darkness. "They mean to burn them."

"*Shit,*" Maeve said. She had been hoping that the appearance of Cutter, the object of his hatred, would have goaded Feledias into doing something foolish, had even gone so far as to entertain the hope that the man might order every armed man with him to chase his brother down in his rage. But even twisted by hatred, it seemed that the man had retained his cleverness. Damn him.

She wracked her brain looking for some sort of answer, but she could find none. There were simply too many, that was all. Even if they somehow managed to take care of the soldiers stationed at the back—another vain hope waiting to be dashed—then it would make no difference, for they would not be able to do so silently, and their efforts would only alert those stationed at the front. Ten against four—one of which knew nothing of fighting and had only just risen from the ranks of childhood into adulthood—were long odds, at best. Twenty-five against four were impossible ones.

"How many can you take?" she asked Priest.

"Done quiet?" he said. He gave a shake of his head. "Two—maybe three. No more than that."

Maeve winced. Perhaps one or two herself, assuming her knees or her back didn't give out on her in the doing of the thing. That left five at best, five for a young boy and an overweight mage who, just then, was looking like he was getting ready to piss himself. Not good odds. Not odds at all, really.

She shook her head. "I don't—"

"I'll need help."

She turned to look at Chall, the mage's face pale but his expression resolute nonetheless. "Help?" she asked.

He winced, clearly embarrassed, as he motioned to the wall the priest had climbed down a moment before. "Getting up. I'll need to be able to see—it helps."

Maeve frowned at that, and it wasn't just at the thought of trying to lever the mage's significant bulk up the wall somehow. Up at the top of the house, he would be significantly easier to spot than Priest had been, not just because of his size but also because he was not exactly known for his stealth. In fact, the only person she knew who lacked subtlety more than the mage was Cutter himself. Despite all her complaints, all the times he made her want to strangle him, she liked Challadius, the man who managed to find a way to make her laugh when no one else could, and she did not enjoy the idea of him climbing up to the top of the building only to get filled with arrows, for she had seen several of the guardsmen with crossbows strapped to their backs.

"Even if we do manage to get you up there," she said reluctantly. "Can you do it?"

He grunted. "I'm a bit out of practice, I'll admit, but...do we have any choice?"

Well, there was no real argument to that, so she sighed. "Don't get yourself killed, alright?"

He gave her a sickly smile. "I'll try my best."

They spent the next few minutes trying to lever the heavy-set man up, the priest giving him whispered instructions for where he should put his hands as they did. It was a miserable, sweaty, straining experience, but eventually the mage was in place, and Maeve was able to dismiss the fear—which had grown with each groaning moment—that the wall, assuming they got the man up there, would buckle beneath his weight.

Thankfully, though, the wall held, which meant that out of all the thousands of ways they might die in the next few minutes, they'd at least avoided death by a crumbling wall.

"So he...he's going to cast a spell then?"

Maeve glanced over at the boy and was reminded, once more, that while she and Priest and Chall had done this a thousand times, been in these sort of situations and survived far more times than anyone had a right to, it was largely new to him. "Yes, lad," she said, softly, "he's going to cast a spell." Or at least, she hoped he was. From what she'd seen of the mage, the only magic he'd performed in the last fifteen years or so was increasing his belly size and, of course, managing to not get knifed in the back by someone he pissed off. Which, of course, was everyone that he met.

"How...how will we know when he does it?"

*If he does it,* Maeve thought. "Oh, lad, you'll know," she said. "Trust me." An easy thing to say, perhaps, but not so easy to do judging by the youth's troubled expression. Not that she could blame him—the fact was, she didn't wholly trust herself.

\*\*\*

Matt's hands were sweaty, his body tense. He was more scared than he had ever been. Even in the days spent fleeing into the Black Woods with Cutter, he had been too busy running and being exhausted to be as scared as he might have been, too busy reacting. But now they were not reacting but *acting.* They were here because of him and him alone. If he had said nothing, only followed, then he and the others would be safely away, leaving the village to its fate, which meant that if any of them died here—if *all* of them died—it would be his fault.

It was the hardest thing he had ever done, crouching there and waiting, and it was all he could do to avoid asking Maeve anymore questions. Instead, he peeked around the corner, watching the soldiers stationed at the inn door. There were four of them there, and others moving around the edges of the inn, stacking pieces of wood along the walls.

He watched the men, wondering how anyone would be willing to kill an entire village of people, and as he did, he remembered what Cutter had said, how he had scolded him when he'd said he wanted to become a soldier. The man had been angry, and he had been surprised by that anger. Now, though, he was not so surprised. He was thinking of that, looking at the grim expressions on the soldiers' faces, when he became aware of an odd sound. It was a sharp, screeching *keening,* low at first, so low that he could almost think he'd imagined it.

But slowly, it began to rise. It was a terrible, somehow unnatural sound, and a chill ran up Matt's spine. And it was not only the sound, as terrible as it was, that unnerved him, that made him begin to shake, for while that was bad, what happened next was worse. Mist started to gather around them, a frigid mist that stole the heat from him where it touched his skin, so cold that it almost seemed to burn.

"*Oh, t-that bastard,*" Maeve said, the words coming out broken as she shivered.

"I-I don't u-understand," Matt managed, his own teeth chattering, "Maeve, wh-what's happening?"

There was a hand on his shoulder, and Matt nearly screamed before he turned and saw the man, Priest, watching him. "Relax, lad. It isn't real, not any of it. Keep telling yourself that."

"B-but the mist," Matt managed, looking all around him, seeing that in the space of seconds, the mist had risen so that it was taller than a man, obscuring the soldiers posted at the back door to the inn from his view, making of them little more than vague shadows.

"They come with the mist," Maeve said, her voice grim.

"W-who?" Matt asked, struggling with a budding panic growing within him. "W-who does?"

Maeve turned to look at him, her expression grim. "The Skaalden, lad. The Skaalden."

Another surge of fear ran through him at that. Matt had never seen the Skaalden, for he had been born here, in the Known Lands. But he had heard some bit of the frost creatures, the monsters who had so easily overridden his people's homeland and forced them to flee to this place. And always, when he did, they were spoken of in hushed whispers. Whispers from men who would not hesitate to talk in raised, angry voices about the Fey.

"B-but they're not here," Matt said, the cold and his own fear making it a struggle to speak, "th-they can't be here—" But then he cut off, the words getting strangled in his throat as he noticed figures moving in the mist. He could not make them out well, no more than vague shadows as they were, but what he could see was enough to know that they were not human. In fact, these figures stood half again or more as tall as any mortal man, even Cutter who was the biggest man he had ever seen—but that was not the worst.

The worst was that their proportions were...wrong. Their figures were slim, their arms far too long for their bodies, hanging so low that they seemed to scrape the ground as they moved. And then, there were their faces, at least what he could see of them. Faces that were long and narrow with mouths which seemed to stretch up on either side nearly to the top of their heads. Mouths that, as he saw their silhouettes, were filled with sharp, razor-like teeth.

"Oh gods," he muttered, "oh gods help us."

Suddenly, there was a face only inches from his own, and he saw that it was Maeve, the woman's own skin pale and waxy. "They're not *real*, lad," she hissed, but despite her words he saw that she too, was afraid, that her words were little more than a harsh whisper. "Remember that—they are not *real*."

At first, Matt's panicked mind could not seem to understand what she was saying, but then he remembered the mage, Challadius, who had climbed up on the ruined house. They'd told him that he would know what the man was doing when it came, but surely this could not be it. No, there was no way a man could create this mist, could form those creatures lurking within it, moving and looking out of it with eyes as pale as hoarfrost. Eyes that, it seemed, were looking directly at Matt.

The soldiers posted at the inn also began to notice those figures moving in the mist around them. And they, like Matt and the others, were afraid. They began to shout and point, drawing their blades, yet despite this, they made no move to charge the figures in the mist, and those at the door of the inn instead remained where they were, their backs hunched against the building's outer wall, frozen in their fright. Matt could not blame them.

He might not have been a soldier or a warrior, but even he could see that such creatures as lurked there in the mist could not be bested in combat, could not be conquered, and a man faced with them could only run. Could only pray.

And indeed, it seemed that as he watched, the men began to do just that. Two of the four turned and with cries of terror, sprinted into the night as fast as their legs could carry them. Matt watched them go, struggling to keep his teeth from chattering and to control the worst of the trembling. That was when he noticed something strange—the mist had risen all the way to the top of the inn and was darker there, thicker.

He frowned at that, something striking him wrong, and then he realized what it was. It was not mist at the top of the inn after all—it was smoke. Which only meant—

"They're firing the inn," Priest said. "We have to go—now."

Before either Matt or Maeve could respond, the man drew the bow from his back and broke into a sprint, directly at the inn and, closer still, at those forms lurking in the mist—in their dozens now—which seemed to have grown somehow, towering nearly to the top of the inn itself, so high that their great elongated faces disappeared somewhere above, in the mist.

"W-what do we do, Maeve?" Matt asked.

"*Damn*," the woman cursed. "Stay here, boy." She gave her head an angry shake. "I'll try to keep that damn man's virtue from getting him killed."

"B-but I-I want to help," Matt said.

The woman glanced back at him from where she'd risen, and he saw that there were two knives in her hands, though where they had come from he could not have guessed. "Help?" she asked, not cruelly, but with what sounded like genuine curiosity. "How? No, lad. You stay here—watch Chall. Best you don't get involved in this. Chall is vulnerable when he's casting, and he'll be weak after he's finished. He'll need looking after. His magic will distract the soldiers—the gods alone know there's few things more distracting than the Skaalden—but if one of them happens on him and puts an end to him while he's concentrating on minding the spell, we're all done."

Matt wanted to protest, opened his mouth to do exactly that, but before he could say anything, the woman was turning and sprinting toward the inn and in moments, she vanished into the mist after Priest. As he watched her go, another feeling crept past the overwhelming fear—anger.

Anger that, once again, he was to be left alone, anger that he, a man grown, was to be treated like a child and left to be a nursemaid to a mage instead of helping to rescue the villagers. Which meant that the others would get all the credit, and he would be left with nothing at all. It wasn't fair, particularly since without him, they would not have come back in the first place, for all the others would have happily left the villagers to their grim fate.

But Matt was not a child. Neither was he a nursemaid. Matt had heard many stories of heroes throughout his life—some from his mother when he was a child, and others he'd discussed excitedly with his friends, and in none of those stories had the heroes of the story ever sat back and hid while others did the fighting, the saving.

Besides, he told himself that Chall was fine—the mage was still hidden on the top of the wall, and the soldiers were far too busy being frightened of the Skaalden to pay him any mind. Matt took a moment to climb up the wall—a far longer moment than the man, Priest, had taken, a thing he noticed and which bothered him—and looked at the mage.

The heavy-set man was hunkered over, staring out at the mist and the creatures moving within it. There was a strained expression on his face and despite the coolness in the air—much of which had been brought on by the phantom mist—the man's forehead was covered in sweat. His hands were in front of him where he lay on his stomach, twisted into what looked like claws, and he was trembling.

Maeve had been right about this much, at least—if one of the soldiers happened on the mage while he was using his magic, the man would clearly be unable to defend himself. Likely, judging by his unfocused gaze, he would not even notice that they had come upon him until he felt the bite of their sword and nothing after.

"Chall?"

"Not now, lad," the mage said, hissing the words through gritted teeth.

"They'll need help, Maeve and Priest, I mean, but Maeve said—"

The mage let out a weary growl, turning to stare at Matt. Suddenly the illusion flickered. Only for a moment, but for a brief instant, the mist, and those figures lurking within it, vanished, revealing Priest and Maeve running toward the soldiers at the inn. "What is it, boy?"

"Chall," Matt said as several of the soldiers began to take note of the two figures rushing toward them, "something's happened."

Chall frowned, looking back toward the inn. "*Shit,*" he hissed. He waved his clawed hands desperately, as if trying to snatch something only he could see out of the air, and then, in another moment, the mist was back, the figures lurking inside it as well.

"Chall," Matt tried again, "will you be okay if I—"

"*Go, Matt,*" the mage growled, "now."

Matt recoiled at the rebuke, hurriedly climbing down the wall of the burned-out house once more. He was standing there, angry at being forgotten, at being left behind, his face heating with a mixture of annoyance and shame, when he thought of something. Yes, the mage's words might be seen as a rebuke. But then, they might also be seen as permission. After all, Chall had *told* him to go, hadn't he?

Matt glanced once more up at the mage. The shadows would cover him, keeping him from the soldiers' view—and anyway they were far too busy worried about the phantom figures lurking in the mist, shouting panicked cries to each other, to go searching for him. What's more, Maeve and Priest would need Matt's help. The woman had told him to stay, yes, but she had told him because she thought of him as a child. But he was not a child, was not helpless. So, he looked at the mist—and the giants moving within it—took a deep breath, and ran forward, leaving the mage and the cover the building provided behind him.

# CHAPTER THIRTY-ONE

*There is no beast more dangerous, than one cornered.*
*No man more dangerous than one with nowhere left to run.*
*—Unknown author*

He could hear the sounds of their pursuit as they approached, the padded shuffle of their footsteps, the harsh rasps of their breath in the cool air as they sprinted to catch up with what they believed to be their fleeing prey. And Cutter had fled, at least for a time, but he had not fled as a deer might when it caught the hunter's scent, wildly and without thought, for whatever else he was, for whatever else he had been, he was not prey, not then and not now.

But the men chased him as if he was, as if he were the fox and they the hounds, barreling after him without caution, without fear. That was their mistake. He stood with his back propped against the wall of a house, the surface still slick with soot, and he listened to them come. Two in this group, judging by the sound. There would be others, of course, spreading out through the village while some moved to surround the village and cut off his exit, making sure that no avenue of escape was left to him. But then, he had never been planning to escape.

So, instead of running for the village edge, an edge which would soon be guarded by soldiers if it wasn't already, Cutter stood at the wall with his massive axe in his hand. And he waited. It had always been the worst part of it for him, the waiting. The doing of the thing was rarely so bad as the fantasies a man created for himself while he waited for it to begin. He knew that, for he had learned it during a hundred other situations like this one, and so he did not concern himself with Matt and the others, did not wonder at whether or not they were safe, at whether or not they would be able to save the villagers. What he could do for them he had done already.

There was only the here, only the now. Only the feel of the axe haft in his hands, its weight a solid, comforting, terrifying presence. When he judged the front man of the two to be rounding the corner, he stepped out, grunting as he swung the axe with all his might. The blow connected solidly, slightly above the man's chin. He did not have time to scream or even slow as most of his head was lopped from his shoulders in a bloody rush. The second man did have time to scream, but no more than that before Cutter pivoted, doing a half-spin and bringing the axe back to bury the blade in the man's forehead.

With a grunt, he ripped the axe free, and the man collapsed to the ground on his back. Cutter started to turn but paused as he caught sight of the man's face. Or, at least, what was left of it. Perhaps by some trick of the light, or his own mood, or perhaps because it was simply the truth, the soldier looked young. In his early twenties, if that. Only a few years older than Matt.

Cutter knew that time was of the essence, knew that every single second he wasted would be paid for in blood, yet he found himself frozen to the spot, staring at the dead man. He remembered the conversation he'd had with Matt what felt like a lifetime ago back in Brighton, when he'd claimed he wanted to be a soldier. He remembered the boy's youthful excitement, his bright-eyed eagerness as he talked about something he did not and could not understand. Had this man lying dead before him been the same? Had he, only a few years recent, left home after having much the same conversation with his mother or father? Left seeking glory and honor and all the other bullshit the bards sang about once the bleeding and the dying was done only to find himself here, a corpse lying broken and forgotten in a dark alleyway of some out of the way village?

There were shouts from nearby. Close. Likely, they'd heard their comrade's shout and would be coming to investigate. It was enough to pull him from his dark imaginings, enough to bring him back to the present. He would die here, that much he knew, but each moment these men spent chasing him was a moment they would not spend hurting Matt or the others. Another moment where his companions, his *friends* might make it away.

And so, he took a brief moment to pause and wipe the blade of his axe clean on the young man's jerkin. No time for sentiment in war, no place for it even if there had been, and the blood would dull the edge of the blade, an edge he'd be using again before he was through.

With that done, he replaced the axe in the sling at his back, and then he was moving again, not away from those men who approached, not this time. There was no hope in running, and he had never been a good runner anyway. He would buy his companions the time he could, but he would do it by doing the thing he was best at, perhaps the only thing he had ever been good at.

He would kill. As many of them as he could. And then, in time, he would die. And with the course his life had taken, he found that the thought was not a very bad one.

\*\*\*

They were all whispering in hushed, frightened tones, huddled in little frightened groups making scared, frightened faces. Hundreds of people—the entire village, Netty supposed—or at least that part of it that had not been killed in the Fey assault. Hundreds of faces all of which she knew, the actors in her small, rural life. Small, rural, but, until the last few days, one she had never regretted.

Berden had been a large part of that. She had not been born to this way of life, this living on the fringes of things. Neither had he, of course, but he had always seemed a natural at it anyway, had, in fact, seemed a natural at anything he ever did. He had never boasted or bragged, her husband, but had simply gone about his life—and what seemed to her to be his inevitable successes—with a quiet dignity that spoke not of arrogance but of confidence in himself, in the world, too.

Berden, had he been here, would have known what to do with all of these people, looking so scared and so desperate. He'd always known what to do. Oh, sure, she'd given him grief enough, but then that was a wife's job, just as it was a husband's to try his level best to drive that wife insane. But she'd loved him, loved him even after more than thirty years. And in the end, when he was gone, after some creature that should never have existed in a right world—though only a fool might claim it as such—had taken him from her, she had realized that he had not just been her husband. Or, at least, that was the least of what he had been. He had been her rock. Her proof that the world was not so terrible after all. He had *been* her world.

And now that he was gone, she felt empty, scoured out and used up. Useless. *Oh, come off it, Netty,* she told herself. *What would Berden say, he could see you now, whining and bemoaning your lot? After all, you ain't the one got killed in the night before you even managed to get out of bed.* And the thing was, that if he *were* here, Berden would not have said anything. Or at least, what he *would* have said would not come from a place of anger or disgust, nor even annoyance. He would speak softly, kindly, *truthfully,* and she would, inevitably, find herself comforted and annoyed all at once. That was Berden. It was why so many of the people in the village had come to the inn so often. They had come for the ale, of course, and for the companionship with their fellow villagers. But they had also come for Berden.

But she was not Berden, and while he might have been chock full of wisdom—she'd always joked he was chock full of shit, but she could tell the truth now, if only to herself—she thought her own life had largely been a succession of one confusing situation after another, all of which she had no damned idea what to do with. And this, with the crying children and their silently sobbing parents, was no exception. She was not the person to lead them, to comfort them. In fact, she figured there were probably thousands of people in the world better suited to the task, just so long as they had a heartbeat.

But no one was stepping forward to take up the task, that much was sure, and yet it was still a task that needed doing. Maybe she wasn't Berden, but she'd known him long enough to know what he would say to that—when a thing needs doin', there's no greater comfort than gettin' started. She was not Berden, but what she was, was *here.*

She moved toward Mack and Will, Cend's hangers-on, and the two who were lucky to still be alive after challenging the Crimson

Prince himself. She thought to ask them where Cend was, but she decided, considering how quickly Prince Feledias had known where Cutter was, that she probably didn't need to. The two men were scared, standing with their wives and their little ones, them scared too, and why not? She knelt before the kids, two girls around eight years of age and thank the gods they didn't get their looks from their fathers. The boy, the youngest, not even old enough to speak, with tears in his eyes, his lip trembling. Not sure why he was scared, maybe, just that his mother and father were scared and so he ought to be too.

Scared just like everyone else, which was a problem. After all, scared people did stupid things, that was another favorite of Berden's, one she'd found to be truer than she'd like. In fact, she would have gone a step further and said that people did stupid things, but being scared certainly didn't help matters. "Mack, Will," she said, "as I recall, there's a couple of decks of cards down in the cellar." She paused, glancing at the children. "Why don't you go and see if you can't fetch 'em for us?"

The bigger of the two—Cend's stand in when the man wasn't around to be a nuisance—Mack, frowned. "Don't feel much like playin' cards just now, Netty, it's all the same to you."

Netty held back a sigh, telling herself that there were other qualities to recommend a man than his intelligence, otherwise the whole damned human race would have ended a long time ago.

Natalie, Mack's wife and therefore to Netty's mind just about as close to godly patience as anyone was likely to get, let out a tired sigh. "She means for the kids, Mack."

"Ah," the big man said, grunting. "Not sure if it's such a good idea, that," he went on, "teachin' the kids to play cards."

Natalie tensed her jaw, and Netty thought that the woman's patience, godly or not, was just about stripped bare, and when the woman spoke she did so in a low tone, without inflection. "I reckon there's probably bigger things to worry about just now than them becoming gamblers, don't you, Mack?"

Perhaps the big man had heard that tone before and recognized it as an alarm bell, for he grunted, turning back to Netty. "In the cellar, you said?"

"That's right."

He grunted. "Come on, Will. Let's see if we can't find 'em."

His friend—the dumbest of the three by Netty's estimation, and that no small accomplishment—frowned. "But I thought you said—"

"Shut up and come on," Mack growled, and then they were gone, heading toward the cellar.

When they were out of earshot, Natalie turned back to her. "Thanks, Netty."

It felt good, that thanks. Good, and by and large unearned, but she gave the best smile of which she was capable. "Don't thank me yet—it'll be a damn shame these pretty little young'uns grow up to be the world's worst gamblers."

The woman laughed at that, one that was pulled from her almost against her judgment, but she sobered up quickly enough, looking even worse than she had before. *Gods, I'm a fool,* Netty thought. A nice little joke, about the kiddies growing up to be gamblers, maybe, but one that wasn't quite as funny when a body stopped to consider the likely proposition that they'd never have a chance to grow up at all.

Netty thought it best to quit while she was behind, and she offered the two women the best smile she could before turning and walking away, trying to look around and decide who else's life she could screw up before it was taken from them. Then an idea struck her, and she moved to Emille. The girl stood alone. A quiet one, Emille, pretty but a little unearthly, some said touched by the Fey. Foolish talk, of course, but there was no denying that she was different, a difference which had only been exacerbated when the girl's father had died to the fever two winters past and grown even more when her mother had been taken by the Fey. The girl was pale, silent tears gliding their way down her cheeks, no doubt still traumatized from the prince's threat.

And then another saying came to Netty, this one not Berden's but her own, passed down to her from her mother, usually accompanied by a whipping, one she likelier than not had deserved at the time. *Idle hands do evil work.*

That was another she'd found to be true. Maybe she couldn't give all the people comfort, maybe it wasn't in her to give, not when she had none of it herself. But she could give them work, at least. That much she could do. And if the work didn't help, well, it was a tavern, after all. There was always ale. "Emille," she shouted.

The girl started and looked up at her. "Ma'am?"

"Come on, girl," Netty said, loud enough for the entire common room, packed full of people, to hear, "I need your help. This is the busiest my and my husband's inn has ever been, and I'll be damned, I don't take advantage and sell all these mopey bastards some ale."

That got a few laughs, and that felt good, felt damned fine, in truth. She moved toward the back of the bar and began pouring drinks, pausing after she'd poured half a dozen or so to look back at the common room, everyone seeming to watch her as if she'd lost her mind. And who knew? Maybe she had. But then, when a person was about to lose her life—and probably in a pretty uncomfortable fashion—she figured there were worse things. "Well?" she demanded, doing her best to adopt her slightly-scolding tone, the one Berden had always joked with her about. "I don't know as I'll be able to drink all this myself, but you all keep standin' there, and I can promise I'll give it a try."

There was some more scattered laughter at that, and people began to move forward, taking the ale, hesitantly at first, but then more, and it was as if a dam had broken, a dam of fear and terror, and they began to whisper again, to talk in hushed tones. And that was good. Netty thought maybe it was the best thing she'd ever done as she continued to pour the ales.

True, they may still die, but then miracles had happened before, hadn't they? Besides, there was always the outside chance that Feledias, once he had his brother—and hadn't that been a shock, seeing the man return as he had?—qould leave them all in peace. And if he didn't, well, there'd be worse things than getting drunk. All in all, she was feeling pretty good, feeling like she had made a difference, not in the way Berden would have, maybe, but in her own way.

That was when she smelled the smoke.

# CHAPTER THIRTY-TWO

*It's not an easy thing, killing a man, watching him bleed out, all his hopes and dreams taken from him until he's nothing but a husk. Not the sort of thing a man gets over, not the dead or the living.*
*No, it ain't easy, taking a man's life.*
*But, then, I figure it's a damn sight easier than dying.*
*—Veteran soldier of the Fey wars*

Maeve wasn't as quick as she used to be, not as fast or as attractive either, but the two soldiers were distracted—as any right-thinking person might be—by the appearance of what appeared to be the Skaalden. They were too busy staring at the looming forms in the mist to notice the considerably squatter, considerably less-terrifying one that approached from behind them, her knives in her hands. The second didn't even so much as look around as her knife slid into the throat of the first and a moment later the two were lying dead at her feet, two down as easy as breathing. Or not breathing.

Maybe she should have felt good about that, but it was hard to feel good about killing terrified men, even if those same terrified men were getting ready to burn an entire village worth of people. She turned, meaning to continue the bloody business, when a man appeared in front of her, a soldier with a sword in his hands, and anger mixed with the fear on his face.

*Perhaps,* she thought, as she watched the sword raise, *not so easy after all.* But just then, an arrow flew out of the thick mist, catching the soldier unerringly in the throat. He staggered, dropping his sword as he pawed uselessly at his throat. Maeve spun to look in the direction the arrow had come from but saw no sign of Priest through the thick fog. Of course, she didn't really need to. The man was out there somewhere, and there was more killing to be done yet. It seemed to her, sometimes, that there always was.

So she took a moment, gathering her breath—didn't remember get winded so easily back then, but then she'd been a lot younger and killing was the type of thing, sadly, that a person did get better at with practice. Then, when the worst of the stitch in her side was gone, she crept forward into the mist. She couldn't be sure, for the fog covered everything more than a few inches in front of her face, but she thought that she must be close to the inn now, not least of which because she thought she could smell smoke. And the last thing she needed was to sprint forward with the intention of saving the villagers only to knock herself unconscious on the building's outside wall and burn to death right along with them.

She eased forward, a knife in one hand, the other held out in front of her. She was moving for a few minutes, struggling to ignore the great forms of the imaginary Skaalden sharing the fog with her. It was not easy. The sight of them was bad enough, but the worst was the sound, the terrible, screeching, keening sound which always accompanied them, a sound which brought her mind back to many years ago, when she'd lost her husband and her child. Still, she gritted her teeth, forcing her reluctant feet forward, telling herself that the sound which filled her ears, the one threatening to make her run in terror, was not that of the creatures which had driven her and her people from their homeland, only their facsimile, one created by the closest thing she had to a friend. But telling herself that as some of those figures loomed out of the mist, walking past her, was not an easy thing, not when she could feel the chill touch of the fog against her skin.

In time, the hand she held in front of her struck something, and she sighed with relief. But it was a sigh that cut off abruptly as what she'd taken to be the wall did something very unwall-like—it moved. "Hey," a voice growled, "who the fu—"

Not a lot to go on, just a voice and a chest with her hand on it, no face, at least none that wasn't obscured by the mist. Not much, but Maeve figured enough. She lashed out with her knife, and the man's words turned into a soft, breathless groan, as her questing blade found its mark. She pulled the knife free, and he collapsed to the ground at her feet.

"*Maeve, help!*"

She froze, a sudden, irrational spike of terror lancing through her. "*Matt?*" she whispered in a harsh voice, sure that, somehow, she had gotten turned around, that she had worked her way back to where the boy and the mage hid behind the house and had, even worse, wounded him.

"*Maeve!*"

But the voice, when it came again, did not come from below her where the man lay, and a quick check showed that he was dead anyway and far past speaking. At least, until he visited her in her dreams like so many others did, but that was a problem for later. The voice was not so close as the man. Instead, it came from somewhere off to her right. Had the soldiers found the mage and the boy, somehow? It would not have been an easy thing, but then it would not have been impossible either. Still, if they had, why was the mage's illusion still working? It didn't make any sense but then it didn't really matter. What did was that she had heard the fear in Matt's voice, and so Maeve abandoned her caution and sprinted into the mist in the direction from which the voice had come.

"*Matt!*" she shouted as she ran. "*Where are you?*"

But the boy did not answer, not this time, and she felt her panic threaten to overwhelm her. Did he not hear her? Was he too busy? Or was there some other, darker reason why he remained silent? "*Matt!*" she yelled again as she narrowed her eyes, struggling and failing to see past the thick fog.

Again, there was no answer. She moved farther into the mist and heard the unmistakable sounds of fighting. She narrowed her eyes, trying to see through the fog, and could just make out the silhouettes of what appeared to be two figures stumbling around with their hands on each other as if in some awkward dance. Maeve hurried forward and saw that, indeed, one of them was Matt. And at a quick glance, she saw, too, why the youth had not answered her—it was not so easy to respond when a man who looked like he outweighed you by a good fifty pounds had his hands wrapped around your throat doing his level best to choke you to death.

The soldier was so intent on killing Matt that he did not notice Maeve's approach as she rushed behind him, burying her knife in his back. The soldier let out a wheeze, and stumbled away, falling. Maeve watched him for a moment, making sure that he was done, then she turned to Matt. "Are you okay?"

The youth was rubbing at his throat, his eyes wide and scared. "H-he was going to kill me."

"It's the thing about murderers," Maeve agreed, "they aren't all that original. Now," she said, "are you okay?"

He cleared his throat, wincing as he rubbed at his neck. "I...I think so."

Maeve nodded. "So what happened? Did they find Chall? Where is he?"

"Chall's fine, Maeve," he said quickly, "he's still at the house."

Maeve frowned. "I don't understand. If no one found you both then why are you here?"

"I thought..." The youth hesitated, as if embarrassed. "I wanted to help."

Maeve blinked, glancing between the boy and the dead man on the ground, the one who had been well along the process of killing him when she'd arrived. "You wanted to help," she said slowly.

"Y-yes."

"Gods, you have no idea what you've done, what you've risked."

"It's alright, Maeve," he said, "I'm fine, really. My throat's just—"

"I don't mean *you*, you damned fool," she snapped. "I mean, Chall."

The youth winced, clearly hurt, but a moment later a defensive, angry look came on his face. "I'm not a kid to be hidden away. I want to help and—"

"You *were* helping, damnit," Maeve hissed, "by keeping Chall alive. Don't you *get* it? If something happens to Chall, it won't just be a friend I'll lose, it'll be all of our lives, for if he dies, the illusion—" And then, as if her worries, her fears, had called it into existence, there was suddenly no need to explain anymore, for the mist, and the imagined creatures lurking therein, suddenly vanished as if they had never been.

Which was bad. What was worse was that, as the mist cleared, Maeve and Matt were left staring at four soldiers with bared blades, no more than two dozen feet between them.

"B-but what happened?" Matt asked. "To the illusion?"

"Don't you see? If something has happened to the illusion, that means that something has happened to Chall, who *you* were meant to watch."

"I-I'm sorry, Maeve," he said, "I thought—"

"It doesn't matter what you *thought*," she snapped, watching the soldiers. "It's done now. The world isn't some fairy tale, boy, where the good guys always win no matter how stupid they are. In the real world, good guys die all the time, if there are even any left. Now, grab that sword," she said, motioning to the blade that had fallen from the dead man's hands.

"But Maeve," he said, "I've never...I mean I don't know how to use it."

"Then you'd better learn, boy," she said. "Learn to fight or learn to die—your choice."

Unsurprisingly, the youth bent and retrieved the sword. Maeve paid him no more mind, however. Instead, her attention was focused on the four soldiers who had overcome the terror that the imaginary Skaalden had caused and were now moving toward them, their blades bared. Relieved, no doubt, to be faced with human opponents instead of the monstrous ones which had lurked in the mist.

Maeve withdrew a second knife, holding one in each hand as she waited for the approaching soldiers. She would do her best, but she knew that she and the boy stood little chance. She had once been known for her deadly skills, but that had been long ago and, anyway, her reputation had not been for standing and fighting as Cutter's had been. Instead, her skills had lain in different areas. Seduction. Assassination. Not an axe to be wielded on some battlefield against countless foes, but instead a knife in the dark, one that might slip in like a thief and do its bloody work without anyone knowing it was coming.

But these four men were ready, and there was no chance for subtlety, no opportunity for surprise. The soldiers gathered speed, coming toward them confidently, aware that they had the upper hand. When they were less than a dozen feet away, something flew out of the night, whistling, and one of the soldiers grunted as an arrow embedded itself in his back. He staggered, a look of surprise crossing his features before he collapsed to the ground.

His fellows let out shouts of surprise, spinning to look around them, and Priest leapt down from where he'd somehow managed to climb on top of the inn's roof in the confusion, landing in a crouch and firing another arrow almost in the same moment he hit the ground. The second missile's path was as true as the first, and it buried itself in the stomach of one of the soldiers who'd turned to look.

Then with a shout of rage and fear, the two men rushed the archer, and Maeve didn't hesitate, charging at their backs. She reached them as Priest was forced to parry one of the soldier's blows with his bow, and she buried one of her blades in the side of the soldier's throat as the second took him in the back, digging up into his chest.

She was just pulling her blades free when she heard a shout behind her and saw that another soldier had come up on them and was rushing toward Matt. Maeve let out a hiss, starting forward at a run but knowing she would be too late even as she did.

***

Matt had always imagined himself as a soldier, as one of the brave knights from the stories his mother had once read him. Knights who never felt fear and who always spoke about things like honor and courage and who would not hesitate at the thought of fighting a single man, who would not hesitate even if he faced ten times that number.

But if the last few days had not confirmed the fact that he was not one of those knights from the stories, then that moment in which he saw the soldier charging at him with a shout, his blade drawn and murder in his eyes, did it well enough. Matt did not feel brave, and honor was the last thing from his mind. What he felt, more than anything, was terror.

The soldier's sword flashed toward him, and Matt raised his own blade, his hands aching where they gripped the handle tight. He let out a whimper of panic as the man's sword came on, and he was just able to get his own blade up in time. But even though he managed to get his sword in line, he was not prepared for the brutal, shocking force of the impact as the two weapons met. Pain lanced up his hands all the way through his arms, and he stumbled, nearly losing his feet as his sword was ripped out of his hands.

The soldier let out a barking laugh. "Time to die, boy."

Here, one of those knights would have said something brave, something to show that he was not afraid, but Matt's throat was dry, and he could say nothing to show that he was not afraid, mostly because he *was* afraid. Terrified, in fact. He wanted to run, but he knew that, if he did, the man would cut him down before he'd made it half a dozen steps.

Yet, that was not the only reason he did not run, for as he stood there watching the soldier and his grin, watching him stalking forward, taking his time, something happened. The overwhelming fear Matt felt began to change, to shift within him, and he found that while he was still afraid, he was not just that. He was angry. Angry at himself for risking them all, for abandoning his post by the mage, angry at Cutter for bringing him here in the first place. But mostly, he was angry at the soldier in front of him, the man who looked so confident, who was staring at him as if he were a bug he meant to squish and doubted he'd have any trouble doing it.

So before he was fully aware of what he was doing, Matt let out a shout and charged forward. The man had not been expecting it—no surprise as Matt hadn't been expecting it himself—so he didn't get his sword up in time before Matt tackled him. The blade flew from the soldier's hands, and then they were both tumbling across the ground, hissing and spitting and struggling.

But while his anger had helped to banish the worst of his fear, to dull the edges of it, no anger, no matter how consuming, could make up for a lack of skill and training, of strength. The soldier was on top of him before he knew it, and Matt cried out as the man's fist struck him a hard blow in the face which rocked him, bouncing his head off the hard ground. The coppery, sharp taste of blood filled his mouth. He fought to dislodge the attacker, pushing against him, yet it was useless, for the soldier was too strong, a man grown with years of experience behind him, and he brushed Matt's meager efforts aside with ease.

The man flashed him a bloody grin, his lip busted, perhaps, when Matt had tackled him, then he wrapped his hands around Matt's throat and began to squeeze. Matt struggled beneath him, trying to dislodge him from his perch as his vision started to fade, shadows creeping into the edges of it, but it was no use.

*I'm going to die here.*

The thought was a shock to Matt, for out of all the things he had imagined, he had never imagined that, had never imagined that his decision to leave the mage behind would lead to his death. Perhaps he should have, but he, like so many youths, had thought, somewhere deep down, that he was invincible, that death was something that happened to other people. He realized now, as his vision tunneled and black specks began to dance in what remained, that he had been wrong. He had been a fool, and Cutter had been right after all.

It seemed wrong to him, perverse, that it should be so easy to die, the easiest thing in the world. He realized, too, that he had been a fool to squander his life as he had, that he had not fully appreciated it and the lives of everyone else until he saw, up close, *experienced* on a personal level, how easily those lives might be snuffed out, with no more effort than a man might give putting out a candle.

Then, suddenly, the pressure eased, and the soldier was pulled back away from him. He saw that Maeve had gripped the man by his hair, jerking his head back, and he saw, too, the blade in her other hand. *No,* Matt thought, seeing what was going to happen, thinking, in that moment, that no life, not even that of the man who had meant to kill him, should be discarded so easily. "*P-please,*" he croaked, "*wait—*"

But Maeve did not wait. Instead, she brought her knife across the grunting soldier's throat, and the blade ripped a deep furrow into the vulnerable flesh there. Blood spewed over him, and Matt gasped at the warm, tacky feel of it, unable to look away as he saw the light, the *life,* fade from the soldier's eyes.

Then, when his weak struggles ceased, Maeve grunted, shoving the lifeless corpse unceremoniously to the side. The body landed on its stomach, the man's face, his eyes, turned toward Matt, a look that seemed somehow accusing on his features. Matt could not pull his gaze away from that face, those features which, moments ago, had been full of life and now were nothing, pale and waxy like the features of a doll, no sign to show that life had ever existed there at all.

"*Why?*" he rasped. "You...you didn't need to. We, we could have—"

"Could have *what*, boy?" Maeve demanded as she pulled him to shaky feet. "Tied him up? Carried him along with us hoping he'd be a good boy while we fought the rest of his friends and rescued those he and the others mean to burn alive?" She gave her head an angry shake, meeting his eyes. "The world is not a fairy-tale, boy, not a storybook. People die—it's what we're best at—and one mistake, one selfish decision, and those people might be your friends."

Matt knew that she was right, knew that he had messed up, and that likely Chall was now dead because of it, so he said nothing. She watched him for a moment longer, then Priest walked up, the man covered in blood and displaying a slight limp. Maeve looked over at him then back at Matt. "How many need to get hurt, boy, how many need to die, before you learn that?"

Still, Matt said nothing, for there was nothing he could say, and she gave a disgusted shake of her head, turning away from him. "Come on—if we hurry, maybe we can at least die with those poor bastards in the inn."

Matt followed silently behind the other two as they crept along the inn's wall, Priest with an arrow already placed on his bow, Maeve with two blood-stained blades in her hands. But as much as he knew he should be focused on the present, for the gods alone knew how many soldiers were left stationed around the inn, he found himself instead thinking of the dead man, of the way his eyes had looked, of how quickly it had all happened. Alive one moment, breathing and thinking with hopes and dreams, perhaps a family, and the next, the man was dead, everything he was, everything he had been, come to nothing.

Matt had seen death before, of course. He'd attended several Sendings during his life in Brighton, most due to old age and some few to men or women who had gotten taken by the elements, by the frigid cold or the unexpected blizzards that sometimes arrived out of nowhere so far north. He had seen more of it in his time following Cutter, the Fey creature who had attacked him, the villagers in Ferrimore who had suffered at the hands of such creatures. But while he had seen death, he had never seen it so *close*, had never felt its breath on his neck, had never felt its hand in his as it considered tearing him away from the world of the living. But he felt it now, and in that feeling, he felt something else—change. He did not know the exact nature of that change, perhaps never would, knew only that he had been irrevocably altered by what he had witnessed, the guard's death, and how close he had come to dying himself. He found himself wondering again at Cutter, at how the man could be so cold and so unfeeling in the face of such death.

They reached the door to the inn moments later. Two more dead men lay here, the arrows protruding from them proof that Priest had come upon them while Matt was stumbling through the mist or perhaps before he had foolishly abandoned Chall. He glanced at Maeve's back, wondering if protecting the mage, protecting *him*, had not been the only reason she had ordered him to stay behind. He wondered if part of that reason had been so he would not see death so close, thought that probably it had been. He wished only that he had listened.

But it was too late now, for what was done could not be undone. Death had caught him in its gaze, he had felt it, and it was not a thing he would soon forget.

"Come on," Maeve whispered to them. "We have to be quick now—Feledias might have left some on the inside."

***

The smoke was roiling through the walls and into the inn, and what conversations they'd had, mostly revolving escape, had devolved into fits of coughing from everyone inside the common room. Several of the men were still trying to break their way through the doors, but whatever the soldiers had used to barricade them was not budging no matter how much they tried.

Netty considered telling them not to bother—after all, she doubted Ferrimore was the first village Feledias had burned and he probably had it down by now—but didn't, deciding that if it helped them, if it allowed them to hold onto a little hope, then there was no point in stealing that from them. She did her best to offer comfort to the others, whispering quiet words, saying quiet prayers, but the fact was that they were scared, and so was she. It was heating up inside the inn, and already her face was covered in sweat, her clothes, like the clothes of those others around her, drenched with it.

Worse, more and more smoke was pouring into the inn by the moment, and it was getting difficult to breathe.

"What do we do, Netty?"

Netty turned to look at Emille, the girl standing beside her, her eyes wide and frightened. Perhaps some of Netty's despair had made it onto her face despite her efforts to hide it, for when she met the girl's eyes, Emille seemed to blanch, her skin going even paler. "W-we're going to die, aren't we?" she asked, keeping her voice low, quiet, so that the others wouldn't hear. Not that there was any real fear of that, not the way the men were banging on the doors, desperately trying to find a way out when Netty was growing certain there was none.

Tears filled the girl's eyes then, and Netty did the only thing she could think to do—she pulled her into a tight embrace. "It's okay, lass," she whispered, her voice feeling raw and sore from the smoke, "it will be okay."

No idea whether such a thing was true or not, for Netty had never died before and so had no idea of what the land beyond the veil might look like. If it were anything like the world they were leaving behind, then she thought she'd just as soon not go there, but then it wasn't as if she had been given any choice in the matter. Still, it was the best she could think of, the best she could offer to the girl.

There was a shout from one of the groups of men at the back door. *What now?* Netty thought, turning to see that, to her shock, the door—which had remained stubbornly closed despite their efforts—was suddenly open, and three men, Mack and Will among them, stood staring at it, stunned.

Netty understood that. It was too much to hope that the soldiers had decided that burning an entire village to death did not sit well with them and had chosen, instead, to let them go. More likely, they had decided to finish it quickly, perhaps to practice their sword work on innocents before they let the fire do its work.

The men must have thought much the same and decided that their only chance—the only chance for their loved ones—was to rush the men who came through, for they started forward, toward the opening. But when a figure stepped through the door and into the inn, Netty was shocked to see that it was not one of the prince's soldiers. Instead it was a woman and a gray-haired man, ones who she did not recognize, though they could have been her closest friends and she still wouldn't have, not with all the blood staining their clothes and faces. It wasn't until the third person stepped through, a young lad that looked no more than fifteen or sixteen years old, that the pieces of the puzzle clicked into place.

"Hold, lads!" Netty shouted at the three men who'd started forward, wielding broken off chair legs. Not that she doubted they would have done much harm to the newcomers who, based on their grim expressions looked like death on two feet. Save the lad, of course, whose face held the dull, vacant look of someone who has felt such fear he has had become numb to it. She knew that look well, for it was plastered across the faces of many of those in the inn.

"Relax, Netty," Mack said, doing his best at a menacing growl, one he'd tried to adopt from Cend but hadn't gotten quite right yet. He turned back to look at the newcomers. "What do you want?"

"Well," the woman said dryly, "we were considering saving you all from certain death, how'd that be?"

He looked a bit flustered at that, as well he should, and Netty used the opportunity of him being distracted by the fact he was a complete fool to step forward. "That'd be just fine with us."

And then they were moving, the villagers, some of whom were crying with shock and relief that it appeared they were going to live after all, staggering out of the inn, coughing and waving hands at the smoke still gathering in the common room.

Moments later, they were outside, panting and gasping as the flames in the inn continued to grow. "Thank you," Netty said to the woman, "for saving us, Miss—"

"Just Maeve," the woman said. "And if you're looking to thank someone..." She paused, nodding her head at the youth who was standing a few feet away, pointedly avoiding looking at them as if embarrassed. "Then that'd be Matt. He's the reason we're back here—him and Cutter, that is."

"Cutter?"

"That's right, though you'd know him by Prince Bernard or 'The Crimson Prince'."

"By the gods, you're the ones that were with the prince!"

"Yes."

Netty grunted. "Almost didn't recognize you, what with all the..." She paused, staring at the blood. "Anyway. I saw him, your prince. He spoke a bit with his brother before they went on about the business of trying to kill each other." A thought struck her, and she blinked. "Wait a minute, are you sayin', he sacrificed himself to save us?"

"Yes."

Netty grunted. "Doesn't seem like the same Prince Bernard I've heard so many stories about, the one known for his love of killin'."

The woman nodded slowly, a thoughtful expression on her face. "No, no it doesn't. Anyway, the prince sent us to get you all out while he's got the others distracted."

"I see. And where exactly does the prince want us to go?"

"Toward the forest."

She nodded at that, opening her mouth to say something more, then she became aware of a crowd gathered at her back. Turning, she saw that it was nearly half the villagers, maybe more, men, mostly, but more than a few women. They didn't look just scared, not now, not like they had when they'd been sure they were going to be burned alive. Now, they looked angry.

"Mack?" she asked the man who stood at the front with his friend Will beside him. "What's all this then?"

"Don't seem right," he growled.

"Oh?" she asked. "And what's that?" Though, the truth was, she thought she knew exactly what *it* was, knew exactly how they were feeling, for she was feeling more than a little bit of it herself.

"Runnin' away," he said. "After the prince savin' us and all."

"Uh-huh," Netty said, nodding thoughtfully. "There's a lot about the last couple days don't strike me as exactly right. Anyway, Maeve here says they've come to save us—says we're to go into the forest, hide out for a while, maybe, until the mad prince is gone."

"Which prince do you mean, Netty?" Will asked.

"Do you suppose it matters?"

The man grunted. "No, no, I don't suppose it does."

"Anyway," she said, looking at the bigger of the two again. "You look troubled, Mack." She glanced behind him at the crowd of men and women. "Matter of fact, you all do. If I didn't know any better, I'd say you look like some folks got violence on their mind." Some of them fidgeted at that, and she grunted. "Oh, don't look so ashamed. Truth is," she said, glancing into the village in the direction Prince Bernard had run, "I do too."

She turned back to Maeve. "Some of us would like to accept your offer now, Marvelous Maeve," she said, grinning as the woman grunted in surprise.

The woman eyed her and the others. "And the rest?"

"Oh, we'll be goin' too," the woman said. "Only, there's somethin' we need to take care of first."

# CHAPTER THIRTY-THREE

*A man came to our village once*
*A Feyling in a cage*
*A coin a look he said to us*
*See its eyes, sparkle gold*
*Its fur sleek and black*
*But do not open up its cage*
*Or the Feyling will attack*
—Rodarian Dalumis, Poet, excerpt taken from "The Ramblings of Life from a Rambling Life"

The net was closing.

Six men lay dead somewhere in the village by his hands, but there were more, many more. Their footsteps were all around him, the sounds of their thudding like the distant thunder of a coming storm as they combed through the streets. But just now, he was not in the street, was instead lying prone on what remained of the roof of what had once been a stable. He was not known for his subtlety, he knew, had a reputation—well-earned—for being a ruthless killer like some mad barbarian.

They did not expect him to hide, to sneak around when he could charge directly into battle. And that was exactly what he was counting on. He focused on controlling his breathing as the three men approached, creeping down the alleyway in front of the stables beneath him. They were careful, scanning the shadows around them, but in time they moved past his spot and then Cutter, his axe in one hand, leapt from the stables, bringing his weapon down in a two-handed grip.

The Fey-crafted weapon cleaved deep into the space between the neck and shoulder of the soldier at the rear in a gout of blood. Cutter tried to pull the weapon free as the dead man collapsed, but the haft, slick with blood from his previous encounters, slipped from his hands, and he was left weaponless as the corpse took his axe with it.

The two soldiers, alerted to his presence by the sound he'd made falling and, no doubt, by the blood of their comrade spattering their backs, spun. Cutter knew he did not have time to retrieve his axe, so he did not hesitate, rushing toward the nearest with a growl. The man raised his weapon, meaning to bring it down in a lethal arc, but Cutter caught his wrist and slammed his forehead into the man's face, felt his nose crumple beneath the impact.

His opponent made a gurgling, choking sound and staggered away, but Cutter was already turning to the last soldier. He caught a glint of metal as the man's blade flashed at his face, and he spun to the side, struggling to get out of the way but knowing, as he did, that he would not be fast enough, a knowledge confirmed as he felt the steel slice through the sleeve of his shirt and cut a bloody line across his upper arm.

Many people, then, having taken a wound, would have retreated, tried to put some space between them and their attacker, but though the wound pained him, Cutter had taken many such wounds before. So instead of retreating or leaping away, he pivoted on his right foot, throwing all his force back toward his opponent who, judging by the grunt of surprise he made, had clearly expected him to back away. Instead, Cutter brought his fist around, burying it in the man's gut. The soldier collapsed over his fist, bending nearly double as the air exploded out of him in a *whoosh.*

Before he could recover, Cutter turned around him, grabbing the back of the man's head and burying his face in the stone wall of the nearest building. With all his not inconsiderable strength driving it, the soldier's face crushed into the stone wall, and as he collapsed on his back, dead, his face was a mess of blood and bone, his features unrecognizable.

His chest heaving with breath, Cutter took a moment to run the fingers of his right hand over his upper left arm where the sword had bit him, and his hand came away red with blood. A bad wound then, hard to tell just how bad in the darkness—not to mention the cold, which had begun to seep in his bones after so long outside, numbing him.

He knew other soldiers were coming, that those nearest could not have missed the sounds of fighting, but he knew also that such a wound, ignored, would sap a man's strength and kill him as surely as an axe to the throat. So he took a moment, ripping a strip of fabric from his sleeve and using it as a makeshift tourniquet, pulling it as tight as he could and holding one end with his teeth as he tied it into a knot. That done, he tried flexing his left hand into a fist and couldn't manage it.

The arm was useless to him then. Still alive, perhaps, but it was a sign that his time—and therefore, the time for his friends—was running out. He was left with a decision then, try to flee the village—and inevitably get killed as those troops his brother would have posted outside of it surrounded him—or do the unexpected and work his way back toward the inn. In such a situation, anyone would expect him to flee, to try to make it to the village's edge and so would position the majority of their troops around the village to make such an escape impossible, which meant that their numbers would be weaker toward the village center. Or so he hoped.

At least if he went that way he might still be able to offer some help to the others or they might, in turn, be able to help him. Assuming, of course, that they were still alive. A big assumption considering the forces arrayed against them, perhaps a vain one, but he decided that he would rather believe in his companions than bet against them and so, taking a slow deep breath, he flexed his useless hand, trying and failing to work some feeling back into it, then he turned and started back toward the inn at a run.

It did not take him long to reach it, and his decision seemed to be confirmed as the correct one as, the closer toward the center of the village he got, the quieter and quieter were the sounds of soldiers until, paused on the edge of where, so recently, Ferrimore's living had burned their dead in a great Sending, he could hear nothing but his own harsh breaths. And the wind, of course, a wind which seemed to cut through his clothes with ease and which carried the smoke from the dying pyre lazily into the sky. In fact, it was almost too quiet.

He frowned, thinking. He could turn back around, could try to work his way toward the inn from another path, but to do so would cost him time—time he could ill afford, for if he didn't see to the wound on his arm soon, blood loss would steal his brother's chance at revenge. Already, crimson droplets were running down his arm, dripping off his fingertips and onto the cobbles of the street. And even assuming he somehow survived long enough to make it to the inn by a circuitous route, there was the other concern, namely that he would increase his chances of being discovered, and wounded as he was, dizzy from cold and blood loss as he was, he doubted he would survive another fight.

Only a short distance separated him from the front of the inn, which he saw had no soldiers there, but several corpses, the arrows protruding from them marking them as Priest's kills. A reassuring sight, at least, that they had taken out some of the soldiers, yet the bodies scattered at the front of the inn did not account for nearly all the soldiers he had seen or that he suspected his brother would have left to deal with the villagers. Where had the others gone, then? Were they even now fighting his companions? No, that didn't sound right, for he heard no signs of fighting, heard nothing at all but his own labored breathing and the wind whistling through the burned out skeleton which was all that remained of the village of Ferrimore. That and the steady plop of blood from his fingers onto the ground. He frowned at the inn, wondering. Had the people been inside when it burned? Had they all died horribly despite his and the others' efforts?

There was no way of knowing for sure—none, of course, except the macabre task of checking the still blazing inn for corpses, and even if he was so inclined, he simply did not have the time. He had left the others at the back of the inn, and with any luck they would still be there. Less than a hundred feet separating him from his destination then, but a hundred feet which he would have to take in open ground with nothing to conceal him from any hidden watchers.

Not that they would need to have tried very hard to hide, for there were a dozen alleys leading into the center of the village, any one of which could conceal soldiers waiting in ambush. But there was no time—he could only hope that Feledias would have spread his troops around the village.

Stifling a grunt of pain as he rose from his crouch, Cutter started forward in a limping shuffle, his axe already drawn and held down at his side in his good hand. He reached the center of the square, near the still-smoldering pyre, when he heard a noise, a slight, almost imperceptible rustle. Another might have attributed such a sound to nothing, perhaps just his nerves, or the wind rustling fabric, but Cutter knew better, knew, in that moment, that he had made a mistake.

He turned to look around him as at least twenty soldiers began to appear out of the alleyways and buildings surrounding the square, their blades drawn. They created a circle around him, penning him in near the pyre, and he grunted. At least they would not have to travel far to burn his corpse—not that he suspected his brother would grant him such an honor. No, it was more likely that his remains would be scattered throughout the kingdom, proof of what happened to any who thought to stand against Feledias.

Feledias who, even as he had the thought, stepped through a gap the soldiers made, walking between it with Commander Malex beside him to stand two dozen feet away from Cutter, studying him with a grin on his face. "Ah, brother," he said, giving his head a shake. "You are nothing if not predictable. You see, Commander Malex here, he thought that you would run, that I should reinforce the outside of the village, but I knew better. There is, for one, the fact that you have never run from a fight in your life, but that is not the only reason, is it? After all…" He paused, his grin widening. "You were alone when you ran. Which meant that you left those fools who follow you here." He shrugged. "Perhaps you might have left the others—it wouldn't be the first time. But I knew you would not leave the boy. Otherwise, you would have done so long before now. No, I knew you would come back and here you are. Here *we* are."

Cutter sighed. "Well. Let's get it done."

Feledias laughed. "Come now, brother mine. It has been so long since we have talked, and now you want to so quickly skip the pleasantries? No, no," he said, shaking his head, "that I cannot allow. And besides, do you not wonder where your friends are, those companions who have so foolishly aligned their stars with your own?"

Cutter said nothing. His brother would gloat, would make sure to enjoy this moment no matter what he did, but he found no reason to make it easier for him.

"Escaped," Feledias said. "Fled toward the forest." He smiled at Cutter as if they were sharing a secret. "Was that your idea, I wonder? Yes, yes, I suspect it was." He shrugged. "It makes no difference, of course. Once we are done here, my men will hunt them down where they have fled like dogs in the streets, and they, like you, will suffer for their crimes."

"And the villagers?" Cutter asked, shifting his shoulder and wincing as a fresh wave of pain ran through his arm. "They have committed no crime."

"Perhaps not," Feledias admitted, "but we both know that makes no difference. They cannot be allowed to spread the truth of what happened here, can they? After all"—he grinned again—"I am the nice brother, the kind one, the one known for his compassion. It would not do for the kingdom at large to believe that I am as bad as you, would it? No, that would not do at all."

"And so you will kill a village of innocents to protect your own reputation."

"Oh, brother of mine," Feledias said, snarling, "I would do far more than that. *Far* more." He took a slow, deep breath as if to calm himself and the madness which had suddenly flashed in his eyes was hidden once more. "Now, then," he said matter-of-factly, "best we be about it. I will make you suffer for taking her from me, brother, for spoiling a thing that was fine, and then I will make your friends suffer as well, your friends who have fled and left you alone."

"Sir, watch out!" Malex leapt forward, grabbing Feledias by the shoulder and jerking him back just as an arrow flew through the space where he had been standing only an instant before.

"No," a voice called, "Not quite as fled as you seem to think."

They all turned and Cutter was as surprised as Feledias and the rest to see Maeve standing at the opening of one of the alleyways, along with Priest and, he saw with heavy regret, the boy, Matt.

Feledias's expression twisted with surprise, but it vanished a moment later as he calmed himself. "So the dogs have returned to their master after all."

"You know us dogs," Maeve said dryly, "stupid, sure, but loyal."

"I see, and yet..." Feledias paused, glancing around them. "It seems that one of you is missing. Where is the mage, I wonder?" Cutter noticed the way Maeve's expression hardened at that, and his brother could not have missed it either. He let out a laugh. "Ah, but it seems poor Chall did not make it out with the rest of you. Well, that is regretful, but I would not mourn for him. No doubt his death was a quick one. The rest of you, I'm afraid, will not be quite so fortunate."

"Ah shucks," Maeve said, "and here I was hoping we could all sit around, have a good chat, talk our differences out over some tea, maybe."

Cutter knew Maeve was brave, few braver, yet he could not help wondering why she did not seem afraid in the face of nearly two dozen soldiers, and it seemed by the way his smile slowly faded that his brother was wondering much the same. "You are a good shot, old man," Feledias said, looking at Priest, "but even you are not good enough to take out so many of us, and I doubt that quiver of yours carries enough arrows to get the job done even if you were. You were foolish to come back, for just the three of you can make no difference, no difference except to die, of course."

It was Maeve's turn to grin at that. "Just the three of us?" she asked. "I don't remember ever saying that."

And as if her words were a signal, people began to materialize out of the shadows behind her. Men and women of the village, wielding kitchen knives, broken-off chair legs, some holding no more than large rocks or burned beams that had once made up their homes.

Feledias grunted, his soldiers glancing around uncertainly as more and more men and women appeared. They did not wear armor, did not have proper weapons, but the villagers did not look afraid. Instead, their expressions were grim, their jaws set. Hundreds of them, it appeared, nearly all of what was left of the village and, at their front, the old innkeeper, Netty, holding a firepoker of all things.

"Prince," Commander Malex said, and Cutter could hear the uncertainty in his voice, "perhaps it would be best if we—"

"*No*," Feledias rasped, his voice raw with emotion. "No, we cannot, we *will* not, go, not when my revenge is so close."

"But, sir," Malex said, "there are too many, they—"

"They're *villagers,* Malex!" Feledias screeched, his voice full of rage, full of madness. "*Farmers with sticks and rocks! Kill them— kill them all!*"

Judging by his expression, the commander clearly did not agree, but he waved to his soldiers, barking orders. The soldiers started forward slowly, obviously hesitant to face the mob that, while it may have been made up of villagers with no training in combat, still outnumbered them five to ten times.

Feledias, meanwhile, turned back to Cutter, his face twisting with rage. "No, brother," he hissed, "you will not escape your fate, not again. This ends, now, and as I told you before, I am not the same warrior you once knew."

Cutter sighed, hefting his axe, for there was no help for it. "Come on then, brother," he said. "Show me."

And then the time for talk was past. Feledias let out a growl more akin to a noise that might come from some feral beast, and he charged, his twin swords held out behind him at an angle. The first blade darted out, lightning-quick, and Cutter grunted as he leaned backward, shifting his axe to knock the questing steel away. He saw another metallic glint and tried to turn to the other side, to bring his axe around, but he was too slow, and he felt the kiss of his brother's second sword as it traced a line of fire across his side.

He grunted, staggering, and then he was dodging and parrying, desperately trying to keep his brother's blades at bay as they moved with the speed of two metallic serpents, striking from seemingly every direction at once. He moved as quick as he could, but he was unable to keep up with Feledias's assault, and he grunted and hissed as he accepted one minor wound after another. It became obvious very quickly that Feledias was toying with him just as it became obvious that his brother had not been lying when he said that he had improved.

But then, Cutter thought, as he staggered away—as he was *allowed* to stagger away—there were few better motivations than hatred, he knew that better than anyone. After all, it had been his hatred for pretty much everyone around him, himself most of all, that had been the number one reason why he had committed the atrocities he had.

He panted, watching his brother dance from left to right easily a few feet away from him, a wide grin on his face, enjoying this moment, this moment which he had looked forward to for fifteen years.

For Cutter, it was all he could do to remain standing. The throbbing in his arm from the wound he'd taken earlier was so strong, so overpowering, that he could barely focus on anything else, not to mention the way the blood loss made him feel light-headed and dizzy.

"Ah, brother," Feledias said, grinning, "I told you that I am not the same man you once knew, not the dog to follow at your heels hoping that you might throw me some scraps. I am my own man. I am your *better*."

Cutter was barely listening though. There was no need to talk, not now, for there was only one way the thing could end. He looked away from his brother, toward the others, his companions, and the villagers who had engaged the soldiers. The soldiers might have been more skilled, but the villagers were angry—no surprise that considering what they'd gone through over the last few days—angry enough that they did not hesitate as most might have at the sight of the bare blades, did not stop to question the fact that they faced professional soldiers while they themselves were farmers with sticks and rocks for weapons.

Instead, they charged the soldiers, as if they were all too eager to come to grips with these men who, had they had their way, would have burned them and their families to death. And while the soldiers gave far better than they got, he saw that the villagers would win out, for the soldiers were quickly becoming overwhelmed by the villagers' superior numbers and their ferocity. Not that it would make any difference for him, of course, for he would be dead long before then.

And that thought did not scare him as it might have. The truth was, Cutter was tired. Tired of fighting, tired of walking the trail of blood which it seemed he had traveled his entire life, one that led from death to more death and nothing else. Matt would be okay, that was what mattered. The others would be okay without him.

They would not just be okay. They would be better. *He* would be better. After all, there was nothing here for him, in this world. Perhaps there never had been.

Feledias started toward him, and Cutter knew that the death he had avoided for so long had finally arrived, could see the pleasure of that knowledge reflected in his brother's eyes. But then, Feledias froze, his face suddenly leeched of all color, and he gasped, his breath catching in his throat as his eyes looked past Cutter.

Cutter frowned. Perhaps it might have been a ruse, one meant to draw his attention, but Cutter did not think so. For one, there was no need for tricks as it was clear to both of them that Feledias could kill him anytime he wanted, but it was more than that. The shock, the pure terror in his brother's face could not be feigned.

Cutter turned to look where his brother was staring and felt his own breath catch in his throat, felt a thrum of emotions—so many that any one was nearly impossible to define—run through him as if he'd been struck by lightning.

She was there, standing only feet away from him, as beautiful, as perfect, as he remembered. She wore the white dress she had worn on her wedding day. Cutter remembered it well, remembered staring at her, *wanting* her as she made her way up the aisle, past those gathered to commemorate the event, to where his brother, Feledias, waited for her.

He remembered the way she had smiled, the way his brother had smiled. It was the last time he had seen his brother happy. And he, too, had been happy for Feledias. At least, he believed so. Mostly, though, he had been jealous. He had wanted her, had thought he *deserved* her, he who had led the assault against the Fey, who had killed their king and sent their forces retreating back into the Black Woods.

It should have been a beautiful moment, as perfect as the world ever allowed, but even then, his lust, his desire had almost been too much to contain. Yes, he remembered it, remembered it all too well. "L-Layna?" he asked.

"*No,*" Feledias rasped, "*no,* it can't be. You're...you're dead. You can't be here."

And yet, she was, standing and saying nothing, watching Feledias. And even now, despite the knowledge of how terrible his crimes had been, of what terrible atrocities they had led to, Cutter found himself jealous of even that much, found himself wishing that she would turn, would look at him. But she did not, only stood and stared at his brother, her husband, saying nothing.

"I-it's impossible," his brother said in a choked, strangled voice. "It must be some trick, has to be, but the mage...the mage is dead."

She did move then, her hand reaching out slowly toward him. She took a step, a single, small step, and Feledias screamed. It was a terrible, heart-wrenching wail that would have sounded more at home coming from some tortured, dying animal.

Then, Feledias turned and ran, sprinting as fast as he could into the darkness. There was a shout from Commander Malex and those few soldiers who had not fallen to the villagers' rage turned and sprinted away, following their prince. Cutter barely noticed. Instead, he was staring at her, marking the lines of her face. And, in another moment, she was gone, vanishing as if she had never been, and he was left standing alone.

There was a scuffling sound behind him, and Cutter turned to see Chall limping up. Each step seemed an effort, and there was a dark bruise around the mage's throat, a bruise in the unmistakable shape of hands. Cutter grunted. "I thought you were dead."

Chall winced, rubbing at his throat. "It was a near thing," he rasped.

Cutter nodded, turning to look at the villagers. What few soldiers who had not managed to extract themselves were currently being thrown to the ground and beaten to death by men and women who had likely never raised a hand in anger and who, in the right course of events, would have lived out their lives quietly and peacefully in this small, out-of-the-way village. But by coming here, he had changed all of that, ruined their lives the same way he had ruined the lives of that happy bride and groom so long ago.

"Chall!"

They both turned at the sound of rapid footsteps and, before the mage could speak, Maeve was wrapping him in a tight embrace. They stayed that way for several seconds, Maeve with her face buried in the mage's shoulder, Chall's expression slowly turning from shock to pleasure.

"Gods, I thought those soldiers killed you," Maeve breathed.

"Wasn't for lack of trying," Chall said softly.

After a moment, Maeve seemed to remember where she was, and she pulled out of the embrace, turning to Cutter, her own face red with embarrassment. "What about you?" she asked in a voice full of compassion, for she could not have failed to see the apparition the mage's magic had created. "Are you okay?"

Cutter forced a smile he did not feel, understanding that she meant more than just physically. "Of course," he said. "I'm fine."

And then he fell.

***

He dreamed of blood and pain and regret. But, mostly, he dreamed of her. Not standing as she had been when she'd wed his brother, nor beside him near the village pyre. Instead, she lay sweaty and weary from her exertions in a bed stained with her blood.

He could hear the newborn babe in the other room, squalling as any should when brought into the world. The nurse maids were gone, for she had dismissed them, and it was only him and her, her watching him with eyes that seemed to know so much, to understand so much.

"I knew you would come," she said, her voice weak and thready.

"Yes."

The baby let out another squall, and she turned, her eyes going to the closed door, beyond which her newborn baby boy was being seen to by the nurse maids, the concern and love known only to mothers showing on her face. "My husband will come for him, will come for me."

"Yes."

She sighed heavily. "It was wrong, what I did. What *we* did. I did it out of a fool's jealousy, I think, tired of coming second in his eyes to you, always to you. I thought..." She shook her head, frustrated. "It doesn't matter what I thought. I love Feledias."

"So do I."

She frowned. "Do you? I am not so certain. I am not so certain that a man like you can love anyone, even himself. Perhaps especially himself."

He said nothing to that, for there was nothing to say, and she let out another heavy, weary sigh. "Do you want to know his name?"

"Who?"

She gave him a small smile, and he realized he was a fool. "The boy," he said, "you mean the boy."

She nodded slowly. "Do not worry yourself, Bernard. You are what you are—perhaps you chose it, perhaps you did not, but it is too late now either way. Yes, the boy. Would you like to know his name?"

"If you would like to tell me."

She gave another small smile at that. "So careful," she said. "It is not like you. If only..." She winced in pain. "If only you—*we*—had been careful sooner. But never mind that. What's done is done. His name is Matthias. I will call him Matt."

Cutter nodded. "A good name."

"Do you know what it means?"

"I do not."

"Peace," she said softly. "It means peace."

"A good name," he said again, because he was unsure what was expected of him.

She gave a weary laugh but sobered quickly. "He will come for him. Feledias. He will hate him because of our sins."

"I can protect you."

Another laugh at that. "Protect me? What do you know of protecting?" She waved a hand. "I'm sorry. That's not fair. I am as guilty as you are. But no, Bernard. Your path is not one of peace, and even if it were, I would not leave him like that, would not complete the betrayal in that way. He deserves better from me, from both of us. No, I will stay. But I have something I would ask of you."

"Anything."

She stared at him then, shaking her head in what might have been disbelief. "If something should happen to me—"

"Nothing's going to happen to you."

"But if it does...will you watch out for him?"

"Of course."

The answer was out of him before he gave it any thought, for he was sure that, whatever she said, he would keep her safe. But he had been wrong. He had been a fool.

***

He did not want to waken, wanted to remain with her, for while the memory brought great pain, it brought pleasure too. Yet, he woke anyway and slowly opened his heavy eyelids.

"Well, well, well," a voice said, and he turned to see the innkeeper, Netty, standing beside him. "I've heard devils can't be killed, and I guess now I've seen the truth of it."

"Where am I?"

She held her hands out to the side. "Our new home," she said. "Like it?"

Cutter glanced around, blinking. At first, he saw only darkness, but then he was able to make out the ruddy glow of torches and campfires and, around them, the great shadowed silhouette of trees. "The forest," he said.

"That's right."

He was about to say something more when suddenly two figures walked up, a young girl he did not recognize and a man that he did, one of those he'd fought with in the inn. He tensed, knowing that if the man chose to press the issue now, to revenge himself, there was nothing he could do in his current state to stop him.

But the man made no move forward, only standing with his hands on what must have been his daughter's shoulders, and it was not he who spoke but the girl. "Thank you," she said, "for saving us."

Cutter found himself staring in surprise. He glanced at the innkeeper, Netty, who gave him a sidelong smile, then back to the girl. Her face was open, honest, and he was surprised by how much those words meant to him, though he knew that, in the end, he did not deserve them. After all, had it not been for Matt, he would not have come back. "I don't..." He hesitated, suddenly not wanting to tell the truth, not wanting to see the smile of appreciation fade from the girl's face. "I didn't..."

"We'll let you get back to it," the man said, wincing. "But...we just wanted to say, you know, thanks. And...sorry. For the inn. Cend shouldn't have..." He paused, taking a deep breath. "*We* shouldn't have done that."

"It's fine," Cutter said, finding that he meant it. After all, the men's reaction to his presence was a far more familiar one than the thanks the girl had offered. The man offered him another nod then he and the girl turned and walked away. Cutter watched them go, then, following the young girl's presence, he found himself thinking of Matt, the dream where he'd promised to take care of him so fresh in his mind.

He started to rise, but Netty pushed him back down with one hand, seemingly with ease. "No, no. You relax. I ain't worked as hard as I have to keep you from goin' through the veil just to have you die anyway."

"But the others—"

"Are all fine," she interrupted. "The boy is fine. I am too, in case you care," she grunted, giving a small smile.

He sighed at that, allowing himself to relax. "And Feledias?"

"Gone into the night," she said. "I suppose maybe we could have chased him down, but we're simple villagers here—killing princes isn't our business." She met his eyes then. "Understand?"

"I do," he said. "And...thank you. For everything."

She grunted again. "Reckon I'd rather have my inn back, have all those dead we've lost back, but if thanks is all I can get I s'pose I'll take it."

"I'm...I'm sorry."

She studied him carefully, as if it had been the last thing she'd expected him to say. "I think maybe you really are. And I thank you for it. Now, that's enough chatting—I've got some frightened villagers need seein' to. I'll go and get your friends. They wanted to hang around, but I told 'em to all go get some rest, or I'd finish what your brother's troops started."

She was gone before he could say anything else, and he lay there, breathing, surprised to still be alive. Soon, the others arrived, Maeve and Chall, Priest and Matt. All of them looking battered and exhausted but all of them, thank the gods, alive.

The bruises had darkened around Chall's throat, an ugly, black and purple mottling, but he smiled. "Done with your nap, then?"

Cutter grunted. "Just about." He turned to Maeve, saw the woman studying the mage from behind, wondered briefly if either of them knew just how much they cared for each other. "Alright, Maeve?"

The woman started as if surprised, turning away from studying the mage with an embarrassed expression on her face. "I'm fine," she said. "Well. Still breathing anyway."

He nodded, looking to Priest. The man nodded at him, the simple gesture and his expression carrying a world of meaning for all the pain and suffering they had witnessed in the last two days.

"Cutter?"

He turned to look at Matt. "You're okay?"

The youth opened his mouth as if to answer, then paused as his face twisted with emotion before clearing his throat. "I...I think so. But...the woman, the one Chall made appear...who was she?"

Cutter glanced at Chall, and the mage winced. "He's thought of little else."

Cutter nodded, turning back to the boy. "She was the greatest person I have ever met," he said simply, "the kindest, wisest person this world has ever seen. And, lad, she was your mother."

The youth's breath caught in his throat at that, and he gave a single nod. "I...I thought maybe she was." There was a moment of silence then as Matt visibly gathered himself, then let out a ragged sigh. "So...is that it? I mean...is it finished?"

Cutter looked over at Maeve and the others, all watching him. "No," he said finally, "not finished, lad. It's only just beginning."

# THE END *of* SAGA OF THE KNOWN LANDS

## BOOK ONE

Now, dear reader, we have come to the end of A Warrior's Burden. It is my sincere hope that you enjoyed your first foray into the Known Lands, but there is more to come, so keep an eye out for book two.

In the meantime, are you looking for something else to read? Don't worry—I've got you covered.

Want another story of an anti-hero in a grimdark setting where a jaded sellsword is forced into a fight he doesn't want between forces he doesn't understand?
*Check out the bestselling seven book series, The Seven Virtues.*

Interested in a story where the gods choose their champions in a war with the darkness that will determine the fate of the world itself?
*Get started on The Nightfall Wars, a complete six book epic fantasy series.*

Or how about something a little lighter? Do you like laughs with your sword slinging and magical mayhem? All the world's heroes are dead and so it is up to the antiheroes to save the day. An overweight swordsman, a mage who thinks magic is for sissies, an assassin who gets sick at the sight of the blood, and a man who can speak to animals…maybe.
The world needed heroes—it got them instead.
*Start your journey with The Antiheroes!*

**Choose your next adventure at JacobPeppersAuthor.com**

If you've enjoyed *A Warrior's Burden*, I'd appreciate you taking a minute to leave an honest review at your favorite retailer. They make a tremendous difference, as any author can tell you, and there are few things better than hearing someone's thoughts on your book. As long as they're good. Otherwise, feel free to lie to me.

If you'd like to reach out and chat, you can email me at JacobPeppersAuthor@gmail.com or visit my website, www.JacobPeppersAuthor.com.
You can also give me a shout on Facebook or on Twitter. I'm looking forward to hearing from you!

*Turn the page for a limited time free offer*!

Sign up for my VIP New Releases mailing list and get a free copy of *The Silent Blade: A Seven Virtues novella* as well as receive exclusive promotions and other bonuses!

*Go to JacobPeppersAuthor.com to get your free book now!*

# Note from the Author

And this, dear reader, brings us to the end of *A Warrior's Burden*. I will not say it was an easy journey, but it is my sincere hope that you enjoyed it. And while this first part of our travels is finished, there is much more awaiting us, awaiting Cutter and Maeve, Chall and Priest and, of course, Matt.

The Fey stir restlessly in the alien darkness of the Black Wood, thirsting for revenge, and Prince Feledias will not so easily cast aside his own quest for blood. After all, a man might try to forget his past—much as Cutter did—but his past will never forget him. It follows him, like a shadow, trailing in his wake. And sometimes that past, that shadow, has teeth.

Yet while a man can never escape his past, the future lies in wait, a path not yet taken, and wherever it might lead, at least Cutter will have his friends with him. And maybe, just maybe, they will even be enough.

I want to take this opportunity to thank all of those people—and there are many—without whom this book would have never been finished or, if it was, would have been far worse.

Thank you, first, to my wonderful wife, Andrea, who attends to the needs of this world so that I can traipse lackadaisically around in others that aren't, strictly speaking, real. Thank you, also, to my friends and family, mostly for not murdering me when having to hear again and again of this plot point or that one. You all endured my droning with a good humor—and steady restraint—that was nothing short of inspiring.

I would also like to thank my beta readers who dedicated their time and energy to making this book far better than it might have been, accepting misspellings and story incongruities as the only payments for their efforts.

And lastly, thank you, dear reader. It is because of you and only you that these stories come to life, that I get to spend my time writing them in the first place. My sincere hope is that you have not found your time here, in the Known Lands, wasted.

And if you have enjoyed the journey thus far, then stick around, won't you? Dark, bloody days lie ahead, it is true, but the fun?

Well, the fun is just beginning.

*Jacob Peppers*

# About the Author

Jacob Peppers lives in Georgia with his wife, his son, Gabriel, newborn daughter, Norah, and three dogs. He is an avid reader and writer and when he's not exploring the worlds of others, he's creating his own. His short fiction has been published in various markets, and his short story, "The Lies of Autumn," was a finalist for the 2013 Eric Hoffer Award for Short Prose. He is the author of the bestselling epic fantasy series *The Seven Virtues* and *The Nightfall Wars*.

Printed in Great Britain
by Amazon